THE PROMISE OF CHANGE

REBECCA HEFLIN

REBECCA HEFLIN BOOKS, LLC

ACKNOWLEDGMENTS

For Mom.
Thank you for sharing your gift.

Many consider writing a solitary occupation, but I couldn't have written this book without the love and support of so many people.

First, to my husband, Ron, who said this was my mountain to climb. I couldn't have reached the summit without your love and dedication. Thank you for giving me the opportunity to pursue my dream.

To my sister, Lynda, who jump-started my love of reading when she gave me a copy of Kathleen Woodiwiss' *Shanna* when I was fifteen. Little did you know that the seed had been planted even then. It just took a while to grow. Thanks for being such an awesome big sister.

To Yvonne, who listened attentively while I talked *ad nauseum* about the trials and tribulations of my characters. You were, and continue to be, my sounding board, my editor, and my cheerleader. But thank you, most of all for being a good listener.

To my "beta" readers, Alice, Susan, Suzie, and Renee, thank you for reading my drafts (sometimes more than once), even those really rough first drafts. Your patience and perseverance are greatly appreciated and will not be forgotten.

To Marie-Claude, who took the time to discuss Sarah's change-aphobia, along with her other psychological glitches. Your knowledge and insight were invaluable.

Finally, to my late mother, Faye, thank you for sharing your gift with me. The only thing that would make me happier is having you here to share this with.

PART I

CHAPTER 1

Sarah Edwards was in the middle of a mid-life crisis, and she had the shiny new Porsche to prove it.

Chin in hand, she stared out the window of her twenty-first-floor office, pondering her current state of mind. Divorced, bored, and twitchy. That about summed it up.

A clap of thunder startled her from her one-person pity-party. A storm was rolling in, turning the sky battleship gray and churning up the waters of the St. Johns River. Afternoon thunderstorms were a common occurrence in summer, building in the warm, muggy Florida climate, only to unleash the accumulated energy just in time for evening rush hour. The predictability of the afternoon thunderstorms had always been comforting to Sarah, but not today. She felt as charged as the atmosphere.

"Excuse me, Sarah." Carlos gave her a sympathetic smile. "I have another contract here from the radiology department."

Ugh. If she had to look at another contract she was going to run screaming from the building. After seven years of legal work, she was beginning to question her sanity for persisting in her apparently dead-end career. Could she do this another *twenty years*?

The phone on her desk rang, momentarily saving her. "Sarah Edwards."

"Yes, Dr. Davids." She rolled her eyes at Carlos, who smiled in return.

"Sarah, I've been waiting for that medical services contract for a week. When do you think your review will be completed?"

"I've reviewed it and my assistant should have the revisions to you by the end of today." She looked at Carlos, and he nodded and left her office to take care of her request.

"Oh. Well. Thank you."

That deflated his attitude in short order, she thought. "You're very welcome. Have a good weekend."

Working as in-house counsel in a small health system, contracts were as common as palm trees in Florida. She had lost count of how many she'd reviewed today. It wasn't as if contracts were the only legal matters the small office handled, they were just the most tedious.

The rain pelted the window like pebbles. Lightning popped all around the city, attracted to the abundant television towers that stabbed the sky from atop the skyscraper rooftops. Rain notwithstanding, Sarah was considering blowing this Popsicle-stand when Ken, her boss, poked his head in her door. "Hi, Sarah, were you just leaving?"

Feeling a guilty flush creep up her face, she sat back down in her chair as she shook her head.

"Do you have a minute?" He stepped into her office.

"Sure. What do you need?"

"I'd like to discuss an office matter with you."

Oh God. She swallowed the lump that suddenly formed in her throat. Was he upset that she was leaving early? Was he unhappy with her work product? Not that she would blame him. She hadn't exactly pursued her work with gusto lately.

"Okay." She tried to sound composed.

He took a seat in one the chairs across from her desk. "You know I've been here since before the steam engine, and I've been thinking it's time to retire. Maybe Cindy and I will sail around the world, something we've always talked about. I've worked hard all my life, and it's time to enjoy the wind in my sails."

Ken and his wife, Cindy, had a fifty-foot Catalina sailboat, hence why he often spoke in sailing metaphors.

"Retiring?" Sarah hesitated, unsure what to say. She had mixed feelings about his announcement. "That's great. I mean, that's great for you and Cindy. You both deserve it. But of course I'll miss you terribly. Do you have a date in mind?"

"As soon as they can find my replacement." He waited a beat. "I'd like for you to be that person." He let that sink in a minute.

This was totally unexpected. The lump of fear turned into a smile of gratification.

"You're the best lawyer in the office. You'll be able to take the helm right away, without any downtime or steep learning curve." Ken stood and paced, his hands in his pockets. "And, a promotion has long been overdue, so I'm recommending you to the board as the next Vice President and General Counsel."

When Sarah didn't speak, Ken continued, "Of course, you're free to take the time to think about it. It will mean increased responsibility and workload, but with a commensurate increase in salary."

Ken took a seat again, waiting patiently for a reply.

"Ken, I'm sorry, I'm . . . speechless. This is a great honor, really. I don't know what to say," she said, faltering.

"Just say you'll think about it and let me know. I hope you'll say yes. You'll make a great captain." He stood, but before leaving he turned and said, "Go, on. Get out of here. I'm sure you're anxious to start your weekend, and perhaps share the news with your family."

"Thanks, Ken. And I'll think about your offer." She hadn't really set her sights on general counsel, but maybe this was exactly what she needed, a new challenge, a new focus.

Before leaving the office, she called her sister.

"Brighton Beach Antiques, Rebecca Kent."

"Hi, Becca. I'm on my way."

"You're leaving early. What gives?"

"I've wrapped everything up for the week, and I could use a walk on the beach. Is it raining there?"

"No. Clear, sunny, and breezy."

It wasn't unusual for downtown Jacksonville to be covered under a blanket of storm clouds, while the beach stayed clear and sunny. The strong easterly sea breezes often held back the western-born thunderstorms, the intracoastal waterway acting as a dividing line between sun and rain.

"Great. Have time for a walk before we meet Ann for dinner?"

"Sure. I'll meet you at the house as soon as I finish up these invoices." Becca owned a successful antiques business specializing in English furnishings. Her husband, a retired financial planner-turned-author and part-time professor, served as silent partner in the business, with an emphasis on silent. Becca was a very savvy businesswoman, with an eye for beautiful, tasteful home décor.

"Perfect."

Sarah picked up her purse and turned off the lights, looking back at her office. Maybe soon she would move to the big corner office with a spectacular view of the River City and its many bridges. On her way out, she stopped by Carlos' desk. "Carlos, can you give this contract to Kim to handle? I've got to get out of here."

"Sure. Have a nice weekend."

"Thanks. See you Monday."

He wore an odd expression, as if he wanted to say something.

"Anything else?" she asked.

"No. Good night." In the hospital parking garage, Sarah slid into the delicious buff leather seats of her ruby-red metallic impulse buy. Too bad it was raining. She would have liked to put the top down. Shifting the car into gear, she pulled out of the garage. Maybe leaving early, she would beat the rush-hour traffic. Anna Nalick sang on the radio entreating everyone to 'just breathe.' Sarah took her advice, drew a deep breath, and let it out on a sigh.

Impulsive. That wasn't an adjective commonly associated with her. Dependable, steady, deliberate. Those were more common. Some would even consider her cautious. She had always considered herself a planner. Until recently. Was she too cautious? Well, this sleek sports car that now called her single-car garage home was anything but.

She cringed when she thought about what her best friend, Ann, and Becca would say when they saw it. Ann would likely think it was cool. Becca, on the other hand, would likely lecture in her give-me-strength mother-of-teenagers tone. Becca took her older sister role a little too seriously at times.

She could also imagine their elation when she told them about her meeting with Ken and their frustration at her need to think about it. The offer was a testament to Ken's faith in her legal skills and abilities. A little nervous butterfly fluttered in her stomach.

The job would mean a lot of change, something she wasn't very good at. She preferred the familiar, the routine. Taking another deep breath, she told herself she would just establish new, higher-paid routines.

After crossing the intracoastal, Sarah pulled over to let the top down for the remaining few miles to Becca's beach house. The sun shone in a brilliant blue sky, the steel-gray clouds she'd left behind reflected in the rearview mirror.

Never mind that her too-public divorce left her shying away from public attention, she noticed heads turned at the brunette in the sexy red Porsche. More for the car than herself, no doubt.

The wind tangled her hair, blowing away the remaining stress of the day. Cool wet sand massaging bare feet, accompanied by the soothing aromatherapy of the Atlantic's salt tang, was almost in her grasp. Nature's most perfect spa treatment.

~

"*I* ran into Adrian yesterday," Becca said with some hesitation, as she and Sarah walked on the beach. "Honey, he's getting married again."

"Oh. Well. Wow." Sarah stopped in her tracks, and bent over as if inspecting a shark's tooth, so Becca wouldn't notice the tears that sprang into her eyes.

"Congratulations to the happy couple, I guess. That didn't take long." Sarah continued, "Is it his nurse?" Adrian's cliché affair with his operating room nurse was the proverbial final straw in their short, troubled marriage. Today marked the six-month anniversary of their divorce.

Becca reached down and took Sarah's hand, pulling her up. "No. She's a pharmaceutical rep he met at the hospital. Pretty, if you like that perfect plastic Barbie look." She gave her a wan smile.

Apparently, Adrian was going through women like he did luxury sports cars. Sarah had heard he'd dated several women since their divorce, well, since *before* their divorce, actually. "It must have been a whirlwind romance . . . kind of like ours," she muttered.

"I'm sorry to spoil our beach time, but I didn't want you to find out from someone else."

"No, it's okay. I appreciate you telling me."

They walked along lost in their own thoughts. The cooling breeze that had kept the thunderstorm at bay had died abruptly. With the absence of the breeze, the Atlantic flattened out, waves barely lapping the shore. The only sound was the laughter of the gulls and the occasional squeals from kids playing along the ocean's edge.

"So she's pretty. What does she look like?" Sarah couldn't resist torturing herself.

"Well, she's tall, statuesque, really, long bimbo-blond hair, blue eyes, 'chicklet-tooth' smile. You know the type."

The exact opposite of her. At five foot four, Sarah certainly couldn't be considered tall, and her petite frame was nowhere near statuesque. Her chestnut hair, which was currently pulled back into a messy ponytail, was thick and wavy. When it wasn't pulled back, it fell in layers to just past her shoulders. Adrian had always been after her to get it cut in a more sophisticated style. And yet, he was marrying a woman with long "bimbo" hair, according to Becca.

"What's her name?"

"Brie something-or-other."

"He's marrying someone named for a cheese?" she asked, with a dash of snark.

Becca giggled. "I never thought of it, but now that you mention it . . . it could have been worse. Her name could have been Muenster."

They both chuckled.

After a long pause, Becca asked quietly, "Do you still love Adrian?"

"I'm not sure I was so much in love with him, as I was in awe of him." She shrugged. If she was totally honest with herself, she didn't miss Adrian. It was sad to say that in the almost three years of their marriage, she'd never developed a genuine connection to him.

Nevertheless, the failure of their marriage was something she was having a difficult time getting over. Failure didn't sit well with her. An impetuous act—and look where it got her. She gave herself a mental shake. Kind of like the one yesterday that led to the purchase a car that screamed mid-life crisis.

"Okay then, why does his remarrying bother you so much?"

"It's just that . . . he's moved on . . . already found someone else. Am I that easy to forget? And why is it so easy for him to find someone else?" She sighed. "My old romantic notion of soulmates is so foolish. If it weren't for you and Mark, and Ann and Rob—"

"You forgot Mom and Dad."

"And Mom and Dad." She smiled sadly, as she thought of her parents, and the recent death of her mother. "I'd completely disregard the concept."

"First, you are not forgettable. Just because Adrian is selfish, and shallow doesn't mean there's something wrong with you. Second, I don't think he's looking for a soulmate. Third, how do you expect to find someone, when you won't even date? Soulmates don't just drop into your lap you know. You have to date a few duds before you find the right guy. Remember Bob?"

"Oh dear." Sarah laughed.

"Exactly."

Becca had dated 'Bob the Snob' in high school. Bob was a member of one of Jacksonville's wealthiest families, and he never let anyone forget it.

"I wish I had a dime for each time he talked about his ski trips to

Switzerland, or his family's vacation house in the Caribbean. What you ever saw in him, no one will ever know."

"Hey, he was good-looking." Becca shrugged.

"Thank God you finally came to your senses and stopped thinking with your hormones."

"Only because he went to Stanford, two thousand miles away."

"What's ol' Bob up to these days?"

"According to his Facebook page, he's an accountant."

"Probably so he can count all his money," Sarah said with a smirk.

"And he's bald and fat."

"No kidding?" Sarah turned to look at her sister. "Now aren't you glad you didn't marry him?"

"No doubt." Becca put her arm around her sister's shoulders. "Never mind my youthful indiscretions, back to you. I think your upcoming trip to England is just what the doctor ordered, uh, sorry, no reference to Adrian intended. Maybe you'll meet your soulmate there, and we'll all visit you at his family's ancient estate."

"Right." Sarah rolled her eyes. "The mistress of Pemberley."

"Keep your mind and your heart open. It will happen. You're too terrific not to find that one person who will feed your mind, your heart, and your soul. And speaking of feeding, let's go eat."

~

"*Y*ou bought a Boxster?"

There it was. 'The tone.' Choosing to ignore it, Sarah said, "Yes. Do you like it?"

"What's not to like? But what on earth possessed you to get rid of your safe, reliable Volvo and replace it with this Cougar Car?"

"It's not a Cougar Car." Sarah's defenses went up. "It's an intelligently designed, precision-engineered sports car."

"Good grief, Sarah, you sound like a car salesman." Becca waved her hand in the air dismissing her sales pitch. "Don't you think it's a bit flashy? Red? Really?"

"You're the one who's always saying I should step out of my

comfort zone." Sarah shrugged nonchalantly, but she was definitely second-guessing her purchase under the weight of Becca's scrutiny.

"The key word there is 'step.' Step. Not leap." Becca whispered her hand across the sleek, curvy lines of the car. "What will the Admiral think?"

Sarah cringed. Admiral George Stovall Edwards, U.S. Navy, Retired, a.k.a. Daddy.

"Sends chills down your spine, doesn't it?" Becca replied with a grin, before Sarah could form an answer.

Avoiding the rhetorical question, Sarah replied, "Do you want to ride with me to the restaurant, or are you just going to stand there being judgmental?"

"Are you kidding?" she said as she opened the passenger door. "Of course I want to ride. But I reserve the right to be judgmental again once the adrenalin wears off."

∼

*T*he trendy new restaurant was in an old warehouse district that was undergoing gentrification, but it could still be a rough area. It would be light until nine o'clock, so long as they left before dark, Sarah, Ann, and Becca felt safe. Parking on the street a block from the restaurant, Sarah put the top up while Becca worked the tangles from her blond hair.

"Okay," Becca conceded, "that was fun, I'll give you that, but not very practical if every time you arrive at your destination you almost snatch yourself bald trying to repair your coiffure."

Sarah laughed as ran her fingers through her curls. "It gives you a nice wind-blown look."

"So does hanging your head out a car window, but I wouldn't do that either," Becca groused as they walked to the restaurant.

The two spotted Ann already seated in a cozy booth. Ann looked up from her smartphone with a frazzled smile. Between her husband and her two kids, she constantly shuffled her schedule to accommodate their many obligations.

Sarah and Ann Parham had been friends since their freshman year of high school. They'd been through the awkward teenage years, the dating, the crushes, the break-ups, and Sarah's agonizing career change. She and Becca were her Gibraltar when she went through her divorce. She couldn't have made it through without their love and support . . . and their occasional well-intended nagging.

"Hey, Sarah, Becca." Even though Ann had lived in Florida since the age of twelve, she'd never lost her molasses-sweet Alabama accent.

"What's up?" Sarah asked as Ann stood up to hug first her then, Becca.

"Oh, Rob just texted me that he wants to invite some potential clients over for a cook-out this weekend. He's apparently forgotten that the kids have a soccer tournament on Saturday, and we're spending Sunday with his parents." She tucked a strand of corn-silk hair behind her ear and tapped out a quick reply.

Although she married rather young, she'd married well. Despite her husband's busy international travel schedule, they'd been happily married for over twenty years. Maybe that was the secret to their success, Sarah thought with a wry grin.

"I don't know how you keep up with everyone's schedules. Thank goodness I only have my own schedule, and Carlos handles that for me," Sarah said with a shrug as she turned to her menu.

Ann gave her a sly look. "How's it going with Carlos? He still giving you puppy-dog eyes? Not that I blame him. After all, you're a gorgeous thirty-eight-year-old divorcee, and you know what they say about divorcees . . ." A grin spread over her face.

Stunned by her comment, Sarah dropped her menu. "What?"

"You know, about divorcees being—"

"That's not what I mean, the part about Carlos—"

"Oh, come on. You can't tell me you haven't noticed. He's got a first-rate crush on you."

"It's true," Becca piped in. "He does. I've seen it."

"Ann, that's not true! Where did you come up with that?"

"It's as plain as the egg on your face," Ann said, shaking her head.

Ann always mixed her metaphors, confused her clichés, and generally mangled the English language. Sarah usually found it funny, but not then.

"He's my assistant, and he's seven years younger than me. I'm no cougar."

Giggling, Ann said, "Oh please. According to Wikipedia, you have to be at least eight years older than him in order to meet the definition of cougar."

"You looked it up on Wikipedia," Sarah stated flatly. Turning to Becca, she said, "Do you believe this girl?"

"Yes. That sounds about right, and I trust Ann."

"That's not what I meant."

"I know that's not what you meant. I just like aggravating you," Becca said with a grin.

"Hey, I was curious," Ann inserted, "and you never know when that information might come in handy. Like, for instance, now."

"Well, anyway, he is definitely not my type."

"Who is your type, honey?" Ann asked sarcastically.

Sarah chose to ignore it. "Carlos is a great assistant, and takes great care of me, but—"

"I bet," Ann said, as she rolled her sapphire blue eyes and looked over the menu at Becca, who snickered in response.

The waitress came over to take their orders before Sarah could respond. The girls made their selections and handed over their menus.

"Anyway, I don't want this," Sarah waved her hand as if shooing a pesky fly, "whatever you're alluding to, to cause a problem with our professional relationship."

Frowning, Sarah wondered if she should say something to Carlos. Talk about awkward. 'So, I hear you have a crush on me.' Then what? 'If so, get over it. If not, please excuse my over-inflated ego for thinking it in the first place?'

No. She was better off taking a wait-and-see approach.

"Speaking of cougars . . ." Becca said, "you'll never guess what Sarah bought. A bright red convertible Boxster—"

"You bought a Boxster?"

"See," Becca said, turning to Sarah, "that's exactly what I said."

"Cool."

"Okay, I didn't say that." Becca gave Ann a stern look. "Don't encourage her."

"Sorry. But I think that's, well, cool. Will you take me for a ride?"

"Of course."

"I think it's a replacement for sex," Becca interjected.

Sarah and Ann turned to look at her.

"Well, I do."

"Who are you, Sigmund Freud?" Sarah scoffed. "Sometimes a car is just a car."

"Except when it's a lipstick-red convertible Porsche."

"It's ruby-red metallic." Sarah's glare indicated she no longer considered this exchange good-natured teasing.

"Red. It's red."

"So," Ann said, as the waitress brought bread and salads, "have you decided what course you're taking at Oxford?"

"Why, Jane Austen of course. A whole week of Jane Austen!" Sarah sighed wistfully then laughed at herself. She was attending a summer adult education program at Christ Church, one of Oxford University's thirty-nine colleges.

Ann laughed too, shaking her head. "I don't know what you see in the dull and proper novels of Jane Austen. Give me a nice racy novel complete with a gorgeous, bare-chested hero and I'm in heaven."

"I'm with you," Becca said, dipping her bread in olive oil before popping a piece into her mouth.

"Jane Austen's heroes *are* gorgeous . . . look at Mr. Darcy," Sarah argued.

"Yeah, but Lizzy never saw him bare-chested." Ann took a sip of her wine. "Speaking of gorgeous, a guy at the bar has been looking at you since you came in. No, don't look, he's coming over."

"Oh God." Sarah could feel the flush creeping into her face. She turned around. Talk about tall, dark, and handsome. He stood right next to the table.

"Hello," he said, first looking at Ann and Becca before finally turning to Sarah. "I hope you don't mind, but I asked the waitress what you were drinking." He placed two glasses of wine and a Cosmo on the table. "I'm Derek. I've seen you here before but couldn't get up the courage to talk to you."

"I'm Sarah." He had a nice smile, but . . . "Thank you for the drinks," she said, as she raised her glass.

"Would you like to go out some time?" he asked quickly, as if he didn't want to lose his nerve.

Sarah's right hand went self-consciously to her now-bare left ring finger. No way to use marriage as an excuse. Times like this she wished she'd continued to wear her wedding band. Before she could stammer out a response, he said, "We could just meet here for dinner or drinks if that would make you more comfortable than going out with a total stranger."

She glanced over at Ann, who wore an impish grin. She didn't dare look at Becca.

She smiled awkwardly, her blush deepening. "Derek, I really appreciate your invitation, but I'm not ready . . . I mean I'm not really . . . thank you, but I have a rule . . . I don't date strangers."

"Well, if you decide to break your rule, I'll be over there." He pointed to the bar and walked away, shoulders stooped slightly.

Ann hunched over the table and hissed, "Are you crazy?"

Sarah closed her eyes. "It must be so difficult to work up the nerve to ask someone out. God, I hate turning men down."

"Then why did you?"

"You know why. I don't date strangers. Besides, I'm not interested—"

"How do you know? He might be a great guy. Honey, when you fall off the bull, you have to get right back on." Ann continued, "At least he didn't try some lame pick-up line." She shook her head.

"Cut it out, Ann. You're my best friend, and best friends are supposed to support each other, not nag each other. And you," she said, pointing her finger at her sister, "don't start."

"Sometimes nagging is supporting," Ann argued.

"Then maybe I could do with a little less support."

They ate in silence for a beat or two. Boisterous laughter broke out at the table behind them.

"Ken's retiring and he's recommending me for the job," Sarah blurted out.

Becca and Ann looked up, mouths gaping, before squeals of excitement emitted from those same mouths.

"You just now thought to tell us that?" Becca said. "What's wrong with you?" She swatted Sarah's arm as she spoke.

"Ouch." Sarah turned and pinched her sister.

"Girls," Ann said, interrupting their playful scrap. "Am I going to have to separate you two?"

"She started it," Sarah said, pointing at Becca. "Besides, I wanted to wait until we were all together."

"So when is he retiring? When do you start? How much are you going to make? Let's toast." Ann raised her wine glass.

Her continuous monologue left Sarah no place for response.

"Ann, take a breath and give Sarah a chance to reply."

Sarah told them about her conversation with Ken and warned that it was only a recommendation. She wasn't a shoo-in for the job.

"They'd be crazy not to hire you," Ann said.

"It's about time. I was beginning to wonder if Ken was ever going to recognize what he had," Becca said, pushing her plate away.

"Congratulations, honey. I'm so happy for you."

Sarah deliberately placed her fork on her plate and folded her hands in her lap. "I haven't thrown my hat in the ring yet."

"What?"

"Are you nuts?" Becca said.

Sarah held up her hands. "Ken told me to take some time to think it over, and I'm going to do just that."

"Why?" Becca's 'tone' returned. "What's to think about? You deserve the job, and I know you can do it. Don't you want it?"

"I know I can do it, but you know me. I have to think it over. Look at it from all angles."

Looking at Ann, Becca said, "A promotion she has to think about.

A pricey ruby-red metallic sports car, not so much. Sarah, your irrational behavior is giving me a mental whiplash."

Sarah sighed. Sometimes she wondered why she told them everything she did. With the two of them ganging up on her, she didn't stand a chance.

Ann's cell phone rang. Saved by the bell again.

In her stern 'mommy voice' Ann said, "Y'all just need to work it out, because neither one of you will like it if I work it out for you."

"Oh well," Ann said after hanging up, "this was pleasant while it lasted. I've got to get home and referee the kids."

Becca pulled Sarah aside. "Promise me you'll seriously consider Ken's offer."

"I will. I promise."

Ann grabbed her hand. "Now show me this Cougar Car."

The three of them walked down the sidewalk in the twilight, laughing and joking.

Sarah stopped suddenly and turned around. She could have sworn she parked right here, in a now-empty space. "What the . . ."

"Sarah, what is it?" Ann asked concerned.

Sarah turned to Becca, whose face also wore a look of confusion. "Didn't I park here?"

"Yes. I'm sure you did, because I remember this black sedan." She pointed to the car parked across the street.

Sarah stepped out into the street to look down the road. Something crunched beneath her feet. Glass. Shards of broken glass. She knelt to examine the pile at her feet. "I think my Cougar Car's been stolen."

CHAPTER 2

What a day. Sarah sat in the passenger seat of Ann's SUV, her eyes closed. It was almost eleven p.m. After calling the police, giving them her report, calling her insurance company, and taking Becca home, she was finally on her way home.

When would she ever learn? Impulsiveness didn't work for her. It didn't work for her marriage. She didn't know why she thought it would work for the car she'd owned less than twenty-four hours.

No more impulsiveness. This was it. She was returning to her usual approach to life, no matter how dull it might be. From now on, she was going to carefully deliberate over every decision in her life, no matter how small.

Except for shoes. A girl could never go wrong with an impulsive shoe purchase. But with everything else, she vowed to be more cautious. And if the police didn't recover her car, she was going to buy another sensible Volvo.

Mentally exhausted, she dreaded dealing with the insurance company, the rental car agency, and all the paperwork and phone calls. She heaved a weighty sigh.

As if reading her mind, Ann said, "You'll need a car if they don't find yours. Do you want me to take you to the rental car agency tomorrow?"

"I'll be okay for the weekend without a car." She turned to look at Ann, without lifting her head from the headrest. "For now, I've decided to rely on Scarlett O'Hara's mantra: 'I'll think about that tomorrow.' It worked for her." She turned her head and closed her eyes. "Can we just not talk? My head is splitting."

"Sure, honey. You just sit there quietly. I'll have you home soon."

*

Two a.m. The lights were finally out and Sarah was in bed, but sleep was long in coming. Her very expensive impulse-buy probably sat in some chop shop being butchered even now. She cringed at the thought. It wasn't a sentient being, but the mental image troubled her nonetheless. Rolling over, she grabbed the other pillow and hugged it to her. Heat lightening flickered through the plantation shutters like a strobe light.

Was Becca right? Had the car been a replacement for sex or for men in general? Not that she'd had many relationships in her life.

Growing up, she'd focused her energy, time, and attention on school and athletics. That intense focus paid off in the form of excellent grades and outstanding athletic accomplishments. She hadn't had time for boys. When she'd become an adult, she'd focused that same level of attention first on college, then her first career as a teacher, followed by law school, and finally on her second career.

She'd never seen any point in dating just for the sake of dating. She always figured when you found 'the one' you just knew. Plus, with all the family moves, she'd rarely had time to make friends, much less form romantic attachments. That wasn't to say she wasn't interested in men, and contrary to her no-nonsense dedication to more practical pursuits, she was a full-blown romantic.

As a teenager, she'd fallen in love with literature's epic romances, like Jane and Rochester, Elizabeth and Darcy, and Cathy and Heathcliff. Seeing those love stories portrayed on the screen only solidified those romantic sensibilities. Add to that her parents' long, happy marriage and those expectations soared.

But she wasn't naïve, either. She knew that marriage came with not only harmony, but with discord; not just with triumphs, but also with tribulations. What made it romantic was overcoming the trials and celebrating the triumphs together. However, her foray into that connubial state had been anything but, and had left her idealistic view of marriage, and relationships in general, in tatters. And she no longer trusted her instincts where men were concerned.

Despite, or perhaps because of, her romantic nature she'd never met anyone who'd fulfilled her expectations of the romantic hero. Until Adrian. After all, he was a brilliant surgeon saving lives. What was more heroic than that?

She'd met Adrian Mills at a hospital function. He was a good-looking, successful surgeon who'd accomplished so much early in his career. Adrian's status as a world-renowned neurosurgeon had the famous, and the not so famous, seeking him out for their care. It was a real coup for the hospital to get him on staff. He'd seemed larger than life, and she'd been dumbstruck that he'd taken an interest in her. By the end of the evening, they had a dinner date planned for the next night. She'd eagerly broken her rule about dating strangers.

The relationship progressed quickly, and the next thing she knew they were married.

Everyone said they were the perfect couple. That is, with the exception of Ann and Becca, who took an almost instant dislike to Adrian. She should have heeded their warnings. After all, both had been happily married for years. Didn't that mean they should be good judges of character?

But she wouldn't listen. Adrian had bowled her over. He was charming, worldly, poised. When he spoke to her, it seemed as if she was the only person in the room. Unfortunately, Sarah hadn't learned until after they were married that shallow brooks babble loudest. The only true substance to Adrian was his surgical skill. If you needed life-saving neurosurgery, he was your guy. If you needed a monogamous mate, look elsewhere.

Despite all the problems, the arguments, the miscommunications, and the bursting of the romantic bubble, she was willing to stick it out, see if it was just a period of adjustment, until the affair, which turned out to be just one of many.

Adrian's social circle, and thus hers, consisted of the city's most prominent citizens, making their divorce a public spectacle. When the news hit, the salacious details became spicy grist for the rumor-mills. Each morsel savored. Each tidbit relished.

The unwelcome spotlight cast on her private life had been almost too much to bear. She withdrew from the social scene, not only to avoid contact with Adrian, but to avoid the knowing looks and catty comments from the city's so-called paragons of society. Soon the invitations dried up, taking with them Sarah's ever-growing need for excuses to decline, and dimming the spotlight, a spotlight she hoped would never shine on her again.

No, she decided, the car was not a replacement for sex, or men. Why would you want to replace something that didn't really hold any interest for you?

At least that's what she tried to convince herself.

CHAPTER 3

$\mathcal{D}$ressed in her best Marc Jacobs power-suit, Sarah checked her appearance in the ladies' room mirror.

The last two weeks had been hectic. Between the aggravations of dealing with the police and the insurance company over the stolen car, and the pressure of polishing her resume and worrying about what to wear for her interview, she'd barely had time to prepare and practice her responses to the usual interview questions: What unique qualities do you bring to this position? If hired, what would be your first priority?

In a few minutes, she'd sit before the selection committee at the boardroom's barge-sized conference table and do her best to wow them. She'd worked with several members of the board on legal matters, but the stakes had never been this high. The job had grown in importance since Ken first approached her.

The Admiral had been as excited about the possible promotion, as he had been appalled over her car purchase and the car's subsequent theft.

Her father's approval had always been important to her. Not that she'd never gained his approval. She could remember countless occasions when her father had been proud of her—when she'd graduated from high school as class Valedictorian; when she'd been accepted to William and Mary; when she'd graduated with highest honors with a degree in literature; and later, when she'd graduated from William and Mary law.

But she could also remember the disappointments—when she'd announced as a college sophomore that she was going to be a writer; when she'd given up on her teaching career after only three years; and of course, when her ill-advised marriage ended in divorce.

Walking to the boardroom, she reminded herself it was these disappointments that made this job so important. It would make her father proud again.

She took a deep breath and knocked on the door. At someone's request to come in, she stepped in and greeted the three board members who served as the selection committee with a warm smile. She was relieved to find that she already knew two of them.

"Welcome, Ms. Edwards." Mrs. Dillard extended her bejeweled hand to indicate the chair across from them. "Take a seat, and we'll get started."

As the mayor's wife, Mrs. Dillard not only served as the city's first lady, but also the Grand Dame of Jacksonville society. She introduced Mr. Cheswick, current board president, to her left, and Mr. Spalding, owner and CEO of the city's largest real estate development company, to her right. Mr. Cheswick, she remembered from her past dealings with him, was a stickler for details, being the head of a large accounting firm, but pleasant and warm. Mrs. Dillard was the consummate socialite, an ideal politician's wife—polished, smooth, articulate. But get on her bad side, and you'd never grace the doors of the city's best country clubs again. Mr. Spalding was an unknown entity. Sarah decided to focus her attention on him.

"Ms. Edwards, why don't you start by telling us a little about yourself?" Mrs. Dillard folded her hands on the table in front of her.

Sarah walked them through her education, her previous career, and her subsequent decision to go to law school, and finally her tenure with the hospital's legal office.

"What motivates you?"

Sarah turned to Mr. Cheswick to answer his question. "I've always been motivated by the desire to do a good job at whatever task I undertake. I want to excel and be successful in my job, both for my own personal satisfaction, and for my employer."

"You certainly come highly recommended. Ken is always singing your praises." Mr. Cheswick's warm smile soothed her jangled nerves.

"What challenges do you expect to face in this job, and how will you handle them?" Mrs. Dillard asked before taking a sip of her coffee.

"I expect I'll have to juggle many priorities—supervising employees, attending meetings, handling complex legal matters, advising clients, not to mention budgetary concerns, resource availability, among many others. But I am quite adept at prioritizing my responsibilities, so I have a clear idea of what needs to be done. I'm a planner."

After about a half hour of questions, Sarah's nerves settled down to a low hum. The interview was going well. So far none of the questions had thrown her.

"You've been here seven years?" Before she could answer, Mr. Spalding continued, "And Ken was here over twenty years?"

"Yes."

"Sometimes it's beneficial to bring new blood into an organization. Get a fresh perspective. Wouldn't you agree, Ms. Edwards?" Mr. Spalding wore a smug smile.

The low hum became a dull roar. If she agreed, she'd be arguing herself out of the running. If she disagreed, she would appear self-serving.

"Mr. Spalding, a fresh perspective is crucial to the success of any organization. But so is institutional knowledge. One is not necessarily exclusive of the other." Sarah paused to carefully formulate her response so that it didn't cast aspersions on Ken's managerial skills.

"An individual who has worked in the trenches may offer a fresh perspective when placed in a management position. The individual who gains experience in the day-to-day routine is uniquely situated to bring an understanding of what works well and what doesn't—what the client likes and dislikes."

Mr. Cheswick looked impressed, while Mrs. Dillard looked at her watch. Mr. Spalding frowned as he flipped through Sarah's resume.

"You don't have a litigation background." It was a statement, not a question.

"No. I came to work here after graduating from law school. Health law is mostly regulatory, so Ken didn't find it necessary . . ." She trailed off, unsure where Mr. Spalding was headed with his comment.

"In today's litigious society, it would be helpful to have someone with a litigation background."

"Ken didn't have a litigation background either, and since our malpractice cases are handled by the risk management department, this office doesn't generally get involved."

"Malpractice isn't the only litigation the health system could face, and an experienced litigator could cut down on our outside counsel bills."

"Most in-house legal offices don't handle litigation because it is frequently more cost-effective to hire outside counsel with expertise in the specific legal matter being litigated." Sarah felt sick. If this is the direction they were headed with Ken's position, then she didn't stand a chance.

"The board hasn't decided yet that this is the direction they would like to go." After exchanging looks with her fellow board members, Mrs. Dillard said, "Unless you have any additional questions gentleman . . ." She turned to Sarah. "Thank you for speaking with us today. As you know, we have two more candidates to interview this week. We expect to have a decision by the end of next week."

Sarah stood and, reaching across the table, shook each committee member's hand, and thanked them for the opportunity to discuss her qualifications.

Well, Sarah thought as she walked to the door, she'd done her best. Mr. Spalding's pointed questions had been disconcerting, but she thought she'd handled them well. The concerns over her lack of litigation experience were troubling, but at this point there was nothing left for her to do but wait.

~

*W*aiting didn't come easy to Sarah. She'd always been patient. She'd make plans, and bide her time, methodically taking the steps necessary to achieve her goal. But when things were beyond her control, when there was no longer anything she could do to affect the outcome, she worried. And when she worried, she didn't eat.

Even the enormous buffet laid before her couldn't tempt her appetite. The family, which included Ann and her husband and kids, were gathered at her father's for his sixty-fifth birthday. The dishes she passed on were a combination of those prepared by her father, who was an artist with the grill, and home-cooked selections from the rest of the family.

The kids splashed in the pool, accompanied by the occasional "Marco" followed by "Polo" as she walked from dish to dish, passing on most of them, and only picking up small portions of the rest.

"Where's your usual appetite? Ah, fretting over the promotion?" The Admiral laid a gentle hand on her shoulder.

She looked up into his pale green eyes, lined from years of squinting at the sun aboard aircraft carriers. Putting her hand on his chest, she leaned her head against his strong shoulder. Those shoulders had carried the burden of commanding men, raising a family, and saying goodbye to his one true love—her mother.

"No reflection on your cooking, but yes." She sighed. "I'll be glad when they've made their decision."

"I know you will, baby, but can there be any doubt that my girl is the perfect candidate?" He heaped a spoonful of potato salad onto his plate.

"Mr. Spalding didn't seem too impressed with me."

"Brett Spalding, of Spalding Development Corporation?"

"Yeah, you know him?"

"Yep. He's a real pain in the ass. A little too slick, if you ask me. Met him a few years ago at a party. He tried to schmooze folks into buying into a retirement community he was developing up in St. Simons."

Piling on mac 'n' cheese, he continued, "Not my cup of tea, but he put on the hard sell. Couldn't take a hint, so I finally had to tell him flat out to take his sales pitch elsewhere."

Sarah frowned. She hoped he didn't hold a grudge.

"Have you decided to buy a more sensible car this time?" The Admiral followed her to the picnic table with his heaping plate of food.

She couldn't figure out where he put all that food. He was still as fit as a thirty-year-old.

"Probably another Volvo." A civil engineer and diver inspecting the footers of the Matthews Bridge had found her Porsche. Sitting at the bottom of the St. Johns River, feeding the fishes like something out of a mobster movie, nothing left of it but the shell. A tragic end to an undeniably beautiful car.

"That's more like my Sarah. Sensible, dependable, and safe."

~

*W*orrying also affected Sarah's concentration. The contract she'd picked up fifteen minutes ago still lay on her desk. She'd read the same provision over several times and yet couldn't tell what it said.

It was Friday. A week-and-a-half after her interview. She felt certain they'd make the announcement today. She looked at the clock. Three. If she had to wait another two hours to find out, her head would explode.

Ken knocked on her door.

Oh God, she fretted, this is it.

"Sarah. I'm glad I caught you. May I come in?"

The tentative smile on his face made her gut clinch. The job she hadn't been sure she'd wanted suddenly became crucial to her.

"Sure."

Hands in his pockets, Ken looked at her framed diplomas, certificates, law license, everywhere but at her. "Sarah, the selection committee has decided to hire from outside the office. They decided to go in a different direction, hiring someone with a strong litigation background."

She hadn't realized she'd been holding her breath, until she felt a little light-headed.

"I'm very sorry. I pushed the board hard to reconsider, but Mr. Spalding's arguments carried the day."

"Who did they hire?"

"A young lady, Patricia Litchkrieg, from New York, worked for Bachman, Seidel, and Schuster in their commercial litigation division . . ."

Ken's voice faded into the background as Sarah's ears filled with white noise. Patricia 'the Bitchkrieg' Litchkrieg? The most hated student in her law school class? How could that be? She didn't even have any experience in healthcare law. What on earth had the board members seen in her? And how on earth was she going to work for her?

~

"I have a new boss starting Monday." Sarah dropped the news like a bombshell. Ann and Becca looked up shell-shocked.

They'd been standing in the middle of the fabric store arguing over whether or not a particular fabric would work in Ann's recently remodeled dining room. Sarah guessed she had their undivided attention now.

"What do you mean? You didn't get the job?" Ann grabbed Sarah's hands.

"I can't believe it." Becca paced the aisle. "Those people are idiots for not hiring you." She stopped in front of Sarah. "Did they say why?"

"They wanted someone with a strong litigation background."

"Whatever for? Your office never handled litigation before." Becca paced away, then back. "What did the Admiral say?"

"He's disappointed." Again. Would she ever make her father proud?

"Oh, honey. I'm so sorry." Ann rubbed her hand down Sarah's arm. "Who'd they hire?"

"Patricia Litchkrieg. She's scheduled a staff meeting first thing Monday morning to meet all of us." Although she already knew Sarah.

"Wait a minute, why do I know that name?" Ann asked.

"She was in my law school class."

"Patricia 'the Bitchkrieg' Litchkrieg?" Ann asked, eyes round as an owl's.

"That's right," Becca said, gaze narrowed. "She was the snotty little bitch who told everyone she beat you out for the trial team, when in fact you withdrew your application to clerk for the federal judge."

"Among other things," Sarah muttered.

"Are you worried?" Ann asked. "You weren't the best of friends in law school."

"More like the worst of enemies, but no, I don't think she's going to come in and clean house, if that's what you mean." Sarah sighed, turning to look at another bolt of fabric. "It's going to be difficult working for her."

"Maybe she's changed, softened over the years." Ann's words weren't exactly comforting. "What's she been doing?"

"Working for a huge litigation firm in New York. They called her the pitbull."

"Okay, maybe not. But you do a great job, and your clients like you. That's got to mean something . . ." Ann offered.

"Well, you'd better put on your best suit and your best game face for your meeting. No point in taking any chances."

Becca. Always the advisor.

CHAPTER 4

Sarah plastered what she hoped was a convincing smile on her face. She and the other attorneys were gathered around the conference table for their first meeting with the Bitchkrieg, er, Patricia. She had to stop thinking of her nickname. One of these days it was going to slip.

So far, Sarah had not shared her specific encounters with the B— or rather, Patricia, only that they went to law school together. Sarah glanced around the table. Everyone shifted nervously in their seats, not making eye contact with one another. Perhaps it was the atmosphere in the office that made everyone twitchy. When Sarah had walked in this morning, all of the administrative staff sat quietly at their desks. There'd been no laughter, no chitchat around the coffee pot, and their hesitant 'good mornings' were barely audible.

Amazing. Patricia had barely been in the office more than an hour, and like the vampire she was, had already sucked the life out of it.

The office had a good group of lawyers. Ken hired well. They'd all gotten along, worked well together. Most of them had served their time in private practice before coming in-house and really appreciated the more relaxed environment.

It was a shame. She was sure the office dynamics were going to

31

change. And the ill wind bringing that change blew into the room, bringing a decided chill with her.

Patricia stood at the head of the table, her well-manicured fingertips touching the surface, as she surveyed the room with an authoritarian air. She was tall, well over five-nine, probably topping out at six feet in her stilettos, and lean.

Her long brown hair was pulled into a sleek ponytail that hung like a curtain down her back. Sharply lined gray catlike eyes that could cut through your defenses like a diamond through glass stared out at the group.

At first glance, some would say she was beautiful, sexy even, in a dominatrix sort of way. But upon closer inspection, they would discover the hard set of her mouth, the cold steel of her eyes, the icy exterior that protected a heart of stone. "Good morning."

Patricia's brow creased at the mumbled good mornings in response.

"I'm sure you're all aware of who I am, so I won't go into a lengthy presentation of my credentials, other than to say that I believe you will find me quite capable of running this office in an efficient and professional manner." Patricia caught the eyes of each attorney in turn, and in turn, each looked away before she did. After all, everyone instinctively knew the consequences of looking into the face of Medusa.

Sarah held her gaze longest. As difficult as that was, she knew the best way to deal with a bully was head on. One of the many things her father taught her.

"Why don't we go around the table, and you can introduce yourselves? Of course I've reviewed your CVs and personnel files, but I'd like to hear from you. Sarah, let's start with you."

Sarah introduced herself, but Patricia occasionally interrupted her with unwelcome anecdotes regarding their law school days.

Katie Butler, Ken's newest hire, came next. Young and pretty, she'd joined the office almost a year ago, passing up a partnership opportunity with a large law firm in D.C. Her sweet, soft-spoken manner would likely make her a target for Patricia's predatory instincts, like a lion stalking an ailing antelope.

"Katie, I seem to recall that you lost your last case with your firm. Is that why you left?" Patricia skewered her with her piercing gaze.

"I—" Katie blushed, looked around the room, swallowed. "It was a very difficult case. The partners knew going in that the odds were against the client."

"Still, I've read the facts of the case, and I'm sure I could have scored a win." Her blood-red lips turned up into a smirk.

Some people never change, Sarah thought. Patricia was still the snide little narcissistic bitch she was in law school. Poor Katie. She'd have to take her out for drinks after work, soothe her wounded pride.

"Let's hope we don't have any repeats of that performance." Patricia turned her cold gray eyes to Steve.

Steve Conrad joined two years earlier. He closed his private practice of more than twenty-five years in the hopes of slowing down. He worked hard, but the current position gave him ample time to spend with his grandkids. Who could blame him? Apparently Patricia could.

"Steve, I'm surprised you didn't retire after you sold your practice, rather than taking this job so you could just skate toward retirement." She arched a brow at him before moving on, not giving him an opportunity to respond.

The most senior person in the office besides Sarah was Kim Chang. She came from another larger health system about nine years ago when that health system got swallowed up by an even larger health system.

"It must have been difficult losing your job in the restructuring. But we all can't be success stories, right?" Patricia said, a note of censure in her voice.

The introductions out of the way and with everyone already on their guard, Patricia continued the meeting by handing out voluminous documents detailing her plans for change.

Sarah stifled a groan. She hated change.

～

"*N*ice to know some things never change." Becca slipped on a supple pair of ballet flats. "The shoe department at Neiman's has always, and ever will be, an oasis for those in need of intense retail therapy."

After Sarah's first week with the Queen of the Bitches, Ann and Becca hauled their friend to Atlanta for a girls' weekend. A little champagne, a lot of shopping, some soothing spa treatments, and a luxurious hotel suite. Who could ask for more?

But Sarah wasn't feeling it, despite the strappy red sandals she had on her feet.

"Some people never change, either," Sarah muttered to herself.

"What did you say?" Ann asked as she dropped into a chair, surrounded by a profusion of shopping bags. "Still grousing about the Bitchkrieg?"

"You'd think someone would have performed a bitchorcism on her by now." Becca handed the shoebox back to the sales clerk. "Do you have these in seven and a half?"

"She's beyond help. You can't exorcise the devil from the devil incarnate," Sarah said, sitting back in her seat. She gave up on the shoes. Even they weren't lifting her mood after her week from hell.

Despite their history, Patricia seemed to have glommed on to Sarah like she was her new BFF. Probably just to torture her.

"The things she said to Katie were inexcusable," Ann said. "Ooh. Look at these." Ann leaned down and snatched up the recently discarded red sandals.

"That's just the half of it. The way she ranted about how the office had been run by the previous general counsel, not even calling him by name, like we didn't know who she was talking about."

"How rude," Ann interjected, as she slipped the sandals onto her feet.

"Not to mention unprofessional," Becca added.

"Anyway, she said she was working on a new organizational structure for the office, and that as a result there would be some personnel changes."

"Oh boy." The clerk returned with the size Becca needed. "What do you think that means?"

"Do you think she's going to fire people?" Ann asked, eyes wide.

"Who knows? But the new structure looks like a multi-tiered bureaucratic nightmare guaranteed to bring the efficiency of the office to a grinding halt." Sarah paced the shoe department as she spoke, arms flailing. "She pulled out a process map that even computer engineers from M.I.T. couldn't read. I'm telling you, she's a classic case of narcissistic personality disorder, possibly with compensatory tendencies."

"Sarah, honey, sit down." Ann pulled her down to the seat next to her. "You're starting to draw attention."

"I mean, what general counsel's office uses a process map?" Sarah sat, but her diatribe continued.

At Sarah's unremitting rant, Ann and Becca looked at one another. "I think this calls for an intervention," Ann said, as she put the sandals back in the box.

"You know what I think we should do? Something really decadent. Let's go have lunch, accompanied by copious amounts of champagne," Becca said, as she grabbed her bags.

"And chocolate. Lots and lots of chocolate," Ann added, pulling Sarah to her feet. "It's a matter of life or death."

CHAPTER 5

Tiptoeing down the carpeted hallway, Sarah attempted to pass Patricia's door unnoticed. It was so quiet. None of the typical office chitchat, laughter, or doorway conversations.

"Sarah, can you step into my office for a moment."

Damn. How did she do that? Either she had x-ray vision or spy-cams in the hallway. Sarah's vote was for x-ray vision.

"I'm headed to a meeting with the Chief of Surgery," Sarah said, half in, half out of the doorway.

"He'll understand." Patricia smiled, but the light never reached her eyes.

"But—"

"It's important." Patricia's false friendly tone turned to steel.

Sarah sat gingerly in the chair across from Patricia's desk, as if afraid she would absorb the taint of evil just by touching the furniture.

"On some level, however conventional, you've always been a woman of taste." Patricia gave Sarah's traditional black suit and crisp white blouse the once-over. "I need you to help me select a paint color for my office redo." She displayed several paint chips as she spoke.

"I'm late for a meeting with Dr. Pendleton, and you want me to help you select paint colors?" What the hell did she care what color Patricia painted her office. She could paint it hot pink and black to match her Chanel suit for all Sarah cared.

Patricia sniffed. "Well, if you think meeting with Dr. Pendleton is more important than helping your new boss settle in, I suppose you'd better go."

Sarah took a deep breath, hoping the action would help avert the scathing remark she so desperately wanted to deliver. "Patricia, I'd be happy to help you select a paint color as soon as my meeting is finished."

"Never mind. The moment has passed." Patricia paused, wearing a petulant expression as she put the color chips into a desk drawer. "I was hoping you and I could bond over redecorating schemes, but I can see now that I was wrong."

Give me strength, Sarah thought.

"Sarah, I don't know why you hated me in law school when I tried so hard to be your friend. It's clear to me that those feelings have not dimmed over the years."

What the hell was she talking about? Sarah struggled to mask her dumbfounded reaction. Tried to be her friend? By spreading rumors that she'd slept with one of her professors? By telling everyone that she was pregnant? She couldn't imagine why anyone wouldn't want to be friends with someone like that.

"Patricia, your statement couldn't be further from the truth." Sarah tread carefully. "Our relationship has been one of the most memorable of my three years in law school."

~

Sarah put the finishing touches on the charcuterie board she'd thrown together. Leave it to Sam to phone at the last minute.

Samantha Bethancourt, Sarah's college roommate, called from the plane to tell Sarah that she'd been flying back to New York from Miami, via Jacksonville, when she decided to take a detour and see

Sarah. Never mind that Sarah might have had plans, or even been out of town. Spontaneity was one of the things Sarah loved about Sam. So different from herself.

The doorbell rang. Right on time. For all her flighty impetuousness, Sam was artlessly punctual.

Amid squeals of delight, Sarah and Sam hugged, complimented, and fawned over one another.

"How long has it been?" Sam asked, as she shrugged out of her suit jacket and slipped off her pumps, before gratefully taking the glass of Chardonnay Sarah offered.

"Four years." Actually, it'd been since Sarah's wedding.

Realizing her faux pas, Sam sat next to her on the couch. "Sarah, I'm so sorry about you and Adrian. I know it must have been difficult. How are you doing?"

"I'm fine." Sarah popped a grape in her mouth before continuing. "I've moved on." Sort of.

"Great house." Sam got up and wandered the spacious living area with its warm, English antiques, soft colors, and traditional brass fixtures, stopping to look out through the French doors at the English garden in full bloom. "Still love all things English, I see."

"How's the job?" Sarah asked.

"It's great. Just came from Miami where I signed a new author." Sam was a literary agent with a large agency in New York. "We don't usually go to our authors, but she's a quadriplegic. Does all of her typing holding a pencil in her mouth. Amazing perseverance. And she's going to be big, you wait and see. The next J.K. Rowling."

Sam circled back to the couch and, plopping down again, spun to face Sarah. "How about you? How's your job?" At Sarah's groan, Sam said, "Uh, oh, tell me all about it."

Pouring herself another glass of wine, Sarah recounted the mess her work life had become in just a few short weeks.

"So, what are you going to do?"

"Do? I'm going to keep plugging away. What else can I do? There's really nothing else here. I don't want to go into private practice, and I don't want to leave my home." After all the moves during her childhood, Sarah had finally put down roots, and she wasn't willing to pull them up again.

"That's too bad. We have a position coming open." Sam must have seen a spark in her eye and pushed a little harder. "It's an entry level position, but it's a great way to get your foot in the door. It's a lot of work, but you'd love it, and you'd be great at it, especially with your legal background."

Sarah bit her lip, tempted. A fresh start, away from the Bitchkrieg.

"And, as an added bonus, we'd get to work together."

Sarah had to admit it sounded great, getting paid to read novels, but she couldn't make yet another career change. More importantly, she couldn't make yet another move. "I won't say it isn't tempting, but, no, I'll stick it out here."

After a beat or two, Sam asked, "Whatever happened to that manuscript you wrote in college? It was good. In fact, as I recall, it was very good."

Sarah had forgotten about her attempt at writing an Austen-style novel. She'd just finished a course on Austen and was hell-bent on becoming a writer. That is, before her father talked some sense into her. "It's probably up in the attic somewhere."

"You should pull it out again." At Sarah's eye-rolling smirk, Sam continued, "You've got a real gift, and you shouldn't squander gifts."

"You're getting preachy on me."

"Sorry, but you wouldn't believe some of the crap I read, and the kicker is, it gets published. Your work is far better. I'm just saying, think about it." Polishing off her wine, she asked, "So, how do you plan to entertain me this weekend?"

~

Carlos opened the door to exit Sarah's office, laughter in his voice over the client's last comment about the federal government being 'here to help' and ran straight into the cold, imposing visage of the Bitchkrieg. His laughter died a sudden, tragic death.

"Sarah, can I see you in my office?" The ice crackled in her voice as she turned on her heel and marched up the hall.

Sarah and Carlos exchanged a knowing look.

"Sure," Sarah said to the now-empty door.

After giving Sarah a sympathetic look, Carlos beat a hasty retreat.

"Close the door, and have a seat, while I finish this email."

Impatiently waiting while Patricia tapped out her email, nails clicking on the keys, Sarah looked out the window at the view that should have been hers.

As if reading her thoughts, Patricia couldn't resist another dig. "Lovely, isn't it? Too bad everyone can't have this view, but then again, with success comes a few perks."

"Patricia, did you call me into your office to discuss the view?" Sarah knew she shouldn't poke at the angry beast, but Patricia really got under her skin.

Patricia responded with her icy stare. "No. I called you in here to warn you about your little office romance."

What the . . .

"Look, as a woman, I understand we all have needs," Patricia's lips turned up into a snide grin, "and Carlos would get any woman's motor running, but as your boss, I must instruct you to break off this relationship." Patricia examined a bright pink nail as she continued, "You know that fraternization is prohibited by hospital policy, and even if it wasn't, I would prohibit it by office policy. It's bad for morale."

Sarah was too stunned to speak. Maybe Ann and Becca were right. Maybe Carlos did have a crush on her and something in his manner gave it away to everyone but her.

"Oh come now, you can't be surprised that I discovered your little secret. The way he looks at you, your gestures of kindness to him, just now the two of you behind closed doors, for over an hour." A well-plucked eyebrow lifted.

"First, of all, I am not having an affair with my assistant. Your conclusions on that point are malicious and unfounded." She would probably regret this, but she'd had enough. "The gestures of kindness are those that I display to any colleague, friend, or family member. But how could I expect you to recognize something so foreign to your own skewed view of the world." Sarah worked up a good head of steam. "Furthermore, we were behind closed doors for over an hour because we were on a conference call with our outside counsel in D.C. and Dr. Crews about a thorny billing matter. And as for the looks he allegedly gives me, I have no earthly idea what you're talking about. Carlos is a respected colleague, an excellent assistant, a genuinely kind and warm human being, and I'd appreciate it if you wouldn't drag his name through the mud like you did Professor Franklin's."

Sarah's heart pounded in her chest. She was probably about to get fired for speaking to her boss like that, but she couldn't help herself. She was not going to stand by this time and let Patricia make unfounded accusations against her or anyone else in the office.

"Well. My, my, my. Sarah has a little temper. Who knew?" Patricia rose from her chair, and walking around her desk, sat on the front of it, arms crossed. Sarah recognized the action for what was—an attempt to intimidate her, encroach on her space. She held her ground.

"You know I could fire you for your little tirade." Patricia let that sink in. "But I'm not. You seem to be the only one around here with a backbone, and while I won't be bullied by my employees, I do appreciate someone who stands up for herself."

Bullied? There's the pot calling the kettle black.

"Let me just put it this way, if you're having an affair with your assistant, then I'm telling you to break it off immediately. If you're not, then no harm done." She gave a little shrug, as if she'd accused Sarah of eating the last cupcake instead of having an illicit office affair.

"Let me put it this way." Sarah rose from her chair as she spoke. "I am not having an affair with Carlos, and I'd appreciate it if you didn't make such false accusations in the future. And you're wrong. There is harm. You've harmed not only my name and reputation, but Carlos' as well. I'm not going to tell Carlos about this. It would be humiliating to him." Sarah continued, "And I'd appreciate it if you didn't say anything to him or to anyone else in the office. Now, if there's nothing else, I'd like to get back to work." Not waiting for a reply, Sarah turned on her heel and left.

～

Sarah closed her door and slumped into her chair, her hand pressed to her stomach. She couldn't believe she just chewed out her boss. Never mind that she hated the woman. She'd never even considered speaking to a supervisor in that manner.

Her father taught her and Becca to respect persons in positions of authority. Even when you disagreed. You politely spoke your mind, judiciously argued your point, and if they still disagreed, at least you'd spoken up.

Sarah also knew that letting people push your buttons only gave them power over you, especially people like Patricia, who were always looking for a chink in your armor.

Taking a deep breath, she closed her eyes, and slowly exhaled, vowing she would remain in control of her temper the next time she had an encounter with the devil made flesh.

～

Things in the office stabilized. Sarah was able to get back into a routine, albeit a new one, which included a heavy dose of avoidance—avoiding the Bitchkrieg, avoiding private meetings with Carlos where possible, and more importantly avoiding thoughts of her own unhappiness. Nevertheless, even avoidance was good when it was part of an overall routine. Routine brought comfort, stability, even if it also brought with it monotony.

Amidst the almost constant upheaval caused by the family moves required by her father's naval career, Sarah's mother worked hard to establish routines, so that no matter where they lived, there would be little constants.

Mornings were for family breakfast. Afternoons were for home-

43

work, chores, and athletic training. Evenings were for family dinners, movie time, or curling up with a book.

Sarah's participation in athletics kept her life regimented, and of course, as a military man, her father lived and died by schedules. So was it any wonder that she sought predictability in her life? Still, predicting the next lottery winner would have been easier than predicting what her erratic boss would do next.

The intercom on Sarah's phone buzzed, making her jump.

"I'm sorry to bother you, Sarah, but Patricia would like to see you in her office first thing tomorrow morning. I've cleared your morning." Sarah could hear the sympathy in Carlos' voice.

Sighing, Sarah said, "Okay. Thanks." So much for avoidance.

∾

Sarah sat across the desk from Patricia, trying to hide her dismay.

From Sarah's perspective, the meeting was going worse than all her previous meetings with her boss. She'd been given two options, neither of which she liked.

After tucking a silky brown strand of hair behind her ear, Patricia folded her hands in front of her on her desk and smiled. The disingenuous smile never reached her glacial gray eyes.

"Well, Sarah, I'm sure I've given you a great deal to think about. But please, take the weekend to consider it."

Her supercilious attempt at graciousness set Sarah's teeth on edge. The Bitchkrieg knew she'd placed her in a difficult position, and clearly she reveled in it.

"Thank you, but I don't need time to think about it, Sarah said, as she looked into Patricia's triumphant face. "You leave me no other alternative."

CHAPTER 6

Sarah, Ann, and Becca walked on the beach in a rare summer nor'easter, bundled in rain slickers and galoshes.

The rain had stopped, but the dark, scudding clouds turned the ocean gun-metal gray. The gusty northeasterly winds churned the water like a washing machine and filled the air with the briny scent of the ocean. Clumps of foam rolled along the beach like tumbleweeds, and Sarah could feel the salt spray coating her face and wind-tangled hair.

"You did what!" Becca and Ann exclaimed simultaneously. Under other circumstances, Sarah would cry 'jinx,' but now was not the time.

"I quit my job," Sarah said, as she shrugged. She had to speak loud to be heard over the wind and crashing waves.

"Why on earth would you do that?" Becca asked. "And without taking the time to find another job first?"

"I had a meeting with the Bitchkrieg this morning."

"What did she want? Was she going to fire you, so you quit first?" Ann asked, hopeful that would explain Sarah's drastic actions.

"She wanted to talk to me about her personnel changes for the office," she said, her fingers making quotation marks around 'changes.'

"Uh-oh," Ann said. Whether it was in response to her story or having to dodge the erratic wave that crashed onto the shore, Sarah couldn't tell.

"Yeah," Sarah responded flatly. "She's equating changing titles with promotions and has plans to change our titles to ridiculously long, over-important ones. None of us ever cared what we were called. We were well-respected by Ken and our clients, and we were well-paid for our efforts."

Seagulls hung in the air overhead, interrupting the conversation with their cries, as if cursing the forces of nature that made their flying so difficult today.

"She'd reviewed some of my work and spoken to my clients, and although she didn't completely agree with some of my advice," Sarah rolled her eyes, "she could see that I was a good lawyer . . . the best in the office."

"How dare she! Of all the nerve," Becca said, tongue in cheek.

"I could do without your sarcasm." Sarah leveled a look at her sister.

"But that's good, isn't it?" Ann asked. "So how did you go from that to quitting?"

"It gets better, or worse, depending on your point of view. She told me she needed a deputy and offered me the position of Assistant Vice President and Deputy General Counsel."

"Wait a minute. She planned to promote you and you quit?" Becca threw her hands up in disgust. "You're right. This does get worse."

"Becca, you don't understand. Not only did she tell me I had to cancel my trip to England, but one of my first duties was to fire Katie. Coward."

"What?" Ann asked, the shock evident on her face.

"Yeah. She wanted me to do her dirty work. It was a test to see if I could become one of her trusted henchman." Sarah picked up a shell and tossed it forcefully into the roiling waves. "She said she had an excellent lawyer who could start in the office right away, someone she'd worked with in her previous firm."

"That is low," Ann said.

"Really low," Becca added.

"In the end, when I said I wouldn't fire Katie, the Bitchkrieg gave me an ultimatum: cancel my vacation and fire Katie—or resign. She gave me time to think about it, but I didn't need it. I told her she would have my resignation by the end of the day."

"Oh my God, Sarah. How did she react?" Ann asked.

"I think she was stunned. Clearly, that wasn't the answer she'd expected, but she'd offered no other more palatable options. I went to my office, closed my door, and began packing my things. My resignation was on her desk by five."

"I sent emails to everyone to tell them. I know," Sarah said, holding up her hands, "that seems cowardly. But I knew if I told them in person, I would get emotional, and I wasn't going to give her the satisfaction of seeing me cry. Everyone has arranged to meet for drinks on Monday."

"How are you going to support yourself?" Becca asked.

"Becca, the house is paid for, and I have the divorce settlement and the small trust fund from Mom. I'll be fine." For a year, maybe longer . . . if she quit eating.

"Yes, but you'll blow through your savings faster than you think. I know you hated her, but at least you had a job. It's easier to find a job when you have a job. Now you have nothing." Becca's tone was like that of a mother scolding her irresponsible teenager. "And the longer you're out of work, the harder it will be for you to find a good job. You'd better start looking right away."

"Honey, I know the last two years have been a mostly downhill roller coaster ride for you, but during all of that, at least you had a good, steady job . . ." Ann's tone was more conciliatory.

"Hey. The two of you have been telling me to shake things up a bit —that I needed a change. Isn't that the reason you persuaded me to go to England?"

"Yes, but by change we didn't mean committing professional suicide. Jesus, Sarah, this is crazy and irresponsible—" Becca argued, arms gesturing emphatically.

"I know. Everything I'm not." She sighed. "Look, I love you both, and I appreciate your concern, but really, I'm going to be okay." She smiled reassuringly. In reality, she wasn't as confident as she sounded.

❧

*T*eacup in hand, the bar journal opened to the classified ads, Sarah picked up her red pen prepared to circle potential jobs that would mean a fresh start for her. At least that was what she tried telling herself.

So much for her moratorium on impulsive acts. Quitting her job had to be the dumbest impulsive act to date.

She couldn't remember the last time she'd looked at the want ads. Probably not since high school when she'd been looking for a job to pay for the car insurance her parents said she had to be able to afford before they would get her a car.

Boutique law firm seeks associate attorney to handle healthcare collections. Five years experience practicing law.

Collections work, Sarah thought. Only if I was starving and my kid was barefoot.

Healthcare firm seeks healthcare attorney to join practice. Must have over five years of solid health law experience and be a member of the Florida Bar.

So far so good. Sarah took a sip of her tea and continued reading.

Successful candidates must have significant experience in various aspects of healthcare law, including contract drafting, contracting, joint ventures, reimbursement, fraud and abuse, Stark and managed care. Litigators need not apply.

She snickered at the last sentence. Circling that ad as a possibility, she moved on.

Experienced, highly competent corporate attorney wanted for small, active transactional firm.

Transactional attorney. Not really her cup of tea, but . . . she continued reading.

Successful candidate will have seven-to-ten years of transactional experience, as well as excellent analytical and legal drafting skills.

She had the transactional experience, and the drafting skills.

Successful candidate will be a self-starter, a team player, and able to manage other lawyers and staff. Bilingual ability in Spanish.

So much for that. If they ever needed a bilingual with French, she would apply. Next.

Work from home. Legal drafters needed. Provide legal research and writing support for law firms. Legal memoranda, briefs, contracts, plus some editing work all on an assignment-by-assignment basis. Qualified candidates must have excellent legal drafting skills, and a minimum of five years practicing law, including legal drafting experience.

That intrigued Sarah. Flexibility. Work from home. And better yet, no bitchy boss.

Circling that one, she picked up her now-cold cup of tea. Only two potential jobs out of the whole classified section. What if she had to move? What if she had no other choice?

She thought about Sam and the job in New York. Assistant literary agent or something like that. But was she ready to give up on her legal career? Would they hire her without any experience, recommendation from Sam notwithstanding? Moreover, could she live in New York? Looking around her cozy, comfortable home, she didn't think she could give it up for a postage-stamp-sized apartment that would likely cost more than her monthly salary.

No. There had to be something she could do and still stay put.

~

She couldn't sleep. Looking at the clock for the umpteenth time, Sarah finally got up to explore the thing that kept nudging her, like a persistent, nagging voice foiling her attempts to sleep.

She woke up at two a.m. thinking about her old manuscript. Wondering where it was, wondering if she still had it, and wondering if it was any good. After all, she'd written it almost eighteen years ago. Now, two hours later and still in her pajamas, she pulled down the attic steps, hoping not to hear any scurrying in her wake.

After yanking the cord, the fluorescent lights flickered and slowly came to life, revealing stacks of dusty boxes, some labeled, some not. At least no unwelcome critters were there to greet her. She shivered as she thought of that possibility.

Heaving a sigh, Sarah's first thought was that it was hopeless. It could take a month of Sundays searching through the multitude of boxes, and she could still come up empty-handed. She didn't even know if she still had it. But she had nothing but time on her hands, and clearly her bout of busy-brain syndrome wasn't going to let her get back to sleep, so she might as well get started.

She needed a plan of attack. Dividing the attic into three sections, she would systematically go through the boxes. She already knew that many of the boxes stacked to her right were Christmas decorations, so those were quickly eliminated. The boxes to her left mostly contained old household items she'd been meaning to donate to the local charity thrift store but hadn't gotten around to it.

It was the third stack, directly in front of her that posed the greatest challenge. Unlabeled, she had no idea what they might contain.

Dragging up an old chair with a missing rung, she pulled the first box off the stack and sat down. Dust floated up to tickle her nose and the smell of musty old books assaulted her, making her sneeze. The box contained her high school yearbooks, some old, worn paperbacks from her childhood, and even some term papers from her high school days. She thumbed through a yearbook before reminding herself that this wasn't a walk down memory lane, but a quest for treasure.

Discarding the box, she wished she'd thought to bring a marker up to not only label the boxes, but also to mark them as searched.

The next box revealed old photos, and the one after that, old tax returns. When she opened a box containing some of her college textbooks and papers, her pulse quickened. At least she was getting warmer, but no manuscript.

It was nearly six a.m. when she opened a box that held no promise whatsoever that it would contain a manuscript. Digging through old athletic uniforms, trophies, awards, and other miscellaneous and sundry items from her days on her college crew team, she found it.

At the bottom of the box, bound in rubber bands that had long since lost their elasticity, she lifted the bulky stack of yellowed pages. The cover page read, *The American Heiress* by Sarah Anne Edwards. Holding it to her chest like a long-lost friend, she nearly wept with relief. And fear.

What if it really sucked?

CHAPTER 7

"Any luck with the job search?" Ann asked. "Way to go, Lily!"

They sat on bleachers in the scorching summer sun watching Ann's daughter's soccer match. Lily ran down the field after scoring a goal, arms raised in triumph. The goal put her team up one-nothing.

Rob, Ann's husband, let out a shrill whistle, followed by a loud *woohoo!*

"Nothing terribly promising." Sarah shielded her eyes from the sun as she followed Lily's progress down the field. "I've got a phone interview next week with a company that hires independent legal drafters for law firms."

"That's good, isn't it?" Ann asked. She pulled out the sunscreen and slathered more on her nose.

"We'll see . . ." Her voice trailed off. "What if I have to move, Ann? What if I can't find anything here?" She looked at Ann, tears in her eyes.

"Oh honey. We'll cross that river when we come to it, and hopefully we'll never come to it."

Sarah rolled her eyes at Ann's muddled cliché.

"That's right." Rob reached over and patted Sarah's leg. "No sense borrowing trouble."

Ann jumped up when Lily got tangled up with another player and fell.

Rob grabbed her wrist and tugged her back down. "She's fine," he told Ann. "Shake it off, sugar," he yelled to Lily.

"Ann, do you remember that manuscript I wrote back in college?"

"Yeah, I wondered why you never did anything with it. You always were a good writer."

"Well, I'd forgotten about it until Sam reminded me of it when she was here last weekend. I found it, and you know something . . . it's not half bad." Sarah smiled as she thought about how she'd read through it after a sleepless night. She couldn't make herself put it down. She'd sat right there in the attic and read at least the first hundred pages, before her stomach spoke up, reminding her that she hadn't had breakfast yet.

"I think I'll work on it again, maybe clean it up, and try submitting it. Sam said she'd thought it was good back in college, and it's something I can do while I'm looking for a job."

Ann's eyes lit up. "I think that's a great idea. You could be the next Jane Austen." She wore an impish grin. "But if you want my advice, I think you should spice it up with a bare-chested hunk or two . . . and a lot of rowdy sex."

～

Sarah had her head in a tall cardboard box when the doorbell rang. Who could that be?

She caught her reflection in the hall mirror. She looked a mess. Her hair was twisted into an unkempt ponytail that hung slightly askew after her submersion into the box. She had on shabby sweats and a ragged, holey T-shirt that didn't match, and her big toe stuck out of a hole in her sock.

She tentatively opened the door and breathed a sigh of relief when she saw Ann's astonished face.

"Well, look at you. Don't you look like something the stork dragged in?" She stepped into the foyer where Sarah was cleaning out the coat closet. "What are you doing?" She looked around in disgust. "Don't tell me you're cleaning out another closet."

It'd been two weeks since she'd told Ann about the manuscript, and she hadn't written or edited the first word, but her closets and attic were well organized, and Goodwill had scored a windfall in donations.

"I thought you were supposed to be clearing your head and getting in touch with your inner Jane Austen. Not cleaning your closets and getting in touch with your inner maid."

"Just because I'm cleaning out closets doesn't mean I'm not getting in touch with my inner Jane Austen. The mindless work gives me lots of time to think . . ." she finished lamely.

"Honestly, Sarah, you're wasting precious time. Once you get a job, you won't have time to devote to creating the sensitive, sexy, well-muscled hero we've all been yearning for."

Ann had been so excited about Sarah's writing scheme, she'd already planned what to wear to the premier of the implausible block-buster movie based on her currently unfinished, unpublished manuscript.

Sarah didn't know what was wrong with her. It wasn't like her to procrastinate. When she set a task for herself, she started on it right away.

"I know, I know. And I leave for England next week." And that's another thing, she berated herself. She should have her head examined for jetting off on a two-week vacation when she was currently out of work.

But the trip was paid for, and she couldn't get her money back at this point, so it was a shame to let it go to waste. At least that's how she rationalized it.

"Hey, maybe that's just what you need to get your creative juices flowing. Your story takes place in England, right? Maybe you'll be inspired . . . and maybe you'll live your own little romance while you're there." Ann waggled her eyebrows.

"You and Becca conspiring again?" At Ann's confused expression, Sarah explained. "She said the same thing. Trust me, with all the upheaval in my life right now, the last thing I want or need is a romance, little or not."

~

"God honey, are you bringing your entire wardrobe?" Ann asked, trying to heave Sarah's steamer-trunk-sized suitcase into the back of Becca's SUV.

"The weather in England is so changeable, I wasn't sure what to bring, so I brought a little of everything." Sarah shrugged as she helped Ann maneuver the suitcase into the car.

"Really? I hope the plane is carrying extra fuel with all this added weight."

"Funny."

"You girls need to stop chit-chatting and let's get on the road before you miss your flight." Becca used the same tone of voice their mother had used when her patience wore thin.

The ride to the airport descended into silliness as the three girls competed to see who could insert the most British colloquialisms into the conversation. Sarah thought she won, but lost track with all the laughter.

"Here," Ann said as she handed Sarah a small, wrapped package. "This is for you."

Sarah unwrapped the package to find a hardcover journal, bound in beautiful handmade rice paper.

"In case you're inspired," she said with a smile.

"Thank you. That is so thoughtful."

"Wait. Me, too." Becca handed Sarah another gift box. This one held a fountain pen emblazoned with the Oxford logo.

"You guys are such givers."

Amid smiles and tears, Sarah hugged Ann and Becca goodbye. "Take care that you don't come back with a stiff upper lip." Becca's parting shot as Sarah went through security made her giggle.

56

"Don't forget to water my plants, fill the feeders, and get my mail," Sarah shouted as she walked down the concourse.

"I know, I know," Ann said.

On the plane at last, Sarah could breathe easy. Preparing for trips always wound her up, but once on the plane, she knew there was nothing else she could do but sit back and relax. Her vacation was mapped out to the last detail, with some unscheduled time allotted for unexpected detours, whimsies, and such. She was determined to put the worries concerning her jobless status out of her mind for the next two weeks.

Before it was time to turn off 'all cell phones and portable electronic devices,' Sarah sent one more text to Ann to remind her to water her plants, fill her feeders, and pick up her mail. She grinned as she turned off her phone. That should do it. She could just hear Ann's groan at the nagging reminder.

∼

Several hours later, the flight attendant announced the preparation for their initial approach into Gatwick.

The patchwork landscape of the English countryside was visible from Sarah's window. Pale green squares, abutted golden patches of hay ready for harvest, and the occasional patch of lavender fields in bloom, all stitched into an irregular quilt, with stands of tall cedars, majestic oaks, and hedgerows creating the seams that held the vibrant patches together. This multi-hued quilt blanketed the undulating hills as far as the eye could see.

Sarah sat back in her seat and smiled. She was already waxing poetic. Ann could be right. Maybe this trip was exactly what she needed.

CHAPTER 8

$\mathcal{A}$ pleasant two-hour train ride from London, Oxford's Town Center was home to Oxford University's thirty-nine colleges, including Christ Church, plus fine restaurants, lovely, old boutique hotels, and a very cosmopolitan population. Matthew Arnold's 'city of dreaming spires' stood much as it had for hundreds of years. Sarah's excitement grew as Tom Tower, the Christopher Wren-designed entrance to Christ Church, came into view.

As the taxi pulled up outside Tom's Gate, a friendly, bowler-hat-wearing porter stepped to the curb to open Sarah's door, offering her a warm greeting and a pleasant smile. "Good day, miss. Welcome to Christ Church. I hope you enjoy your stay with us."

With her first glimpse of Tom's Quad, she had an almost spiritual experience. Smiling broadly at the porter she replied, "I have no doubt I will."

$\mathcal{T}$ he week was off to a good start. Interesting and diverse people filled Sarah's class, including a few men.

Her Victorian Era dorm was on the fifth floor of a five-story walk-up, so there would no lack of exercise, and the weather was unusually mild and sunny.

After sumptuous dinners in Tudor Hall, the evenings were filled with activities ranging from poetry readings to croquet and sparkling wine in the Master's Garden, or in less highbrow pursuits like sampling Guinness at one of the local pubs.

Class discussions were lively and stimulating, and the added male viewpoint was enlightening. The two Austen books under consideration during the course were *Sense and Sensibility* and *Mansfield Park*.

Sarah sat among her classmates, pen and paper in hand taking notes as their tutor, Mr. Byrne, raised the question whether Austen's male characters lack depth; whether they are worthy of the women who win them in the end.

Sean Daly spoke in his lyrical Irish burr, "Austen's men are not flat, depthless characters." Sean looked like the last person you'd expect to see in a class on Jane Austen's heroines. The twenty-something pub-owner looked as if he would be more comfortable behind his bar building pints of Guinness than in a class at Christ Church discussing Regency novels. But underneath his tattooed and pierced exterior, he harbored a great love for literature. His pub, Brophy's, was on the Dublin Literary Pub Crawl.

His brows puckered in concentration, drawing his eyebrow ring down, as he continued, "Austen's men have the maturity to recognize the profundity of the women they come to love. Edward and Edmund couldn't appreciate Elinor and Fanny, respectively, if they lacked the same discerning character themselves."

Everyone's brows shot up in response to his use of the word 'profundity.' It was a little like watching a biker discussing Wharton.

"That's right. It takes a good man to recognize a good woman." Mitch, wearing a silly grin on his face, put his arm around Darla and tugged her closer to him. Darla and Mitch, an American couple, who when asked what brought them to Christ Church, explained that about four years ago they promised each other to take an active interest in the favored passions of the other. Last year, Darla spent a week with Mitch at an NFL football camp. According to her, she'd ended the week bruised, battered, and sore, but having loved every minute of it. This year, Mitch was joining her for a week at Oxford. He had never read much of anything, much less Jane Austen. It was going to be interesting to see if he ended the week with the same enthusiasm with which Darla ended the NFL camp.

"Or, another good man," Guy interjected with a mischievous glint in his blue eyes. Openly gay, Guy was the kind of guy that could be a girl's best friend. He'd never had any interest in Jane Austen, or literature for that matter, until he saw Colin Firth in *Pride and Prejudice* and, in his words, "fell arse over tip in love." This confession had broken the first-day ice, and had everyone laughing.

"I don't think it's fair to lump Edward and Edmund in with the likes of Willoughby and Henry Crawford." Guy continued, "Those two are as shallow and feckless as they come. I wouldn't give either of them the time of day, and I can't understand why Marianne and Maria did either."

"Sarah, you're awfully quiet. What are your thoughts on Austen's male characters?" Mr. Byrne had a way of pulling everyone into the discussion.

Sarah gave her response some thought, before responding. "Although Edward and Willoughby are guilty of the same sin—courting a woman when they are already attached—in the end, Edward redeems himself, albeit because his vapid little fiancée runs off with his brother. But once he is free of his prior obligation, he is still willing to live on a small annual sum in order to marry Elinor, his true love. Willoughby, on the other hand, chooses wealth over the woman he professes so adamantly to love."

"Well, ladies and gentleman, on that note, it is time for lunch." Mr. Byrne gathered his books and notes as he spoke. "Before I forget, we leave Thursday at eight-thirty a.m. sharp. The coach will be waiting at the Tom's Gate, so please be on time."

Thursday was the class excursion to Chawton House and

Winchester. The ladies in the class considered it their pilgrimage to Austen. The men in the class considered it an opportunity to visit the pubs in Winchester.

"Oh, Sarah, may I delay your lunch a moment?" Lady Clara Fraser, Dowager Countess of Rutherford, rounded out the class. According to Mr. Byrne, Lady Clara was considered the matriarch of Oxford.

She'd taken classes every week of Oxford's five-week program for the last three years. Her effervescent personality and genuine warmth won the immediate affection of everyone in the class, but for some reason, she'd singled Sarah out as her 'particular friend.' This pleased Sarah greatly, since she felt an instant connection to her.

Sarah smiled into the sparkling eyes of a woman who reminded her a little of Queen Elizabeth II, matronly, but regal, sure of who she was and her place in the world.

"Do you have plans tomorrow afternoon?"

"No. Some of the others are taking a tour of the Oxford breweries at the request of the men, but I wasn't planning to join them."

"I would like to have you to tea at Rutherford Hall, if you're so inclined."

"I would love to. Thank you for your kind invitation."

"Lovely. My car will pick you up at two-thirty at the Canterbury Gate."

"Thank you." Sarah already knew better than to argue with Lady Clara about the transportation arrangements. Once Lady Clara made up her mind, not even the Queen herself could change it. "I'll look forward to it."

～

The smells of hops and barley, cigarette smoke, and fish and chips filled the low-ceilinged, wood-beam and plaster room. The sixteenth-century pub overflowed with both Oxford locals and international visitors. The ladies sat on barstools, while the men hovered, sampling pints of stout and cracking good-natured jokes.

Sarah sipped from a pint of ale and listened to the boisterous conversation of her newfound friends.

Kim Haynes, a fellow American, sat next to Sarah. Her small frame, delicate coloring, and pixie features seemed out of place with what they'd come to call her Texas-sized personality. Kim graduated from high school and was taking a year off before going to college at Yale University. Sarah smiled as Kim flirted outrageously with the handsome young man behind the bar. Those Ivy League boys were in for a surprise when they encountered this steel magnolia.

Sean wore a slight frown as he watched the exchange. It looked to Sarah like a crush had developed there, at least on his side.

Marie Gaudet sat on the other side of Kim. Her lovely French accent stood out among the various English dialects spoken by the other pub patrons. She was a lovely young woman from the South of France whose midnight black hair, ultra-short fringe bangs, and patrician features reminded Sarah of a young Audrey Hepburn. Her flamboyant Bohemian dress was in direct contrast to Lady Clara's somewhat matronly style.

Guy sipped his beer, making a face, while Sean and Mitch laughed, obviously at his expense. Sean and Mitch treated Guy like, well, one of the guys, regardless of his sexual orientation. It pleased Sarah to see the camaraderie among them. She overheard snippets of their conversation. Despite their reminders that Colin was a married heterosexual, Guy hadn't given up hope.

"If the handsome, rich Mr. Darcy can fall for a woman purportedly beneath his station then, Colin Firth can fall for a lovesick gay guy from the East End," he said, taking another sip of his beer, shuddering this time as it went down.

Their little group had become tight knit in a short period of time. They ate all their meals together, and yesterday toured the other Oxford colleges, between the compulsory stops to the city's oldest and most renowned pubs. On Friday, weather permitting, they planned to have a picnic in the Master's Garden, their own private goodbye.

Sean squeezed between Sarah and Kim, trying to commandeer Kim's attention, but she continued her banter with the bartender.

Hoping to distract Sean, Sarah asked, "Your love of literature notwithstanding, what made you pick up Jane Austen?"

"I've read all the great male writers, James Joyce, Henry James, Trollope, so I thought it was time to see what the Jane Austen craze was all about. All the women I know go all dreamy when they talk of her novels." He wore a roguish expression as he continued, "I'm after thinking I could learn a thing or two."

Sarah laughed. "Are you sure it wasn't just an excuse to meet women?"

"Ah, Sarah, you've got me pegged," he replied before a question from Kim captured his attention.

Just then, someone bumped into Sarah causing her to spill the beer she held to her lips. A sharp rebuke on her lips, she turned and looked into the warmest coffee-brown eyes she'd ever seen. The words froze on her tongue.

"I beg your pardon." He spoke in a refined British accent, a dimple forming at the corner of his mouth. When Sarah didn't move to clean up the spill, he picked up a napkin and taking her hand, began the task himself.

"Please, allow me. Although I'm afraid your hand will be rather sticky until you wash up with soap and water." His hands were warm on hers as he gently wiped her wrist and hand.

"I suppose if I'm holding your hand, I should at least introduce myself. I'm Alex Fraser."

She noticed his eyes crinkled around the corners when he smiled. Sarah still couldn't find the function of speech.

"Hey, Mick, hand me a clean damp cloth." He spoke to the bartender who'd been the focus of Kim's attention, and Sean's ire.

"And you are . . ." he asked, his brow lifted.

"Oh, I'm Sarah, Sarah Edwards."

"Thanks, Mick," he said, as he took the damp cloth and cleaned the remaining beer residue from her hand. "Well, Sarah, the least I can do is buy you another drink." Before Sarah could protest, Alex turned back to Mick. "Mick, bring Sarah here another of what she was drinking."

"Sure, mate." As Mick worked the tap, he asked Alex, "How've you been? Any new movies in the works?"

"Thank you," Sarah said, as she took the glass from Mick. She frowned. Was he an actor? A bit embarrassed, she wondered if she should recognize him.

He smiled at Mick as he spoke. His charming British lilt carried the cadence of the British upper class, not unlike that of Prince William or Prince Harry, in a voice smooth as satin against silk. Dimples framed an engaging smile. Casually tousled, his dark wavy hair evoked thoughts of discarded clothes, rumpled bed sheets, and whispered promises. Sarah realized the bed she pictured in her juicy little imagination was hers. She looked down as he glanced at her, mortified at the direction of her thoughts.

She risked another glance, and found his attention directed at Mick once again, giving her an opportunity to further examine his features. A clean-shaven face stretched taut over a strong, square jaw enhanced all the aforementioned male beauty.

Her attention returned to the conversation when Alex said something about filming a BBC adaptation of one of the many so-called Darcy novels, which re-imagines *Pride and Prejudice,* from the perspective of Mr. Darcy.

"I'm sorry I don't recognize you. You're an actor?"

"Yes, and no apologies, please."

His polished manners were out of place in the decidedly unpolished atmosphere of the pub and seemed more fitting for a waistcoat and trousers rather than the blue jeans and navy T-shirt he wore.

"My work hasn't made it across the pond yet. But to answer your question, I have been in three BBC adaptations of somewhat obscure literary works. Rather stodgy plots by today's standards."

"What is obscure to some may not be obscure to others. Are we talking really obscure works like *Abelard and Heloise,* or just mildly obscure works like *Middlemarch?*" She'd recovered her footing now that they talked literature.

Alex was pleasantly surprised to find such erudite conversation in his favorite pub. The large student-population notwithstanding, the conversation of even the most educated in Oxford often turned to more base topics when alcohol was involved.

Who was this beautiful American, and what was she doing in an Oxford pub discussing literature as if she were an academic? She was a far cry from the bookish tutors with whom he was familiar.

Her hair fell in mink-colored waves around her shoulders, and he imagined they were just as soft and silky. He longed to brush the heavy locks back so he could catch a glimpse of that lovely neck. Her green eyes sparkled like emeralds that changed with her emotions. First fiery when she'd turned to deliver a set-down at his now-fortuitous collision, then warm as the conversation turned to literature.

No. He was sure he'd never felt this attraction for any of his female tutors.

"Well, my first role was as Jude Fawley in Thomas Hardy's *Jude the Obscure*," he grinned and shrugged when he said 'obscure,' "followed by Angel Clare in *Tess of the d'Urbervilles*, also by Hardy. But my most recent role was in a remake of *Mansfield Park*, in which I played Edmund Bertram."

She raised a neatly trimmed brow. "I gather you enjoy period pieces."

"Certainly. It gives me an opportunity to explore history and culture in a way my imagination never could. I get to live it, if only for a short time. I enjoy the experience of being transported to a world that no longer exists."

"Everything okay, Sarah?" The burly, tattooed man next to her asked. Her boyfriend perhaps? He didn't seem at all her type.

"I'm fine, Sean, thank you."

She turned back to face him. No. Their body language wasn't that of a romantic couple, and his interest appeared to be on the young woman sitting to her right.

Taking a sip of his beer, he continued the discussion, hoping to satisfy his curiosity. "So, obscurity is in the eye of the beholder, to butcher an old cliché. What is it you do that Jude Fawley is, well, not so obscure?"

"I'm a lawyer, er, well, currently I'm an out-of-work lawyer."

He raised his eyebrows, not expecting that response, neither the fact that she was a lawyer and not some literary scholar, nor the fact that she was unemployed. The light in her eyes momentarily dimmed when she mentioned her employment status.

"But I majored in literature in college, and love to read books with stodgy plots," she said, eyes bright again.

"What brings you to Oxford?"

"I'm here studying at Christ Church. These are some of my classmates." She waved her hand, indicating her friends gathered at the bar.

Ah, yes, of course. Spending much of his time in London, he forgot about the summer educational programs offered by the various colleges.

"Sarah, we're leaving. You coming then?" the burly guy asked as Sarah's classmates paid for their drinks and vacated their spots at the bar. He gave Alex the once-over that seemed to indicate he wasn't leaving without Sarah.

"Sure." As much as she enjoyed talking with Alex, it was rather late.

As she reached for her wallet, Alex touched her wrist stopping her, "I've got it. I owe you a drink after making you wear your other one."

"That's not necessary but thank you." She looked up into his laughing eyes. "I enjoyed our conversation." She was reluctant to leave, but it was probably for the best.

He didn't know why, but he couldn't let her just walk away. "Would you like to go to dinner tomorrow evening?"

She certainly hadn't expected that. "Thanks, but I have plans. Besides, I have a rule . . . I don't date strangers." The brilliant smile tempered any offense her words might have caused.

She threw one last look over her shoulder before exiting the pub.

Didn't date strangers. He grinned as he fished money out of his pocket. He could solve that.

*A*s promised, Lady Clara's car waited at the Canterbury Gate the following afternoon.

The chauffeur introduced himself as Charles, and after settling in the back seat, Sarah couldn't resist talking with him. She wasn't sure if that was appropriate, but he didn't seem uncomfortable with her attempts at conversation.

She asked him what he knew of the history of the area and how long he'd been with Lady Clara.

"My family has been with Lady Clara's family for seven generations, miss," he said.

Sarah was genuinely taken aback. "Wow!" came her inarticulate response. She quickly did some math in her head and guessed that would be about two hundred years of service to Lady Clara's family.

He smiled at her reaction. "All of the men in my family have served either as coach drivers in the days of horse drawn carriage or chauffeurs in the days of motor cars," he responded with pride. "The women in the family have served as chamber maids, ladies' maids, and more recently as cooks. Now with women taking on more men's work, some of the women even work as gardeners."

"Then your family has seen a great deal of change throughout the last two centuries."

"Oh yes, miss. Some good, some bad. But change is the one constant in life. I believe it was the Greek Philosopher Heraclitus who said, 'Nothing endures but change.'"

Hmm, she thought, a philosophy-quoting chauffeur. Sarah turned to look out the window. The ride to Lady Clara's ancestral home took only half an hour. They arrived at the gates and drove for another quarter mile to the main entrance of the imposing structure. She wasn't sure what she'd expected, but those expectations couldn't possibly live up to the reality.

Although the home would not be considered grand when compared to Blenheim or Althorp, it was quite large by most standards. The residence was constructed of a mellow golden brick fashioned in the form of the letter 'H' with a center portion and two wings. Large, mullioned windows lined the front of the house at regular intervals, giving the house a very orderly appearance.

Sarah was astonished that a woman of Lady Clara's apparent means and status took such a liking to her.

The chauffeur escorted her to the massive wood-paneled foyer, and from there, another gentleman escorted her to an elegantly furnished sitting room where Lady Clara waited. The Countess stepped forward, taking Sarah's hands and kissing her cheek. "Welcome to Rutherford Hall, my dear. I am so happy you agreed to have tea with me this afternoon."

"Thank you for the invitation, Lady Clara. I wouldn't miss the privilege. You are so thoughtful to think of me."

"Oh, pish-tosh. You do me the honor of keeping an old lady company. And please, call me Clara."

"Thank you. I'll try." Sarah looked around the room, all rich golds, warm reds, and deep blues. The lapis fireplace served as the focal point of the large room, but several small furniture groupings lent an intimacy to the space.

"Before tea, would you like a tour of the main rooms?"

"That would be lovely."

The ancestral home's proportions were generous, but the country style architecture and warm, inviting rooms made it comfortable. As Lady Clara presented her home, she talked of her family, her life, and her marriage. She pointed out this artifact or that antique, and Sarah couldn't help thinking how awe-inspiring it must be to walk in the footsteps of generations of ancestors.

Lady Clara Fraser was born Lady Clara Sutherland. "My family's estate has a long and storied history. Once quite prosperous in the seventeenth, eighteenth, and nineteenth centuries, the estate fell on hard times during the early part of the twentieth century, not uncommon in Great Britain."

Climbing the stairs to the second floor, Sarah measured her steps so as not to outpace her hostess. "Without the support of its tenant farmers, estates had little revenue. Many were sold off and divided up into smaller parcels, while others were turned into inns by their owners."

"My father, Lord Rutherford, the seventh Earl of Rutherford, tried desperately to hold onto the family estate by any means possible, including opening it up to tourists."

They walked along the large gallery looking at portraits of Lady Clara's ancestors, before stopping in front of a painting of a beautiful young woman. Pale blue eyes set in a face of English rose skin and framed by golden blond hair stared back at Sarah with a subtle, but impish smile.

"Is that you?" Sarah asked, admiring the portrait.

"That was me at the age of twenty, not long before I met my Jonathan. He was a brash young upstart from Leeds, and I fell head over heels in love with him."

They walked farther down the gallery until they stood in front of a portrait of Lady Clara and Jonathan.

"He was very handsome," Sarah said, admiring his well-balanced features, hazel eyes, and sandy blond hair. "I can understand why you fell so hard."

"My father did not approve of the match initially. My family is one of England's respected and titled families. Jonathan was from a family of unknown origins, and although we were bordering on impoverishment, my father believed I was marrying beneath my station. My goodness . . . sounds rather like an Austen novel, doesn't it?"

She turned indicating the door opposite the one through which they'd entered. "Shall we go down to tea?"

Walking along, Sarah paused in front of the portrait of another couple. She could see the resemblance of the man to Lady Clara's late husband. However, the woman bore no resemblance to either Lady Clara or her husband, so she assumed the couple pictured was husband and wife, rather than brother and sister. There was something about her, something around eyes the color of dark chocolate, which reminded her of someone.

"That is my late son and his wife." Lady Clara's expression turned sad. "I lost my son twenty-four years ago in a plane crash in Africa."

"I'm so very sorry." Sarah hesitated. Then putting her hand on Lady Clara's arm, she said, "Losing a child must be a grief like no other."

"I can attest to that." She reached up and laid her hand over Sarah's. "However, my grandsons bring me comfort." Lady Clara indicated the last two portraits along the wall. One was a slightly stockier version of Lady Clara's son. The other was Alex Fraser.

CHAPTER 9

Sarah's breath caught in her throat. He stood, one hand in his pocket, the other hand resting on the back of a chair, with golden oak-paneled walls serving as the backdrop. The dark blue suit deepened his brown eyes to almost black. His hair was shorter and more formally arranged, leaving very little evidence of the tousled waves that had elicited her mortifying thoughts. There was no question it was a slightly younger version of the man she'd met last night. The engraved brass plate beneath the portrait confirmed it: Alexander Tristan Sutherland Fraser, Ninth Earl of Rutherford.

"My dear, are you quite well? You look as if you've seen a ghost."

Lady Clara's look of concern forced Sarah to regain her composure. "I'm fine. Perhaps I'm just hungry."

"Of course, my dear." Lady Clara directed Sarah through the doorway. "How impolite of me to keep you wandering these drafty halls, when we have tea waiting for us."

They left the gallery and returned to the sitting room where the teacart was set up.

"Did your father finally give you his blessing?" Sarah asked, resuming the story to take her mind of the disingenuous Alex Fraser.

Actor my ass, she thought. At least he hadn't lied about his name.

What on earth was an earl doing in an Oxford pub? She gave a mental snort. Wasn't it obvious? Trying to pick up women. The old accidental bump routine. She should have recognized it for what it was.

She returned her attention to Lady Clara. It wasn't her fault her grandson was a jerk.

"My father relented when I threatened to elope if he withheld his consent. It pained me to put this ultimatum before my father and risk the alienation of my only parent, my mother having died when I was but fifteen. But I loved Jonathan to distraction and knew he could make me happy."

"As luck would have it, my Jonathan had a sharp mind and became enormously successful in Leeds' flourishing banking and finance industry."

But Mick had asked him about his movies. Well, maybe he lied to Mick as well. Or maybe Mick was part of the game. After all, it's hard to lie about being in a movie, or three, when a fellow countryman like Mick could check it out for himself.

"Do you take cream in your tea?"

Lady Clara's question interrupted her internal discourse. She needed to pay attention. In spite of her current preoccupation, she was genuinely interested in Lady Clara's story.

"Yes, thank you." Sarah took the proffered cup of tea and helped herself to a couple of the finger sandwiches and a teacake.

"Sadly, my father died a year later, six months after my marriage. When the estate passed to me, Jonathan provided an infusion of cash needed to refurbish Rutherford Hall and reassert its place among Oxfordshire's small, but illustrious estates. Between my drive to restore my family's legacy and Jonathan's acute business acumen, Rutherford Hall once again became a thriving, self-supporting estate."

"You must be proud and pleased to see what you and Jonathan accomplished."

"I am." She looked melancholy. "Jonathan and I had a wonderful forty-five-year marriage. He died of a heart attack three years ago, just a few days after our anniversary."

"I am so sorry," Sarah said, quietly. "I remember when my mother died, my father seemed so lost. We were very worried about him for a while."

"Oh, I gave into my grief, cocooning myself in the private apartments we shared, refusing visitors and condolers for over a month. But when I emerged, I was determined to live the rest of my life with the same joy and eagerness I always had. Jonathan wouldn't want me to just exist. He would want me to live."

"Would you ever consider remarrying?"

"Oh yes, my dear . . . if the right man ever came along. I don't know that I could ever love anyone as I did Jonathan, but I wouldn't deny myself that possibility, even if I am a bit long in the tooth." She was thoughtful a moment. "Not a day goes by that I don't expect Jonathan to walk into my study, kiss my cheek, and invite me for a stroll around the gardens. But I am quite happy with my situation. I am never lonely and always with some purpose or other."

She flashed Sarah a sad smile. "Enough about me. I have rambled on incessantly. Tell me about you my dear. Is there a special person in your life?"

It was a mild afternoon, so they'd moved to a terrace overlooking the rolling green hills of Oxfordshire.

"Actually, I'm divorced . . . eight months ago." Sarah smiled wanly. Divorced. A word that seemed synonymous with failure.

Lady Clara colored. "I'm sorry, my dear, I didn't mean to bring on unhappy thoughts."

"It's okay."

"So, the trip to Oxford . . ."

"Initially it was the result of an intervention of sorts by my best friend, Ann, and my sister, Becca."

"How so?"

"Tired of my moping, they showed up at my door one day and told me to snap out of it and start living. That's when they gave me the information on the Oxford program, with a warning that they would not accept any excuses for not going, including cost." Sarah shook her head at the memory. "They'd even spoken to my boss at the time and cleared my vacation time with him."

"Sounds like two people who love you very much."

"Yes, I'm lucky to have them, although there are times . . ." Sarah smiled through her exasperation.

"I'm very glad they convinced you to come to England, otherwise we never would have met, and that would have been unfortunate indeed."

She fell silent a moment, but Sarah could feel her eyes on her.

"Sometimes it takes a regrettable event to shake us out of our complacency, and good things often follow."

When they said goodbye, Lady Clara hugged Sarah to her and held her there momentarily. "I think it was George Sand who said, 'There is only one happiness in this life, to love and be loved.' Don't despair, my dear, it will happen."

leading a headache, Sarah sought the privacy of her room after dinner.

Packing the last few items of clothing, she wondered why her encounter with Alex troubled her so. After all, they'd only just met. He didn't owe her anything. Not even the truth. He was just another guy trying to impress a woman he'd met in a bar.

Just another guy. *Right.* He was an earl for God's sake. An earl slumming it in a pub. One that was obviously a favorite haunt of his.

Forget him, she scolded herself. She was certain he'd forgotten her the minute she'd walked away. Moved on to his next target. What did it matter anyway? She was never going to see him again.

I am sad today. This, my last day of classes, has come all too soon. I wish I'd signed on for two weeks of classes. Next year. This has truly been an experience of a lifetime. I must remember to thank Becca and Ann for encouraging, and sometimes pushing, me outside my boundaries.

Seated at her desk in her dorm before class, Sarah recorded the thoughts in her journal, wanting to jot them down while they were still vivid in her mind.

I can't explain what it is like walking the grounds of this venerable institution. I admit to feeling a wicked sense of superiority as I walk across Tom Quad in the early morning, where the tourists press their faces against the iron gates to catch a glimpse inside of Christ Church, or later in the day as I blithely walk through the hordes of tourists past the signs that read "Private. No admittance."

Entering Tom's Gate is like stepping back in time, or like Alice stepping through the looking glass, isolated from present day reality, where you can choose to ignore the real world, if only for a short time.

When I climb the stairs to Tudor Hall, where the college has served meals to Christ Church residents since 1529, I feel the indentations worn into the stone steps by the centuries of footsteps from the scholars who'd tread the same path.

Tonight is the final reception and dinner. In the morning, I'll leave these magical walls for a week alone in Oxford. It will seem all the lonelier for having spent this week in such engaging company. But for today, I will enjoy the atmosphere of Christ Church: the sense of stillness I find in the Master's Garden, the hush of the Picture Gallery, and the peace and tranquility within the walls of this college, not passing through Tom's Gate into the noise and chaos of the city until I leave tomorrow morning.

Closing her journal, Sarah picked up her copies of *Sense and Sensibility* and *Mansfield Park* and headed to class, ready to make the most of her final day.

~

The temperature rose into the upper seventies, a heat wave by England's standards. She'd even had to remove her otherwise obligatory cardigan while she and her classmates picnicked in the Master's Garden. She should be relieved it hadn't been too warm this week since none of the dorms was air-conditioned.

Glancing at her watch, she realized she'd dawdled in the Picture Gallery too long, and hadn't left herself much time to change for the reception. After a week of wearing conservative trousers and cardigans, she'd selected a lovely, feminine black and white floral silk sundress with a lemon-yellow pashmina and black strappy sandals. She left her hair loose around her shoulders. Satisfied with her appearance, she spritzed on a little *Voile De Jasmin,* grabbed her bag, and hurried over to the Cathedral Garden.

From the volume of voices drifting through the door to the Garden, everyone had already arrived for the reception. She stepped through the doorway, looking for her group. Almost every head turned in her direction, eyes wide, some with frank approval, some with disapproval.

Compared to everyone else in the Garden, she looked as if she were going to a garden party rather than a gathering at Christ Church. She couldn't have stood out more if she'd been wearing a hat befitting Her Majesty and the races at Ascot. Clearly, she should have asked around about the attire for this evening. Most of the tutors wore dark conservative suits, including the women.

Alex watched as she stood, rooted to the spot, a becoming blush coloring her cheeks. His memory had failed him. She wasn't beautiful; she was breathtaking.

He was pleased now that he'd accompanied his grandmother to the reception. He'd planned to offer his services as her escort for the evening and was surprised when she beat him to the punch and asked him instead.

"Lord Rutherford," Mr. Phillips, the program director, interrupted Alex's observation of the clearly disconcerted Sarah. "May I introduce you to Mr. George Sommers? He's visiting us from New Zealand. Mr. Sommers is the Minister of Education."

Alex reluctantly turned his attention to the two gentlemen but kept an eye on Sarah.

His interest in the conversation waned again as he watched his grandmother approach Sarah. Perfect. He smiled at his own good fortune.

As if sensing her discomfiture, Lady Clara had rushed to Sarah's side, effusive in her praise of her appearance. "My dear, you look absolutely stunning—a breath of fresh air in this otherwise stuffy gathering." She turned her considerable frown upon those with disapproving looks. "Stodgy old codgers," she mumbled.

"Thank you," Sarah murmured. "I certainly stand out." A waiter walked by with a tray of champagne, and she grabbed a flute off the tray and took a gulp.

As the gawkers returned to their own conversations, Sarah spoke to Lady Clara a few minutes. Just as she thought she'd recovered her aplomb, she spotted Alex speaking to Mr. Phillips and another gentleman. What on earth was he doing here?

He watched her, an amused expression on his face as he raised his champagne flute in a silent toast.

She turned away, chin lifted, pointedly dismissing him. Joining the remainder of her group who were discussing their plans for the near future, she tried to ignore his presence. Not very successfully.

While some of her classmates were returning to jobs and families in their respective countries, others were continuing their travels. Kim was going to Italy to meet up with a boyfriend, much to Sean's dismay, while Marie was meeting friends in London for one more week before returning to France.

The gavel banged promptly at seven, announcing dinner. Sarah made a swift departure, hoping to avoid Alex. He must have come with his grandmother, but why? Thankfully, the class would be seated together this evening, so he wouldn't be seated with Lady Clara. Determined to enjoy the evening's pomp and circumstance, she put him out of her mind. Almost.

Tudor Hall was regally dressed for the elaborate four-course dinner. The dark-paneled walls, adorned with portraits of such illustrious Christ Church alumni as W.H. Auden, William Penn, Charles Dodgson—a.k.a. Lewis Carroll—and John Wesley, glowed in the late summer light streaming through the stained-glass windows.

Alex watched from his place at High Table as Sarah took her seat among her classmates. He noticed as his grandmother and Sarah put their heads together conspiratorially, wondering what they were talking about, and selfishly hoping it was him.

His grandmother had evidently taken a liking to Sarah. Having her to tea, sending her car for her, saving her from the effects of her grand entrance. She'd clearly been mortified, but what did she expect? She'd swept into the garden like a sweet summer breeze. Of course, every red- or blue-blooded male was going to take note.

Following the last course Mr. Phillips garnered everyone's attention, thanked them for participating in the programs, and welcomed them to return for future programs.

Students received their certificates without much fanfare, unless one counted the frequent camera flashes as people took pictures with their cherished certificates. Now they could all claim attendance at the revered Christ Church. Concluding the evening's presentation, Mr. Phillips wished everyone safe travels, and the dinner conversation resumed.

After dinner, many of the students adjourned to the Buttery, the college's private bar just outside the hall, for a final night of revelry. Sarah found herself chatting again with Lady Clara. She enjoyed her company so much and would miss her when she returned home. Over the past week, she'd gotten to know her well, and she'd taken on an almost motherly, or grandmotherly, role to Sarah.

Sarah noticed her tutor, Mr. Byrne, speaking with Alex. Was there anyone Alex didn't know? His warm smile reached his eyes, crinkling them at the corners. His dark gray suit and deep blue tie enhanced his regal bearing, making him look every inch the Earl.

Lady Clara noticed her slight preoccupation, and following her gaze, said, "Oh, I see you've spotted my grandson. He is a handsome lad, although I suppose I am biased. Would you like to be introduced?" she asked, a sly smile on her face.

"Oh. No." Sarah said, a little too emphatically. "That's okay." Too late . . . he walked toward her. It seemed that every head in the room turned to watch him, and consequently, Sarah. For the second time this evening, she wished a hole would open up and swallow her.

As he sauntered in her direction, she couldn't help but admire the way he moved, with the easy grace of an athlete. His well-tailored clothes fit his powerful frame as if made for him. And most likely they were.

"Some escort you are. You've left me to fend for myself all evening," Lady Clara chided her grandson.

He leaned in to kiss her cheek. "Yes, Grandmother, but if anyone can fend for herself, it would be you." He smiled down into his grandmother's beaming face. "You'd have Henry VIII himself wrapped around your finger in a moment."

"You're a good grandson." She reached up to pat his cheek as she said it.

Sarah tensed. Would he refer to their meeting the other night?

"May I introduce Sarah Edwards? Sarah was one of my classmates this week." Lady Clara turned to her. "Sarah, this is my grandson, Alexander Fraser, the Ninth Earl of Rutherford."

"How do you do?" He took her hand, never taking his eyes off her face.

Sarah smiled tentatively.

He couldn't resist. "You look familiar." Her hand tensed in his. "But then again, if I had met you, I'd have remembered eyes as lovely as yours." Her hand relaxed a little, but there was a spark of fire in those green eyes.

She pulled her hand from his, with the memory of their warmth uppermost in her mind. Was he being considerate, she wondered, or worse, did he actually not remember meeting her?

Lady Clara's eyes sparkled mischievously as she looked between the two of them. "Ah, there's Mrs. Talbot. I must have a word with her. Will you excuse me?" She strode off before either of them could object.

"So, we meet again," Alex whispered conspiratorially.

His breath tickled Sarah's face, suffusing her cheeks with warmth, and raising another blush.

"I thought—"

"I know, you wondered if I'd actually forgotten you." He took her now-empty wineglass, which she turned nervously in her hands and placed it on the table behind her. "The answer to that is of course not. But my grandmother told me of your visit to Rutherford, and I gathered from that conversation that you did not reveal our previous meeting." He tilted his head. "I wondered why that was."

With nothing left to fidget with, she folded her hands in front of her. "Because I didn't want to tell your grandmother what a liar you are."

"A liar?" He frowned. "What are you talking about?"

"You told me you were an actor."

"No, you asked me if I was an actor."

"So that makes lying about it all right? Did you lie about accidentally bumping into me, too?" Her ire was up. How dare he play semantics with her, as if that excused his dishonesty.

"No. I can assure you the collision was accidental. If I'd set my sights on meeting you, I wouldn't have resorted to dousing you with beer. I would simply have introduced myself." The corner of his mouth lifted in a slight grin. "As to the bit about being a liar, I can assure that I am not. I am an actor." He turned to indicate Lady Clara's approach. "You can ask my grandmother if you wish."

"Ask me what?" Lady Clara asked as she rejoined them.

"Sarah expressed an interest in my acting." Alex said, eyebrow arched in Sarah's direction.

"Ah, his acting." Lady Clara waved her hand as if the subject were a disagreeable fly she was shooing away.

"Grandmother doesn't approve." He observed Sarah's chagrinned expression and the pretty blush that accompanied it. He must remember to make her blush regularly and often.

"It isn't that I don't approve of acting. I think it a noble profession. Look at Sir Laurence Olivier and Dame Judi Dench. I just disapprove of my grandson, the Earl, acting." Lady Clara turned to Sarah. "That isn't to say he's not good. I think him quite good. But you can judge for yourself. When you return to the States, you should get the BBC videos and watch them at your leisure. I'm sure they are available on DVD."

Taking a sip of his wine, Alex asked, "When do you return to the States . . . which state, by the way?"

"I return to Florida the end of next week." She found herself wishing again for a wine glass, something to hold so she knew what to do with her hands.

"How will you be spending the remainder of your holiday now that your classes are over?" he asked with great interest.

Before she could answer, Lady Clara interjected, "She is planning to tour Oxfordshire and the Cotswolds—all alone."

Sarah blushed again; nothing obvious about that response.

"Did you hire a car?" he inquired, again enjoying the pink in her cheeks.

"No, I took the train from London."

"How did you plan to tour the countryside and take advantage of all it offers without a car?"

"I planned on one of the touring companies."

"That's no way to see the Cotswolds," he said, shaking his head in mock horror. "If I'm not being too presumptuous, may I offer my services as a tour guide for the week?" he replied. "After all, we are no longer strangers," he added with a subtle grin.

Before Sarah could respond, Lady Clara declared, "Oh, I'm sure she would enjoy your company! Wouldn't you, my dear?"

"Um, thank you. Are you sure? I wouldn't want to impose." Sarah looked down trying to hide her embarrassment over Lady Clara's transparent matchmaking.

"It would be my pleasure," he replied warmly. "Where are you lodging after tonight?"

"The Old Parsonage on Banbury Road."

"Ah, yes. Very nice hotel. May I call you there tomorrow?"

"Oh, yes. Or you could call my cell phone, or my mobile as you call it, in case I'm not in my room."

"Even better."

After providing him with her cell phone number, Sarah realized that the room was nearly empty, except for the staff who clearly hoped they would leave so they could clean up. Apparently they'd overstayed their welcome. Although she was now reluctant to leave, she indicated that perhaps the evening was at an end.

As they walked out of the Buttery, Alex offered to walk Sarah back to her dorm.

Wow! Talk about a flashback to college. She felt like she was nineteen again, and Dan Acosta had asked her the same thing. With one glaring difference: Dan had not been an earl.

When she said good night to Lady Clara, the Countess grinned broadly. "My dear, I will be in touch in a day or two regarding our planned lunch date."

They'd already planned to meet for lunch while Sarah remained in Oxford, but now she clearly had another motive for their lunch date. Lady Clara was worse than a teenager, but that's what Sarah loved about her.

Alex and Sarah descended the stairs and stepped out into the cool evening. She wrapped her pashmina tighter around her shoulders, prompting Alex to offer his jacket.

"No, thank you," she replied. "It was just the sudden difference in temperature. I'm fine." She realized that it had been rather warm in the Buttery. Or perhaps the warmth was in response to Alex.

It was a beautiful night. The stars were visible, the air perfumed and gentle. She closed her eyes and lifted her face to the night air, thinking how it was vastly different from the climate in Florida this time of year, where you had to wring out the air in order to take a deep breath.

"Where is your dorm?"

Alex's voice gently pulled Sarah back from her thoughts. "Not far. I'm in Meadow Five."

They turned and walked slowly in that direction. The resonant tolling of Great Tom punctuated the quiet. The seven-ton bell housed in Tom Tower rang one hundred one times each night at five after nine in honor of the original scholars of Christ Church College.

"What am I to call you? Lord Rutherford?" A little embarrassed by her question, she half expected him to laugh.

"You may call me Your Lordship," he returned in his haughtiest voice, his tone dead serious.

Sarah turned to him appalled, eyes flashing.

"I'm only teasing." He chuckled, a warm, melodic laugh that went straight to her head like a shot of whiskey, making her woozy.

"Please call me Alex."

"Oh." Astonishment turned to embarrassment once more. She seemed destined to make herself look foolish in front of him. "Alex, I owe you an apology for calling you a liar and assuming the worst."

"Apology accepted."

They walked very slowly, meandering through the vaulted corridors, taking the long way to the Meadow Building.

"But why did you focus only on your acting?"

"I'd rather be known for something I've worked to accomplish, rather than a fate of birth. Besides, if I'd told you I was an earl, would you have believed me?" he asked, his expression dubious.

Sarah laughed good-naturedly. "I suppose not." A breath or two later, she asked, "Do you think that means I have deep-seated trust issues that have only now come to light?"

He laughed, deep and rich. "Perhaps it means you have a healthy mistrust of strangers in pubs who bump into you, clumsily sloshing beer on you, before asking you out on a date."

"I've seen that technique work before."

"Have you?"

"Not on myself of course," she said rather primly, although with a slight smile, "but certainly on other women. It even has a name: the Bump and Spill. It's patented."

"Hmm. And I thought I'd invented it. Just goes to show there's nothing new under the sun."

The gravel crunched under their feet, signaling their arrival at her dormitory courtyard.

"How—"

"When—"

They both spoke at the same time.

"Go ahead—" Sarah said, a little flustered.

"Ladies first."

"I saw you speaking with Trevor Byrne, my tutor, how do you know him?"

A smile flickered at the corners of his mouth. "Trevor and I shared a dorm in Peckwater Seven, where I believe your class meets."

So he was a Christ Church man. Not surprising.

"You were going to ask a question . . ."

"Did you find your experience worthwhile?"

"Oh, yes. I'd like to return next year, but, of course, my job and economics will dictate that."

There was another pause in the conversation.

"When did you arrive? Did you spend time elsewhere before your classes started?"

"No. I arrived early to spend a day in London, but that was all."

They'd arrived at the entrance to her dorm. "Here we are," she said inanely as she turned to face him, her hands clasped nervously behind her back.

"Yes, well, good night." He hesitated, as if unsure what to do next. He leaned forward, as if to kiss her, but then stepped back. "I'll ring you tomorrow."

"Good night."

She watched as he turned and wandered slowly in the direction of Tom Quad, hands tucked casually in his pockets.

She sighed, punched in her door code, and slowly climbed the five flights of stairs to her room.

Well, that was certainly an interesting evening. She wasn't sure what she thought of Alex Fraser, Lord Rutherford, not to mention Lady Clara's overt matchmaking. But one thing was for sure, the week ahead was definitely looking up. She pulled out the week's carefully planned itinerary and balled it up, tossing it into the wastebasket.

That simple act was rather liberating.

CHAPTER 10

*A*fter checking into her room in the Old Parsonage, Sarah noticed she had a message on her cell phone. Anxious to see if it was Alex, she checked the minute the bellman left.

She groaned a bit in frustration. The first message was from Becca, not that she wasn't happy to hear from her, but it wasn't the message she'd hoped for. The next was from Alex.

"Good morning, Sarah, this is Alex. Unfortunately, I had a change of plans." Instant disappointment. "I had to return to London to take care of some business. But, if you are available for dinner, I will be back in time. How does seven at the Old Parsonage sound? Ring me on my mobile and let me know, although you may have to leave a message. I hope to see you tonight."

She slumped down on the bed. Okay, well, at least he hadn't cancelled completely like she'd initially thought, although the potential was still there if his business took longer than expected. She would wait a bit and then call him. Why make him think she's sitting around anxiously awaiting his call?

She unpacked and settled into her room for the week. It was a lovely room, bright and sunny, furnished in an eclectic mix of modern and antique furniture, upholstered in soothing tans and whites with punches of grape-colored accents. Two wingback chairs sat in front of a small fireplace that likely wouldn't find much use this time of year.

That task completed, she plopped down on the bed again, crossing her legs, and texted Becca and Ann that things were going well, classes were over, and that she looked forward to the remaining week to tour Oxford and its environs. She didn't mention Alex. No need to stir anything up. She sent them love and kisses and a promise to update them soon.

Well, she sighed, what to do with myself now? Although she'd planned from the very beginning to vacation alone, after making plans to spend the day with Alex, she found herself at loose ends with the loss of his company. And since she recklessly tossed out her itinerary, she'd have to make it up as she went along.

She went to the desk and, opening her journal, concluded her musings on her Oxford experience. So far, she'd managed to keep her promise to herself to write every day.

Task completed and promise kept, the sunny day called her outdoors. A walk along Oxford's busy streets would provide an excellent afternoon diversion.

~

*S*he dressed carefully that evening, choosing a pair of black slacks and a silk blouse in rich emerald green. Pulling the front of her hair back, she let the rest fall loose. Even with all the care she took with her appearance, she didn't want to look as if she'd tried too hard.

After anxiously checking her appearance in a hall mirror, she descended the stairs into the lobby, thinking she was a bit early, but Alex stood by the desk chatting amiably with the clerk. He certainly defied all previous notions on the behavior of British aristocracy.

Alex saw her out of the corner of his eye and turned in her direction.

She blushed under his appreciative gaze. His smile broadened as he walked over to greet her.

"Hello, Sarah. You look lovely."

Hearing her name in that charming British lilt made her melt inside. What is it about that accent? His hair was tousled the way she remembered it from their first encounter, with a dark brown lock falling across his forehead. He wore charcoal gray slacks, a white shirt open at the neck, and a blue blazer, looking like he'd just stepped out of an ad for Ralph Lauren.

"Hi, Alex," She breathed, sounding like a lovesick schoolgirl. Get a grip, she admonished herself.

"Shall we?" He took her elbow and escorted her toward the inn's walled garden. The hostess greeted them enthusiastically, although Sarah thought the enthusiasm was directed more at Alex than at her. Adrian used to get the same adoration from women, but his response to it was quite different. Where Alex was humble and a bit bemused by it, Adrian almost expected it.

Giving herself a mental shake, she wondered why she'd compared him to Adrian. Comparisons were always unfair to all parties involved.

The hostess was clearly a little star struck. With just the briefest glance in Sarah's direction, she said, "Lord Rutherford, I just loved you in *Mansfield Park.*" She hesitated and then asked, "Could I have your autograph?"

He willingly obliged her. After she left with her prize, he turned back to Sarah. "Sorry about that."

"Oh, it's no problem," she said, opening her menu. "Does that happen often?" She lifted a brow in question.

"A little more often with the release of each film. I am surprised, and pleased that young women are watching and enjoying film adaptations of great works of literature. It's an encouraging sign."

She smiled. He apparently had no idea that they were watching and enjoying him, not necessarily the great works of literature. How many young women, her nieces included, never gave a second thought to Jane Austen until seeing Colin Firth as Darcy?

The waiter came over and took their drink orders, and their conversation stopped while they perused the menu.

"What did you do today?" he asked after making his choice and setting aside his menu.

"I wandered the streets of Oxford like the tourist I am. First, I visited the Ashmolean Museum then, Carfax Tower. After that, I walked up High Street to Queen's Lane and took photographs of the gardens and the New College gargoyles, and of course, the Bridge of Sighs, and from there I walked to the Bodleian Library, finally stopping for tea at the Randolph before returning to the hotel."

"Hmm, you've had a very busy day, and it sounds like you made the most of it."

"I try to get my money's worth from my vacations," she said with a self-conscious shrug.

The waiter brought a basket of bread to the table. Suddenly, she was famished. She'd skipped lunch, and although she did stop for tea, the teacakes hadn't lasted long. Trying not to pounce on the bread basket like a fox on a hare, she delicately selected a soft roll.

Remembering part of Alex's conversation with Mick, she asked, "Did I understand correctly that you were undertaking the role of Fitzwilliam Darcy in your latest film? Is it based on Pamela Aidan's trilogy?"

"Yes, you are correct on both counts, which is a convenient segue into my apology for abandoning you today. I had to return to London for a final costume fitting before filming begins. Will you please accept my apology for this abominable treatment, and allow me to make it up to you?"

"I don't know . . . I suppose if I must, but I warn you, it will take a great deal to make up for your un-chivalrous behavior," she bantered with feigned disapproval. *Don't look now, but she was flirting outrageously with a member of the British Peerage.*

"Well, I shall endeavor to behave in a more gentleman-like manner."

They both laughed at his clever use of Jane Austen.

"I take it that you have read Aidan's trilogy?" he asked, returning to their previous conversation.

"Yes. I really enjoyed reading it. Reading Aidan is like reading Austen. She captures Austen's style with impeccable accuracy."

"I agree. I was impressed with the books from the moment I read them, and writing the middle book, *Duty and Desire*, as a gothic novel was a stroke of genius on her part. That's why I decided to produce it."

"You're producing it? That's impressive."

"Or daft," he said with a frown. "I haven't figured out which yet."

"So . . . Darcy . . . one of literature's most beloved characters," she said with raised eyebrows.

"Yes . . . no pressure there, especially following Colin Firth's definitive Darcy," he replied with self-deprecating humor. "But there is nothing more I love than a challenge," his look seemed to imply he wasn't just talking about the role of Darcy, "and next to Rochester, Darcy, is the character I would most like to tackle."

Taking hold of a rare opportunity to discuss literature, she jumped in with both feet. Adrian had never been interested, and made no pretentions about it, and while Ann and Becca patiently sat through her mini dissertations on this novel or that character, it was only out of love for her. Finding someone with a passion for literature that apparently matched her own was like hearing someone who spoke English in the midst of a crowd of Chinese. Finally, someone spoke her language.

"I can certainly understand the desire to play a character with such depth and complexity as Darcy, but I'm not certain about Mr. Rochester."

"Darcy is not without his flaws. He is brooding, introspective, and moody. And, of course, his major flaw—his pride, exposed so eloquently by Elizabeth—makes him the subject of disdain among those in Meryton. But he does redeem himself, most nobly in the end, and the reader falls in love with him much the same as Elizabeth." She looked up to see if he was paying attention, or if her ramblings had begun to bore him. He appeared interested anyway.

He enjoyed the way her brow furrowed when she paused to think, and the passion and insight she applied to her topic. The combination of her sharp intelligence and her subtle diffidence delighted him. He longed to push past her reserve and ignite the passion she concealed just below the surface.

"Mr. Rochester, on the other hand, well, I'm not sure I can find anything in him to admire. While he is rather complex, he has, to my mind, no redeeming qualities. His deceitful attempt to enter into a bigamous marriage with Jane is outrageous, especially when he professes to love her so."

He grinned at her conclusion.

"I'm sorry." She blushed and shook her head. "I get on a tangent sometimes."

"No. I quite enjoyed your tangent and will respond with one of my own." These days, blushing women were as rare as the Queen's smile. It intrigued him.

Taking a sip of his wine, he continued, "It is precisely Rochester's complexity that makes his portrayal a worthy endeavor. He is the archetypal Byronic hero. Flawed, to be sure, but then aren't we all? His flaws tend to the darker side of literary heroes, but that only serves to add depth to his character. He is moody, arrogant, and self-destructive, and his social and sexual dominance both repel and attract the reader." He paused, thoughtful. "No, I would very much enjoy delving into the intricacies of his personality." His eyes were alight with excitement over the thought.

"Hmm," she said, her chin in her hand, "you've devoted a great deal to the study of his character. I wonder, are your daily observations of human behavior that thorough?"

He held her eyes for a few seconds and then looked down as the waiter returned with their salads.

"Yes." He looked up, his brown-black eyes capturing hers. "And now it is time to begin my study of you."

The heat rose to her cheeks. That one statement felt like a caress. Until then, she'd never felt that depth of interest from another human being. It was a little disconcerting, as if he intended to reach the darkest depths of her soul.

"Tell me about yourself . . . I've learned that you're a lawyer." At her frown, he added, "Okay, an unemployed lawyer, and that you have a literature degree. Do have family back in the States?"

After taking a sip of her wine, she replied, "Well, I have a sister, Rebecca, or Becca as her friends and family call her. She is four years older and doesn't look a thing like me."

"Really?" he interjected. "How so?"

"She's blond with light brown eyes, and her hair is straight as a board. She's a bit taller than I am, and more athletically built. She's a surfer chick." She smiled indulgently. Even at forty-two, she still looked like she was eighteen.

"And the two of you are very close."

"Yes, does it show?" she asked, her brows arched in surprise. Perceptive. She mentally added that to his other superlative qualities, along with intelligent, handsome, funny, charming, polished, well read . . . and did she say handsome?

"I can see it on your face when you talk about her. I'm a devoted observer of human behavior, remember?" He tilted his head. "Do you have any other family?"

"I have twin nieces, who are as beautiful as their mother, and who are currently home from college for the summer, my brother-in-law, Mark, who's a great guy, and my father, whom we affectionately call the Admiral—he's retired Navy. My mother passed away last year."

"I'm very sorry," he interjected with sincerity.

"Thank you. Being in the world without your mother is a very lonely feeling. You feel somewhat adrift without her to anchor you to your family, your history . . . I'm sorry, I don't know why I'm rambling on about that." She looked down, embarrassed.

"No, you're not rambling." He leaned across the table. "I'm very interested. I know how difficult it was when I lost my father."

The waiter came to take their salad plates away.

"Lady Clara told me about that—a plane crash. That must have been horrible for your family."

"It was, but it seems so long ago now."

"Do you have other family?" she inquired, hoping to change the subject to a more cheerful topic.

"I have a brother, Robert, younger by three years, who lives in London. He's a Barrister, believe it or not, so you two have a little something in common."

"It's nice that you have a brother. I've always wanted a brother."

"If you say so." The edge in his voice brooked no further discussion on that topic.

"And your mother?" she said, probing further.

"My mother, Emma, is still with us." He explained that Emma kept a bag packed with essentials so she could leave at a day or two's notice. She'd traveled all over the world at deeply discounted rates, not that she couldn't afford it otherwise, because she was on the list of a variety of travel companies. When travelers had to cancel, they'd call her to see if she'd like to go. Apparently she rarely refused.

"She's been on African safaris, floating down the Yangtze River in China, hiking the Milford track in New Zealand, dog sledding in the Arctic, cruising in the Mediterranean, and who knows where else. It is often hard to keep up with her. If it weren't for her mobile, we might go weeks or even months without talking." He shook his head and smiled.

"Sounds like she's having a lot of fun."

"Oh, no question." He didn't seem put out by his mother's vagabond ways. "I'm glad she's enjoying herself."

They turned their attention momentarily to the entrées the waiter placed in front of them.

"She was never really comfortable in her role as countess, and if it weren't for my brother and me, when my father died, she would have moved back to Leeds. However, she knew my brother, but especially me, needed to grow up in our ancestral home. As soon as we were adults, she moved to a small flat in Leeds."

The life of a countess was so far beyond Sarah's comprehension that she might as well imagine living her life as a Martian. The only thing she knew about it was garnered from her reading of Regency romance novels.

"So your mother was a commoner?" As soon as the words were out, she wished she could rewind the tape. "I'm sorry. That was rude."

"No, don't be silly. It seems to run in my family," he said with a smile. "I'm sure you didn't get out of hearing my grandmother's narrative of her love story." Sarah noted it wasn't said with any hint of disrespect.

"How did your parents meet?"

"Are you sure you want me to bore you with the details?"

"Yes, I'm very interested," she said, echoing his previous sentiment.

"My maternal grandparents had a men's clothing store in Leeds, where my mother grew up. The shop was quite humble, catering to the modest clothing needs of the men who worked in the various factories. When my mother started working in the shop as a young woman, she tried somewhat unsuccessfully to get my grandfather to upgrade the clothing lines to cater to the city's up-and-coming financial sector." He paused to take a bite of his fish.

"My mother finally took over the business when my grandfather became ill, and she took the opportunity to renovate the interior and the storefront and began carrying higher end clothing lines for business men." He continued, "She took a financial risk in doing so, but it paid off. The shop established a clientele of bankers and other high rollers in the financial industry."

"Men from all over England learned of the quality of goods and services and flocked to the shop. That's how my father met her. He frequented Leeds on business, buying his clothes almost exclusively from my grandfather's shop."

"Well, that explains it," she said, tilting her head.

"Explains what?" he asked, eyebrows drawn in confusion.

"Why you have an innate sense of style and excellent taste in clothes," she said, laughing.

He actually blushed. "Thank you."

She wasn't sure if she'd ever seen a grown man blush. It endeared her, and made her feel a little empowered.

"Does your mother still have the shop?" she asked.

"No. She finally sold it to a clothing conglomerate for a small fortune after my brother and I came along."

The remainder of dinner passed pleasantly with additional shared stories of families, childhoods, and life in general. She loved watching him eat, using knife and fork in tandem, European-style.

Over dessert and tea, he asked, "Do you have a wish list of sights and activities for this week?"

"Well, this is not the first time I've been to Oxfordshire, but on my previous trip I only passed through the city briefly and did not see much of the countryside other than from a car window."

"Did you come with your family?"

"Um, no, my ex-husband," she answered, swallowing hard.

"Oh . . . I see." He wore a slight frown.

Great. Why did I say that? she admonished herself. Why wasn't I more circumspect?

"Well, there's a great deal to see and do." His face brightened and his smile returned. "I'm sure a smart girl like yourself has done her homework . . . what's on your list?"

"Oh, I guess the usual sites: Blenheim Palace, Woodstock, the Cotswolds, Chipping Campden, Castle Combe . . . and I think you've got some rather old stones south of here that are a big tourist attraction."

Playing along with her banter, he responded, "Ah yes, I believe those rather old stones are called Stonehenge, or something like that. I'm sure we can find them. If not, we'll ask the locals." He grinned playfully, making her heart do a little tap dance in her chest.

"Let me give some thought to the best route in order to take in all the things on your wish list, and perhaps some things that aren't on the list but should be." He tilted his head, "I could pick you up out front at, say, nine?"

"That sounds perfect." She couldn't hide her enthusiasm.

When the bill came, she reached for it to put it on her room bill, and he politely but firmly grabbed her wrist and took the bill from her hand. His firm hand left a warm, but invisible impression on her skin.

"What do you think you're doing?" he asked, his tone reproachful. "Your Yankee dollars are no good here. It's my treat."

"Alex," she said with a sigh, "you don't have to buy my dinner. Believe it or not, I do have meals budgeted into my vacation."

"I'm sure that you do, but I cannot allow you to pay. It's a guy thing, something about the Y-chromosome."

"Well, genetic or not, I cannot allow you to pay for everything this week, and if that's your plan, we should get that straightened out here and now. If you're acting as my tour guide, shouldn't there be some remuneration for those services?"

"Oh, we can discuss remuneration for my services later," he teased, looking up from the bill he held in his hand.

She sat back in surprise. Was he suggesting that she repay him by jumping into bed with him? Even from the little she knew of him, that seemed out of character. Was she wrong about that? "I beg your pardon?" she asked in dismay.

He looked up again and read the expression on her face. He actually blanched. "Sarah, I didn't mean . . . well, what I meant was, you buying lunch or something along those lines. I can see how that sounded. Please accept my apology. My attempt at a joke was in poor taste."

Sarah didn't doubt his sincerity. This was more in line with what she'd learned of his character thus far. "Apology accepted. Perhaps I wasn't far off about those deep-seated trust issues," she sighed, shrugging her shoulders.

"No, just cautious, as any woman traveling alone should be. Which begs the question: why did you agree to have a strange man chauffer you around all week? Aren't you breaking your rule about dating strangers? And didn't your mother teach you not to accept rides from strangers?" he asked with a devastating grin.

She had to look away a moment to get a grasp on her thoughts. "Is this a date?"

"Of course. What else would it be?"

She wasn't sure how she felt about that. "Well, I guess after dinner tonight, we are no longer strangers. Besides, you came with the Lady

Clara stamp of approval," she explained, quite pleased with her rational response.

"Yes, I've succeeded in pulling the wool over my grandmother's eyes," he said, wringing his hands like a diabolical villain. "I am an actor, you know," he said, turning his attention back to the bill.

She noted he was left-handed, like Adrian. Stop! Again with the comparisons.

"I doubt anyone could pull the wool over Lady Clara's eyes," she said, dubious, as he walked around to pull out her chair for her.

"No. Even the great Houdini couldn't deceive that dear lady."

It was much later than she thought. Since the light this time of year lingered well past nine-thirty p.m., it was easy to lose track of time. Of course, she'd also been so absorbed in their conversation that she didn't realize how late it was. Oh, who was she kidding? She'd been absorbed in Alex.

He walked her to the lobby. At the foot of the stairs leading to the guest rooms, he reached out, and, taking her wrist, leaned down to give her a very sweet kiss on her cheek as he whispered, "Good night, Sarah Edwards. Pleasant dreams."

CHAPTER 11

Sunday morning dawned cool and damp, so Sarah dressed in layers in case it warmed up later. Wearing trouser jeans, a sleeveless blouse, and a sweater, she grabbed a jacket and hurried down the stairs, feeling like a teenage girl on her first date, slowing as she came through the lobby and out the door, not wanting to appear too eager.

Alex waited outside the hotel, leaning up against the passenger door of a car, arms casually folded across his chest. The Ralph Lauren image came to mind again. "Good morning," he said, beaming, as he pushed off the car and opened the door for her. "'She looks as clear as morning roses newly washed with dew,'"

"Good morning," she said, then added, "Thank you," feeling a blush crawl up her face at his compliment.

He wore a pair of jeans and a cashmere V-neck sweater in dark blue, with a white T-shirt underneath. She noted with curiosity that his hair was still damp, like he'd just towel-dried it on his way out the door. He walked around to the driver's side.

"Whose car?" Sarah asked as he climbed into the driver's seat.

He turned to look at her before pulling away from the curb. "I borrowed Trevor's car for the day."

It was a Renault of some kind, rather small by American standards, but not atypical for European cars. She could smell his scent in the coziness of the warm interior. It was woodsy, with notes of bergamot and cinnamon—a rich, masculine scent.

"That's very generous of him."

"He doesn't have any plans for today, so is in no rush to get it back. Besides, Oxford is a cycling city. If he does need to run out, he'll use his bike." He turned to her. "By the way, tell me again why you didn't hire a car . . ."

"I don't think I told you at all, but the reason being that I didn't want to drive on the wrong side of the car down the wrong side of the road."

"You Yanks, you think unless the thing is done your way, it's done wrong." His teasing look took any sting from the comment.

"'One man's ways may be as good as another's, but we all like our own best,'" she quipped, quoting Jane Austen, then winced. Two literary quotes in less than five minutes. "Don't you just hate those pretentious intellectuals who go around quoting literature?"

"Yes," he replied with a grin.

"How many do you think we'll have by day's end?"

"Between the two of us, I'd venture at least seven, maybe more."

Her laughter bubbled up like champagne, sweet and effervescent.

"Oversleep this morning?" she asked, pointedly referring to his still damp hair.

"Er, no," he said, appearing somewhat chagrinned, "actually Trevor and I went for a run this morning and ran into an old friend, uh, no pun intended, and got waylaid for a bit."

"You stayed with Trevor last night?"

"It was easier than driving a half hour to Rutherford and then back this morning."

"I see." His damp, tousled hair was sexy. She wanted to run her fingers through it. "Where are we off to today?" she returned cheerfully.

"I thought we would set off in search of those mysterious stones to the south," he said, "and then head back north to the prettiest village in England, Castle Combe, perhaps stopping at a lovely little spot in between."

"In between?" she questioned.

"Oh, I have a little surprise I think you'll like."

They headed south out of town. She wasn't good with surprises. She would needle the person planning the surprise until she got it out of him or her. Ann and Becca gave up a long time ago. "Don't I even get a hint about where the in between is?"

His cryptic hint of 'think *Pride and Prejudice*' did not help. "Just so you know, I've already been to Chawton House and Winchester as part of the Oxford course on Jane Austen," she supplied, hoping this would narrow the possibilities.

"Oh, I know. It's neither one of those places," he responded vaguely. He wore the grin she was beginning to recognize as mischievous. "You might as well give up and enjoy the trip, because you won't be able to guess."

She sat back in her seat in a huff, and to her annoyance, he turned and laughed at her. She pointedly ignored him, as if that were even possible, instead staring out the window at the passing scenery. The sun began to burn off the morning mist. Perhaps it would be another nice day after all. Silence filled the car, but it was a companionable silence.

~

When they arrived at Stonehenge, the morning mists had not yet lifted from the surrounding grasslands, giving the mystical site a strange, ethereal quality befitting its fabled history.

As they strolled around the ancient monoliths, a fresh breeze began to push the damp mist away, allowing more of the sun to penetrate, but not enough to chase away the chill.

Using Sarah's camera, Alex took the obligatory goofy touristy pictures of her, including the one that looked like she was holding up one of the leaning stones. Another couple visiting from Ireland offered to take their photo, and they exchanged the favor by taking a photo of them with their two redheaded kids.

The cold wind picked up across the plains, sending a shiver through Sarah, prompting Alex to ask if she was ready to return to the car park. She nodded. "'I have no enthusiasm for nature which the slightest chill will not instantly destroy.'"

"George Sand. That's three." He smiled and he took her elbow, guiding her across the uneven ground.

She could feel the warmth of his hand through the layers of clothes. Once at the car park, Alex opened the car door for her. Before she could swing her legs into the car, an errant gust of wind blew something into her eye.

"Oh!" she gasped. She immediately lifted her hand to it.

Alex pulled her hand away and asked with concern, "What's wrong?"

"It's nothing . . . I think something blew into my eye."

"That doesn't sound like nothing . . . let me take a look," he said as he knelt beside the car and gently placed his thumb on her upper eyelid, telling her to look up, then to look down.

She tried to hide her embarrassment by joking, "So, although you're not an eye doctor, you've played one on TV?"

He chuckled and replied, "Be still. I need total concentration while I examine my patient."

She obeyed.

"I don't see anything obvious. Perhaps it was a grain of sand." He released her eyelid but kept his hand on her face. "How does it feel now?" he asked, cocking his head to the side.

She blinked it a couple of times. "It feels better. Thank you." She thought to swing her legs into the car, but his warm, coffee-colored eyes held hers, his thumb caressing her cheek, arresting any thoughts of further movement on her part.

His gaze slid to her mouth and his thumb followed, brushing ever so softly across her bottom lip. Mesmerized, she held her breath. Just the anticipation of the coming kiss was as potent, as intoxicating, as any kiss she'd previously experienced. Her lips tingled with it.

He leaned in, hesitated briefly, looking into her eyes again, before gently kissing her mouth.

She sighed, closing her eyes. His warm and soft lips tenderly captured her lower lip. He pulled back, his eyes on her lips again.

As she leaned in and cautiously returned his kiss, he placed his hands on the sides of her face and pressed his lips to hers.

Her arms rose of their own volition, clasping her hands around his neck, running her fingers through his hair. All thoughts of her self-imposed impulse-embargo fled. Why deny herself something so delectable? What was the harm?

She didn't know how long they kissed. An eternity, yet not long enough. The sound of laughter from kids returning to the car park brought them back to reality. One more brief kiss and he was on his feet as she swung her legs into the car, allowing him to close the door.

She didn't take her eyes off him as he walked around the front of the car. He climbed in, started the car, and backed out of the parking space before looking at her, flashing a wary smile. She tentatively returned the smile as he pulled out of the car park.

They rode in silence for a few minutes, each lost in their own thoughts.

She didn't know what his thoughts were, but hers were chaotic. Her first thought: *Wow! That kiss was . . . delicious!* She couldn't resist the urge, so she pulled her lower lip between her teeth and ran her tongue across it. She could still taste him . . . could still feel the warmth and pressure of his mouth on hers. Consequently, she could also feel the heat rising in her face from her unruly thoughts.

Her second more rational thought: *How did this happen?* She mentally shook her head, admonishing herself. This . . . whatever this was . . . acquaintance; friendship; fling; one-week-stand . . . was dangerous. She was not ready to face this dilemma. She'd been diligent since her divorce not to place herself in this situation.

"So," his voice punctured the silence, "are you ready for your surprise?" he asked with boyish enthusiasm.

"You mean the kiss wasn't my surprise?" she asked, turning to face him with one brow arched.

He had the grace to flush a little, but then his mouth lifted, flashing a dimple. "Okay, your other surprise."

"Well, in that case then, yes, I'm ready for my other surprise. What is it?"

"Remember the hint I gave you?"

"The one that was useless?"

He chuckled. "Yes, that one. There is a little village north of here whose claim to fame is having been one of the locations for the 1995 BBC production of *Pride and Prejudice*. Lacock village had the honor of being 'cast' as Meryton. In fact, the Red Lion in Lacock served as the exterior of the assembly rooms for the Meryton dance where Elizabeth and Darcy first meet. I'm sure you'll recognize it." Turning off the main road, he continued, "I thought you would enjoy seeing it and walking the streets where Lizzy and the Bennett sisters met up with the likes of Wickham, the officers, and of course, Darcy and Bingley."

She sat there a moment, open-mouthed, pleasantly surprised by his thoughtfulness.

"Of course, if you would find that boring, we can to go to Castle Combe straightaway . . ." His voice trailed off.

"No, I would love to see Lacock. I was just thinking how thoughtful your surprise was."

He smiled, appearing relieved. "Good. We can stroll the streets of Lacock and have lunch before we continue on to Castle Combe."

The sun shone in earnest now, and Sarah felt more lighthearted than she'd felt in a long time. So much for her avowed disinterest in men. For better or for worse, all concerns over protecting her heart were forgotten.

~

*L*ater that night, she looked back over the day she'd spent in the company of the charming and amiable Lord Rutherford.

Lacock had been a wonderful side excursion. She truly couldn't remember the last time she so thoroughly enjoyed a day.

There was no schedule, and although they'd tentatively planned to visit Castle Combe after Lacock, nothing was compulsory.

The thirteenth-century village with its quaint streets lined by row upon row of beautifully preserved cottages, some lime-washed and half-timbered, others of golden stone, made Lacock the perfect example of an English country village. Besides *Pride and Prejudice,* it served as a location for *Moll Flanders, Emma,* and most recently, for the Harry Potter films.

They lingered in Lacock, lunching at a fifteenth-century inn with charming wood beam ceilings, stone fireplaces, flagstone floors, and horsehair plasterwork.

Alex was so patient, even while she dallied in Lacock's shops. She purchased a book on the making of *Pride and Prejudice* from the National Trust Store, intending to savor it on the flight home. They stopped at the various locations used in *Pride and Prejudice,* tossing out remembered lines from the movie, with him laughing at her lame acting skills.

His portrayal of the ridiculous Mr. Collins launched her into unrelenting giggles. But even with the absurdity of Mr. Collins' proposal to Lizzy, her heart fluttered when taking her hand in his, his other hand to his heart, Alex said, "'And now nothing remains, but to assure you, in the most animated language, of the violence of my affections!'"

She hugged a pillow to her chest. She didn't know the violence of Alex's affections, but the violence of her own affections was growing, and it was only the third day since she'd met him.

Of all the unexpected events for which she had contingency plans —lost luggage, missed connections, stolen credit cards—meeting and falling for an earl was not among those events.

She didn't want to engage in too much introspection, because she was having too much fun. Ann deemed that one of her character flaws, over-thinking things, when she should just go with the flow. Ironic, because she hadn't over-thought Adrian, and look where that had gotten her.

She sighed. Alex was refined and intelligent; masculine and athletic; funny, gregarious, and sweet; she could go on and on. She'd already learned to recognize what his smiles meant. There was the sweet smile, which he wore when he talked about his mother or grandmother; the mischievous smile, which appeared just before he said something he knew would aggravate her; and there was the self-conscious smile he wore after the episode in the Stonehenge car park.

She felt both comfortable around him and giddy at the same time. There was no denying his sex appeal. Every time he touched her, even an innocent hand on her back when he guided her through doors, sent shivers along her spine.

She was always very much aware of his presence. His scent, which still lingered on her clothes when she'd taken them off tonight, was delicious, a subtle blend of his cologne and his own masculine scent.

She realized that her notion of Adrian as romantic hero paled in comparison. Alex was Darcy, Knightly, and Captain Wentworth all rolled into one appealing package. That, more than anything else, worried her most. Alex embodied all of her romantic fantasies, so how could she not fall for him?

But on a deeper level, she already felt as if she could tell him anything. He was such a good listener, making her feel as if there was no one else in the world, much less in the room, but her. He wasn't judgmental, only supporting and understanding.

She groaned. This was insane. She wasn't ready for a relationship, any relationship, much less a long, no, really long-distance relationship. They lived four thousand miles apart. Tomorrow she was going to tell him that this . . . thing couldn't go anywhere.

But then what if she's making more out of it than he is? That would be humiliating.

She groaned again and rolled over. What should she do? She wished she could talk to Becca or Ann about it . . . but then again, they would only encourage it.

Wrangling with this Gordian Knot she'd gotten herself into was going to keep her up all night, and short of the bold stroke of telling him she didn't want to see him anymore, which she was not willing to do, she saw no resolution that would safeguard against a broken heart.

CHAPTER 12

After a sleepless night, Sarah rose at dawn. Ordering a breakfast tray, she set about making herself look rested and refreshed, a Herculean task since her eyes were puffy and her head ached.

The breakfast tray arrived, along with a copy of the *International Herald*. Sipping her hot, sweet Darjeeling tea, she picked up the paper, hoping there was some news that could distract her from the troubled thoughts still plaguing her.

A headline on the inside of the front page caught her eye: *Renowned U.S. Surgeon Saves Prince's Sight*. Her breath caught in her throat when she recognized the smiling face staring out of the accompanying photo. Adrian.

Prince Asad, a member of the Saudi royal family was recently diagnosed with a rare benign, but progressive, brain tumor that was pressing on his optic nerve. Left untreated, the Prince would lose his eyesight in a matter of months. However, surgery to remove the tumor was predicted to be complicated and very risky. The Saudi family turned to Dr. Adrian Mills, recognized internationally as the preeminent neurosurgeon for deep-brain tumors.

Mills flew to Riyad earlier this week to perform the grueling sixteen-hour surgery.

It wasn't unusual for Adrian to fly to some foreign country to perform surgery, but the previous surgeries hadn't resulted in an article in an international paper. Skimming over the parts of the article with the Prince's bio and more medical information about the brain tumor, the article continued on another page:

The surgery postponed Mills' upcoming nuptials to fiancée, Brie Wood. Following the successful surgery, the Saudi family offered one of their yachts to the couple. The couple will take a two-week honeymoon on the yacht, sailing the Mediterranean, all at the expense of a grateful Saudi family.

There were other photos: one of Adrian with the Prince's father, the other of Adrian with a beautiful, plastically perfect blonde.

"He's marrying the cheese. On a yacht. That belongs to a Saudi prince." She could feel the tears stinging her eyes, blurring the photo. So he's remarrying up or down, depending on how you look at it.

Why? Why did this bother her? And why did it magnify her uncertainty? Because, like her hasty romance with Adrian, this one was destined to break her heart, before she'd even begun to pull the pieces back together.

Pressing her fingers to her aching head, she resolved to keep the charming Lord Rutherford at arm's length, both literally and figuratively. As if that were even possible.

~

"What a breathtaking view." Sarah and Alex stood on the top of a knoll just outside the town of Stow-on-the-Wold, the highest town in the Cotswolds, looking out over the deep green valley below, dotted with sheep. The morning was absolutely glorious, sunny and a little warmer than the previous day.

Alex's warm greeting and tender kiss on her cheek that morning had made her forget all about the sleepless night, the headache, and the potential heartache. She could hear Ann and Becca's voices in her head telling her to just enjoy herself. That was easy to do with Alex.

"This is one of my favorite overlooks," Alex said.

She turned in his direction. He was looking out over the valley, his handsome face in profile. "I can see why. I don't think I have seen a more picturesque view. Thank you for sharing it with me."

"It's my pleasure." He turned to her, taking her hand. They walked a few minutes in silence.

"Alex . . . what are we doing?" She looked up into his face. She wasn't going to bring it up, but she couldn't help herself.

"We're taking a walk," he said, joking. And evading.

"You know what I mean. I leave on Sunday, and as much as I'm enjoying your company, I just wonder what this," she held up their joined hands, "is."

"Sarah, can't we enjoy each other's company without reading anything else into it?"

She blushed. It was exactly as she'd feared. She was definitely making more out of it than it was. She cleared her throat. "Of course. You're right." She looked down before he could see her chagrin.

Damn, he thought, when he saw her crestfallen expression. Instead of lifting her mood, he'd just added another layer of anxiety.

When he'd arranged to meet her again through his grandmother, he hadn't expected to be so captivated by her. He sure as hell wasn't ready to confront his feelings for her. In fact, he'd been doing a damn good job of avoiding them. Until now.

How could he be falling in love with her? They'd just met for heaven's sake. He might be a romantic, but that didn't mean he believed in love at first sight, despite his grandmother's arguments to the contrary. Utter nonsense.

He'd take his own words to heart: enjoy the time they had together.

"Are you ready to see the idyllic village of Chipping Campden?" he asked, eager to save her from further embarrassment and himself from further introspection.

As they drove toward Chipping Campden, he attempted to bridge the distance between them by asking about her education and interest in literature.

"After graduation, I taught literature to middle school students."

"Wait, I thought you were a lawyer—"

"I am, or was, or I don't know." She grimaced. "Anyway, I had a previous career."

"I think I would enjoy teaching literature, filling those eager minds with Shakespeare, Milton, and Donne. Why did you change careers?"

She looked at him as if he'd sprouted two heads. "Clearly you've never taught hormonal, silly teenagers *Romeo and Juliet.* Believe me, it's not all it's cracked up to be. Listening to their nervous titters and giggles when one of them read from the balcony scene set my teeth on edge, so after what seemed like three long years of that, I went back to law school," she explained with a shrug. She made it sound so simple, when in fact she'd agonized over the decision to abandon her teaching career for law school.

After a few seconds of silence, she laughed out loud.

"What's so amusing?" he asked, turning to look at her, with a questioning smile on his face.

"Oh, I was just imagining you reciting Romeo's final lines to a room full of impressionable teenage girls." She giggled like the schoolgirls she referred to.

"What's amusing about Romeo's death?" he asked, appalled.

"Nothing . . . it's tragic, but I was envisioning the wistful expressions on the girls' faces, and their sighs of longing."

He still looked confused.

"You may not realize it, but you are devastatingly handsome, and I am sure every girl in the class would have had a crush on you. Add to that the tragically romantic lines spoken by Romeo as he looks upon Juliet for the last time, and you would have had every girl in the room eating out of your hand."

He turned to her again, this time with a brilliant smile, "You think I'm devastatingly handsome?"

"Yes." She blushed at her open admission. "I can't think of a red-blooded female who wouldn't think that."

He turned his eyes back to the road, still smiling, seeming quite pleased with himself.

"So, an earl-come-actor. How does that happen?" A little chagrined at her blunt question, she sought to soften it. "I mean, I imagine you have plenty of responsibilities as Earl, how do you have time to work elsewhere?"

"The estate has a manager to handle the day-to-day operations, so quite frankly I didn't have enough responsibilities to occupy my day. And the monotony of the tasks was not my cup of tea." He sighed, as if remembering the boredom of which he spoke. "I enjoy working with people, but I also need the flexibility of working with ideas. More importantly, gone are the days when the aristocracy can sit on their plump bums with their gouty feet propped on a pillow in front of a fire. Most have to work hard just to keep their estates afloat. And besides, I'd always wanted to act. I performed in some community theatre productions while I was at Oxford, thinking that would satisfy me. It wasn't until the role of Claudio in *Much Ado About Nothing* that I realized acting was my calling. I auditioned for small parts in BBC productions until I landed the role of Jude. And the rest, as they say, is history."

"Funny, I'd always found the monotony of my jobs comforting somehow . . . predictability I guess." She said the last as if to herself. "Anyway, it's great that you found your calling. Not everyone is lucky enough to love what they do." She sighed and turned to look at the countryside. She'd been so engrossed in their conversation, that she'd missed most of the passing scenery. It flew by in a green blur.

"You're not happy in your career." It was a statement, not a question.

"My second career. I wouldn't say that I'm not happy. I've been quite lucky . . . until now."

"Being lucky with your situation and being happy with it are two different things," he interrupted gently. "Do you mind telling me why you find yourself unemployed?"

She told him about Ken's retirement, her shot at a promotion and her subsequent failure to get it, her horrible boss, and the final straw.

"So you just quit, right there on the spot?" He didn't look horrified, as she'd expected. He looked impressed. "Good for you." He paused. "So what will you do when you return?"

"I have an interview with a company."

"You don't sound altogether happy about that." After a waiting a beat, he asked, "If you could do anything you wanted, what would it be?"

She gave it some thought. Not that she didn't know her answer. She just couldn't decide whether to tell him. "Well, I've always dreamed of writing." There . . . she'd said it, and he didn't even laugh at her.

"What's stopping you?" His eyes lit with interest.

She contemplated his question a moment before answering. "Fear, I guess." Despite the completed manuscript from college, she couldn't get past her fear. Being older only made her more cautious, less sanguine of the possibilities that as a twenty-something had seemed infinite . . . and attainable.

"Fear? Fear of what?"

"Fear of failure, I suppose. If I don't write, then I don't risk failure."

"But by not even trying, haven't you already failed?"

She sat bewildered for a moment. She'd never thought of it that way. But then she shook her head. "Perhaps the irrational fear of failure that stops me in my tracks is stronger than the rational argument that you don't know until you try." The manuscript was decent but needed some editing. What if she succeeded only in making it worse?

"Just write about what you know," he returned. "I believe it was Frank McCourt who said, 'you are your own best material.'"

"I don't aspire to be another John Grisham. Legal dramas would not be my thing, and health law isn't exactly rife with danger." She rolled her eyes at the absurdity of it. Although the Bitchkrieg's murder might make for an interesting plot twist.

"The law is not the only thing you know. Don't sell yourself short. You're not one-dimensional. Even in the short time I've known you, the brilliance of your character is apparent. You are a well-read, well-traveled, intelligent, funny, interesting, and might I add, beautiful woman, who has experienced life's ups and downs, and who happens to also have a profound love of literature. Put those thoughts on paper, even if only for yourself. You never know where it will take you. But don't give up on your dreams."

"I'm already on my second career—"

"So?"

"It seems a little late in life to think about changing careers again, and anyway, my family was so proud when I became a lawyer. I wouldn't want to disappoint them. Of course, that presumes I'm capable of making a career out of writing. Besides, I would have to plan."

"Plan?" he asked, confused. "What do you mean plan?"

"I'm a planner." She shrugged. "I try not to do anything without a plan first."

When she'd made up her mind to abandon her carefully mapped out teaching career to return to law school, she put a well-constructed plan in place. She determined how much money she needed to save and how much longer she would need to teach in order to save that money. Then she stuck with the plan. Of course, since she'd already quit her job, she didn't have to worry about that minor detail this time.

"My motto is 'failure to plan is a plan for failure,'" she said, somewhat sanctimoniously.

He looked incredulous for a moment, and then chuckled. "I'd say I'm not a planner, but rather a preparer. If things don't go as antici-pated, I reassess. I guess my motto is 'luck is what happens when preparation meets opportunity.'"

He was silent for a few minutes, watching the road ahead. When he finally spoke, his voice was soft, entreating, "Real living is about accepting challenges and making changes . . . taking risks. You've already taken the first step by quitting a job you'd grown to hate. Don't stop there."

She didn't respond.

"Sarah, don't stare so long at a door that is closing that you fail to see the door that is open."

CHAPTER 13

"$\mathcal{I}$'m afraid that I have to return to London this evening for a photo shoot in the morning," Alex announced.

Sarah tried to hide her overwhelming disappointment, apparently not too successfully.

"But I'll be back tomorrow afternoon, and to make it up to you, I have a very special evening planned."

"What kind of special evening?" she asked, sounding like a petulant child.

"It's a surprise—"

"Again with the surprises?" She rolled her eyes.

"Why, do my surprises disappoint you?" he asked with a concerned look.

"No," she replied quickly, "of course not, it's just that you seem to have an affinity for them."

"I do," he affirmed, "so, just be ready by five, because we have a bit of a drive. Oh, and it's a dressy occasion."

"Dressy? Just how dressy?"

"I'd say a nice dress . . . something like you wore to the Oxford reception would be appropriate," he replied with a gleam in his eyes.

Super. Since that was the only dress she'd packed that fell into that category, she now had some shopping to do. She hoped she could find something within walking distance. She recalled Queen Street had some lovely dress shops.

"Did I ever mention how spectacular you looked that night? I couldn't believe my eyes when you stepped into the garden. I noticed more than one approving eye was turned in your direction."

"Yes, and some disapproving eyes as well," she returned. "How could I forget? But thank you."

"It was all I could do to make some pretense of listening to those with whom I was supposed to be conversing. I am surprised you didn't feel me leering."

"That's what that was. I knew I felt something," she said, giving him a teasing look. "Ugh. Right now all I feel are my aching feet." It was a warm day and they'd walked the grounds of Blenheim for what seemed like hours.

"Here," he said, taking her hand and leading her to the shade of an ancient horse chestnut tree. "I can fix that, I think." Pulling her down on the grass beside him, he pulled her feet onto his lap and removed her shoes. He massaged her tired, sore feet with the expertise of a masseuse.

"Let me guess, you were a massage therapist in your previous life." She closed her eyes, leaning against the tree, enjoying the feel of his hands caressing her feet.

"No, but I used to watch my father massage my mother's feet. I guess I learned a thing or two."

The tree beneath which they sat was perched on a small hill above Blenheim's extensive parkland, the River Glyme visible as it wound its way through the magnificent lawns, like a silver ribbon, sunlight glinting off the water. A warbler of some sort serenaded from the branches above.

"'I shall soon be rested. To sit in the shade on a fine day and look upon verdure, is the most perfect refreshment.'"

"Well said, Fanny Price," he said, his hands gently kneading her feet. "How many does that make today?"

"I do believe that was the first, but I thought you might appreciate that particular quote, Edmund," she replied, waiting for a response, but none came. "At least I have no Mary Crawford to distract your attention," she teased, although something clearly distracted him.

"Yes." He had something infinitely more appealing to distract him, the sight and feel of her beautiful, shapely legs and silky skin. The soft moans of pleasure when he found a particularly sensitive spot and worked the tension from it. He massaged her feet for a few more minutes, admiring the gold toe ring on her right foot, before his hands advanced to her ankles and then her calves. *Lovely, lovely, Sarah. So fit, so trim, so sexy.*

Her eyes flew open, but he wasn't looking at her, he was looking intently at his hands on her bare calves.

"Were you an athlete in school?" he asked.

Odd question, she thought. "Yes, why?" she asked, curious, and not a little excited. His hands caressing her calves made it difficult to carry on a casual conversation.

"Because you have an athlete's legs . . . beautifully muscled." He still frankly appraised her legs.

She gulped, blushing profusely. She sat up and removed her legs from his lap. "Thanks for the massage. My feet feel much better." She slipped her shoes back on and sat with her knees drawn up under her chin. So much for keeping him at arm's length. Her erratic heartbeat subsided now that his hands no longer stroked her legs, leaving disappointment in its wake.

He stood, holding out his hand to help her up. "We'd better go. I have to catch the train to London."

"Oh. Right." She'd almost forgotten that he was leaving tonight.

He obeyed the urge to pull her into his arms and kiss her. Soft and tender, his lips found hers. She tasted of warm sunshine, smelled of sweet jasmine. He could get drunk off both.

Taken by surprise, she nevertheless melted against him on a sigh. Raising her arms, she draped them around his shoulders, her fingers caressing his neck.

He shivered when her fingers found the hair at the nape of his neck. Her soft moans nearly brought him to his knees. He pulled back, looked into her face, her eyes closed, expression all dreamy. "Sarah. Sarah?"

"Hmm."

"Open your eyes. Look at me." He gave her a gentle shake.

She reluctantly opened her eyes, a sexy smile flirting with the corners of her mouth. "Sorry, I momentarily lost all higher brain function."

Chuckling to cover his own similar reaction, he draped his arm around her shoulder and started down the hill. They walked in silence for a pace, each trying to recover the power of cognition.

"What sport?" he asked, once the blood returned to his brain.

"I'm sorry . . ."

"What sport did you play in school?"

"I crewed in high school and college."

His brows shot up in surprise. He'd expected gymnastics, or cheerleading. Something a little more . . . girly he supposed.

"What about you, did you participate in a sport?"

"My brother and I played rugby."

"Tough sport . . . I mean, I don't know that much about it, but from what I've seen it looks more dangerous than American football."

"Yes. That's how I got this scar," he said, pointing to a small scar underneath his chin. "One of these days he'll pay for it." He wasn't joking.

"Your brother did that?" she asked in surprise.

"We're very competitive." There was a slight edge to his voice.

They drove back to Oxford in a subdued atmosphere.

She wasn't looking forward to the lonely evening ahead.

He wasn't looking forward to the family meeting.

～

A short time later, Alex walked Sarah into the inn's lobby. "I'm sorry I'm leaving you to dine alone. I had intended to have an early dinner with you, but we tarried at Blenheim longer than I expected—not that I minded." He smiled, but the light never reached his eyes. "It was a wonderful way to spend the afternoon."

"Thank you for such a lovely day." She hesitated, not sure what she should do. Talk about mixed messages. First he tells her not to read anything into the relationship, then he kisses her to the point of disorientation. She stood on tiptoe to kiss his cheek. Instead, he took her face in his hands and kissed her tenderly on the lips.

Pulling back so that his face remained just inches from hers, he said, "The pleasure was all mine. Tomorrow at five." He kissed her once again before he turned and walked away.

CHAPTER 14

"You're late."

"My apologies, Grandmother, but I had a late meeting in London." Robert Fraser bussed his grandmother's cheek before taking a seat at the table in a small parlor reserved for intimate family meals. He shook out his napkin and placed it on his lap, while the footman filled his wineglass. "Some of us do have schedules to keep."

Alex ignored his brother's dig. "Good evening to you, too, Robert. So good to see you." Alex's mouth turned up into a sardonic smile.

"Boys, do try to behave, at least through dinner," Lady Clara admonished.

"Have you seen the latest tabloid articles? Here, let me oblige you." Robert rose from his seat and walked to his briefcase, pulling out a newspaper, before sticking it beneath Alex's nose.

"I try not to read those rags. I suggest you do the same. They really are a waste of your money." Taking the paper, Alex tossed it on the table.

"My secretary feels an overwhelming need to keep me informed," Robert said, taking a bite of his fish.

"You should be happy. My relationship with Clarice is over. No more potential for tainting the Sutherland bloodlines with a Lib-Dem."

His brief relationship with the Prime Minister's daughter had ended, much to his brother's relief. Of course, if her father had been from the right side of the aisle, quite literally, Robert would likely have encouraged the relationship. The rags were having a heyday with the story of their 'break-up,' prompting Alex to take an unplanned holiday in Oxford.

The morning he and Sarah went to Stonehenge, he'd told her he'd run into an old friend, but he'd actually run away from a tabloid reporter. Although the relationship had ended amicably, that didn't prevent the tabloids from making up all manner of stories about their 'tumultuous relationship.'

"What would make me happy is for you and your . . . girlfriends to stay out of the tabloids."

"Do you think I go around waving my arms at tabloid photographers and reporters saying 'please, write more rubbish about my life?'"

"Of course not. But your career choice and your penchant for high-profile women make you a favorite target."

"Yes, Robert. You'd be much happier if I buried myself here on Rutherford and came out only for occasions of state."

"Don't be obtuse. Grandmother, may we take Brandy in the study?"

Lady Clara looked between her grandsons, "Whatever you like."

"Yes, by all means, let's get this family meeting underway. I have to be in London tonight for an early call tomorrow morning."

"Your tailor?" Robert asked snidely.

"No, your advisors. They're trying to determine how to make you more agreeable to voters."

"Funny."

The insults continued until they were settled in the study.

"Well, Robert. You called this meeting. Let's have it." Alex stood in front of the window overlooking his grandfather's rose garden, his back to the room, a frown playing across his features.

After their father died, Alex and his mother had protected Robert.

Sometimes to a fault. Alex tried to assume the role of father, but a lenient one. Robert had taken the death of their father especially hard, and bitterness in one so young was especially painful to observe. When Robert took an interest in estate matters, Alex was only too happy to oblige. For one thing, it made Robert happy in a way he seldom was, and for another, it gave Alex time to pursue his own interests.

After Robert read for the law and took a position as a barrister in London, Alex had to assume the reins again, choosing to hire a manager to handle the day-to-day tasks of estate management.

Over the years, Robert had come to resent Alex's hands-off approach. His brother felt he neglected his duties as Earl to pursue an acting career, which in his eyes was synonymous with playboy. It didn't matter that the estate and all its interests were meeting, and in some cases, exceeding expectations. From vineyards to media companies, from shipping to publishing, the diverse portfolio greatly reduced the risk and provided a steady income to the estate.

"I'm planning to run for Prime Minister."

Ah. There it was. The true reason for Robert's disapproval of Alex's life. His political ambitions.

Proud of her grandson, Lady Clara rose and kissed him soundly on the cheek. "That's wonderful. Your father would be so proud." But Alex knew her enthusiasm was tempered by the additional animosity she realized this course of action would inevitably cause between the brothers.

"And?" Alex turned to Robert.

"And, what?"

"We've known this was coming. This announcement is no great revelation. There must be more." Alex poured himself another two fingers of Brandy, before tossing it back.

Damn, he thought, he wanted to be proud of his brother. He wanted to clap him on the back and congratulate him. Drink to his brother's success instead of to steady his own temper. If Robert wasn't so damned sanctimonious.

"Your career is a detriment to mine. I'd like to ask you again to reconsider. Take up full-time residence once more at Rutherford as the Earl." Robert took a deep breath, and dragging his fingers through his hair, faced his bother. "And if not, I'm asking you to relinquish the title. To me."

Alex heard his grandmother's sharp intake of breath.

Before Alex could respond, Robert continued, "It would greatly help my chances, and you've never wanted it . . ." His voice trailed off.

"I am the Earl of Rutherford!" Alex's booming actor's voice resonated in the wood-paneled room.

"Then start behaving like it!"

"Fine. I'll begin by asking you to leave. Now." His voice subdued, he turned back to the window.

"You don't mean that—"

"Yes. I do. Please leave."

Lady Clara rose and quietly asked Robert to leave. She would call him later. "It is for the best," she told him.

Alex waited a beat or two, until certain Robert had left. "Do you have concerns about the financial stability of the estate?" He didn't turn to look at his grandmother.

"No." Lady Clara walked up behind Alex and reached up to put her hands on his taut shoulders. "But Robert is right," she said quietly. At Alex's sharp look, she clarified, "Not about relinquishing your title. I will speak with him about that. But you do have a duty to your family and to your title. Stop all this nonsense and direct your inimitable skills to sustaining our heritage . . . your heritage."

Alex turned to look at his grandmother, his face grim. "Grandmother, you of all people should know the importance of following your dreams."

"You're right. I followed my dreams and married the love of my life, but I also did my duty and saved this estate from going to the highest bidder." She sighed. "I'm not going to tell you who you can marry, but find an agreeable woman, and if you're madly in love with her, so much the better. Settle down." A mischievous smile smoothed her knitted brow. "Sarah Edwards would make a lovely countess."

"Grandmother," Alex said, frowning.

"I like her. She's got pluck. But she's also attractive, bright, and personable."

As if he needed to be reminded of her best qualities. He was all too aware of her superlatives, and many more than his grandmother enumerated. But he didn't see how it would work. Why would she abandon her life in the U.S. only to be placed under a microscope by the British tabloids?

As if reading his mind, Lady Clara said, "Listen to me, my boy. You may be the Earl of Rutherford, but don't think I won't take you down a notch or two if you hurt her." She patted his cheek just as she'd done when he was a child. "If you have no serious intentions toward her, then let her down easy, stop seeing her, and move on to your next flighty conquest."

"Clarice was not flighty." She was quite smart, in fact.

"No, but she doesn't have the best reputation, either."

That part was true enough.

"I know you mean well, but stay out of my love life." He kissed her cheek before leaving.

❧

*S*arah woke at first light. Again. She rolled onto her side and grabbed the pillow, hugging it to her. There were times . . . like now, when she was on vacation that she wished she could sleep in. She sighed, closing her eyes and hoping sleep would overtake her. After lying there a half hour, she finally got up. Her disobedient mind would not settle down, especially where Alex was concerned.

Generally, she was happy in solitary pursuits, but last night and this morning she found herself anxious for his company. The thought of spending her day without him was daunting.

Luckily, she had lunch with Lady Clara to look forward to.

After breakfast, she sent a text message to Ann and Becca to tell them she was enjoying herself, an understatement. And that she missed them, also an understatement. She, Ann, and Becca, saw one another at least weekly, and spoke almost daily. It was strange to only communicate by abbreviated text messages all this time. On second thought, maybe it was better that way. She knew if she spoke to them by phone, she would never be able to keep Alex a secret.

Since she had some time before lunch with Lady Clara, she sat down at the desk with her travel journal and the beautiful fountain pen. She'd been somewhat faithful in keeping her promise to herself, if not writing each day, at least writing about each day. She discovered enjoyment in the process of capturing her daily activities, recollections, thoughts, and fears. Some days the entries were a sort of stream-of-consciousness exercise, where she wrote as fast as the thoughts entered her head; other days the entries were a travelogue, detailing the wonderful places she'd been, the memorable meals she'd eaten, and the history of the area. In some ways, those entries resembled a travel guide. Of course, her most recent entries included her interactions with Alex. Those resembled a lovesick teenager's diary.

～

*L*ady Clara was already seated when she arrived at the cafe. She glanced up and smiled as Sarah approached.

"Am I late?" Sarah asked, concerned that she'd kept her waiting.

"No, my dear," she replied, as she rose from her seat to take Sarah's hands and kiss her cheek. "I arrived a little early to claim my favorite table." It was located in a quiet corner of the restaurant, with only one other table nearby. Sarah sat down across from her as the waiter hurried over with menus. He greeted Lady Clara by name.

"Good afternoon, Richard," she responded cheerfully. As soon as the waiter left, Lady Clara leaned in conspiratorially and asked, "How is my grandson?"

Sarah blushed and murmured, "Fine," looking down at her menu as if it was the most interesting thing she'd ever read.

"Come, come, my dear." She sat back in her chair, eyebrows raised. "I can see by the blush that he is more than fine."

Sarah sighed in exasperation. She knew the conversation would include a probing inquisition from Lady Clara, she just didn't expect it before they'd even placed their lunch order.

"Okay," she blurted out, "he's charming, handsome, dashing, intelligent, witty . . . and a great tour guide, as you well know." Following her outburst, she was a little embarrassed.

Lady Clara wore a self-satisfied expression. "I knew you two would hit it off. So, tell me, what adventures have the two of you undertaken?"

Before Sarah could respond, Richard returned to take their orders. Despite her attempts to use the menu as a subterfuge, she'd barely given it a glance, so she just ordered the same item as Lady Clara.

She then proceeded to give Lady Clara a synopsis of her visits with Alex to Stonehenge, Lacock, Castle Combe, the Cotswolds, Blenheim, and Woodstock, carefully leaving out the parts that involved kissing, foot massages, and other romantic activities.

"It sounds as if you two have been quite busy," she responded innocently.

Why did she doubt that ingenuous expression? If she didn't know any better, she'd think Lady Clara had some clandestine report of their activities, complete with compromising photos. Lunch arrived, and they turned their attention to their meal.

"Alex told me that your late son purchased his clothing from his grandfather's store in Leeds."

"Yes. That is how my son met Alex's mother. Every time he traveled to Leeds on business, he paid a visit to Mr. Sheffield's shop."

"I think my son fell just as hard, and just as unexpectedly in love with Emma, as I did with Jonathan." She smiled. "Most people think love at first sight is a silly, romantic myth, but I know from experience that it's quite real."

"Alex told me that Robert is a barrister in London. Do you see him often?"

"Just last evening." Lady Clara frowned. "He's not pleased with Alex's career choice."

"Why not? Why should it matter what Alex does as long as he's happy?"

"Robert has political aspirations. Next to the two royal princes, Alex is the most eligible bachelor in the Kingdom. And we both know that even the Royal Family can't avoid the unflattering headlines, even if there isn't any truth to the stories. Add acting to the mix, and Alex becomes ideal fodder for the tabloids."

She remembered the edge to Alex's voice yesterday when he mentioned his brother. "In the U.S., we elect our actors Governors and Presidents," she shrugged.

"Yes," Lady Clara said archly. Changing the subject, she asked, "Did Alex tell you about his mother, Emma?"

"Yes. He said she was quite the world-traveler, and often has a difficult time keeping track of her." Sarah smiled as she remembered his fond stories of his mother.

"When will you see my grandson again?" Lady Clara asked.

Sarah laughed at Lady Clara's transparent attempt to sound casual. "He's picking me up at five. Although I don't know what we're doing. He said it was a surprise," she continued with annoyance. "Which reminds me, I need to buy a dress, since the only one I brought I've already worn."

"Alex always did love surprises," Lady Clara smiled at some memory. "There is a lovely shop on Queen Street that sells fine ladies clothing suitable for a young woman like yourself. I'm sure you will find a charming selection. Besides, my dear, you could make a nun's habit look like the Queen's robes." After hesitating a moment, Lady Clara said, with an earnest expression, "For someone who puts on a nonchalant face when it comes to discussions of my grandson, you seem excited about your date tonight."

Sarah stared down at her plate of food, and then looked back at Lady Clara. "I confess I am." Her brow furrowed, as she tried to decide whether to confide in Lady Clara. She didn't want to put her in an awkward position with her grandson. "Can I share something with you?"

"Of course, my dear," she said reassuringly, reaching across the table to touch her hand.

"Since my divorce, I thought it would be a very long time before I would even consider dating. I've been asked out many times in the months following my divorce, but I've always said no. Alex is different. I haven't felt this way about anyone, ever, and it scares the hell out of me," Sarah finished with a wan smile.

Lady Clara squeezed Sarah's hand. "Having never been through a divorce, I cannot begin to know what that feels like. But I do know this . . . when the right man comes into your life, it is like nothing you've ever experienced. The feelings of trust, respect, admiration, and intimacy are indescribable." She smiled with obvious fondly recalled memories. "I know you will find this. You are too dear not to." She hesitated again, adding, "Had Jonathan and I been blessed with girls, I would have wanted a daughter just like you."

Sarah could only squeeze her hand in return, tears in her eyes. It was a touching ending to an already poignant lunch. This would likely be the last time she saw Lady Clara before returning to the U.S.

They exchanged their contact information, with promises that they would stay in touch. Sarah vowed this was not just an empty gesture, whatever might happen with Alex.

Once outside the restaurant, they hugged one last time then, true to her British roots, Lady Clara squared her shoulders and turned to walk up the street.

Sarah tried to follow her lead, turning to walk in the opposite direction.

CHAPTER 15

$\mathcal{L}$ady Clara was right. The shop she'd recommended had some lovely dresses. Sarah had chosen a violet shantung silk sleeveless dress with a modest jewel neckline, but a deeply scooped back that left much of her back bare. A shimmery new silver wrap and the strappy sandals she wore to the reception finished the ensemble.

She was pleased with the way the rich, saturated color of the dress made her green eyes stand out. She pulled her hair up into a simple twist using a silver-jeweled clip she'd also purchased from the shop, letting a few stray tendrils frame her face. She didn't know why, but this felt more like a date than any of the other activities they'd enjoyed the last few days. Having most of the day to think about it only gave her more time to get nervous. Picking up her purse and wrap, she walked down to the lobby.

Alex waited near the foot of the stairs, with a gaze so intense she felt the frisson of pleasure down to her toes.

He had resolved to show her a good time tonight, and let her down easy with some story about leaving on pressing business. That, he figured, would be that. But one look at her, her eyes shining, her face radiant, he saw his resolve dissipate.

Sarah paused on the bottom step with a soft smile on her face. Even standing a step below her, he was taller than she was. Her admiring gaze started at his feet, clad in classic black wingtips, and swept up his athletic frame to his charcoal gray suit, the pale purple stripe in his white shirt, and to her surprise, his matching purple silk tie. They looked as if they'd coordinated their attire. If he noticed the coincidence, his face didn't reveal it. He looked at her with such frank admiration, her knees felt weak.

"Sarah." He stepped forward to take her hand. "You are breathtaking. I didn't think it possible to surpass your entrance to the reception, but I stand corrected." He leaned down and nuzzled the hollow beneath her jaw. He inhaled, murmuring against her skin, "Ah, sweet jasmine."

She shivered at the intimacy of his gesture, making her breath catch in her throat and her pulse quicken. Blushing with pleasure, she thanked him. "You're not bad on the eyes yourself."

He gave her a provocative smile, holding her hand to his lips for a kiss. "Shall we go?"

They walked out to the street, his hand on her back guiding her to a sleek silver Mercedes coupe. He had a delectable view of her bare back, and he found it sexier than even the most revealing neckline. He longed to glide his fingertips down her spine and feel her shiver in response.

"Is this yours?" she asked, surprised. She didn't know why, she just assumed he'd left his car in London, seeming to prefer the train.

"Yes. Trevor needed his car this evening, so I drove out from London."

The plush leather interior of this car was a far cry from the serviceable Renault they'd been using all week.

"Where are we going again?" she asked after he climbed in behind the wheel.

"Nice try, but it's a surprise, remember?"

She sighed in frustration. "Well, you can't blame a girl for trying."

～

"*I*'m probably stepping far outside the boundaries of propriety, but may I ask you about your marriage?" he said, his voice soft and searching. He hadn't planned on probing any further into her previous marriage, but for some inexplicable reason, he needed to know what happened.

They lingered over dessert at a restaurant overlooking the Avon River.

"There's not much to tell, really," she replied hesitantly.

"Ouch," he muttered, behind a wry grin. "I'm sure your ex-husband would be disappointed to hear that. How long were you married?"

"Almost three years. Our divorce was final one month before our third anniversary."

"How long have you been divorced?"

"Seven months, but we were separated the last six months of our marriage. Turns out wealth can really complicate an otherwise uncontested divorce."

"His wealth or yours?"

"Oh, definitely his."

"Was he a lawyer like you?"

"No, a neurosurgeon."

"So, you were married to the proverbial brain surgeon?" He chuckled. "How did you two meet?"

"At a hospital function shortly after he moved to town. It was a real coup for the hospital to get him on staff. Adrian's skill is world-renowned."

"Why did you get a divorce? He sounds like a great fellow," he said, his brow knitted.

"He'd be the first to tell you he's a great fellow."

"Oh, so he has more front than Brighton."

"Pardon?"

"Sorry, he's, uh, excessively self-confident."

"Oh. Yes, you could say that."

"But that's not why you divorced."

"No." A wave of emotion crossed her face. "Another woman."

They lapsed into an uncomfortable silence.

What man in his right mind would think he could do better than Sarah? He supposed he should be thankful she married an arrogant fool; otherwise, he wouldn't be sitting here with her now, watching goose bumps rise on her bare arms as he softly stroked the back of her hand with his thumb.

She cleared her throat.

"I'm sorry. This is supposed to be a right royal night out, and here I am making you sad."

"Right royal?" she asked, confused.

"Oh, a fun, memorable night."

"It is so far . . ." Sarah said, hoping Alex would give in and tell her what else he'd planned. He didn't take the bait. "Enough about my lackluster marriage, now it's your turn. Have you ever been married?"

"No. I'm a bachelor. I've never met anyone with whom I thought I could spend the rest of my life. I guess I have high expectations after watching my parents and my grandparents." He smiled as he stood and walked around to pull out her chair, effectively ending any further discussion on that topic. "Are you ready? We'll be late for the next surprise."

"Do the surprises ever stop?" she asked, a little exasperated. Not that his surprises were disagreeable. Although she typically didn't like them, his were more enjoyable than most.

He shook his head in feigned disappointment, placing his hand on the small of her back and directing her out into the pleasant evening.

◠

*T*hey walked down the aisle to their seats in the stall, or orchestra pit as it was known in the U.S. Sarah wondered if he'd relied on his position as Earl or his celebrity as an actor to acquire such choice seats at the last minute.

This was indeed a pleasant surprise. Attending a performance of Shakespeare's *As You Like It*, performed by the Royal Shakespeare Company, was not something she'd thought to do. The road sign announcing their arrival in Stratford-upon-Avon, the birthplace of Shakespeare, should have provided her with some clue.

"How familiar are you with *As You Like It?*" He thumbed through the program.

"A little. I only read it once, a long time ago. My assigned play in my college Shakespeare class was *Othello.*"

"Your assigned play?" he asked, confused.

"Yes. My Shakespeare class was not typical of most college literature classes. I had a drama coach as my professor. She assigned groups of students to perform selected scenes from Shakespeare's plays, complete with costumes. After all, she said, Shakespeare intended his plays be performed, not read." Her tone held a hint of disdain.

"You disagree?"

"No. My professor was absolutely right, but I was mortified by the thought of acting. I almost withdrew from the class after the first day."

"Why was that?"

"I'm not fond of being the center of attention, and to be graded on it, well, that was daunting. Plus, as you saw from our antics in Lacock, I'm not an actress."

"But you survived the ordeal."

"I did. And to this day, I still recall my most dramatic lines: 'I care not for thy sword. I'll make thee known though I lost twenty lives!'" she said with a theatrical flourish, then blushed, suddenly embarrassed by her display.

"As they say, don't give up your day job." He chuckled, shaking his head.

She smacked him with her program before the house lights dimmed, postponing any further discussion.

~

*I*t was another lovely night, each night getting progressively warmer. Alex asked if she'd like to walk a bit before the drive back to Oxford. She agreed. As they ambled along in silence, Alex took her hand and placed it in the crook of his arm, "The cobblestones are a bit wonky along the walk," he said by way of explanation.

Since the play had just let out, there were many couples walking hand in hand on the sidewalks, along with some families, among the assortment of people enjoying Stratford this mild evening. They walked for a few minutes talking about the play.

Music spilled out into the street from one of the pubs featuring live music. The singer was quite good. He sang a popular American song. Alex asked if Sarah would like to go in and have a glass of wine.

They found a small table in the front by the door. Just as he had done all week, Alex pulled out Sarah's chair for her. The smiling waitress came over and they each ordered a glass of wine and then sat in silence for a few minutes just listening to the song.

As the song came to its end, the waitress brought their wine. "You're Alex Fraser, er, Lord Rutherford, right? The bartender, Vicki, said no, but . . ."

Alex looked up and confirmed her suspicions. "Did you have money on it? If so, you can tell your friend to pay up."

She blushed shyly and hurried back to her friend to proclaim her victory.

"'May you be merry and lack nothing,'" he said, quoting, appropriately enough, Shakespeare.

After the toast, they turned their attention back to the entertainment and sipped their wine. Sarah was unfamiliar with the next song, but Alex seemed very familiar with it, as he tapped his fingers on the table to the upbeat tempo. It was followed by another American song, slow and romantic. Sarah could feel Alex's eyes on her.

He stood up and held his hand out to her. "Dance with me?"

She smiled up at him as she placed her hand in his and let him lead her out to the small area set aside for dancing, where a few other couples swayed to the music. Alex pulled her to him, wrapping one arm around her waist, as he placed his other hand on her bare back, bringing her even closer. Her skin was as smooth as warm satin beneath his hand, her body as supple as a ballerina's in his arms.

The hand on her back was strong and protective. She laid her head on his chest, while he gently rested his chin on her hair. It seemed like a lifetime since she'd felt the combination of both joy and contentment of being in someone's arms. They began the slow, swaying motion of a couple more interested in holding each other close than in actually dancing. His hand drifted up the back of her neck and lingered there, gently caressing the curls that escaped her clip.

The song ended far too soon. He stepped back, tilted her chin up, and, searching her face, twisted a stray tendril of hair around his finger. Brushing his knuckles across her cheek, he looked down at her lips, which were slightly parted in surprise, before bending down to kiss her tenderly on the lips. She hadn't realized that she'd been holding her breath, until it escaped on a sigh.

"Shall we go? I have a big day planned for us tomorrow, so we need to get you back and into bed." He stammered as soon as the words left his mouth. "I mean — I didn't — that came out wrong. I meant that it's getting late and you should go to bed, not that we should go to bed. Well, not that I wouldn't want to join you—bloody hell! I just need to stop talking." He smiled sheepishly. He didn't know why the unintended double entendre had him as nervous as a schoolboy. Any other woman and he'd have played the rogue to the hilt.

He was not the only one flustered. Sarah could feel the heat in her face, and it wasn't righteous indignation she felt. Her heart skipped a beat when he referred to getting into bed. The idea was far from unpleasant. Obviously, since one of her first thoughts upon seeing him when they met involved a rumpled bed. Hers.

"It's—it's okay," she stammered. "I didn't think anything of it. I mean, not that the thought of going to bed with you—now I just need to stop talking." It was her turn for the sheepish smile.

He chuckled. "Let's go before we say anything else that leads to a stammered and ineffective explanation." He walked back to the table, threw a bill down for the wine, picked up her bag, and handed it to her, before placing her wrap around her shoulders and hugging her to him.

～

*A*lthough it was well past midnight, Sarah was too keyed up to sleep. Tonight's good night kiss had taken on an entirely different tenor.

When they'd reached the lobby, it had been dark and abandoned with the late hour. Rather than kissing her at the bottom of the stairs, as he usually did, Alex had pulled her into a darkened corner and proceeded to kiss her with barely restrained passion. He had taken her completely by surprise. She found herself gasping for breath, yet unable to get enough of his lips on hers. Her fingers found his thick, dark curls and grasped them like a lifeline, tugging his face down to hers. He pulled away, his lips moving to the hollow beneath her ear, giving her a chance to catch her breath, but not for long. The length of his body pressed hers against the paneled wall.

He let down her hair, dropping the clip to the floor with a clatter, before wrapping his fingers in her unbound hair, and pulling her head back to kiss her along her neck to her jawbone.

A moan of unadulterated pleasure escaped her lips.

Releasing her hair, his hands moved to her waist, pressing her closer still, leaving no doubt as to the intensity of his desire. Then he turned her around in his arms and began to rain hot kisses down her bare back. One arm wrapped around her waist, the other brushed her hair aside. "I've longed to do this all night," he said as he kissed and nipped at her bare shoulders.

Her breath came in short pants, making her dizzy with both longing and hypoxia.

Sarah was on the verge of asking him up to her room when he suddenly pulled away and turned her to face him, searching her eyes, before releasing her and stepping back, his breath raspy.

He whispered, "I'd better go," then kissed her chastely. "Good night, Sarah. Sleep well."

She stood, dazed, watching him as he strode out of the lobby. She remained there, trying to control her pounding heart, for what seemed like several minutes, before pushing off the wall she'd used to support herself, and staggering up the stairs, down the hall, and, after fumbling with the key, into her room.

Closing the door quietly behind her, she leaned against it for support, trying in vain to figure out what had just happened. Where had that come from, and why had it ended so abruptly, leaving her both frustrated and confused? There was no way she was going to find sleep anytime soon. Hoping she wouldn't disturb the other guests in the hotel, she ran a hot bath in the hopes of soaking away her agitation.

She slid into the hot bubble bath and sighed, thinking back on the evening. It had been wonderful, sexual frustration notwithstanding. She couldn't remember when she'd last felt so completely admired, respected, and desired by another man. Especially desired. She shivered at the memory of his lips on her bare back. Those kisses seemed more intimate to her than any others.

She should be angry that he'd left her like that, but she actually found his restraint sexy. Not too many men would have walked away from a woman who was as obviously willing as she was.

Adrenaline still pulsed through her body. The zing of electricity she felt whenever he touched her, the breathlessness when he kissed her, was unlike anything she'd ever known. Her lips still tingled where he'd gently nibbled them. She hadn't realized just how much she'd missed being wooed, pursued, and yes . . . seduced.

She groaned and slid deeper into the bubbles. What was she doing? That seemed to be a constant refrain this week. Her life was so confused right now, and Alex only added to the confusion.

I'm thirty-eight years old, she thought, newly divorced, out of work, and trying to figure out what I want to do with my life. She didn't need another man . . . not now.

But what a man he was. Strong, yet sensitive; in control, but not controlling; worldly, tolerant, and insightful.

He understood her in a way few others did. His eyes revealed flashes of intuition when she exposed some other aspect of her character. Add to all that, the rare and beautiful combination of masculinity and grace, and you had the total package. "Oh God," she moaned. "I'm in deep trouble."

~

*J*t wasn't a hot bath that Alex sought but a cold shower. His high-minded plans to let her down easy had dissipated into an all-out seduction. What the hell was the matter with him anyway? One minute he'd been embarrassed by his innuendo and the next minute he'd been trying to bring it to fruition.

He stood in the small guest-bath shower at Trevor's, arms braced against the wall, letting the cold, stinging spray cool his blood. His grandmother was right. He needed to be careful where Sarah was concerned. She was recovering from a divorce, a husband who'd cheated on her, and she didn't deserve yet another heartbreak.

He never set out to hurt the women he dated. He respected women. With examples like his grandmother and mother how could he not? He was careful to avoid those looking to marry into money and title. That's why he only had 'relationships,' if that's what they were, with women who could hold their own—women who were only looking for a casual fling.

Sarah wasn't one of those women. She was so easy to read, she'd get beat at poker even if she were holding a royal flush.

Warm and tender, sophisticated yet reserved, and the kind of woman who'd put everything she had into what was important to her. She was the first woman in recent memory, perhaps ever, who didn't give a damn about his title, his money, or his relative fame.

He toweled his wet hair before discarding the towel and climbing into bed. He had to make up his mind. Either he must let her down easy as he'd previously intended or pursue her with all the seriousness she deserved. The question that would plague him all night was which one would it be?

CHAPTER 16

*H*arry, the desk clerk, called Sarah's name as she walked out. He wanted to know if she'd lost a hair clip, saying he'd already asked the other guests, and no one had claimed it, so she was the last logical choice.

In his hand lay her errant clip. Mortified, she said, "Ahem, yes, I wondered where that had disappeared to." When she didn't reach out to take the clip, he gently placed it on the desk. "Thank you."

"Yes, miss. I wondered how it got there . . ."

"I'm not sure," she muttered, looking back down quickly, and striding out the front door. She wasn't looking up as she exited the building in haste, so she was surprised when she ran right into a hard, masculine chest.

"Hey, where's the fire?" Alex laughed, grabbing her shoulders to prevent her from falling.

She looked up into his grinning, handsome face. Her blush deepened. "The desk clerk apparently found my hair clip on the floor this morning," she replied, looking into his face with an arched brow.

"Well, he could think you simply dropped it," he said unconvincingly.

"Right . . . I dropped my hair clip on the floor . . . against the wall . . . in the darkest corner of the lobby," she retorted with an embarrassed laugh.

"That is probably a very popular location for passionate late-night kisses, so I'm sure they find all manner of interesting items there," he said, nuzzling her neck. "A hair clip is probably the least incriminating item." He grinned devilishly against her skin.

Sarah wanted to kick him in the shin. She was a little grumpy this morning after going to bed alone and sexually frustrated. "Are you planning to stand there all day holding my arms, or are we going on that bike ride we discussed?"

He released her shoulders, stepping aside to reveal two bicycles.

Each bike had a basket on the front. One basket looked to have a picnic lunch, while the other basket contained a blanket.

"Your chariot awaits my lady," he said with a grand, sweeping gesture, turning on the devastating charm.

"Very original," she said, giving him a withering look.

~

Their bike ride took them past Radcliffe Infirmary and then briefly up Walton Street before turning onto Jericho Street and into a suburb of the same name.

Now one of Oxford's most sought-after residences, Jericho had a storied past. In the Victorian Era, it was notorious for poor quality housing. It is said to be the model for Thomas Hardy's fictional slum, Beersheba, in *Jude the Obscure.*

Alex pointed out one of the terraced houses. "That's where Trevor lives." They breezed past on their bikes, giving her little time to study the house.

They made their way back to Walton Street and then to Walton Wells Road, which came to a dead end at Port Meadow, a large common area of grazing land still used for horses and cattle. It was also a favorite area for walking or biking. The Thames, or the Isis as it was called at this point, ran along the unfenced land. The meadow had never been ploughed, maintaining its treasure of archaeological remains.

It was sunny and hot today, a little more humid, too, making Sarah glad she'd packed a pair of shorts and a tank top for the trip just in case.

Alex slowed, and she pulled up next to him.

"I thought we would go punting," he said.

"Huh?" she asked, her thoughts running to football.

He laughed at her expression. "Punting. A punt is a flat-bottomed boat used in shallow water. Punting refers to boating in a punt." He explained as if lecturing a student.

"Like a gondola?"

"Somewhat, except you use an oar to propel a gondola. In punting, you use a pole."

They rode next to each other, arriving at the launch shortly.

After hiring the aforementioned punt and pole, they put into the river. Alex looked like he knew what he was doing, so she just did her best to stay out of his way. He'd already loaded the picnic basket and blanket in the punt, before reaching into the picnic basket and pulling out a bottle of champagne and a rope.

Sarah was totally befuddled thinking the rope was to tie up the punt, but there was already a rope lying in the bottom of the boat. Rather than sounding ignorant again, she watched quietly as he tied one end of the rope to the punt and the other end of the rope to the neck of the champagne bottle. He gently dropped the bottle over the side into the river.

"For a second I thought you intended to christen the boat," she said, laughing, her mood lightening with the sun, fresh air, and soft breeze.

He returned the laughter. Moving to one side of the boat, he tipped it slightly, and grabbing the pole, gently pushed along the river.

Sarah sat facing the stern watching him. He had superb balance and looked like he was thoroughly relishing the physical activity. His dark brown hair ruffled by the gentle, cooling breeze; his T-shirt hugging his sculpted arms and chest; his muscular legs flexed, facilitating his balance. He wore shorts for the first time since they met, giving Sarah her first view of bare legs, and it was a pleasing view indeed.

The scene in the lobby last night came flooding back. What would have happened if he hadn't been such a gentleman? She sighed, thinking a little less gentlemanly behavior would have been welcome.

"Why aren't you viewing the scenery?" he asked, referring to the fact that she faced the stern where he stood, rather than the bow.

She raised her hand to shield her eyes from the sun as she looked into his face, "I am." Did she just say that out loud?

"All right." He grinned, a little self-conscious. If she didn't stop looking at him like he was a luscious piece of Godiva chocolate, he was going to have to find a secluded spot and finish what he'd started last night. That, or take a swim in the Isis.

After another few minutes, he asked, "Are you enjoying yourself?"

Startled, she looked up at him. For a moment, she thought she was busted . . . that he had read her wayward thoughts. "Oh, um, yes," she said, looking out at the cool water. The sun wasn't the only thing making her hot.

A little while later, he startled her again. "Are you hungry?" he asked, tilting his head to the side, giving her his most charming grin. He felt a little like a juicy piece of meat hanging in front of a salivating dog.

Again, she thought she was busted, but he was talking about a different kind of hunger. Maybe. Either way, the answer was the same. "Yes."

"We'll moor the punt and find a shady tree for our picnic," he said.

They were both quiet for a time, soaking up the sun and enjoying the gentle breezes off the river. Despite her recent wicked thoughts, she felt quite content. She pointed out a couple of ducks swimming along behind the punt and asked if they could share a little of their lunch with them.

"I wouldn't do that if I were you."

"Why not?" she asked, puzzled. He didn't seem the type to dislike animals. In fact, he had stopped a man on the street in Castle Combe to pet his border collie.

"You'll attract every waterfowl within a fifty-mile radius. Trust me. It loses its charm after five minutes."

"Oh."

He continued to pole the boat up the river. "Did you know that *Alice in Wonderland* was inspired by a punting trip?" Not waiting for her reply, he continued, "Reverend Charles Dodgson, a.k.a. Lewis Carroll, and Reverend Robinson Duckworth were punting along the Isis with three young girls, including the story's namesake, Alice. The girls asked him to make up a story for them. He later expanded that story into the current tale as we know it."

"If you ever decide to forsake your acting career, you have a promising career as a tour guide."

"I'll remember that. Tour guide by day, masseuse by night." He waggled his eyebrows.

～

They lounged side-by-side on the blanket beneath the sweeping arms of a primordial oak tree, the remains of their lunch spread around them. The picnic basket had been thoughtfully packed with fresh strawberries, sweet grapes, fine stilton cheese, sliced ham, and hearty Irish soda bread. The bottle of champagne, chilled in the water as they punted down the river, was now more than half empty.

Alex reclined on his side facing Sarah, propped up on his elbow. "Can I ask you . . ." he drew in a breath, "the night we met in the pub, you blushed at one point, quite charmingly I might add. Why was that?"

"How can you possibly remember that?"

"I remember everything about our first meeting."

So did she, including what he was alluding to. "You caught me staring at you, and as our mothers always taught us, it isn't polite to stare," she hedged, not meeting his eye.

He shook his head, "No, that wasn't it. There was something more to make you blush that deeply."

Remembering her thoughts, she looked away, blushing again.

"That's it!" He pointed his finger at her face, as he laughed. "That's the blush—like you've just got caught with your knickers down."

"Do I really have to tell you? It's just too mortifying."

"Oh, I really want to know now that I've seen the blush again," he insisted.

"Um, well," she hesitated, "since we'd just met, I was studying your appearance," she hesitated again, "and when I got to your hair, I thought that it was . . . charmingly tousled."

"That's not it, there's more to it," he said, his voice coaxing.

"Okay! I thought it looked like you had just gotten out of a bed. And I wished it had been mine." She looked him straight in the eye on the last part, her brow raised with a bravado she didn't really feel. The look she saw there made her heart race.

His eyes widened, and then he broke into a broad, suggestive smile. "Why, you saucy minx!"

"What did you just call me?" She frowned up at him in surprise.

"A saucy minx. Is that a problem?" He looked askance.

Thoughtful, her brow creased, and she said, "Well . . . I don't know . . . I've never been called a saucy minx before. I'll have to think about it." She tried to hide her smile, to keep up the offended façade, but to no avail. She burst out laughing.

He visibly relaxed, throwing a grape at her.

"I want to apologize for last night . . . in the lobby," he said, his brow creased, all teasing gone.

"Oh." Did he regret it now? "Are you apologizing for the seduction or the callous desertion?" she asked in annoyance.

"Did I desert you?"

She snorted in response.

"I suppose so. Then I should apologize for that as well. I guess both were ungentlemanly of me, but I'm especially apologizing for seducing you." He paused, his brow furrowed in thought. "In my defense, it wasn't my plan to seduce you. I was quite carried away by . . . your taste, your scent, your texture."

She drew in her breath at his arousing confession.

His eyes became intent as he crooked his index finger at her. When she hesitated, he reached out, wrapping his free hand behind her neck, pulling her toward him. He kissed her gently at first. When she returned the kiss, he rolled her onto her back and slid his hand down her arm to rest on her waist, his tongue parting her lips.

A throaty moan escaped her. His warm mouth tasted of strawberries and champagne. Her hands went to his hair, grasping it with a need so strong, all thoughts of their rather public display fled.

"Apparently, I'll be apologizing often," he murmured against her lips, as he reached down and pulled her leg up over his hip. His hand on her bare thigh sent a hot frisson of desire through her.

His mouth traveled down to the hollow of her throat, as he rained sensual kisses up and down her neck, inhaling her signature fragrance of sweet jasmine.

"Sarah," he breathed. He withdrew a few inches from her face and reached out to trace her collarbone with his fingertip. "You are so beautiful."

She felt like her bones had melted, like she had no substance. His brown-black eyes searched her face, making it difficult to control her erratic heart. A rumble of thunder broke the spell. They hadn't noticed that the sun had disappeared, the sky had darkened, and the air smelled of ozone.

"Uh-oh. We might be in for a little English shower," he said, his voice husky.

They didn't move though. Another rumble of thunder, more insistent this time, rolled across the open meadow, prompting him to sit up.

He glanced in the direction of the approaching storm. "We'd better pack up."

~

By the time they reached the launch, they were soaked through.

Alex was exhausted, having poled upwind through the driving rain back to the launch.

Sarah helped him get the picnic basket and now-sodden blanket out of the boat, and started walking toward the bikes; after all, what was the point in running? They couldn't get any more drenched than they were.

"Where do you think you're going?" Alex asked as she felt his arm snake around her waist, stopping her.

She looked up in surprise, the rain running down her face, making it hard to see the expression on his face. "To the bikes," she said, as if it should be obvious.

"Are you daft? We're not going to ride the bikes in this downpour." He sounded annoyed. He pulled her in the opposite direction toward the Perch Inn near the boat launch.

"But how are we going to get back to my hotel, and how are we going to get the bikes back to Trevor?"

"Let me worry about that," he said dismissively.

They stood under the inn's overhang, out of the rain.

"I'll be fine. I'm not a cupcake." But this was not like the summer storms in Florida that left the atmosphere like a sauna. This storm ushered in a bone-chilling cold.

"Sarah, you're shivering." He grabbed her shoulders. "You're covered in goose bumps." He ran his hands down her arms, chafing them for warmth. "And your teeth are chattering." He brought his hand up to cup her face, rubbing his thumb across her chin. "Your lips are turning blue." Her lips parted, and he leaned down to touch his warm lips to hers.

A loud clap of thunder made her jump.

Pulling away, he said, "Here, let's go inside the pub where it's warm."

There was a crackling fire in an oversized fireplace, surrounded by other wet boaters, in varying stages of drying out. An older man saw them enter and vacated his seat next to the fire for Sarah.

"Th-thank y-you," she stuttered through her chattering teeth.

"Wait here," Alex said, then turned and left. He returned a couple of minutes later with a thick wool blanket in his hands, unfolding it as he walked. He wrapped it around her shoulders, pulling it up under her chin. "Better?" he asked, the concern evident in his voice.

"Y-yes."

"Good. I'll be back."

Not long after he left, a waitress walked over with a steaming mug of tea. "Here you are, miss. This should help."

"Thank you." Sarah noticed her teeth no longer clattered uncontrollably. She gratefully took the hot mug and wrapped her hands around it.

She didn't know how long she sat in front of the fire, but gradually she thawed out, her tense muscles relaxed, and the shivering abated. She shook out her hair, running her fingers through it, hoping it would dry a little. I must look like a drowned rat, she thought.

She looked up to see Alex striding toward her. She might look like a drowned rat, but he looked like the clear winner of a male wet T-shirt contest. His hair was soaked, and his sodden T-shirt clung to his broad chest and flat stomach, revealing even more of his pleasing athletic frame. Water dripped from the hem of his shorts, running down his legs in rivulets.

"Did you go out in the rain again?" she asked, trying somewhat unsuccessfully to hide her frank admiration of his body.

"Yes. I had to take care of the bikes," he said matter-of-factly. "I'm glad to see your color has returned." He reached out to touch her face. "I was beginning to think you were going into hypothermia."

"Playing doctor again?" she asked, teasing.

"I'll play doctor with you anytime." He broke into a seductive smile. He held out his hand to her. "It's still raining cats and dogs out, so I've hired a taxi to take us back."

Once seated inside the warm, cozy interior of the taxi, he drew her to him and wrapped his arms around her.

She didn't bother to tell him he was cold and wet. It didn't matter.

"Old Parsonage, please."

CHAPTER 17

They dashed into the lobby of the inn. The rain had not
let up.

"Good afternoon, Ms. Edwards," the desk clerk said cheerfully. "I
see you got caught in the rain, too." There was a roaring fire in the
inn's sitting area, with a few dampened guests gathered around it.
"We've laid a fire in your room. All it requires is a match," she added
with a quick glance at Alex, followed by a knowing smile.

Walking past the desk, Alex took Sarah's hand and drew her
toward the stairs. She threw him a questioning look.

"You need to get into dry clothes, right?" he asked with a sweep of
his hands indicating her crumpled, clammy clothes.

"Yes, but what about you?"

"I'm English. I'm used to being cold and wet." He shrugged his
shoulder. "They have dressing gowns in the room?"

"Yes—"

"Then I'll be fine. I'm more worried about you right now." He
directed her upstairs as they had this conversation. The thought of
him in her room made her shiver, but not with cold.

Once inside her room, he walked over to the fireplace and, kneeled
down, and pulled out a match to start the fire. Without looking at her,

he said, "Why don't you take a hot shower? I'll make sure the fire catches."

Sarah hesitated. The intimacy of the scene was hard to miss.

"Go ahead, you're safe. I won't invade your privacy. Unless you ask me to," he added with a grin.

Even amidst the nervous flutters in her stomach, she noted his pronunciation of 'privacy' with a short 'i.' Perhaps a hot shower would help calm her agitated nerves.

After starting the fire, Alex found himself alone in the room, and used that opportunity to strip off his wet clothing and rummage in the armoire for a dressing gown. He tried not to think of her naked in the shower, just a few steps away. Instead, he occupied himself with ordering hot tea for the room.

Standing beneath the hot spray, Sarah finally warmed up for the first time since the rain started. She'd hoped it would steady her erratic pulse, but no such luck. The thought of him in the next room . . . her room . . . was intoxicating. She stayed in the shower longer than necessary, unsure what she would find when she opened the bathroom door. She turned off the water before he thought she'd washed down the drain. She'd failed to bring a change of clothes into the bathroom, so putting on her robe she took a deep breath and stepped out of the bathroom, toweling her hair casually, like it was perfectly normal to have him in her room.

She stopped in her tracks. Seated in one of the wing chairs in front of the now-blazing fire with a small tea tray on the side table, he wore the inn's complimentary robe, his rumpled clothes lying on the floor by the fire to dry, making the fact that the robe was the only thing he wore even more obvious.

The deep breath she took before she opened the door left her in an audible sigh. He looked up. It was dim in the room with the storm still darkening the sky, the fire the only source of light. It cast a golden glow across his handsome face, where a series of emotions flickered. First, surprise, then admiration, and finally desire.

He crossed the ample room that suddenly seemed small. He placed his hands on her shoulders. "Better?"

"Yes," she breathed, tilting her head up, his face so close to hers. He leaned down, taking her face in his hands, kissing her softly. She dropped the towel she held and threaded her fingers around his neck, pulling him closer. His hair was still damp.

He coiled his fingers in the wet hair at the nape of her neck, moving his lips over hers with increasing intensity. Her damp skin smelled of jasmine and rain.

A voice in the back of her head said this was insane. She ignored it. Instead, she took his bottom lip gently between her teeth. He groaned. Sarah sighed in return.

"Sarah." He spoke her name against her lips. "Sarah." He pulled back, his hand cupping her throat, caressing her staccato pulse with his thumb. "Sarah, tell me now . . . is this what you want? If not, I will leave. All you have to do is ask. But thirty more seconds of this, and I can't vouch for my self-control." He searched her face with his fathomless eyes, almost black now with desire.

She took a deep breath, as if she was about to dive into the deep end of the pool. "Yes," she said with a sigh. "This is what I want."

He kissed her again, more urgently this time. Retreating a step, he took her hand and led her to the bed.

~

She didn't move, afraid that she would wake up from this dream. Her murmured, "no apology necessary," and Alex's seductive grin and tender parting kiss were part of that dream.

She sighed, trying to keep consciousness at bay, but she was pulled inexorably to wakefulness. She rolled over and caught his scent. The other pillow had an indentation where his head had lain. It wasn't a dream. Of course, how could she expect it to have been a dream, when she'd hardly slept long enough to enter that state?

She waited for the panic to set in. This was completely out of character for her. She wouldn't think about the only other time she fell this fast for someone. No panic. She stretched like a satisfied cat, smiling at the memories. For someone who had slept very little, she felt remarkably well.

Alex had snuck out of the inn in the pre-dawn with a promise to be back by nine. He thought it best that he didn't come down for breakfast in his stiff, rumpled clothes from yesterday, murmuring something about her reputation. He's such a gentleman, she thought.

She reluctantly climbed out of bed and tried to locate her robe. It lay in a pool on the floor a few feet from the bed where Alex had slipped it off her shoulders. She staggered to the bathroom as if she was drunk, stopping in front of the mirror.

She stared in dismay at the image. There was no denying what she'd done last night. It was readily apparent in her face. Her lips were swollen, her eyes too bright, and her cheeks flushed. Add to that her wild, tangled hair and she was a walking billboard for sex. She cringed. A little butterfly fluttered in her stomach. Was that panic, or excitement? Definitely a little bit of both.

Sex was not a recreational activity for her. She knew this was a bit old-fashioned, but according to the Book of Sarah, sex was more than just a physical activity, a union of two bodies. It was an emotional, spiritual, and even intellectual merging of two people who cared deeply for one another.

So how did her actions of last night fit with her feelings for Alex? Or vice versa? And how did Alex feel about last night?

The shower cleared her head and calmed some of the rising panic, but the consequences of last night's events chipped away at the bliss she initially felt when she woke.

What was I doing? she asked herself yet again. How many times this week did I ask myself that question, and how many times had I shoved it aside? There was no shoving it aside anymore. She only had two more days in England, and she didn't know how this would end, but it couldn't end well. Could it?

Thrusting further introspection aside, she looked for something to occupy her mind until it was time to meet Alex for breakfast. She wondered if they were fooling anyone by putting on this charade.

Picking up the TV remote, she clicked on the news. She hadn't seen the TV news since she'd been in England, and come to think of it, she hadn't missed it. As the news played in the background, she grabbed her phone, and with her tongue firmly in her cheek, texted Ann and Becca: "Having a wonderful time. Wish you were here."

Laughing at her foolishness, she turned back to the TV in time to catch the name 'Fraser.' On the screen was a heavy-set man, his broad face capped by slightly thinning brown hair, dressed in a conservative suit. He stood at a podium surrounded by a few dour looking suit-clad gentlemen.

The caption on the bottom of the screen read: "Robert Fraser to run for Prime Minister." Sarah gasped. Alex's brother. Grabbing the remote, she turned up the volume, catching him mid-speech. ". . . announce my candidature for Prime Minister under the Conservative Party. I will support the principles of Thatcherism: free markets, deregulation, financial discipline, tax cuts, and weaker trade unions. It was the dedication to these principles that cured Britain's economic decline in the 1970s. It is the dedication to these same principles that will cure Britain's current economic crisis."

Ironic that Robert criticized Alex's chosen profession, when he had quite a flair for the dramatic himself. Then again, didn't all politicians, she thought a bit cynically.

He wasn't as good-looking as Alex, but that could just be her bias. She wondered whether Robert had told his brother before making the announcement and if so, what Alex thought about his brother's decision. More importantly to Robert, she supposed, was whether Alex would vote for him.

Turning off the TV, she grabbed her bag and headed down to meet the politician's handsome brother.

CHAPTER 18

"What would you like to do today?" Alex asked as he buttered a slice of toast, a hint of a smile teasing the corners of his mouth.

Seated at a small table in the inn's garden, they shared a light breakfast, both clearly relaxed and at peace with their world. Sarah didn't know how it was possible, but he looked even more handsome today, and she wondered if she had anything to do with that.

Alex's warm greeting this morning erased any concerns she'd had earlier. He'd taken her in his arms and discreetly whispered in her ear that he couldn't stop thinking about her, sending shivers of desire from her head to her toes.

Yesterday's storm had heralded a brilliant blue sky, cooler temperatures, and a whisper of a breeze. Birds sang in the trees, and the garden fountain seemed to chuckle with joy, even as Oxford's morning traffic was underway just beyond the walled garden.

Considering a response, she sipped her tea. "I'm not sure there's a site in Oxfordshire we haven't seen."

"I know one," he replied with a smile. "You haven't seen Rutherford."

"I've been to Rutherford," she said, a little confused. "Remember, that's when I figured you for a liar."

He laughed. "Yes, but you haven't seen the grounds. Do you ride?"

She frowned. "A little, and not since college."

"Let me guess, you played polo in college."

Laughing, she said, "No, but I needed a basket weaving class."

"What does basket weaving have to do with riding?" he replied, obviously confused.

"Nothing." She laughed lightly. "Basket weaving is an expression for an easy class. I wanted an easy 'A' my last semester, so I signed up for English riding."

"Was it an easy 'A'?"

"It was an 'A,' but it wasn't easy." She chuckled, remembering the sore knees and quads from all that posting.

"Well, it's a shame to waste that training." He smiled, slow and easy.

"I'm afraid I left my jodhpurs and riding jacket at home," she said with a little smirk.

"Jeans and T-shirt will suffice. I'm sure I can find a pair of my mother's riding boots. Size thirty-six, I'd guess."

She raised her eyebrows in surprise. "Yes."

"Perfect."

~

*S*itting astride a lovely dappled gray mare, Sarah looked out over the land that was Rutherford. She was having a Jane Austen moment. Beside her on an enormous black gelding sat Alex, looking like a modern-day Darcy in his riding pants and boots.

Alex indicated the various points of interest: the ruins of an ancient castle, the caretaker's cottage, the pond where he and his brother fished as boys, and some small caves where he and his brother often hid out playing a game of Robin Hood.

The pride he took in his family's estate was obvious, but his was a quiet pride, that of someone who knew how easily it could all be lost, as it almost was but for the hard work of his grandparents.

"Please forgive me. I have probably bored you to tears with all this talk of my ancestors."

"No," she hastened to assure him, "I have thoroughly enjoyed it. Truly." She smiled tenderly.

He turned his horse to face hers and carefully sidled up to her. Leaning from the saddle, he pulled her to him for a deep, yearning kiss.

She was the first woman he'd brought to Rutherford. After last night, and being with her today, having her by his side as he rode the grounds, he realized that he'd already made up his mind. This was not his usual fling. She was what he wanted. What he'd been waiting for. And he would tell her tonight.

～

"Grandmother! We've returned," Alex shouted to the house.

"In here, darling," Lady Clara called from the same room where she and Sarah had had tea.

Alex and Sarah entered the room holding hands and laughing. "Grandmother, Sarah and I would like to stay for dinner if you don't mind?"

"Mind? For heaven's sake boy, this is your home, too. I'll just go tell Martha," Lady Clara said as she left the room.

"Did you enjoy today?" Alex asked, drawing Sarah into his arms before kissing her.

"Oh, yes!" she replied, breathless from the kiss. "I must confess, I felt as though I'd walked straight into the setting of a Regency novel." She blushed a little at her confession. "And you, Lord Rutherford, you were quite dashing on your dark steed, looking every inch the lord and master."

Alex pressed her denim-clad hips to his, the corner of his mouth tilted up at a rakish angle. "How about I throw you up on the back of my horse and carry you off to those ancient ruins and—"

"Ahem." Lady Clara stood in the door, hands folded primly in front of her.

Sarah's blush deepened to full-on red. Alex didn't seem the least bit perturbed. When Sarah attempted to pull away, he kept his arm at her waist, holding her firmly by his side.

"Dinner will be served soon. You two must be parched after your long ride today. Martha is bringing refreshments shortly."

"I'll just go freshen up, if you'll excuse me." Sarah got to the door before she realized she didn't know where she was going. "Where . . . ?"

"Down the hall, my dear," Lady Clara said, coming to her rescue. "Second door on the left."

Alex watched her trim figure disappear through the door. He didn't know which was better, the elegant backless dress, or the snug jeans and riding boots. A soft smile played across his features. Last night, he'd witnessed, and, to his extreme pleasure, experienced, the passionate side that formed the underpinnings of his sweet, reserved Sarah. A side he looked forward to exploring even more.

He'd also witnessed a bit of her stubbornness earlier when he tried to help her mount and then give her a brief review of the mechanics of riding English. A smile ghosted across his face at the memory. Her eyes flashing green sparks, she'd said, with a stubborn set to her chin, "I can do it myself. Don't help."

"So, it looks as though you two are having a nice time," Lady Clara said, archly. "She is a lovely girl."

"Yes, Grandmother, you don't need to sing her praises. You'd be preaching to the choir at any rate."

"Oh, Martha, set the tray there. Thank you."

"Lemonade, dear?" Lady Clara asked, as she poured a glass.

"Yes. Thank you."

"It is a shame that she is leaving on Sunday," Lady Clara nudged.

"Yes. I wanted to speak with you about that. Do you, that is, would you mind if I asked Sarah to stay a little longer . . . here . . . at Rutherford."

"Oh, I think that is a lovely idea. She could have the Rose Room," she said.

Alex couldn't help the grin at her pronouncement. The Rose Room happened to be conveniently located across the hall from his room.

Lady Clara still beamed when Sarah returned. "Here you are my dear, a lovely glass of lemonade."

Gratefully, Sarah took the glass as Martha came to announce dinner. Sarah hadn't realized how thirsty she was, and she was unsure whether to bring the drink with her or leave it.

"Come, my dear. Bring the lemonade with you."

Thank God. She controlled the urge to guzzle the icy drink in a very unladylike manner. Alex wrapped his arm around her waist and guided her to the family dining room.

Dinner was a lovely affair. Sarah enjoyed watching Alex and Lady Clara interact. It was easy to see the love and affection they had for one another.

Alex was not immune to observations of his own. Sarah and his grandmother laughed over some Oxford anecdote, and he was reminded of his own mother's interactions with his grandmother. The two women genuinely enjoyed one another's company. He hoped his mother would feel the same when she met Sarah.

"Oh, my dear, I never will forget how beautiful you looked at the final dinner," Lady Clara gushed.

Alex smiled at the praise. "You should have seen her Wednesday evening. She put heaven's stars to shame."

Sarah blushed at the profusion of compliments.

"Grandmother! Where are you?"

"Heavens! You'd think these boys were never taught any manners. In here, Robert."

"Robert? What the hell is he doing here?" Alex's face grew thunderous.

"Now, now," Lady Clara placated.

Robert? Alex's brother was here? Sarah's blush turned into a blanche. Her mouthful of food went down like a rock.

The man Sarah had seen on television just this morning entered the room. He paused when he saw her, then nodded his head before grazing his grandmother's cheek and stalking past her to stand beside Alex's chair, where he threw a pile of tabloids onto the dining table with a *thwack*, making Sarah flinch and the dishes clatter.

"Hello, Robert. So good to see you again." Alex's voice was sarcastic as he raised an eyebrow at his brother.

Robert didn't bother with a greeting. "This," he said pointing his finger at the papers on the table, "this is exactly what I was afraid of. This," he stated, pointing again at the papers for emphasis, "is my worst nightmare!"

Sarah's first impression was correct. Robert had a taste for the melodramatic.

Alex started to brush the papers aside when the photo caught his attention. Picking up the paper, the thunderclouds returned. He shifted his eyes to Sarah, and then back to the paper he held. His mouth flattened out into a frown.

"Your worst nightmare, what about Sarah?" he said, indicating her presence.

Sarah? What did this have to do with me? she wondered.

Robert didn't even bother to look in her direction. "Sarah isn't running for parliament on a conservative ticket. Supermodels, actresses . . . that singer, your playboy lifestyle is going to crush me," he growled.

Dramatic flair or not, she winced at the bitterness in his voice. Still confused over what this had to do with her, she reached for the paper Alex discarded.

Something about the grainy photo looked familiar. She continued staring at it until it dawned on her with sickening clarity. She and Alex lying beneath an oak tree in an intimate embrace she remembered only too well. The caption read, 'Port Meadow Picnic.' She didn't bother to read the story below the fold that accompanied the photo.

Her hand flew to her throat as her face grew ashen.

"My dear." Lady Clara laid a hand on her shoulder. "My dear, are you okay?"

Sarah's ears buzzed, the room grew dim, as everyone around her seemed to recede into the background. Memories of the knowing looks and snide public comments about Adrian's affair and their divorce flooded her brain. Reminded of the article about Adrian earlier in the week, Sarah also recalled her fears of rushing into a relationship with Alex. A relationship that could plainly have another very public end.

Alex was remarkably calm as he rose from his seat, glancing at Sarah with concern. "Robert, do you ever think of anyone besides yourself?"

"I'm supposed to sit back and watch my political aspirations go down the toilet just so you can cop off with this woman?"

Sarah snapped back to the present. She didn't need a translation to understand the insult. Everything happened so fast after that.

Alex drew back his fist and punched his brother in the stomach.

Sarah gasped as Robert doubled over with a strangled groan.

"That was for insulting Sarah," Alex ground out before dealing an uppercut to Robert's chin, opening a gash that started bleeding almost immediately. "That was for the rugby match."

Robert brought his hand up to his chin to staunch the blood. "You bloody-well better be prepared to fight. Let's take this outside."

Sarah was so shocked she couldn't even articulate a plea for Lady Clara to do something. No need, because Lady Clara was already intervening.

"Boys! Enough. Will you have Sarah thinking I have two hooligans for grandsons?" She stood between them like a referee at a boxing match telling the opponents to go to their respective corners.

"Robert, go wash up that cut and bandage it. Alex, I'm sure your hand could use some ice." He winced when she mentioned his hand. "Now," she urged when they continued to face off at one another. She followed Robert out of the room.

Sarah shook with anger, fear, and the fight or flight response caused by the altercation. She'd never seen Alex so angry, so . . . violent. She heard ice rattling in the ice bucket as Alex put some in his napkin to wrap around his hand. The sound broke through her inertia.

"Alex, is it broken?" she whispered, anxious, but afraid to touch his hand for fear it might cause him more pain.

"I doubt it. It's not the first time I've clouted my brother, Sarah, and it probably won't be the last . . ." His voice trailed off.

"But why did you do that?" she asked, incredulous.

"He insulted you. Do you think I would let him get away with that?" He frowned at her, his brows knitted together. "And the rugby retribution was long in coming," he muttered almost to himself.

"But you could have . . . I don't know . . . cursed at him or something . . ."

He raised his uninjured hand to her cheek. "Sarah, it's how we settle things." He shrugged. "Don't worry, later we'll reconcile over a pint."

This was a side of Alex she had yet to see, nor ever had imagined existed. Oddly, she rather liked that he stood up for her. Not being a violent person herself, this was an unexpected side of her as well. But the fact that it was his brother, and that she had been the impetus for such behavior, was mortifying to her. Her eyes cut back to the tabloid lying on the table, a concern creasing her brow.

"Are you okay?" Alex asked, as he pulled her to him, wrapping his arm around her. "I'm sorry about the photo. I thought I'd outsmarted the guy, but it seems he has made it his personal mission to invade my privacy."

Sarah pulled back. "You knew about this? You knew we were being . . . stalked by this photographer, and you didn't tell me?"

"I didn't want to worry you, and I thought I'd evaded him." Alex reached for her again, but she stepped back.

"You really should have warned me, Alex. Don't you think I had a right to know that a consequence of dating you might be to find myself in the . . . spotlight?" She picked up the tabloid again and flipping it over saw the headline "The Other Woman?"

He grimaced at the expression on her face.

"The other woman? Me? Am I the other woman?" Her voice rose

with her hysteria. Her throat tightened and tears threatened to spill down her cheeks.

If Alex was dating someone, or worse engaged . . . she felt sick. However unwitting her role as the other woman might have been, the thought of it filled her with revulsion. But no, his grandmother never would have stood by and let him . . . unless she doesn't know.

"No! Of course not." Alex raked his good hand through his hair. "Listen . . . Sarah . . . you can't believe everything you read."

"Then why don't you enlighten me?" she asked, as she swiped angrily at a tear.

Alex sat with a sigh. "I had been dating the Prime Minister's daughter. The tabloids practically had the wedding planned." At her horrified expression, he raised his hands, entreating her to wait. "We never had any intention of getting married, and we ended the relationship amicably."

Alex stood to pace the length of the room. "But that doesn't sell papers, so they create stories out of whole cloth, with absolutely no basis in fact." He stopped in front of Sarah, and tossing the makeshift ice pack on the table, placed his hands on her shoulders. "Sarah, you are *not* the other woman. You are the *only* woman. And I am so sorry that you've been thrust into the ruthless public eye."

This brought a fresh round of tears. In front of her stood a contrite, and no doubt sincere, man. A gentleman, who personified all her romantic notions, however silly those notions might be. But she couldn't do this. She couldn't live her life wondering if some tabloid photographer was snapping her photo at some inopportune moment. More importantly, she couldn't bear to see her relationship with Alex reduced to a tasty tabloid tidbit.

"Is this what your life is like?" she whispered.

"Yes. I'm afraid it is. For now. You might not like it, but you learn to live with it." He gave her a half smile and a slight lift of his shoulder.

Sarah closed her eyes. "No, I don't think so," she whispered, despondent.

CHAPTER 19

The wheels of the jet touched down on the runway, startling Sarah. She didn't even remember the flight attendant announcing their initial approach into Jacksonville. This had been the longest flight she'd ever experienced, and the eight-and-a-half-hour flight time and five-hour time difference had nothing to do with it.

After spending the last day and a half crying, vacillating between anger, shame, heartbreak, and remorse, she was emotionally and physically drained. Angry at herself for getting into this situation. Ashamed that she'd slept with a man with whom she should have known an ongoing relationship was nearly impossible, the tabloid photo broadcasting her indiscretion to the world like some sort of sick joke. She was heartbroken, with only herself to blame this time. But mostly she was remorseful for having hurt Alex the way she did, and it was clear from the look on his face that she had hurt him. Let him down.

The drive back to the inn had been the most awkward experience of her life. Thinking the tabloids might be camped out at the inn, Alex convinced Robert to drive her to Trevor's, who would then take her to the inn via a back way. As it turned out, it appeared to be all quiet on that front.

Surprisingly, Robert had apologized to Sarah for his crude remark, and even tried to console her in his stiff-upper lip manner. Under any other circumstances, she might have found his feeble attempts endearing, but she couldn't get past the pain. Her heart was in tatters. Again.

The loss of Alex was only half of it.

Lady Clara's goodbye had almost been more difficult than Alex's. She'd been tender and yet subdued, trying to convince Sarah to stay at Rutherford, but Sarah refused. Postponing the inevitable would only make it worse. And it was inevitable. She saw no other alternative. She was not cut out for life center stage.

Alex had argued and cajoled, ranted and pleaded, finally giving in with the resignation of a patient who's been given bad news, his face wearing the same sad, shocked expression as that same unfortunate patient.

But it was the memory of their last kiss that would never leave her. Filled with yearning, anger, sadness, regret, and loss. Whose emotions were whose, she couldn't say.

Her eyes welled up. She had to stop thinking about it. It was going to be hard enough to convince Ann and Becca that her red swollen eyes and lack of enthusiasm were from jetlag.

They waited for her at the end of the concourse with broad smiles on their faces. Ann bounced up and down like an eager child. This at least brought a tremulous smile to her face. As soon as she cleared the security barrier, Ann ran over and gave her a big hug and kiss. Becca followed more sedately, but hugged her with just as much affection.

"So, how was your trip? Did you have a great time? Did you take lots of pictures? Did you meet interesting people?" Ann's continuous stream of questions didn't allow for a response.

"Ann, give her a minute to answer . . ." Becca chided.

"Oh, sorry. I just can't wait to hear."

Sarah had missed them both: Ann's bubbly personality and her sweet, Southern accent; Becca's sound advice and steadying influence. But she wasn't ready to talk about the trip. Maybe if she stuck with safe subjects, like the university, the students, and the classes . . .

"You both were right. Oxford University was a wonderful experience. I met smart, engaging people, and immersed myself in Jane Austen." That should be safe enough. As they walked to baggage claim, she proceeded to tell them a little about the campus, her dorm room, and her classmates.

They stepped out into the oppressive heat of a Florida summer, the weight of the atmosphere as overbearing as her misery. Sarah hoped if she stuck to her friendship with Lady Clara, an only slightly less painful topic, she would have a wealth of anecdotes that would keep them entertained for the duration of the drive home.

Ann was very impressed that Sarah could count a "real-live Earl's daughter" among her friends. Sarah didn't bother to clarify that Lady Clara was a countess in her own right. Ann proved an unwitting ally in prolonging Sarah's tales of Lady Clara by asking lots of questions about her house, whether she's met the Queen, and how the whole English title system worked.

"Did you have to curtsy in her presence?" Ann asked in awe.

"No." Sarah couldn't refrain from laughing. "She's not royalty."

"Well, I didn't know." Ann said with chagrin. "I probably would have curtseyed . . ."

"And Lady Clara would no doubt have been charmed," Sarah said, reaching into the backseat to squeeze her hand.

Ann and Becca helped her get the luggage in the house.

"The mail is on your desk. You'll also be happy to see that your plants survived in your absence," Ann said, indicating the still-healthy plants in her study, "and that the backyard birds didn't starve."

"Thanks Ann. I really appreciate it. Which reminds me, I have gifts for you both, but they're buried in my luggage somewhere . . ."

"You're such a giver. That's why we like giving to you in return," Ann said, with feeling.

Before Ann could return to her interrogation about the trip, Becca said, "You must be exhausted. We'll let you get unpacked. Get some rest," she finished, giving Sarah another hug. Ann followed suit, leaving her alone with her broken heart.

Sarah looked around her house. She hadn't realized how much she had missed it. Tomorrow was Monday. Her telephone interview with Harper Legal Consultants was at two, giving her less than a day to rest and catch up on things, before circling back to the more pressing matter of her unemployment.

Last week had been a wonderful fantasy . . . well, up until Friday night . . . but it was time to close that door and come back down to reality. Return to being sensible Sarah. She'd get a job, put her nonsensical past behavior behind her, bury her ridiculous dreams for the future, and get over Alex. In that order.

PART II

CHAPTER 20

*A*s much as Sarah dreaded returning to the job search, she found she was fortunate to have something to take her mind off Alex, if only for a while. It had been almost two weeks since she'd left England, but he proved difficult to forget, even though four thousand miles separated them. In Guy's words, she'd fallen 'arse over tip' in love with Alex.

She knew now that what she'd taken for heartbreak after her hapless marriage to Adrian ended had only been wounded pride, a deflated ego, and of course the shame of having failed. What she suffered then paled in comparison to what she suffered now. This was the real thing.

Subtle reminders taunted any attempt to put that perfect week behind her: the faint scent of his cologne that lingered on her clothes when she'd unpacked; the cheesy Jane Austen replica cross he purchased for her in Lacock; other small, inconsequential souvenirs like the program from *As You Like It;* the notorious hair clip; and, of course, the photos of them from the trip.

Stop, she admonished herself. She promised herself she would close the door. Alex would get over it. He's a handsome, charming, sweet, sexy . . . Stop! Someone with an open heart, minimal baggage, and a strong constitution for public attention would come along and make him forget about her.

She was confident he would get over it, but would she?

~

"*D*o you want to get together this weekend, maybe do a little shopping?" Ann asked with her usual buoyant enthusiasm, but Sarah knew she was just trying to cheer her up.

"Sure," she said with feigned interest. "Where should we go?" she asked, idly flipping through a catalog that sold books, videos, and other gifts as she spoke to Ann on the phone.

"Let's go to the new outdoor shopping center. It's supposed to be enormous."

"Sure. That sounds great."

Both she and Becca had been poking and prodding her into various social activities. After finally breaking down and telling them about Alex, they'd been especially solicitous, but also extremely meddlesome. They had been hurt at first that she hadn't fully disclosed all the details of her vacation. Then they couldn't understand why she refused to contact him again, to get over her fear of public scrutiny and apologize for leaving him. Wasn't he worth overcoming her trifling social anxiety disorder?

She'd finally had to put her foot down and threaten that if they didn't stop nagging her, she would stop talking to them altogether. And it wasn't social anxiety disorder. It was simply an aversion to public attention.

Ann rambled on about the kids and Rob. Even though she felt guilty about it, Sarah only listened with half an ear. Suddenly, there it was: Alex's movie, *Jude the Obscure*. Sarah's heart skipped a beat and her eyes welled with tears.

"Sarah . . . Sarah . . . are you there?" Ann's insistent voice yanked her back to the present, reminding her that she was still on the phone.

"Sorry. I gotta go. I'll talk to you later." Sarah hung up before Ann could answer.

Was *Mansfield Park* also in the catalog, she wondered? She flipped quickly through the pages. After turning a few more pages, she found it. His handsome face graced the cover of the DVD. He was attired in Regency garb, facing the actress who she assumed played Fanny Price, his arm around her waist. She felt an irrational stab of jealousy for the actress. She flipped a few more pages. *Tess of the d'Urbervilles* was also in the catalog.

She hadn't forgotten that his movies were likely available, but some vestiges of self-preservation had prevented her from tracking them down. Now, out of the blue, here were all three.

On a whim, she went to her computer and ordered them, paying the excessive cost for two-day shipping, so she would have them by the weekend. So much for self-preservation.

*L*ying on the couch, still in her pajamas yet having never gone to bed, Sarah wiped the tears from her eyes. She'd just finished watching *Jude the Obscure* . . . for the second time. Seeing Alex in the romantic period costumes was agony, hearing his beautiful voice, the flowing lines spoken in his clipped accent, torture. Yet, she couldn't help herself. She'd already watched the other two movies twice each.

Her doorbell rang. Reluctantly, she went to see who it could be. Ann. She groaned. She'd completely forgotten about their shopping date. Shame-faced, Sarah opened the door.

Before Sarah could apologize, Ann blurted, "Why aren't you dressed? Are you sick? What's the matter?"

She held the door wide for Ann to come in. "I'm sorry. I completely forgot . . ."

"You look like something the cat dragged in," she said without mixing her metaphors for once. "And you've been crying."

She plopped down on the sofa, pulling Sarah down with her. That's when she saw the DVDs on the coffee table.

"Is this him?" she said picking up the cover for *Mansfield Park* and examining it. "Oh my. He is gorgeous! I'm sorry, that slipped. Isn't it unusual for an earl to have a . . . profession? I mean, shouldn't he be, I don't know, managing his Earldom?"

"Flogging his serfs, conspiring to usurp the crown, locking virgins in the tower?" Sarah shook her head. "You've been reading too many bodice-rippers."

Ann swatted at her. "No but, it just seems weird that he would be an actor."

"Many titled men and women have professions outside their estates, from publishers and journalists to broadcasters and artists." Sarah sniffled. "Oh, Ann. I miss him so much."

"Honey, why are you doing this to yourself?" She took Sarah's hand in hers. "I've already told you I think you should call him, but if you're standing by your stubborn refusal, why are you torturing yourself this way?"

"I don't know." Sarah looked down and a crystal teardrop fell on their hands. "Maybe I just need to get him out of my system, and this is the final cleansing self-flagellation."

"Ah. Come here." She gave Sarah a big hug. "My Aunt Bertie always said, 'When life throws you a curve ball, make lemonade.' I'm still not sure what that means, but it seems appropriate."

Sarah laughed out loud. It felt good. "Thanks."

"What are best friends for, if not to make each other laugh?"

CHAPTER 21

The in-person interview with Harper Legal finally came through. Next week Sarah would fly to Atlanta, the company headquarters, for a full day of interviews, including lunch and dinner, before flying home the next day. It was a grueling process, and one she was not looking forward to. It didn't help that the potential job just wasn't doing it for her. But it was income, and distraction, both of which she could use right now.

Ann came over to help her decide what to wear: the conservative black Tahari suit with the Stuart Weitzman python pumps, or the slightly edgy chocolate-brown Marc Jacobs, with the Crocs peep toe flats.

"Oh, definitely the Marc Jacobs," Ann confirmed. "Gives you an I'm-confident-yet-understated look. And the shoes add a little sex appeal," she added as she stepped into the shoes and struck a pose in front of the mirror. "A girl's gotta use all the weapons in her arsenal."

Sarah chuckled at her friend's antics.

The phone rang. Ann followed Sarah into her sitting room strutting her stuff like a runway model. "Ooh. Love these shoes. If you ever decide you don't want them anymore, remember me, your best friend in the whole world."

"Hello," Sarah said into the phone while shaking her head at her friend.

"Hi, Sarah, it's Kim."

"Oh, hi, Kim. What's up?"

"Listen, I've got some horrible news. Ken's dead."

"What!" Sarah collapsed into the armchair, her hand to her chest.

Ann gazed at her in alarm.

"When?" Sarah asked.

"They found him on his sailboat this morning. They think it was a heart attack." Kim was crying on the other end of the line. "I gotta go. I'll let you know when the arrangements have been made."

"Right. Okay. Let me know when you find out. Okay. Bye."

"Sarah, what is it? You look like you've seen a ghost."

"Ken's gone."

~

Perched on the sofa with a cup of tea, Sarah surveyed the other black-clad mourners who had come to the post-funeral gathering. Some assembled in groups of three, talking in somber tones, others in larger groups, joking and laughing. All had some form of refreshment in their hands.

She'd always thought it was an odd tradition. Someone dies, and the grieving family invites the hordes back to the house and feeds them.

Her wandering gaze landed on Ken's wife, Cindy. Only now she was his widow. She still looked dazed, like she'd woken from a bad dream only to find it wasn't a dream at all. Her eyes were red-rimmed and swollen, but she managed to play the consummate hostess, ensuring that her guests wanted for nothing.

Sarah realized then how self-absorbed she'd been the last year. Her heartaches, discontent, and mid-life setbacks were nothing compared to Cindy's devastating loss. Sarah's marriage was long over, and any possibility of a relationship with Alex non-existent, so she needed to get over herself. Move on.

She also needed to come to a decision about her career. If she was going to continue to practice law, then she needed to recommit herself to finding a job and then give one hundred ten percent. If she decided to give writing a try, then she needed to devote herself to that task with the same level of dedication.

Life was too short. Ken's death so soon after his well-earned retirement had made that all too clear. No one knew how much time he or she had left, and she wanted to leave this earth with the knowledge that if she didn't accomplish her dreams, at least it wasn't for lack of trying. As Alex said, in not even trying, she'd already failed.

What was that saying? Be bold and courageous. When you look back on your life, you'll regret the things you didn't do more than the things you did.

She didn't want to look back and regret that she'd spent this opportunity tidying her closets, instead of pursuing a dream. On a more practical level, her savings weren't going to last forever. Time was not a luxury she could afford at this point.

~

"*B*aby, we're worried about you," the Admiral said, his voice filled with concern. "We thought you'd return from England recharged and renewed. Instead, you seem even more miserable than before you left. And Becca tells me you've cancelled the job interview."

Sarah and her father sat in her garden taking advantage of the unusually dry, temperate August dusk. Citronella torches flickered, keeping the ravenous mosquitoes at bay.

"What's happened to my steady, sensible Sarah?" He nudged when she didn't respond.

Sarah tucked her legs up under her chin and wrapped her arms around her knees. "Oh, Daddy, it's everything. Alex, my love life in general . . . or the lack thereof." Sarah blushed to the roots of her hair to be discussing her love life with her father. "Ken's death, my career, in that order. I've just got a lot on my mind."

The decision to cancel the interview had felt like cutting a lifeline. Biting her lip, she finally said, "I think I need a change . . ."

"You need a change. But, baby, you hate change."

"Yeah, I know. But maybe it's time." They listened to the first cricket song of the evening. "I'd just like to take a little more time, you know, figure out what I want to do. Maybe the time will give me some perspective."

She knew he wanted to protest, to talk her out of it, but he held his tongue. She hesitated, wondering if she should confess her real plans. "You know, Dad, I've always wanted to write. Maybe I'll give that a try for a while."

Her dad looked up, pain and uncertainty flashing across his face. "What would you write about?"

"You remember my sophomore year when I said I wanted to be a writer? Well, I'd actually finished a manuscript."

"You did? You never told me that?"

"You weren't too thrilled with my revelation. In fact, you talked me out of it, remember?"

"Oh, baby." He put his arm around her shoulders and pulled her close, trying to hide the unmanly tears that threatened his composure. "I thought it was just a silly flight of fantasy that would soon pass. I never considered that you might be serious."

Sarah could hear his heart beat reassuringly where her head rested on his chest. She felt so secure in her daddy's arms. There was only one other pair of arms which made her feel so protected, cherished.

"Okay. Then I think you should do it."

"Really?" She sat up in surprise. "But, Daddy, I don't want to disappoint you."

The Admiral, brow creased in worry, sat back, pushing her away so he could look directly into her eyes. "Disappoint me? Baby, you could never disappoint me. Your mother and I were always the proudest parents on the planet. You and Becca turned out better than any parent could have hoped for. I'd like to believe I had something to do with it, but it was all your mother's doing."

"But I thought . . ." She looked down, picking at the frayed hem of her old cut-off shorts.

"Thought what?"

"When I said I wanted to be a writer, when I gave up teaching, got divorced, didn't get Ken's old job . . . that I'd disappointed you."

"Baby, I've never been disappointed in you. I've only been disappointed *for* you. And afraid."

"Afraid?" She looked up, confused.

"I only wanted you to have a good, steady career, something that would always provide you with stability." He took her hand in his calloused one. "Your heart is so easily broken and becoming a writer, and staying successful is fraught with so many disappointments that are completely out of your control. Failure has never been an option for you."

Thinking of Alex's challenge, she said, "A wise man once pointed out that not having tried is the equivalent of failure."

The Admiral considered this a moment. "That is wise. Who said that? Churchill? Kennedy?"

She chuckled. "No, Fraser." At his puzzled look, she said, "Oh, never mind."

Her father's face grew serious again. "I'm so sorry. I never knew that I'd effectively crushed your dreams. The only thing your mother and I ever wanted for you and your sister is your happiness. In career, in love, in life."

"Oh, Daddy." Sarah leaned over and kissed his weathered cheek. "I love you."

He cleared the tears from his throat, giving her a gruff "I love you" in return. "While you've always been cautious, you've never been afraid. Don't let fear of the unknown get in the way of your dreams. Sometimes the reward is worth the risk." He chuckled.

"What's so funny?"

"Oh, I was just remembering when I tried to teach you to ride your bike. You were adamant that I not hold on to your seat, wanting to do it all on your own. You always were a stubborn little thing when it came to accepting help. What you never knew was that I was no more than a breath away, ready to grab you if you started to go down."

Sarah smiled at the memory.

"You know, too much self-reliance can often be mistaken for stubborn pride. Remember, baby, we all need help from time-to-time. There's no shame in asking, and no shame in relying on those around you once in a while."

They sat quietly as the birds settled in for the night, Venus shone on the horizon, and the sky turned from dusky violet to black. Fireflies flickered like little sparks.

"Well, no point in putting it off," he said suddenly, slapping his thighs. "What is right to be done cannot be done too soon."

"You just quoted Jane Austen," she said in astonishment.

"I did? Well, what do you know?" He grinned at her obvious approval. "So, tell me, what's this book of yours about?"

She looked dubious, "Really? Are you sure you want to hear about it?"

"Of course."

~

Seated at the breakfast table, Sarah stared in bored fascination at a squirrel sitting on the windowsill tearing apart a sweet gum ball to get to the seeds inside. After a couple of minutes, the little tree rat hopped away, apparently exhausting the supply of seeds, taking her excuse to procrastinate with it.

She couldn't postpone this any longer. It was time to put words to paper, or rather pixels to screen. She would never know if she could really write, if she didn't start writing. There was no other way.

Grabbing her cup of tea and the yellowed, dog-eared manuscript, she sat down at her desk and began to write.

CHAPTER 22

Summer passed into fall, such as it was in Florida. The flora remained green, the air continued heavy and warm, necessitating the steady hum of air conditioners, and the swimming pools still enticed their owners to dive in and splash around.

Sarah padded around her house in shorts and bare feet, picking up the mess that was strewn about. By nature and by nurture she was a tidy person, but she'd been so completely absorbed in her manuscript that she'd become the slob she never was in college. She hadn't done laundry in so long she'd feared she wouldn't have anything clean to put on. As it was, she wore a pair of shorts with a hole in the crotch and paint stains on the seat.

But today that would all change. She'd finished the rewrite of her old manuscript, and was awaiting a return phone call from Sam, who'd been in a meeting when she phoned to tell her the news. Remembering her father's advice, she'd decided to seek Sam's help. Sarah had no idea if her novel was any good, but she knew she could trust Sam to tell her the truth. Friends or not, Sam wouldn't risk her reputation on a manuscript that sucked.

Sarah tried to still the flutter of nerves in her stomach. She had so much riding on this. Not a gambling woman, this long shot she'd bet her career and her savings on would either make or break her. She knew the odds of getting struck by lightning were better than getting a first manuscript published, or even a second . . . or third. But no matter the outcome, she tried to tell herself, she'd proven that she could do it. She could write a full-length novel. And not just once, but twice, if you counted both manuscripts. That had to count for something.

She still missed Alex. In the months since she'd left, she'd been tempted to call him, but she always stopped short. She had to get her life in order. Figure out what it was she wanted, before she could be any good to anyone else. Which would likely mean Alex would be lost to her forever, and in all likelihood already was, but she was determined to accept this. Sort of.

The phone rang, making Sarah's heart leap to her throat.

"Hello."

"Hi, Sarah, it's Sam."

"Sam." A hummingbird fluttered in Sarah's stomach. "Thanks for calling me back. Do you have a minute?"

"Sure. What's up? Did you change your mind about the job?"

"No, or rather I have changed my mind—but not about the job. About writing."

Sam squealed on the other end. "Really? Great. Send me the manuscript. I'll get it to our agent who handles historical romance—"

"Sam. Take a breath. It's not the college manuscript. At least not anymore. I rewrote it . . . in the twenty-first century." Silence reigned on the other end of the line, and panic socked Sarah right in the gut. "Sam? Is that bad?"

"No. Of course not. It just took me by surprise. Listen, send it to me via email. I've got a transcontinental flight this weekend. I'll read it on the flight and get back to you next week."

"Okay. I'll send it this afternoon. And Sam, you'll tell me the truth, right? I mean, just because we're friends doesn't mean you can't be brutally honest with me." Well, maybe not *brutally* honest, Sarah thought, sugar coat it a little.

"Sarah, I'll be honest, but remember this isn't my genre. I'll have to get it to Elizabeth Bouchier for her read. But I'll let you know if I think it needs work before we go there."

"Thanks, Sam." Sarah hung up the phone and finally let her legs give out, slumping to the sofa. This was it. So why did she suddenly feel like a death row inmate who'd just lost her last appeal?

~

Sam turned on her laptop as soon as the flight attendant gave the all-clear. She hated red eyes, but oftentimes they were the only way she could wade through her gigabytes of electronic submissions. Unable to sleep on planes, the dark, quiet aircrafts provided her with uninterrupted reading time.

Clicking open Sarah's manuscript, she chewed her lower lip, nervous for her friend. She knew that having one's first manuscript read was like standing naked on a street corner. For writers, good and bad, allowing someone . . . editor, friend, or both . . . to read the words the writer labored over, anguished over, was deeply personal, soul baring. Sam thought it was nothing short of brave. For that reason, she gave each submission the respect it was due.

Sarah had had such a gift for the language of the Regency Period, so Sam was surprised that she'd chosen to write a contemporary novel and was a little concerned that Sarah wouldn't be able to pull it off.

The American and the Aristocrat. Catchy title, she thought. She clicked on page one:

"It is a truth universally acknowledged that a single female in possession of little fortune must be in want of a rich husband. A title didn't hurt either."

Good start, Sam thought, loving the allusion to Jane Austen. Sipping on her wine, Sam settled in for what she sincerely hoped was a good read.

~

A fretful week passed with still no word from Sam. Sarah didn't want to nag her about it. She was busy, right? And not just avoiding her. Maybe.

With the manuscript completed and no job, Sarah found herself at loose ends. The glut of nervous energy meant her house was spit and polished, her running shoes worn out, her legs toned from frequent endorphin-releasing runs, and her weeds afraid to show their faces for fear of being yanked out of her garden by their roots. She'd had lunch and dinner with Ann and Becca so many times, that they, and their husbands, were probably sick of her.

It also meant she had more time for introspection, particularly where Alex was concerned. She often wondered what he was doing. Was he working on his next film? Had he mended the rift with his brother? Were the tabloids still dogging his well-heeled heels?

More importantly, did he have some glamorous supermodel, actress, or entertainer on his arm—or worse—in his bed? Someone who could handle the heat of the limelight?

She frequently questioned what he saw in her, given his apparent penchant for illustrious, sophisticated women, and what Robert called his "playboy lifestyle." Of course, from what she'd seen of his conservative brother, anything short of the priesthood would be deemed a playboy lifestyle.

The phone rang, startling her into awareness. She hadn't realized she'd stopped in front of the French door with a load of laundry in her arms and stood staring out at her garden. Dropping the laundry on the sofa, she dove for the phone, thinking it must be Sam.

"Sam?"

"Er, no. Sarah, it's Albert Cheswick."

Mr. Cheswick? What could he possibly want? Dejected, Sarah said, "Hello, Mr. Cheswick. What can I do for you?"

"I was calling to ask if you were available for lunch tomorrow. We can meet wherever is convenient for you," he continued, as if she'd refuse otherwise.

"Sure." Even more confused, and not a little curious, she said, "We can meet at J.J.'s Grille on Park, if you'd like."

"Okay, say around noon?"

"That's fine. Mr. Cheswick, what is this about exactly?"

"Sarah, I don't mean to be so secretive, but I'd rather discuss it in person."

"Okay. I'll see you tomorrow then." She hung up the phone and plopped down on the couch. Had they found a problem with one of the legal matters she'd handled before resigning? Maybe he needed some legal advice. But no, he probably had a team of lawyers who advised his accounting firm. He couldn't be offering her job back. Impossible. The Bitchkrieg would never stand for that.

She'd just have to wait until tomorrow. Just one more thing she'd have to wait for. And whatever it was would be a surprise. Waiting and surprises. Neither of which sat well with her.

CHAPTER 23

Sam sat in her hotel room, a hard copy of Sarah's manuscript on the desk next to her. She'd finished it about an hour earlier, but not soon enough. She'd hoped to have finished it in a day or two, as per her usual routine, but other obligations interfered.

She'd apparently fallen asleep with it on her lap. The plopping of the pages as the entire second half of the manuscript slid onto the floor woke her. After the frustrating process of arranging the pages back into numerical order this morning, she'd finished it.

Drumming her fingers on the desk, she waited, impatiently listening to what was supposed to be soothing 'hold music,' but it only made her count the seconds as they ticked by. She had a flight to catch and needed to get this ball rolling.

"Sam. Sorry for the delay. I couldn't get off the phone with one of my more needy clients. What's up?"

"Marlene, do you still have that client who's in the market for an adaptable novel?"

"Sure. He's always in the market for good option opportunities. What do you have?"

"I'm sending it to you now, and I'll give you the synopsis in a hundred words or less." Sam clicked 'send' on her email and began her sales pitch.

~

*M*r. Cheswick was already seated when Sarah arrived. She'd had a sleepless night, wondering and worrying over the reason for this meeting.

"Mr. Cheswick," Sarah said, extending her hand for a shake. "Good to see you." So far, anyway.

"Please, call me Albert."

After taking her seat, and a sip of her water to clear her parched throat, she started to make small talk before he interrupted her.

"Sarah, I'll get straight to the point, then we can discuss the more salient aspects of the topic."

Sarah's hand shook a little as she replaced her glass of water. "Okay."

"Patricia resigned last week." He wore a sour look on his otherwise affable face.

Shocked, Sarah blurted, "The Bitchkrieg resigned?" Mortified by her flub, she colored as Albert's eyebrows shot up in surprise. Feeling the heat rise to her face, she stammered, "Er, Patricia. Sorry." She shrugged a shoulder. "It was a law school nickname," she muttered, chagrinned.

"Well, apparently very apropos," he whispered conspiratorially, a slight smile on his face.

Now it was Sarah's turn to raise her eyebrows. There must be more to the story than he was willing to discuss. Kim would know the scoop. She always did. But what did this have to do with her?

"The board asked me to meet with you, well, to ask if you'd like to come back . . . as the General Counsel."

"What?" Sarah never saw that one coming. A jumble of emotions collided in her stomach. Excitement. Resentment. Dread. Going back as GC would make her dad proud, but the fact that she was second choice didn't endear her to the offer. Sensible Sarah would be jumping at the offer. It's what she'd wanted, wasn't it? But she was tired of settling. Tired of giving up her dreams.

"Look, I'm sure there are hard feelings, but the board realizes its mistake." When Sarah didn't say anything, he nudged, "We'll double your salary . . . and the staff really wants you back."

Oh sure, she thought, throw money at me, then jab me with a little guilt trip. "May I take time to consider it?"

"Of course, take the weekend." He looked at Sarah with the sincerity of a father. "But I hope you'll say yes." Picking up his menu, he continued, "Now, what shall we eat?"

~

A few hours later, Sarah waited anxiously in the same restaurant for Kim. When Sarah had called Kim, she'd been more than eager to share the story with Sarah, but not at work. Thus, the clandestine meeting in the back booth.

Sarah waved her arm as soon as she spotted Kim. Her silky black hair was shorter, but she still looked great. After hugs and squeals, inspections and compliments, they sat down to share gossip that was juicier than any steak in the restaurant.

"Let's have it. What happened to the Bitchkrieg?" Sarah asked, with uncharacteristic avarice.

"What goes around comes around. She was asked to resign before they fired her for 'inappropriate use of hospital resources,' which is a euphemism for sending naughty photos of herself via email." Kim snickered as she lifted her just-served cosmo for a sip.

"She sent a nude picture of herself . . . on the hospital computer?" Sarah asked, incredulous. There were a lot of things she wouldn't put past Patricia, but that wasn't one of them.

"Pictures, plural. Apparently she intended to send them to some guy who was sadomasochistic enough to date her, but the email address that auto-populated was that of . . . drum roll please . . . Mr. Spalding." Kim's cool blue eyes glittered with amusement.

Sarah choked on her chardonnay. "Mr. Spalding!" she all but shrieked once she regained her breath.

"Shhh," Kim warned, looking around the restaurant to make sure no one took an unwelcome interest in their conversation. "Can you just imagine the apoplectic seizure? It's a wonder he didn't end up in our ER."

"Good thing his wife didn't see it."

"No kidding. Anyway, the day she resigned, we all went around the office singing *Ding, Dong, the Witch is Dead*." Polishing off her cosmo, she added, "I know I have to be careful. Fate could come back to bite me on the ass, but I tell you, Sarah, I've never been so happy to see someone go. And that includes my mother-in-law after a recent two-week visit."

Kim always knew everything, but Sarah wondered if she knew about her meeting today with Mr. Cheswick. "I had lunch with Mr. Cheswick today." At the shocked expression on Kim's face, Sarah gathered she didn't have this tidbit of information.

"What for?"

"He came on behalf of the board to offer me the GC position."

Kim squealed with delight.

"Before you start re-decorating the corner office for me, I haven't made up my mind yet." Sarah couldn't help but laugh at Kim's deflated expression. "You know me. I have to think about these things. Weigh the pros and cons." At this point all she could see were cons. Other than the income, that was.

"Okay. Well, let me say this . . . you'll be the greatest boss ever, and I'm not just saying that because we're friends."

"Sucking up already?" She laughed. "I knew there was something I liked about you."

The waitress came to take their dinner orders. Watching her walk away, Sarah leaned over the table, and asked, "So, these pictures . . . just how naughty were they?"

"Let's just say they involved lots of bare skin with a hint of leather."

∼

The phone rang as Sarah jiggled her key in the lock. Dashing into the kitchen, she dropped a bag of groceries on her foot. "Ouch!" Grabbing the phone, out of breath and moaning, she said, "Hello."

"Um, Sarah, did I, uh, interrupt . . . something?"

"Sam! What? No. I hurt my foot running for the phone." Oh God. Her heart thudded in her chest like a pile driver. This was it.

"Sarah, I'll just get to the point, since I know waiting isn't your strong suit. I've found a publisher for your book, or I should say Elizabeth Bouchier found a publisher . . . and I found someone who wants to option the screenplay."

Sarah felt the blood drain from her face, and her ears began to ring. She thought she might actually faint.

"Sarah. Sarah. Are you there?"

"Yes. Yes. I'm here. Can you . . . can you say that again? I think I might have misunderstood you."

"No you didn't. I said what you thought I said." Sam laughed. She loved giving this kind of news, especially to her dear friend. "You did it, kid. Congratulations!"

Sarah's legs finally buckled, and she sank with a *thunk* to the kitchen floor, where she finally noticed the broken eggs among the pile of groceries she'd dropped.

CHAPTER 24

"Grandmother, I'm home!" Alex shouted to the house as he stepped into the vast foyer.

"Lord Rutherford, welcome home." The butler, Mr. Fletcher, greeted Alex. "Lady Clara is out, but I expect her back soon."

"Oh, Fletcher." Alex responded with pleasure. "How are you? How are the grandchildren? Timothy still tearing up the turf playing polo?"

"Yes, sir." Fletcher blushed. "He's doing me right proud."

"Good, good. I'll wait for my grandmother in the library, if you wouldn't mind letting her know when she returns."

"Yes, sir."

Alex strode down the hall in high spirits for the first time in months.

Since Sarah left, the months of work on location had kept him busy, but they'd been dismal nonetheless. Once the project was completed, loneliness, something Alex had never experienced, had descended with a vengeance. In search of companionship, he'd gone out with a couple of starlets, but they'd seemed such shallow, vapid creatures compared to Sarah's rich intellect and depth of character that he'd stopped dating altogether.

When other previous relationships had ended, he'd look back on them with fondness, but never with the desire to renew them. Sarah was different. He looked back on their relationship, as short as it was, with longing. Longing to tell her how he felt, longing to feel her in his arms again, and longing for what the future could have been.

After pouring himself a snifter of brandy, he sat in his favorite chair in the library and looked around at the vast collection of books. To his shame, he'd avoided Rutherford. That one day when Sarah was there, that one day when he thought he could see the future, their future, and her subsequent absence, made what had once been a refuge, a prison instead.

But quite by happenstance, an opportunity to get her back just dropped in his lap. His agent had called to sing the praises of an unpublished novel for adaptation to the screen. Alex had been looking for a contemporary novel to produce, and possibly to star in, one that would reach a larger audience than the literary adaptations he'd previously undertaken.

At first, Alex wasn't too keen on the idea of an unpublished novel, but when his agent mentioned the author, Alex requested the manuscript immediately, reading it from beginning to end in one sitting.

Sarah had written her novel, and what a novel it was. He was enormously proud of her, not only for accomplishing her goal, but for doing such a stupendous job of it.

He'd told his agent to make an offer on the option, and they were off to the races. Alex wasted no time in getting a screenwriter and director, and, as part of the deal, he wanted the author involved from the start. And on the set to advise.

All involved were sworn to secrecy, although they didn't know the reason for it. Sarah could not know anything about his involvement other than the coincidence that he was playing Christen. He didn't want her to think he'd only offered the option to get her back. The stage was set, so to speak, for a surprise reunion between Alex and Sarah. Knowing her aversion for surprises, he couldn't help but grin.

"Alex, what are you grinning about?" Lady Clara greeted him. As she walked into the room, the scent of Lilies of the Valley brought back warm memories.

"I should be angry with you for deserting me these months past." She patted his cheek with just a little too much gusto.

"Grandmother." Alex laughed as he rubbed his cheek.

"Ah. There's the smile I've been longing to see. What is the reason for that Cheshire cat grin?"

"Just a new project in the works. Come sit and catch me up on all the news of Oxfordshire." Knowing his grandmother's attachment to Sarah, he didn't want to put her in a difficult position by making her a co-conspirator. So for now, his secret would remain just that. A secret.

CHAPTER 25

The holidays were an anxious time for Sarah. Elated over the book and movie deal, she, Ann, and Becca indulged in countless conversations over who would play Christen and Amelia, giggling and giddy over the possibility that Sarah might get to work with the likes of Colin Firth, Hugh Grant, or Hugh Jackman.

But not even all the parties, family functions, and holiday preparations could keep Sarah's loneliness at bay. She'd always been content with her friends and family for company, and with herself, as well. Not anymore. She felt it with an acuity she'd never experienced, and it unnerved her. The highs and lows were emotionally dizzying, as if she could never quite get her mental feet under her before another dip or rise affected her.

She'd resolve to focus on the business at hand, then something would trigger her melancholy. Hanging ornaments on the Christmas tree, she'd wonder what Christmas at Rutherford was like. Seeing a luxurious smoky-blue cashmere sweater, she'd think how incredible Alex would look in it.

But she made it through the holidays, and then through the post-holiday doldrums. Her thirty-ninth birthday came and went, with

Ann and Becca throwing a small party including close friends and family.

April ushered in Sarah's favorite time of year. Spring. Snowy dogwoods bloomed, followed by showy azaleas then redbuds and wild plum. The oak trees wore a coat of spring green as they shed their old leaves for new. And coated every surface with pollen.

She would miss most of it this year, trading spring in Florida for sunny California to begin work on the pre-production phase of the movie. She vacillated between excitement, nervousness, and outright terror. Yet another challenge. Yet another change. The only difference, this time she welcomed it.

PART III

CHAPTER 26

Sarah woke at dawn in her own bed for the first time in almost two months. It was a beautiful late spring morning, the kind of morning that reminded her why she lived in Florida. At least she would catch the tail end.

The birds already sang, and a gentle breeze stirred the sheers at the open window. She rolled over and grabbed the other pillow, hoping to fall back to sleep, but thoughts of the last few months, and the whirlwind that her life had become, dashed those hopes.

Her dream had become a reality in a big way. *The American and the Aristocrat* had not only garnered a book deal, but a movie deal.

In homage to the writings of Jane Austen, the novel tells the contemporary story of the beautiful, unmarried twenty-eight-year-old Amelia Hampton, who spends a year in England to fulfill her late Aunt Millie's wishes before inheriting her estate, the value of which is unknown to Amelia. During her stay in England, she meets the handsome and aloof Lord Christen Hare, a member of one of Britain's noble families and respected member of the House of Lords. In true romantic fashion, the two clash repeatedly.

She sighed, rising from the bed. She was wasting the day, and after

"

all the time away, she had a stack of mail, and various other chores waiting for her.

Her decision to turn down the hospital's offer disappointed her former coworkers and frustrated Mr. Cheswick, who, despite her protests to the contrary, believed her decision was based on lingering resentment over being second choice in the first place. He'd get over it, and so would her former coworkers. Maybe the board would be more careful about who they hired next time around, but Sarah argued it should be Kim. By the time they'd hung up, she thought Mr. Cheswick had come around.

Positioned at the breakfast table with a cup of tea and the mound of mail, she sorted through it, creating separate stacks by levels of importance. There was a letter from Lady Clara halfway through the pile. Lady Clara disdained email, insisting that meaningful correspondence be in the form of pen and paper. She shoved the other mail aside and opened it immediately. It had been written shortly after she'd left for California, so Lady Clara was probably wondering why she hadn't responded. She'd do that first thing.

Dear Sarah,

I hope this letter finds you and your loved ones happy and well. Life here is clacking along at its usual measured pace.

Her letter continued for another page informing her of the goings on at Hawthorne Hall and in Oxford. Sarah skidded to a halt at the top of page two:

I was recently in London visiting a dear friend when I ran into Alex. He spends most of his time there now. It's a shame that I have to run into my own grandson on the streets of London in order to see him, but he's been filming on location.

Sarah's heart stuttered. Though she'd thought about him almost daily over the past nine months, she hadn't spoken his name, and neither had Ann or Becca.

He is looking very well, but of course, that could just be my bias. He's finished filming his last movie and is planning a little holiday for himself. His mother invited him along on one of her adventures. I believe they are taking a walking tour of Tuscany. What do you think of that? He asked after you, and of course I told him that as of your last letter, you were in excellent health.

Sarah could hear the insinuation even in her written lines. None of their previous letters broached the subject of Alex. She knew that was difficult for Lady Clara, but she seemed to understand Sarah's desire not to poke that particular wound.

Write to me soon, my dear. I want to know all your comings and goings. They're always vastly more interesting than my dull country life.
    Yours,
    L.C.S.F.

Time had softened the pain to a dull ache, though it had not yet healed the self-inflicted wound. Sarah wasn't sure it ever would. Sometimes she thought she'd imagined that perfect week, but then the pain would return, and that was not her imagination.

He'd asked about her, but did he think of her, or was he merely being polite? If he did think of her, was it with loathing, or perhaps worse, indifference? She cringed, reminded of a line from the *P&P* movie: 'I cannot bear to think that he is alive in the world and thinking ill of me.'

Shaking off the gloomy thoughts, she retrieved stationary from her office.

Dear Clara,

    I apologize for the delay in responding to your letter. When you read this, you will understand why it has taken me so long to write. I have so much to tell, that I don't know where to begin.

    I just returned last night from California, where I met with the director for the movie based on my book. Can you believe it? It's true! Someone's making it into a movie!

My literary agent and dear friend, Samantha Bethancourt, is a genius! She took the manuscript to another friend and agent at the same time it was accepted for publication, rather than waiting for its release. Her friend apparently had a client who is always looking for adaptable novels. The client loved it and bought the option right away. Things moved quickly after that. The screenplay was drafted, a studio accepted it, and now we're off and running.

I've spent the last two months with the director, screenwriter, and pre-production team reviewing the screenplay, looking at the storyboards, set designs, and locations photographs. I leave for London in six weeks, after another two to three weeks in California, to begin production. I'll be in London for a time, and then we'll be filming in Oxfordshire, and I would dearly love to see you.

I would have to kill a few trees to tell you the whole incredible story, so I'll save it until we're together. I have to run. Becca and Ann are throwing a party for me tonight to celebrate.

Sarah read over the letter. Maybe she should say something about Alex. Lady Clara will think it odd if she completely ignores it.

I'm glad to hear that Alex is well, and that he and his mother are going to spend some quality time together.

Although slightly lame, that should do it. She finished the letter by adding her arrival date and a promise to call her after she knew her schedule.

CHAPTER 27

When she arrived in London, a car waited to take her to the rented flat that would be her home off-and-on during the film's production. She couldn't believe production would get underway this week. She also couldn't believe she'd get to see her manuscript come to life on the proverbial silver screen. It was times like this when she needed to pinch herself.

The flat was spacious and inviting, and more importantly, it was on a quiet side street in the exclusive Knightsbridge district of London. Tastefully furnished, with clean lines, neutral colors, and little clutter, it was decidedly masculine.

On the foyer table sat a basket of fruit and a bottle of champagne with a note attached. It was from Michael Williams, the film's director, welcoming her to London and explaining that a detailed schedule was on the desk in the study. She already knew her first meeting would be tomorrow afternoon to review the casting decisions, followed the next evening by the introduction party, where she would meet most of the actors and crew.

The schedule was on the desk in the study where Michael said it would be. It looked demanding. Didn't they believe in sleep? Placing the schedule back on the desk, she noted the study's floor-to-ceiling bookshelves were lined with books, mostly great works of literature from Austen to Wordsworth. The owner was well read, or at least wanted to appear so.

Picking up the basket and the champagne, Sarah carried it into the well-equipped kitchen. Clearly the apartment belonged to someone who loved to cook. The cabinets and refrigerator were thoughtfully stocked with the essentials. There were also some of her favorite foods: fresh strawberries, grapes, mascarpone cheese, seven-grain bread, fresh juice, stilton cheese, English Breakfast tea, and of course chocolate. She didn't recall providing a list of her food preferences but perhaps it was the work of her fabulous agent. At least she didn't have to go out for breakfast in the morning.

Michael, or most likely his assistant, had been attentive to every detail. The phone rang. Other than the studio, who else knew the number there?

"Sarah Edwards," she answered, just in case the caller expected the owners to answer.

"Sarah? It's Michael."

"Michael, hi. I was wondering who would be calling me here."

"How was your flight? Is the flat to your liking?"

"My flight was fine, and yes, everything is perfect. Thank you for the fruit and champagne."

"How about dinner tonight?"

She gave a mental groan. All she wanted was a hot bath and a comfortable bed. "That would be fine . . . if you don't mind making it an early one. I'm afraid if I wait too late, jetlag will descend and I'll fall asleep in my plate."

"Seven then?

"Seven is fine.

"See you then."

The doorbell buzzed. The luggage she'd had shipped over had arrived. Perfect timing. Now she had something to wear to dinner.

～

*A*fter years in the business, Michael Williams had a lot of insight into what makes a memorable romance on paper an even more memorable movie. And he didn't mind telling Sarah that. She was lucky to have gotten such a great director, especially since she was an unknown entity. And he didn't mind telling her that either. He wasn't bad looking. In his mid-fifties, he had thick salt and pepper hair surrounding a tanned face with chiseled features. Tall and fit, he had a confident bearing that commanded attention when he entered a room.

They sat sipping after dinner drinks in a trendy restaurant not far from the apartment.

"I can't believe I haven't thought to ask you before, but how did you come up with the plot for your very first book? What inspired you?"

That would be because you're too busy talking about yourself, she thought. They'd spent weeks together and this was the first interest he'd shown in her craft. Not that he hadn't shown an interest in *her*.

"Um, I'm not sure I could point to any one thing, but the inspiration to actually write came from a friend's very wise words about doors." If she could still count Alex as a friend. She didn't want to go into the whole Bitchkrieg-unemployment-college-manuscript thing.

"I don't follow."

"I needed a change, and he helped me see that." She shrugged, as if it were that simple.

"Well, whatever it was, I'm glad for it. I'm excited about this project, and I haven't been this excited since I directed *From Cairo with Love*." He laughed, his blue eyes sparkling, while laugh lines formed parentheses around his mouth.

She didn't have the heart to tell him that she'd never seen the movie. Before he could ask, she jumped in, distracting him with another question. "Are you pleased with the cast?"

At present, the cast was an unknown to her, but the big reveal would be tomorrow. She'd been involved in many aspects of the pre-production, with the exception of the cast. It was to be a surprise. What was it with men and surprises?

"The cast is top-notch. You'll be pleased, I'm sure."

Of course she would. She was mortified when she could no longer stifle a yawn. Between the jetlag, the wine at dinner, and the glass of port with dessert, she was suddenly wiped out. "I am so sorry. It's not the company or the conversation, I assure you," she laughed sheepishly.

"I shouldn't have kept you out so long. Please forgive me." His voice was kind, but he looked mildly annoyed. "Would you prefer that I call the car, or would you care to walk back?"

"No, a walk would be nice."

He walked her to the door of the apartment building. "Thank you for dinner, Michael. I had a very nice time. I look forward to working with you." She added the last as an afterthought, hoping to reinforce the label she put on their relationship.

"Good night then." He waited until she was safely inside before walking away.

CHAPTER 28

Sarah sat rigid in her chair, wondering why she was so tense. It was absurd. She looked around the generic conference room at the faces of the casting director, Edra Moore, two of her assistants, and an intern. She was about to see, for the first time, the actors who would breathe life into the characters she had so lovingly created.

"So Sarah, I thought we'd start with the minor characters and work our way up. How's that sound?" Edra's musical Irish accent made her sound perpetually cheerful. Sarah had liked her on the spot. From their previous conversations, she could tell she'd clearly put a great deal of thought into the character's personalities, blemishes and all.

"Sounds great." Breathe, she told herself.

"For the role of Aunt Millie's voice, we have Audrey Cole." She placed a headshot on the table in front of Sarah. Of course, it didn't matter what Audrey *looked* like, since they were only casting her voice.

"Okay," was Sarah's only response. It wasn't as if she had veto power over who was cast for the movie. This was simply a courtesy.

Edra proceeded to place additional headshots in front of her identifying the other minor roles each would play.

"Now we've come to the major roles. This is where it gets exciting. Robert Chesser has been cast as Roderick and Angela Freeman as Margaret." She placed two photos on the table, side by side.

Margaret Fitzsimmons, an American ex-patriot, was Aunt Millie's dearest friend. She and her husband, Roderick, a British diplomat and wealthy businessman, 'chaperone' Amelia throughout her stay in England. It is through them that Amelia and Christen are introduced. Christen and the Fitzsimmons travel in the same social circles, throwing Amelia and Christen together more often than the two would like.

After giving Sarah a moment to review the photos, she took them away.

"Lady Victoria Markham will be played by Cynthia Hollingsworth."

Sarah looked at the photo of a young woman with long, straight dark brown hair and indigo blue eyes, framed by dark lashes. Lady Victoria is the daughter of a wealthy titled gentleman who was best friend to Christen's late father and, as Christen's equal in society, is the expected choice as his wife.

"Good?" Edra asks.

"Yes. Thank you."

"The role of our lovely heroine, Amelia Hampton, has gone to Brooke Bellamy. Brooke is a rising star in the U.S. and should be a good draw." The photo was of a lovely champagne blonde, with crystal blue eyes set in an oval-shaped face with delicate features. Her glossy lips were turned up in a soft smile. She looked very much as Sarah had envisioned Amelia. More importantly, Sarah hoped she could portray the sharp-witted Amelia, who was particularly close to Sarah's heart. Although a woman from the American middle class, Amelia is not awed by the social circles of the British upper class. Always forthright and honest, she holds her own, sometimes to the dismay of those around her.

"She appears ideal," Sarah said, reserving judgment.

"Finally, in the role of our handsome hero, Christen Hare, we have," with a flourish worthy of Vanna White, Edra placed a photo on the table, "Alex Fraser."

Sarah's breath skidded to a halt. Alex's handsome face stared back at her with his warm, coffee-colored eyes, slightly crinkled at the corners, and the engaging smile she'd committed to memory, punctuated by irresistible dimples. His hair was a little tidier than she remembered it. He wore the black T-shirt typical of an actor's headshot. She'd never seen him in black. The color made his eyes even darker.

Sarah didn't know how long she sat there trying to keep her hand from reaching out to trace the familiar lines of his face, but apparently long enough for Edra to grow concerned. Edra cleared her throat.

"Isn't this movie a little outside his genre? I mean, doesn't he generally prefer literary adaptations?" Sarah struggled to sound neutral. She hoped Edra didn't hear the quaver in her voice.

"True, but Christen is an allusion to Mr. Darcy is he not, and we think he's perfect for the part," she said, seeming unsure of Sarah's reaction. "It's as if you had Alex in mind when you created Christen."

Sarah suppressed a nervous titter. Edra's comment couldn't be closer to the truth. After she'd revised Christen's character profile from the previous manuscript, she'd realized Alex was her model, at least for the physical characteristics. Alex was too open and amiable to serve as the model for Christen's aloof personality.

"No. You're right. He's . . . perfect."

"Good." Edra heaved a sigh of relief.

s soon as Sarah got back to the flat, she shot off a text to Ann and Becca:

You'll never guess who's playing Christen!

Ann:

Colin Firth! No, Hugh Grant!

Sarah:

No, Alex!

Ann:

OMG! Alex! SRSLY? How does that make u
feel? BTW, is he still gorgeous?

Sarah:

IDK. Haven't seen him F2F.

Becca:

OMG! Apologize. Groveling should be
involved.

Sarah:

Right. Thanks.

Curled up on the sofa, Sarah poked at her Chinese take-out between text messages. She'd been invited to dinner after the meeting, but she didn't have much of an appetite, or much interest in making small talk with people she'd only just met. Her stomach had been doing somersaults since the meeting. The insects in her stomach seemed more like bees than butterflies.

What were the odds? Of all the British actors, Alex was cast in the role of Christen. Of course, why should that really surprise her? It's no one's fault but her own. She created Christen in Alex's physical image.

Obviously, when she'd written the book, the odds of winning the lottery were better than getting her book published, and the odds of getting hit by a meteor were better than someone believing in the manuscript enough to produce a movie.

He had to know it was her book. Everyone involved in the film, from the set designer to the locations manager, were required to read it. If he knew it was her book, would he have accepted the role if he hated her? Maybe he didn't think she'd be on the set. What would he say when he saw her? What would she say when she saw him? How would he behave? Would he acknowledge their previous time together, or would he pretend they'd never met? Worse, would he bring some leggy supermodel? So many questions, so many uncertainties, many of which would be answered tomorrow at the party.

She wished they could meet alone first, so she could prepare herself. Then again, maybe a public meeting would be better; no opportunity for him to tell her what he really thought of her. Regardless of his reaction, she was determined to handle herself in a professional manner. No drama on the set. A nervous giggle escaped at her pun.

The bees in her stomach buzzed again, attacking the honey chicken she'd barely managed to swallow. *Ugh.* Sleep was going to elude her tonight.

~

*S*arah planned to meet Lady Clara at eleven that morning at the National Gallery in Trafalgar Square. The National Gallery, which housed paintings by the world's renowned painters, including Botticelli, da Vinci, Michelangelo, Raphael, Titian, Rembrandt, Vermeer, and Monet, among others, was one of Sarah's favorite London haunts.

She arrived early at the square, giving herself time to gather her thoughts before greeting that all too-perceptive lady. Sleep had been long in coming last night, and when it did come, it was fitful. Lady Clara would see immediately that she was troubled. Could she avoid talking about Alex? Not likely.

Sarah meandered around Trafalgar in the unusually warm weather, admiring the two huge fountains flanking Nelson's Column. Trafalgar was the fourth most popular tourist attraction in the world, and as she looked around, she could certainly see proof of that claim. The square teemed with both tourists and locals. Among the throng, Sarah heard a variety of foreign languages, from the familiar languages of Europe to the unfamiliar languages of the Middle and Far East. She could also detect the various accents of Great Britain, including Irish, Welsh, and Scottish, as well as some of the accents of the U.S. regions.

She turned back to the north side of the square facing the National Gallery, which had previously been the site of the King's Mews since the time of Edward I. On the lawn in front of the gallery were two statues: one of James II and the other of George Washington. Washington's was said to be built on soil imported from the U.S. so to honor his declaration that he would never again set foot on British soil.

She directed her steps to the main entrance where she and Lady Clara planned to meet. It was cool by comparison inside the gallery, and it took her a moment to adjust her vision to the relatively dim interior.

"Sarah, my dear." Lady Clara walked toward Sarah, arms outstretched.

"Lady Clara . . . I mean, Clara," Sarah corrected at her frown.

"It is so good to see you." She hugged Sarah close before stepping back just enough to examine her appearance. "You're lovely as usual, although I must say you look a little peeked dear. Jetlag?" She tilted her head with her inquiry.

"Yes, jetlag." Sarah latched on to the excuse she provided. "You're looking well. I've missed you so."

"And I you. Come, let's walk the gallery. Shall we go to the Sainsbury Wing first for a taste of the Renaissance?" She hooked arms with Sarah, leading the way.

As they strolled through the understated, intimate rooms admiring the exalted paintings of da Vinci, Raphael, and Botticelli, among others, they caught up in a way letters could never accomplish.

They talked of Rutherford, Oxfordshire, and Lady Clara's recent travels to Italy, then moved to discussions of Sarah's family, the book, the movie, and the enormous changes her life had undergone in a year's time.

"Where are you staying?" Lady Clara asked.

"I've been provided a flat in Knightsbridge for the duration of the filming."

"Oh! Alex lives in Knightsbridge. What a happy coincidence."

Alex lives in Knightsbridge? Was she just being paranoid, or were there too many coincidences involving Alex? Lady Clara had asked another question. What was it?

"I'm sorry Clara, I was lost in Botticelli's *Adoration of the Kings.*"

"I asked if you were going to see Alex while you were here."

The question she'd been dreading. "Um, yes . . . every day on the set."

"Why Sarah! He's in the movie? Why didn't you tell me?" she scolded. "For that matter, why didn't *he* tell me?" Her cheerful expression turned to exasperation. "Wait until I see my grandson. The tongue lashing I will give him."

"I learned only yesterday he was in the movie. Besides, he probably hates me, or worse, doesn't even think about me," she muttered.

"Sarah, he doesn't hate you. He couldn't. His expression when he asked after you was one of genuine concern, not indifference." She touched Sarah's cheek. "From the little I've seen of him these months past, I can tell you he's different. No longer the playboy. He's very focused on the estate business, and his filmmaking. He's even managed not to irritate his brother more than necessary." She smiled. "I think he misses you."

Sarah's heart gave a little squeeze. "Well, I'll find out soon enough, I guess. I'm meeting the cast and crew tonight. It will be the first time I've seen him," . . . in person anyway, "since . . . well, you know, and I'm terribly nervous."

"Things will work out as they should." She patted Sarah's arm reassuringly. "They always do. You will see."

~

*A*n elegant Georgian townhouse on Grosvenor Square served as the setting for the Fitzsimmons' London home, the location for Amelia' and Christen's first meeting. It was an appropriate venue to hold the introduction party, since filming would begin there before moving into Oxfordshire.

Michael escorted Sarah through the home's carved oak door and into the foyer. Sarah looked around with pleasure. The interior was elegantly furnished in the Queen Anne style, noted for its graceful cabriole legs, and simple fan or scallop shell embellishments. From the foyer, she heard the hum of voices drifting from the drawing room and saw the room's soft, pale creams, roses, and sages common to that era of design. It was indeed a lovely home.

She caught a glimpse of herself in the huge gilt-framed mirror in the entrance. She'd paid special attention to her appearance when dressing for the evening, knowing she would see Alex. Tastefully clad in a black sheath dress with pearls at her throat and ears, her now-long hair fell in soft waves down her back. In the months she'd been unemployed and working on her manuscript at home, rarely leaving the house, she'd paid little attention to maintaining her previous hairstyle, letting it grow until it hung to the middle of her back.

She entered the crowded drawing room with Michael's arm encircling her waist and immediately saw Alex standing across the room directly opposite the door through which they'd entered. His face was an inscrutable mask until his eyes flashed to Michael's arm. His dark eyes narrowed briefly, before the mask returned. Michael's once-comforting arm now felt heavy and cloying. As they approached, Alex was as cool and aloof as the character he was cast to portray.

"Alex." She couldn't help the breathless pronunciation of his name, as the bees took up residence in her stomach again. Classically dressed in black slacks and a blue dress shirt that was open at the neck, he was striking. She realized her memory had not done him justice. Or was it possible he'd just grown more handsome? He looked tan, perhaps from his recent walking tour of Italy.

"Hello, Sarah. You're looking well," he said with polite reserve. He nodded a curt greeting at Michael. The gulf between them stretched as vast as the Atlantic Ocean and seemed just as impassable. "Congratulations on your success."

"Thank you." She smiled tentatively. Before she could say anything further, a tall willowy young woman joined the group.

"Ms. Edwards, I hope I'm not being too forward, but I couldn't wait to meet you. I'm Brooke Bellamy." She extended her hand. "I recognized you from the book jacket, and I just had to come over and tell you how much I loved your book. When I read it, I knew I had to play Amelia. She is the perfect heroine." She gushed. "I'm hoping we can sit down together so I can pick your brain and get more inside Amelia's head."

She was even lovelier in person than in her picture. A good four inches taller than Sarah, notwithstanding the stiletto heels she wore. Beneath the lights from the crystal chandelier, she virtually sparkled, with her champagne blond hair and gold sequined halter top. The skinny jeans she wore hugged her long gazelle-like legs. Standing next to her in her little black dress, Sarah felt almost dowdy.

"Yes, Brooke," Sarah said as she took her offered hand. "I recognized you from your picture. And please, call me Sarah." She examined Brooke's face. "Honestly, you are my image of Amelia." Brooke blushed under the praise, though there was something about it that appeared contrived. Was it possible to fake a blush?

"And Alex is the perfect Christen. I think we will make a great couple—on screen, I mean." She blushed again as she looked at Alex's impassive face. Sarah thought she saw a flash of disdain. Was that directed at her? Or Brooke? Or both?

Michael was saying something about his experience with creating the perfect on-screen couple, but Sarah wasn't paying attention. She was trying to decipher the meaning behind Alex's unapproachable demeanor. It was so unlike the Alex she knew. *Isn't it obvious?* she thought. *He hates me.* But even if it was her he hated, he was cool to Michael and Brooke as well.

After a few more minutes of conversation, Alex excused himself, leaving no doubt that she was the reason. He walked across the room to a bar set up in the corner, ordering something from the bartender. The bees fled, leaving only an empty ache in her stomach.

"I think it is time to formally introduce you to everyone," Michael said as he led her over to stand in front of the empty fireplace, the room's focal point.

"I wish you wouldn't . . ." But before she could finish, he clinked his ring against his wine glass.

Once he had everyone's attention, he announced in a theatrical voice, "Ladies and gentlemen, I am pleased to introduce the charming, talented and very beautiful Sarah Edwards." He wrapped his arm around her waist again, pulling her close. "She is the reason we are here engaged in this worthy endeavor."

There was a round of applause and raised wine glasses. Sarah could feel the heat rising to her face for more reasons than her aversion to being the center of attention. For one, Michael's arm felt like he was staking a claim. For another, from his taut expression, Alex had witnessed that claim. He turned on his heel, leaving the room.

Distractedly, Sarah said her thank-yous to the crowd, was inundated by people coming forward to introduce themselves and shake her hand. The only names she managed to remember were those of the actors whose photographs she saw yesterday. The rest were a blur as she tried to monitor the room for Alex's return.

The introductions seemed interminable. She thought she'd never be able to escape to look for Alex. He hadn't come back to the party. Had he left?

Slipping out the door, she searched the unfamiliar rooms, hoping to find him alone. She was about to give up when she found him standing in the dimly lit study with his back to the door.

"Alex," she said so softly that she didn't think he'd heard her at first.

He turned, and for an instant, she saw something in his eyes before they were shuttered again. Anger? Warmth? Longing? She wasn't sure. He took a sip from the whiskey glass he held, but he didn't speak. She approached him slowly, stopping with a few tense feet separating them.

"It's so good to see you." She hesitated when that didn't elicit a response from him. "I want to apologize . . . what I did, leaving like that, must have seemed . . . cowardly to you." That was eloquent, she thought castigating herself.

"Don't give it another thought, Sarah. I haven't." His voice was flat, but the meaning behind his words made her flinch. She'd wondered if he thought of her with derision. She had her answer: apparently he hadn't thought of her at all.

"Well, I'm very sorry," she finished quietly.

"It's late, and I have an early call. I'll see you on the set." He placed his glass on the table and stalked past her.

She stood in the study rooted to the spot. He left no doubt as to his feelings toward her, but why? Why was he so angry? So distant? Being on the set together was clearly going to be awkward, but maybe they could reach some kind of detente over the next few weeks. It was obvious a truce was all she could hope for at this point. If that.

"Sarah." She jumped at the sound of her name. It was Michael. "I wondered where you'd disappeared to. Are you okay? Did the crush get to you?" he asked in concern, wrapping his hands around her shoulders. She wanted to shrug them off.

"I'm fine. I was a little overwhelmed by all the attention and needed some time to myself."

"You're tired. I'll take you home."

The ride back to the apartment was quiet. She wasn't in the mood for conversation, but hopefully Michael attributed it to fatigue.

He got out of the car and walked her to the door of the building. "Thank you, Michael. I enjoyed the evening, and I'm eager to see the first scene tomorrow." Before she could turn to enter the building, he leaned down to kiss her.

"Michael." She put her hand against his chest and lowering her face, stopped him from coming any closer. "I think we just need to keep this professional. I don't know about the movie industry, but where I come from office romances are frowned upon." She smiled to soften the edge in her voice.

He pulled back reluctantly, and taking her hand from his chest, he kissed it instead. "Good night then. I'll send a car for you in the morning. Seven-thirty."

~

What did she mean waltzing into the party with Michael draped all over her? Alex slammed the door of his rented flat. The happy reunion he'd hoped for had been shot all to hell.

She'd clearly gotten over him, and Michael apparently worked fast. Weeks of leaning over storyboards and locations shots, dinners afterward to discuss 'business,' being thrown together on an almost daily basis. What had he expected? Michael had a reputation for this sort of fraternization, didn't he? But he was also a great director, and Alex wanted him for the film.

Striding to the kitchen, he pulled down the bottle of whiskey and poured two fingers into a glass. Tossing it back, he let the warmth slide down his throat, flooding his stomach, before scrubbing a hand through his hair.

He'd have to find a subtle way to warn Michael off without seeming like the jealous spurned boyfriend. His breath left him in a rush. That's what it was, wasn't it? Jealousy. Sarah had a way of bringing out never-before felt emotions. Love, despair, jealousy. What was next?

Well, he wasn't over Sarah Edwards, and he'd be damned if he let her get over him.

CHAPTER 29

he first two weeks of filming have been a learning experience for me, but to my inexperienced eye, it seemed to go smoothly, she wrote in an email to Ann and Becca.

It was almost midnight, but she'd been so busy that she'd been unable to do anything more than text Ann and Becca now and then. With BBC News on the TV for company, she finally sat down on the sofa to fill them in on her daily activities.

> *I'm amazed how many takes are required to shoot one short scene. Filming more than a few scenes makes for a very long day. In the evenings, we watch the dailies, the raw, unedited footage shot that day. Anyone who thinks actors have it easy never saw the hours of work it takes to shoot a movie.*
>
> *I sit quietly in my chair next to Michael. He occasionally leans in close to explain some point or another to me. Although after his second unwelcome attempt to kiss me the other night, I can't help but wonder if he's using his whispered explanations as an excuse.*

Alex had witnessed more than one of these little conferences, which only added to her discomfort. She'd learned that Michael had a reputation for pursuing his leading ladies, but had now apparently turned his attentions to her.

I am thankful for one thing: other than the occasional glare at Michael between takes, Alex has been too busy to do more than briefly acknowledge my presence, but at least those acknowledgements have been getting progressively less severe. He actually smiled at me today, evidently before he remembered he wasn't supposed to be nice to me. Nevertheless, it is getting a little easier to be around him.

Overall, I've been pleased with Michael's direction and the actors, especially Brooke and Alex. In keeping with the book, the friction and intensity between Christen and Amelia has been palpable.

We leave for Oxfordshire in two weeks. Some of us will be staying in a wing of the country house that serves as Wilcox Manor, Christen's estate. The house is a sprawling eighteenth-century Palladian structure whose owners have turned it into a luxury hotel, but we've taken over the entire place for the duration of the filming. Although I've seen the photos taken by the locations manager, I'm looking forward to seeing the real thing.

Tomorrow we skip ahead to Chapter Thirty-Five, where Christen returns to London in search of Amelia. I realize filmmaking is not a linear process—neither was my writing, for that matter—but it is a little disconcerting to jump around the story. I'm not sure how the actors manage to get into the mood for such disparate scenes.

Before she could finish her email, a news story caught her ear. She heard the name 'Fraser.' Robert, Alex's brother, was apparently giving a campaign speech. She recalled what Lady Clara said about Alex not irritating his brother. Likely by avoiding the tabloids.

Turning off the TV, she finished up her email and headed off to bed. It was another early call in the morning.

*C*hristen: *"Ms. Hampton, what you consider hauteur is merely my abhorrence for any actions remotely beneath my dignity to* acknowledge."

Amelia: *"Lord Hare, your perfection continues to be an inspiration to me."* Brooke's tone was teasing, not serious as Sarah had intended.

They were in the middle of shooting one of Christen and Amelia's many sexually charged disagreements, when Michael's "Cut!" startled her. She was not happy with Brooke's interpretation of the line, but she hoped that Michael would say something.

"Brooke, Amelia's response isn't intended to be flirtatious. It is intended to be a scathing rebuke of Christen's self-righteous attitude, an attitude he seems to reserve only for her."

"Michael," she said, using her most flirtatious manner, "As a woman, I would respond to his comments in a teasing manner, hoping to take the edge off—"

Before she could finish, Michael said, "Amelia doesn't want to take the edge off. She wants to impart the full measure of her contempt."

Their argument went on in the same manner for another minute, before Alex interrupted. "Why don't we ask Sarah what she intended? After all, she wrote it."

Sarah's head snapped up when Alex said her name. Other than the obligatory polite exchanges, he'd carefully avoided speaking to her directly. Everyone turned to look at her.

"Well, when I wrote it, the feeling I'd intended to convey was Amelia's disdain for Christen's superior attitude. I believe the adverb I'd use is acidly."

Sarah was uncomfortable at first with giving her opinion, but she warmed to it in short order. "Amelia may be lively and witty, and in other circumstances, and perhaps with another kind of man, she might flirt, but at this juncture, Christen is the last man in the world with whom she would want to flirt."

"Okay, that settles it." Michael said. "Let's do it over—Sarah's way."

Brooke gave Sarah an irritated look. Good, Sarah thought, maybe she could channel that irritation into the appropriate delivery of her line.

After a few more takes, Michael called for a break. The caterer kept food and refreshments available in the kitchen at the back of the townhouse, and since Sarah had skipped breakfast, she headed in that direction. She was just placing a scone on her plate when Alex walked in. He walked over to the coffee pot with his back to her. So much for her appetite.

Alex wasn't in the mood for coffee. He just wanted an excuse to follow her into the kitchen, and once there, he needed something to distract him while he worked out what he wanted to say. Tongue-tied. Another first for him.

His jealousy had cooled. Watching Michael's excuses to touch her, his attempts to kiss her, were like taking a knife in the gut. But witnessing Sarah's gentle rebuffs of those advances, and of course they would be gentle, as would be expected from one so gracious, he now thought there was still a chance. Though after his abominable treatment of her these two weeks, he couldn't blame her if she didn't want anything to do with him.

Sarah couldn't stand the cold shoulder anymore. "Alex, I want to thank you for asking my opinion on that last scene. I didn't like the first take, but I didn't want to butt in . . ." She trailed off, unsure what else to say.

"You shouldn't be afraid to speak up. It *is* your book."

"Well, thank you anyway." She turned back to her now-undesirable scone, thinking that was the end of their conversation.

"Sarah." He said her name so softly that she was startled when she turned and saw how close he was. "I want to apologize for my inexcusable behavior the night of the party, and well, these last two weeks. It was rude and uncalled for. Will you please forgive me?" His eyes were sincere but guarded.

"You're asking *me* to forgive *you*," she asked in disbelief, "after I ran out last year?"

"Yes." He gave slight shrug. "I suppose I am."

"Does that mean I'm forgiven?"

"Don't push it." His teasing look took away any sting the words themselves might have inflicted. "But it's safe to say I'd like to call a truce." He extended his hand.

Sarah hesitated, not sure how she would react to his touch. "Truce then." She shook his hand. His grip tightened when she tried to pull her hand back, causing her to look up into his eyes in confusion.

He wanted to lean in, to brush her lips with his.

"Oh. I'm sorry, am I interrupting?" Brooke stood in the doorway wearing a disingenuous polite expression.

Sarah jerked her hand away as if it'd been burned. "No." She grabbed her plate and returned to the sitting room for the next scene.

The beautiful Brooke Bellamy is starting to get on my nerves. She's a good actress, I'll give her that. No one who sees her portrayal of the quick-witted Amelia would ever know what a self-centered, insipid little creature she is.

She'd just finished her word-for-word email account of the kitchen encounter with Alex when she began venting her frustration with Brooke to Ann and Becca.

I hate to admit it, but I'm jealous of her interactions with Alex. I know they are only acting, but she gets to spend time with him in rehearsals and be close to him on the set, while I sit back and pretend that we are only acquaintances. I don't know what I'll do the first time they kiss. I may have to absent myself from the set that day.

We leave tomorrow for Oxfordshire. I'll write again from there. Hugs and kisses.

Your fickle friend and sister,
Sarah

CHAPTER 30

The location chosen for Wilcox Manor was a former abbey built in the mid-seventeen hundreds. The central block with its temple-like portico flanked by two sprawling wings was constructed of weathered creamy Headington Stone, a type of limestone common to Oxfordshire. The façade was lined with Palladian windows, which provided spectacular views of the grounds.

The thousand-acre parkland, all that remained of the original three thousand acres, featured the rolling lawns and extensive views out to isolated groups of trees, typical of the famed landscaper Capability Brown. The effect made the landscape seem even larger. The grounds also boasted beautiful formal gardens complete with Greek temples of the same soft limestone as the house.

"May I join you?"

Sarah looked up with a start to see Alex standing there. She sat on a bench beneath a large maple in the garden behind the house, legs curled under her, reading the script for the next day's shoot. The first unit filming was cut short today, because Brooke claimed a migraine. Second unit was somewhere on the grounds shooting inserts and cutaways.

"Of course."

He took a seat at the other end of the bench, toying with a leafy twig in his hand, silent for a few moments. The détente that began in London had become a full-fledged normalization of relations in Oxfordshire. "I haven't asked you yet, how does it feel?"

She tensed at his question. There were so many ways to interpret it. How does it feel to have run out on him? How does it feel to have to face him again? She looked up in confusion.

"To option your first book? To watch it come to life in film?"

"Oh." She smiled in relief. "It feels amazing!" She could feel the blood rise to her face after her effusive outburst.

He turned to face her and his expression opened up. The Alex she knew suddenly returned. "I'm so proud of you, Sarah."

She looked into his eyes and, instead of cool distance, she saw genuine warmth. "I have you to thank for it. No," she held up her hand when he would have interrupted, "listen. I need to say something, and it may not come out as eloquently as I would like, but it is the truth and it is from my heart." He waited patiently while she tried to find the words.

"Notwithstanding my cowardly retreat last year, I owe you a great deal. I've lived most of my life with caution and timidity. It served me well most of the time. I made it through my teenage and young adult years with my heart intact, but that's easy to do when you don't let anyone in. The first and only time, until last year, that I threw caution to the wind . . . well . . . as you know, it didn't end well." She smiled ruefully. "I'm ashamed of my behavior. I was so afraid of opening my heart again, and then having it all become . . . so public. It was just easier to leave. It was easier to stay broken."

She took a deep breath. "But I've learned that I can't plan every-thing . . . that I have to take chances, even if I get hurt in the process. That's just part of life. I'm just sorry if I hurt you in the process."

He was quiet. She couldn't tell if he was considering her long confession, or whether he was contemplating a response.

"I was hurt and angry, I admit, but I suppose on some level I understood. We'd only spent a week together, you were recovering from a dreadful divorce, and there I was putting pressure on you—moving too fast and dragging you into my very public life."

"I should never have allowed it to happen," he continued, frowning. "I couldn't slow down where you were concerned . . . there just wasn't enough time. Not that I regret our night together, but I should have taken a page from your playbook and moved more cautiously."

"You're very forbearing." She hesitated, confused by his kindness and understanding. After a few moments of silence, she asked, "Not that you weren't justified, but why did you react so angrily that first night in London?"

"To be honest, I was surprised by my own reaction. I was prepared to remain distant, wait for some sign from you as to where things stood, but when I saw Michael's arm around your waist as if marking his territory, I assumed that's where things stood. Watching his continued fawning only fueled my anger. When you came to apologize, I'd almost made up my mind to pull out of the project. I wasn't sure if I wanted to watch him with you every day. But I always finish what I start." He paused before continuing.

"Over the weeks that followed, it was very difficult. He appeared to look for every opportunity to lean in close and speak to you. But your reaction the day he attempted to kiss you gave me cause to hope . . . to hope that I could try again but take it a little slower this time . . . allow you to set the pace." He took her hand in his and turned the full weight of his tender gaze on her. "Sarah, tell me . . . if you want me to leave things be, I will, but if you'll allow me, I would like to try again."

"I'd like that very much." She had to look away before her eyes filled with tears. I don't deserve him, she thought.

~

She returned to her room that night to find a box on her bed. Once she saw the return address, she quickly tore open the box. It was the first run of her book. She couldn't begin to express what it was like to pull out a beautifully bound copy of her own book.

If she wrote a hundred books, she didn't think that experience would ever grow stale.

The book jacket included some of the better reviews. Not surprising, the first was her favorite:

Not since the days of Jane Austen has a novel introduced such brilliant characters, sparkling dialogue, and unforgettable romance. A must-read for Austenites everywhere.

Of course, not everyone loved the book. After all, even Jane Austen had her detractors. There was one particularly scathing review she recalled, which, of course, was not on the back cover. She did take some level of satisfaction that the reviewer lacked originality, relying on a Mark Twain quip on Austen to sum up his critique of her book:

I go so far as to say that any library is a good library that does not contain this volume by Sarah Edwards. Even if it contains no other book.

That was okay. At least he kept her in good company with Jane Austen.

She couldn't wait to show Alex.

CHAPTER 31

Over the following two weeks, Sarah began to see a number of interesting parallels between the development of Christen's and Amelia's relationship and the rekindling of hers and Alex's relationship.

Just as with Christen and Amelia, hers and Alex's first meeting in London was awkward and fraught with tension, but before departing for the Oxfordshire countryside, there was a thawing in relations, a crack in the icy reserve of both Christen and Alex. Likewise, as a mutual understanding developed and grew between Amelia and Christen during their time in the country, so, too, had a mutual understanding developed and grown for her and Alex.

He had limited free time, with most of his attention consumed by the movie production, but the free time he did have, he spent with Sarah. Some of that time was spent in the former manor's well-stocked library, where they read to one another from books recently discovered or re-discovered.

It was purely selfish on Sarah's part because not only did she get to be with him, she got to listen to him read to her. His warm satin voice, lilting accent, and pleasing intonation brought life to the beautiful words and captivating characters.

Walking the inviting grounds of the estate was another favorite activity. With nothing to distract them, they caught up on the year they were apart. He explained how many times he'd thought of calling her, writing to her, or even emailing her, only to change his mind, thinking she would find the communication unwelcome.

She explained how she'd made the decision to write and the influence he had had on that decision. He was surprised, but pleased, to learn that their previous conversations had inspired her to take a chance on her dreams.

Although they had not resumed physical intimacy, their emotional intimacy was deepening, and all of their encounters were accompanied by subtle gestures of tenderness: a guiding hand on her elbow when they traversed the wilder parts of the park; a hand holding hers as she stepped over a fallen log; a solicitous question about her comfort in the evening air. This attentiveness was a welcome change to the cool distance of a few weeks earlier.

Yes, she could see many pleasing parallels. She only hoped there would be no comparable displeasing parallels.

Living within the confines of the estate, spending nearly every waking hour together, the cast and crew became a family. Evening meals were often raucous, convivial affairs. Seated at the enormous formal dining table, everyone joked and laughed over the day's trip-ups, flubs, and bloopers. Sarah found herself enjoying everyone's company, even Brooke's on occasion. Tonight, however, she enjoyed herself at Brooke's expense.

During the brief shoot for the scene with Amelia and Cat on horseback, Brooke's horse became uncooperative. The videographer needed only a quick shot of Brooke mounting the horse, the rest of the scene being shot with a stunt woman, but every time Brooke tried to put her foot in the stirrup to mount, the mare took a step or two forward, causing her to hop after her on one foot.

This happened a few more times, until finally, in a fit, Brooke demanded a more submissive animal. Laughter rang out around the table with the account of the story, and despite her participation, Sarah detected Brooke's annoyance at being the butt of the joke.

"And did you see Alex slip during the fencing scene? It looked like he'd stepped on a banana peel, arms flailing, foil wobbling in the air." Mel, one of the more outgoing members of the crew, recounted the story, arms gesticulating wildly. "I was afraid he would lose his grip on the thing and skewer us all like a shish kabob."

Alex joined in, his eyes alight with mirth. "Yes, well, I was attempting to execute a picture-perfect flèche, which failed on a monumental scale. Though you can't say I didn't warn you to give me a wide berth. Swordplay is not my forte. I'm a lover, not a fighter," he said with a devastating grin, as his eyes caught Sarah's across the table.

She sucked in her breath while her heart did a little quickstep. How did he do that, she wondered, how did he make her heart race with just a look?

The remainder of the meal carried on in the same vein, getting more boisterous as the wine flowed, and they were a thirsty bunch. Although it had been a long day, Sarah was inexplicably keyed up. She excused herself from the table, intending to find some quiet in the library. She was scanning the titles on the shelves when the muffled sounds from the dining room suddenly grew louder. She looked up to see Alex closing the door behind him.

"I thought I might find you here." He wanted to talk to her. To finally own up to the conspiracy that resulted in their reunion. "Am I disturbing you?"

"No. I was just looking for a book to take up to my room."

"Looking for anything in particular?" he asked as he crossed the room to stand next to her. "I've become quite familiar with the library," he replied to her unspoken question.

"Oh, I don't know . . . something light." Her pulse fluttered in response to his proximity.

"Well, let's have a look. There's the Brontë sisters—"

"That's light?" she asked with a laugh.

"I guess you're right. How about James Joyce?"

"Lighter."

"Scott?"

"F. Scott or Sir Walter?"

"Sir Walter."

"Lighter."

"All right, Dr. Seuss?"

"They don't have Dr. Seuss—" She rolled her eyes.

"It's right here," he said, reaching down to the bottom shelf.

"Okay," she said with a laugh, "maybe not quite that light. How about Alcott?"

"*Little Women*? That's light?"

"Light enough."

"If that's what you want . . . it's here right above you." He stepped onto the library ladder reaching for a volume one shelf up. His cologne wafted past Sarah, bringing memories flooding back. She recalled his smoldering look across the table earlier and her heart skipped a beat.

He stepped off the ladder, holding the book out to her. "Frankly, I don't know what's wrong with a little Sir Walter Sco—"

She cut off his words with a kiss. She didn't know what happened. One minute they were talking the classics, and the next she was grabbing his face and kissing him. She'd acted completely on impulse. And instinct.

At first, his arms remained unresponsive, but he quickly recovered from his shock at her inexplicable behavior, dropping the book to the floor with a *thwack*, and wrapping his arms around her waist. He pulled her into the alcove behind the ladder, his fingers fisted in her hair, pulling her head back, and running his lips down the column of her throat. "God, Sarah. How I've missed you. Your smell, your taste." He moaned, claiming her mouth again, his lips branding her.

Her hands knotted in his hair, drinking in the taste of him, nibbling his lower lip, until she finally retreated, gasping for breath. "Come to my room. Now."

"So much for taking it slow," he said with a wicked grin.

"You said I could determine the pace, right?" She ran her hands down his neck, inside the collar of his shirt.

"Yes." He shivered when her fingers touched his bare skin.

"Well, I've decided to pick up the pace a bit." She unbuttoned one button then another, pressing kisses onto his exposed skin with each button she popped open.

"A bit?" he asked skeptically. "The velocity at which you're moving now is making me dizzy."

"I hope that's not the only thing making you dizzy."

"Sarah." He drew in a ragged breath. "What about the others . . . ?"

"It's early. They'll be at the table for several more hours," she murmured between kisses. "Send in a few more bottles of wine. That should take care of it." She had reached his navel.

"Dear God, Sarah. If you don't cease this instant, there won't be time to get to your room." His hands were on her shoulders as he gently pushed her away. "I'll be up in about fifteen minutes." He re-buttoned his shirt as he spoke. "I'll need that time to compose myself. I certainly can't be seen in this condition," his added, his meaning obvious.

"My room is on the left, at the end of the hall." Breathless, she kissed his chest once more before he could finish buttoning his shirt.

❦

*S*arah hadn't planned on seducing anyone during her stay in England, so she didn't have any lacy lingerie to slip into. Remembering Oxford, she put on the same robe she wore that night . . . and nothing else. Hopefully he would remember, too, since the robe itself was about as enticing as a flannel nightgown.

She was anxious. Why did it seem longer than the promised fifteen minutes? Had he changed his mind? Decided that her sudden unpredictability was more than he'd bargained for?

There was a knock on her door so soft she thought she'd imagined it. She hurried over and opened it. He stood there looking so . . . delectable. She grabbed the front of his shirt and tugged him through the door. His eyes opened wide in surprise. Then his hands found her face, pulling her lips up to meet his, molding her body to the length of his, as he leaned against the now-closed door. He slid his hands down to her waist, untying the sash, slipping his hands inside her robe. His breath left him in a soft hiss when he encountered the bare skin underneath.

He smiled against her lips. "I have rather fond memories of this robe." So alluring in a simple white cotton robe. He swallowed hard when he imagined her in a lacy bit of nothing. He'd have to see what he could do to fulfill that little fantasy later.

She sighed when his hands found the bare skin at her waist. He pressed her hips to his, kissing her along her collarbone to her shoulder. She wanted to remove his shirt, but her arms were useless, like they'd melted into nothingness. She reveled in his touch, his kisses, his warmth, his desire. The robe glided to the floor, pooling at her feet.

"Oh God," he breathed as his scorching eyes blazed a trail along her skin. "You are so beautiful. Sweet Sarah, my love." He picked her up, carrying her to bed, her legs wrapped around his waist.

~

"*Y*ou know, I see a lot of myself in Christen . . . well, apart from the fencing skills." He chuckled.

Lying in bed, bodies intertwined, they listened to the great house settle as the occupants drifted to their rooms. Alex reclined on one elbow, playing with a lock of her hair, brushing it along her collarbone.

"That's not surprising."

"The part about the fencing?"

"No, the part about seeing a lot of yourself in Christen . . . at least physically." She hesitated before making her confession. "After all," she said, smiling sheepishly, "you were my muse. Although mere words failed to adequately capture your devastating good looks and irresistible sex appeal."

He pulled back, surprised. "Really? Huh." He ignored her effusive compliments.

"You're not upset?"

"Why should I be? I'm flattered, actually."

She shrugged. Before she could articulate a response, he pulled her face around to look at him, his hand cradling her neck. His eyes were troubled. She tensed in reaction to his knitted brow.

"Sarah, at the risk of scaring you off . . ."

Her tension increased ten-fold. He drew in a deep breath, as if preparing to take a plunge into deep water.

He'd waited too long to tell her and could wait no longer. It didn't matter whether she could return the sentiment or not. "I love you. I think I've loved you from the instant we met, your hand covered in beer, your eyes snapping with indignation." He chuckled softly. "And from the moment we kissed goodbye that night at Rutherford to this moment, a day has not gone by that I didn't think about you, miss you, hope that you were happy . . . even if it meant you weren't mine."

Sarah stared at him, her eyes wide with wonder and shimmering with tears. She'd never expected to hear those three words from him. She let them sink in. She'd fallen in love with him during that short week a year ago. Had loved him all along; and loved him still more now; knew it with the certainty with which she knew she needed to breathe.

She grazed her fingers across his lips. He shivered. "Alex. I love you." She wrapped her hand around his neck, drawing his mouth down to hers.

～

"Sarah . . . aside from the tabloid article, what precipitated your . . . um . . ."

"Cowardly retreat?"

"Yes, well, retreat. There had to be more to it than that, although I confess, seeing your photo like that for the first time can be somewhat disconcerting."

"Alex . . ."

"I want to know . . . so in the future, I can avoid doing whatever it was that I did." He wore that boyish grin she loved so much.

As they walked along the moonlit gravel path of their favorite garden, she thought about how to respond to his question. "What if I told you it was nothing you did?"

"I'd still want to know what it was that made you throw a wobbly that resulted in a miserable twelve-month separation." He stopped and turned her to face him, tucking a strand of hair behind her ear.

She swallowed hard. Then took a deep breath. "When Adrian and I were married, we traveled in loftier social circles. Later, when we separated then, divorced, the dirty laundry associated with it became quite public, subjecting me, not him," she said, laughing contemptuously, "to ridicule and catty remarks." She dropped to a garden bench to finish. "I swore I would never allow myself that kind of public scrutiny again. When I saw our picture, my picture, in the tabloid along with the article calling me the other woman, I panicked." Tell him everything, she admonished herself. "But that's not the only reason."

"What's the other reason?" His voice was flat, his brow knitted.

"There was an article in the *International Herald* that morning." She pulled her knees under her chin, wrapping her arms around them.

"I don't understand. About us?" His face was wary.

"No. It was just a story about how Adrian had saved a Saudi Prince's sight and about his upcoming wedding."

"And, what, you were regretting your divorce, you were jealous?"

"No."

"Then you need to explain, because I'm feeling a little uneasy." He frowned, deep in thought. "Sarah, I need to know . . . if there is still something there, because I don't do anything by halves, and apparently that includes love. If you don't feel the same way I do, please tell me now so I know what to expect."

"First, I love you in a way I never thought possible. In a way I never loved, nor ever could love Adrian. Second, there is nothing there. I haven't seen or heard from Adrian since our divorce was final a year-and-a-half ago."

She paused, afraid that what she was going to say wasn't going to make him feel much better. "Something you don't know about my marriage to Adrian . . . we'd only dated a few short weeks before he asked me to marry him. This impetuous behavior was completely out of character for me, and look where it ended . . ." she trailed off.

It dawned on him, "And you saw our relationship as a potential repeat performance." He frowned again.

"What I thought was . . . I don't know what I thought. My reaction was idiotic. I was just trying to protect my heart. I couldn't take another life-altering disappointment, and I couldn't face the potential for an exposé on our failed relationship if it didn't work out." She stood up, touched her hand to his face. "There isn't a day that goes by that I don't regret hurting you . . . regret the lost time . . . time that we'll never get back . . ." She sniffed as a tear rolled down her cheek.

He captured the tear with his thumb. "Okay. I'm sorry I dredged it up." He wrapped his arm around her and hugged her to his chest, holding her there for a few more sniffles. He tilted her chin up and kissed her lips, a soft whisper of a touch. What began as a tender kiss, blossomed into something very different. Ardent. Intense. "I guess we'll just have to make up for lost time," he groaned against her lips, as he pulled her into the perfumed shadows.

CHAPTER 32

This was it. The day Sarah had been dreading. The day she'd have to watch Alex kiss Brooke in the pivotal scene in the library; the scene where Christen acknowledges his feelings for Amelia. Another parallel, however faintly drawn, between the fictional relationship and the real-life relationship: the library. And to think some people find libraries boring.

After the events of the past week, all the passionate nights they'd spent together, it was going to be torture. Part of her wanted to avoid the scene, but the other part of her, the part that won, wanted to be there, to ensure that Brooke didn't take advantage of the situation. It was clear she'd had her eye on Alex from the beginning, and despite his rebuffs, her advances grew more calculated by the day.

Sarah sat in her customary seat next to Michael, although lately she'd surreptitiously put a little more space between them. She tried to act nonchalant as Michael called 'action.'

The scene began with Cat confronting Christen about his feelings for Amelia, encouraging him to tell her. He argued that he had no such feelings, and he didn't know what she was talking about. Unbeknownst to them both, Amelia was curled up in a chair, where she'd tried to hide when she heard them enter the library, clearly having an argument. She doesn't know the argument is about her, until she hears her name.

Cat: *"Oh, Christen, it's as plain as the nose on your aristocratic face. Admit it. You're in love with Amelia."*

Christen: *"I most certainly am not. What nonsense. Besides, she positively detests me."*

Cat, with a smile: *"Why would you say that? You're very loveable—when you want to be."*

Christen: *"Are you blind? We can barely speak two civil words to one another—"*

Cat: *"I spent a long, cold night in the woods with her, remember?"*

Christen winces at the memory.

Cat: *"Trust me, she doesn't detest you. In truth, I think it is quite the opposite."* *She walks over and stands on tiptoe to kiss his cheek.* *"Tell her . . . soon."* Cat exits the library.

Amelia remains frozen in her chair, hoping that Christen will follow, leaving her to make her escape. Unfortunately, she hiccups, a nervous reaction she's had since a little girl.

Christen, voice severe: *"Who's there? Show yourself this instant."*

Amelia hiccups again then, hesitantly reveals her presence, her eyes wide with shock and embarrassment.

Christen, steps back in shock: *"Amelia."*

Amelia hiccups again: *"Christen . . . I'm so sorry"* (hiccup) *". . . it wasn't my intention to eavesdrop"* (hiccup) *". . . I'll just be going . . ."* *In a rare moment of chagrin, she attempts to walk past him.*

Christen, grabbing her shoulders, stopping her, looks into her face only inches from her mouth: *"How much did you hear?"*

Amelia: *"Everything."* (hiccup) *"I heard everything."* (hiccup)

Christen, in frustration: *"Confound it. Could you please stop hiccupping?"*

Amelia: *"Sorry."* (hiccup)

Christen, first in exasperation: *"Oh, blast."* *Then murmurs:* *"Perhaps I can cure those."* *He takes her face in his hands and lowers his lips to hers. They kiss. She wraps her arms around his neck, and he pulls her closer.*

Sarah's hands gripped the arms of the chair so tight she expected to hear a snap—either the chair or her hand breaking. Hasn't this gone on long enough? She wanted to yell 'cut!' Alex still kissed Brooke. What the hell was Michael waiting for anyway?

"Cut! Print."

Thank God. She could breathe again. She hoped that was the only take, but of course she knew better than that. Michael liked to get shots from a variety of angles.

"Okay, let's shoot the scene from Amelia's perspective." Michael turned to Sarah. "I think that went well, but we'll get a few more takes so the editor has several to choose from."

Sarah closed her eyes and groaned. Out loud.

"Sarah, you okay?" Michael asked with concern.

Sarah could feel Alex's eyes on her.

"Yes. It's just a headache." She grimaced.

"Maybe you should take something and go lie down. These lights can be brutal," Michael said indicating the lights surrounding the set.

"No," came her emphatic response. As much as she hated watching it, she hated not watching even more. "I'll be fine. Maybe I just need some caffeine."

"Could someone get Sarah a Diet Coke?"

With a tequila chaser, she thought. "Thanks," she said lamely.

She scanned the room for Alex, finding him in the makeup chair. She longed to tell the make-up artist to erase the amused expression from his face.

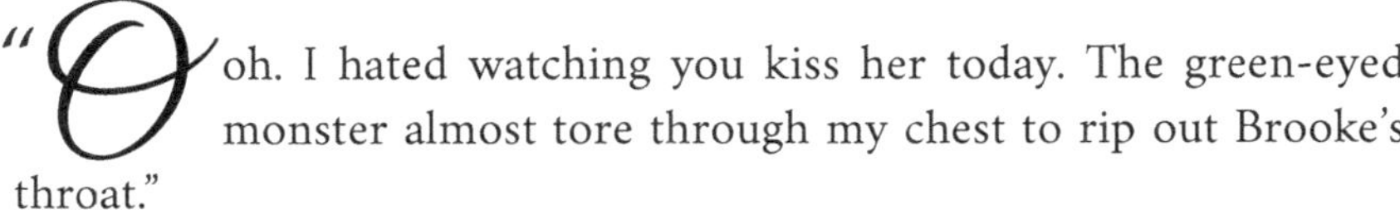

"Ooh. I hated watching you kiss her today. The green-eyed monster almost tore through my chest to rip out Brooke's throat."

Sarah's evening pursuits had changed drastically in the past week. Instead of just reading a romance novel, she lived her very own romance with Alex joining her every night after the house fell quiet. He'd even moved some of his personal items to her room, while still maintaining a plausible presence in his own. They both agreed they should keep this to themselves, at least until the filming was completed, afraid that their relationship might provoke discord among the cast and crew.

She could think of one cast member she'd like to provoke. But the movie was more important than her immature desire to rub this in Brooke's face.

She'd told Ann and Becca but swore them to secrecy. She could have sworn she'd heard Ann's shriek of elation all the way across the Atlantic.

Alex stayed with her until morning now, waiting until she gave him the all-clear, via text message, before he'd quietly exit her room and saunter nonchalantly down the stairs.

"If it's any consolation, I didn't enjoy it one bit. Her kisses are too wet." He shuddered.

"Maybe that's because she drools," Sarah said snidely.

He chuckled. "Sarah, you've nothing to worry about. What can I do to calm the green-eyed monster before she rears her ugly head again?"

"Take me to bed and tell me you love me."

"Since we're already in bed, how about I tell you how much I love you."

"That will do . . . for now." She snuggled closer, her face buried in his neck, breathing his wonderful spicy, citrusy scent.

"'I love you without knowing how, or when, or from where . . .'" His voice was husky with emotion.

His recitation left her breathless. She buried her face in his chest so he couldn't see the tears welling in her eyes. "That was beautiful," she breathed. "Did you write that?"

He laughed softly, wrapping his arms around her. "No, I only recite great lines, I don't write them. It's from a sonnet by Pablo Neruda, the Nobel prize-winning poet."

He tenderly kissed her lips, her throat, her hair, and she shuddered under his caress.

With one smooth motion, he tossed the blankets aside, revealing their naked bodies, making her gasp in shock, then his teeth grazed down her body to her quivering stomach.

Her breathing grew ragged.

He gently rolled her onto her back, his eyes black with desire, and captured her mouth in a kiss so tender yet fierce she thought it would consume her.

CHAPTER 33

Sitting at a delicate writing desk in one of the manor's many rooms, Sarah responded to an email from Ann, contemplating how to answer her question about what Brooke was like.

Not to put too fine a point on it, but 'she is a woman of mean understanding, little information, and uncertain temper.' Despite her frequent declaration that she just adores Jane Austen, she wouldn't get an allusion to her if it came up and slapped her on the back of her vapid little head. Uh-oh. Speak of the devil . . .

"Oh, Sarah. I thought you might be Alex. Have you seen him?"

"I haven't seen him. Did you check the library?"

She made a little face before saying, "Thanks."

Brooke clearly couldn't understand their fascination with the collection of essays, novels, and poetry the well-stocked library offered.

Sarah returned to her email, finishing with a rundown of the schedule over the next week. If all went as planned, the crew would wrap up the shoot here and return to London soon. However, she would be returning to London tomorrow. Elizabeth, her agent, was stopping over on her way to Hong Kong to meet with her about another two-book deal. She sighed, as if that were a bad thing.

She hated leaving Alex, especially with Brooke on the prowl. Even with her previous experience with infidelity, it wasn't that she didn't trust Alex. She didn't trust *Brooke.* She reminded herself it was only for one night. She'd return on the early morning train the following day and stay for the remainder of the shoot.

She looked forward to the end of the filming. She was tired of sneaking around with Alex like they were having some sort of torrid affair. The pretense was wearing on her. She couldn't believe she hadn't already slipped. It was hard to believe her love for him wasn't tattooed on her face for all to see.

She closed her laptop before returning to the library in search of her script to review it before tomorrow's shoot, particularly since she wasn't going to be here. Would there be any kissing tomorrow? Speaking of kissing, if she got lucky, she might run into Alex and corner him for a little make-out session before dinner.

Opening the library door, Sarah froze. Brooke stood close to Alex, face lifted to his. He held her wrists up in front of his chest. Sarah gasped.

"Sarah." He dropped Brooke's wrists, pushing her away from him. "It's not what you think . . ." He grimaced at the trite expression.

"I know—"

"I was trying to remove her unwelcome hands from my chest—" The anguish was plain on his face.

Sarah glared at Brooke, gritting her teeth to hold back the unlady-like string of expletives that threatened to erupt.

"Now I know why you're producing this claptrap." Brooke returned Sarah's astonished look with one of smug satisfaction.

"What?" Sarah looked at Alex, confused. "What did she just say? What did she mean?" It finally dawned on her. She was more shocked by the revelation that Alex was apparently producing the movie, than by Brooke's blatant attempt to seduce him. "I thought Michael was the producer . . ." Her voice trailed off. She already knew the answer. "Alex?"

He opened his mouth to speak, but nothing came out.

"All this time, I thought I'd succeeded on my own merits . . . someone had read my book and genuinely loved it enough to make it into a movie . . . and all along it was you," she said as if to herself. "I should have known. The coincidences were so obvious." She shook her head.

"Bloody hell. Sarah, can you just forget your damnable pride for one minute." He strode over to her, his hands raised as if to grab her shoulders.

"My pride?" She took a step back. "This isn't about my pride." She smacked his hand aside as he tried to reach for her again. "Why didn't you tell me? Was this supposed to be another of your surprises? In case you've forgotten, I don't like surprises."

"Sarah. I'm sorry. I'd planned to tell you . . ."

"Does everyone else know?" She could feel angry, humiliated tears filling her eyes, blurring her vision. "I feel like such a fool." The tears rolled down her cheeks, temporarily clearing her vision.

"No," he said softly. "No one else knew, except . . . Michael . . ." He turned to glare at Brooke, understanding mounting. "A little pillow-talk, Brooke?"

She at least had the grace to blush.

"Please leave," he said to her, his voice barely audible. She turned on her heel and left, giving Sarah a baleful look as she stalked out the door.

"Sarah." Alex's hands were on her shoulders. "Look at me, please."

Sarah stubbornly shook her head, more tears spilling down her cheeks.

"I need to leave."

"Is that your solution to everything—run?"

"Don't worry Alex, I'm not going to run off again," she said with a little sarcasm. "Give me a little more credit than that. I just need to get some air . . . preferably alone." He dropped his hands, and, stumbling out of the library, tears blurring her vision, she all but ran out the front door into the cool summer evening.

≈

*A*lone in her room later that night, she saw with clarity how perfectly the pieces fit. The fact that he was cast as Christen —I mean, let's face it, she thought, what were the odds of Alex being cast out of the blue, perfect or not?

As producer, he could cast himself. The deference Michael paid him on the set; his involvement in almost every aspect of the production, including his regular viewing of the dailies, even when he wasn't in the scenes. Although she was a novice to the movie industry, she was surprised she hadn't seen it before. She was surprised everyone didn't see it.

She was going to London as planned. Maybe a little separation would do them both good . . . give them some time to think. Besides she wasn't sure she trusted herself around Brooke without wringing her swan-like little neck.

Cried-out and exhausted, she turned in early, trying not to think about how cold and lonely the bed was without Alex.

≈

*H*e'd screwed up. He knew that. But damn it, if she wasn't so stubborn, so determined to do everything on her own, maybe this wouldn't have gotten blown out of proportion.

Of course, it didn't help that Brooke had been the one to reveal it. He sighed, sat on the edge of the bed. It only added to Sarah's humiliation. He wanted to belt Brooke, and he wasn't too happy with Michael at the moment either.

He stood, paced his room, scrubbing his hands through his hair. He should have told her. Of course, he should have. If he'd told her weeks ago, maybe she'd have been miffed at first, but after he'd explained to her why, they'd had a good laugh over it and moved on.

He stopped in front of the window and looked out at the black night. He wondered if she were still out there. He didn't like the thought of her out there at night alone. Should he go to her? Apologize? Apologize, yes, but go to her, no. She said she wanted to be alone. If she wanted to speak to him, she would have let him know.

Tomorrow he would grovel. Perhaps crawling on his knees would be in order. After what promised to be a long, lonely, sleepless night.

CHAPTER 34

On the crowded southbound Piccadilly line, her mind was not where it should be: her upcoming meeting with Elizabeth. Instead, it was on Alex. She was hurt that he didn't tell her the truth, that he'd led her to believe it was all a coincidence, that he was merely a member of the cast. But was that the only reason she was upset?

She'd always had trouble accepting help. Even as a child, she'd stubbornly refused help tying her shoes or doing her homework . . . or learning to ride her bike. She thought if she didn't do it by herself, without assistance from anyone, she hadn't succeeded. This hadn't changed as she grew older.

Was that part of the issue here? Did it really matter who produced the movie? Did it lessen her satisfaction of having written her first novel? After all, she likely wouldn't be here if she hadn't asked for Sam's help.

Instead of making her doubt her success, his investment of time and money should reinforce her accomplishment. He loved her, but she didn't think he would throw good money after bad if he didn't believe in the project. He was too driven for that.

She also realized that she found great satisfaction in working with Alex. His insight into the characters she developed, his creativity in fleshing out the scenes, and his ability to lift the story from the pages of her book to make it compelling and real were a gift. They made a great team.

Then there was his acting. She could watch him all day, except for the romantic scenes with Brooke, and never tire of the experience. He was so . . . believable. Genuine. That was the word.

The train stopped at Green Park Station, but instead of emptying, more people got on, jostling for space in the tiny, crowded car. Reluctantly, she stepped closer to the man behind her.

There was still the little issue of trust. If they were going to have a relationship, she needed to know he was secure in her love for him that he could tell her anything.

Maybe that was her fault, too. Maybe he hadn't told her because he was afraid she would react, well, exactly the way she did. She didn't have the best track record with him. Clearly, she needed to work on her fight-or-flight response. She groaned, eliciting an apprehensive look from the well-dressed businessman holding the strap above her head. She met his frown with a tentative smile, and he returned to his newspaper.

As soon as her meeting with Elizabeth was concluded, she'd call him. Of course she'd only get his voicemail since they were filming, but she could at least tell him that she loved him and that she couldn't wait to see him tomorrow.

That issue resolved for the moment, she pulled the copy of her contract for the book deal out of her tote. There were a few provisions she wanted to discuss with Elizabeth. She bet Elizabeth just loved having a former lawyer as a client.

The next stop was Hyde Park Corner, one more stop before Knightsbridge. The car's doors opened, expelling most of its commuters, but still not enough for Sarah to take a seat.

The train had barely pulled away from the station before a series of explosions shook the tracks, filling the car with acrid smoke. The train ground to a halt with an angry jolt. Screams erupted, followed by deafening sirens. Sarah lost her grip on the handle and her world seemed to turn on its side. There was a sickening crack as her head hit the seat behind her. Just moments after landing on the floor of the train, someone fell on top of her, forcing the air out of her lungs with a *whoof.*

Her last thoughts were of Alex—and regret. She wished she'd kissed him goodbye. Then darkness . . .

~

*A*lex paced his brother's office, scrubbing his hand through his already disheveled hair. "Damn it, Robert! I've got to find her."

"Calm down. We'll find her. Just give my people time." Robert walked over and closed his door on the chaos outside his office. People running about, phones ringing off the hook.

"You don't understand, the last time we saw one another we'd had . . . words." Alex sat down, his head in his hands.

Robert walked around his desk and, reaching out, tentatively touched his brother on the shoulder. "You love her, don't you?"

"Oh God, Robert. I love her. I don't know what I'd do without her." He looked up at Robert, his face tense with worry and uncertainty.

Thoughtful, Robert sat in the chair next to Alex. This was a side of his brother he thought he'd never see. For his brother's sake, he fervently hoped Sarah was safe.

~

*S*he floated up from the murky depths to a shaft of light shimmering above her. It reminded her of summers spent in the tea-colored lake in front of the family's vacation house. Diving down to the lake's gloomy depths, she would let the buoyancy slowly lift her to the surface, challenging herself to hold her breath. Only this time she didn't feel the water's weightlessness, only heaviness. Her body ached with the burden of gravity.

The light grew brighter, forming a pinpoint that sent a stabbing pain to the back of her head. She wanted to retreat into the darkness, away from the pain, but a sweet, familiar voice coaxed her up to the surface.

"Sarah. Sarah, sweetheart?" Alex sat beside her bed, urging her to come to.

She felt someone squeeze her hand. Memories flashed through her brain, adding to the pain. Some memories were visual, others auditory, and still others olfactory. They were jumbled, out of order: acrid smoke burning her lungs before the air was forced out of them; a series of loud bangs; flickering lights; screams; violent lurching; pain; blackness.

"Sarah." The sweet voice again, closer this time, tinged with concern. She wanted to comply, to respond. She wanted desperately to break from the confines of gravity, but it was too strong. Her eyelids felt as if they had been sealed shut.

"Allow her to come to on her own. Her brain will determine when it's ready," the nurse said as she came into the room.

"Alex." Her voice was raw and scratchy. She swallowed, trying to clear her throat, but her mouth was so dry. *He's here*, she thought. A tear leaked out, sliding down the side of her face. *He still loves me.*

Alex shot out of his seat as if he'd been ejected. "Sarah," he breathed close to her ear.

He sounded relieved.

She groaned, and his voice grew anxious again. "Are you in pain?"

She ignored his question. She had more pressing matters. "Where am I? What happened?" She furrowed her brow and the pain in her head returned.

"You're in hospital, love. You don't remember what happened?"

"No," she replied, wincing again as she tried to remember.

"There was an accident on the Underground tube. From what the media reports have said, there was a massive power surge, causing a series of explosions. There was chaos at first, with rumors of a terrorist attack."

Train. She vaguely remembered being on the train . . . going somewhere . . . the only thing she could really remember was the noise, the smoke, the pain.

"Mr. Fraser, please excuse me while I check her IV."

He released her hand reluctantly before moving to the other side of the bed.

His hand was replaced by the gloved touch of the nurse. "How are you feeling, Ms. Edwards? Can you open your eyes for me?"

Sarah tried, but only succeeded with a couple of ineffectual blinks. The light was painful. Someone flipped the light switch, turning off the light, taking the sharper pain with it. "How's that? Better?" the nurse asked kindly. She had no accent. American, Sarah wondered?

"Yes." Her voice croaked again. "Could I have some water?" She opened her eyes, hesitantly at first. All she saw was a blurry face, surrounded by red hair. Blinking some more, the nurse came into focus. She had a plain, but kind, face, and her nose was covered in freckles. No offense to her, but she wasn't who Sarah wanted to see. "Alex?"

"I'm here, Love." Taking her unfettered hand, he held it to his lips. Though his brow was creased with worry, he wore a small smile.

Sarah was so relieved to see his dear, sweet face. A face she thought she'd never see again. Closing her eyes, she licked her dry lips. The nurse held a straw to her mouth, cautioning her to take small sips. It was so cool and sweet as it passed down her raw throat, she wanted to gulp it, but the nurse pulled the straw away.

"You can have more in a few minutes. The doctor will be in soon," she said, stepping away from the bed.

"How long?" She hoped Alex understood her disjointed question. Her throat still burned.

"The accident was yesterday. You've only been out a little more than twenty-four hours." He brushed his free hand tentatively across her cheek, his other still holding her hand.

"How many . . . hurt?" Another inarticulate question.

"About a hundred, but most were treated and released. Cuts, scrapes, things of that sort. Only a few were hospitalized."

"Any . . . dead?"

"No. They're saying it's a miracle the injuries weren't worse."

"Good afternoon, Ms. Edwards."

Sarah tried to turn her head in the direction of the voice, but the pain returned with a vengeance and the room tilted slightly.

"I'm the neurologist, Dr. Smithwick. It's good to see you awake. How are you feeling today?" He stood on the side of the bed opposite Alex, Sarah's chart in his hand. He appeared old enough to be her father, with a shock of white hair, and pale gray eyes. His face looked worn, but friendly.

Awake? Just barely. She felt like she could sink into the darkness again at any time. "Fine. My head hurts. My throat burns. My body aches."

"Sounds about right. You've suffered a concussion. You've got a nasty bump at the base of your skull. Do you remember hitting your head?"

She winced as the memory of the sound of her head hitting . . . something . . . reverberated in her brain. "Yes."

"Your throat is likely raw from the smoke inhalation. That should go away soon. You're sore both from the fall and from cushioning the fall of a rather burly gentleman." The doctor had a lovely bedside manner and a pleasing sense of humor. Too bad Sarah didn't feel like laughing.

"Do you remember anything about the accident?"

"Not really. Just disjointed images, sounds . . ." Her voice trailed off as she tried again to remember.

"Some level of memory may return, or it may not return at all. It's nothing to worry about either way. Despite your harrowing ordeal, you are in good shape. Your head CT shows no signs of bleeding in the brain. No skull fracture."

"That proves it," she croaked, with a slight smile. "Becca always said I was hard-headed."

"Well, in this case, I'm grateful for your hard head," Alex said, a smile flickered around his mouth.

"X-rays are negative for any broken bones, just some pretty ugly bruises." He put Sarah's chart down, reached into his pocket, and pulled out a pin light. "I'm just checking those baby . . . greens," he said as he shined the light into her eyes.

Sarah winced.

"I'm sorry. I know the light is painful. It will only take a second."

He finished his examination. "Everything looks fine. You may have some dizziness and headaches, possibly some memory loss of the events surrounding the accident, but otherwise, you should be fine. The light sensitivity will recede as well."

He made notes in the chart. "We are going to keep you one more night for observation. If you feel nauseated," he turned to Alex, "if she seems uncharacteristically confused, or if her speech becomes slurred, let the nurse know right away. Any questions for me?" He looked at Sarah and then Alex.

"No. Thank you," Sarah said.

"Can she have something to drink?" Alex asked. "She's very thirsty."

"Yes. I think we should stick with water for the time being. See how she keeps that down. I'll be back tomorrow before we release you."

"Thank you, Dr. Smithwick." Alex picked up the cup Sarah had been drinking from before and held the straw to her parched lips.

Grateful, she took the cup from him and carefully sipped the water as instructed by the nurse.

Alex leaned his hip against the bed watching her carefully. "I hope you don't mind, but I took the liberty of calling Rebecca and Ann. I rummaged around in your purse, I know," he held up his hands, "a woman's purse is sacred, but I found your mobile and looked up their numbers . . ."

"Thank you." She had hoped they would be blissfully unaware, but she supposed the story had been on the news, and they both knew she was supposed to be in London today, or rather, yesterday. "How did they react?" She could just imagine Ann would be frantic, while Becca would be worried, but all business.

"Frantic and concerned. They'd tried calling you, but of course you didn't answer, so they couldn't get you, which made them even more frantic. I assured them that you were okay. They both offered to fly over. I told them I would leave that up to you." He softly stroked her hand.

"I'm fine. They don't need to leave their families to come over here." They were both silent a moment.

"Tired?"

"You have no idea." She tried to laugh but winced instead. "But I want to talk to you."

"Later. You need to rest. Would you like me to read to you?"

"You have nothing to read," she said, pouting.

"All right, how about I recite to you then?" He flashed his brilliant smile.

"Okay. But I want you to lie next to me."

"Sarah, I don't think that's a good idea—"

"Yes. It's what I want." She sounded like a toddler who wasn't getting her way.

He chuckled, lowering the bedrail and climbing in next to her, gingerly wrapping his arm around her shoulders. "What should I recite? Shakespeare?"

"Hmm, that would be lovely," she answered drowsily.

He was silent, deciding which of the countless beautiful sonnets or soliloquies to select. He inhaled, and then in his beautiful voice, softly spoke the words of Sonnet 116:

"Let me not to the marriage of true minds
Admit impediments. Love is not love
Which alters when it alteration finds,
Or bends with the remover to remove.
O no, it is an ever-fixed mark
That looks on tempests and is never shaken;
It is the star to every wand'ring bark,
Whose worth's unknown, although his height be taken."

Alex had chosen this poem deliberately. Even with her scrambled brains, its meaning was clear. True love—their love—was deep enough that circumstances, unkind words, nor age would disrupt it. He was right. They would work out their issues.

Now as her eyelids fluttered closed, his silken voice continued softly:

"Love's not time's fool, though rosy lips and cheeks
Within his bending sickle's compass come:
Love alters not with his brief hours and weeks,
But bears it out even to the edge of doom.
If this be error and upon me proved,
I never writ, nor no man ever loved."

He kissed her tenderly on her head before she slid into oblivion. "I love you, sweet Sarah."

~

Dressed and anxious to leave, Sarah sat on the hospital bed, waiting for Dr. Smithwick to release her. Her head still ached, and although she had to turn her head slowly to prevent the room from dipping crazily around her, she was ready to get out of the hospital.

Alex gathered the myriad bouquets of flowers and balloons that arrived during her short stay there. Ann, Becca, Lady Clara, her former colleagues, the cast and crew, and Michael all sent the customary flowers or balloons. Brooke sent nothing.

Her agent, who according to Alex stayed long enough to determine Sarah was going to be okay before catching a flight a day late for her meeting in Hong Kong, gave her a bottle of fine Cognac. Leave it to Elizabeth to break the mold when giving a get-well gift, or any gift for that matter. For her last birthday she'd given Sarah a tandem parachute jump. As if Sarah would ever voluntarily jump out of a perfectly good airplane.

"Good morning, Ms. Edwards. It appears you are eager to leave us." The effervescent Dr. Smithwick approached the bed, looking at her meager belongings gathered on a cart. "I can't imagine why, what with our five-star cuisine," he said blandly. He picked up her chart, looking it over before turning to her. "How are you feeling?"

"Sore. Like I've been hit by a train rather than just having hit the floor of one."

"And the head?" he asked, pointing out the most serious injury, since she hadn't.

"It aches, but I'll live."

"Glad to hear that you'll live. Always like to have my prognosis confirmed." He smiled. "You're free to go, but you have some limitations.

"First: rest, rest, rest. Second: stay away from aspirin, ibuprofen, or other anti-inflammatory drugs. Panadol, or Tylenol, as you call it, is the ticket. Third: avoid vigorous activity for at least two weeks. No aerobics, running, or other activities that may bounce your brain around. Finally, if any of your symptoms return, seek medical attention immediately."

Before Sarah could respond, Alex spoke, "Thank you Dr. Smithwick. I'll make sure she follows all of your instructions."

She rolled her eyes before she realized that made her dizzy. She swayed a little on the bed, but caught herself before either Alex or Dr. Smithwick could change their mind about springing her.

"Goodbye, Sarah. Take care." Dr. Smithwick gently shook her hand before leaving. "Lord Rutherford."

"I'll bring the car around and see you out front."

"I'll be the one in the wheelchair," she said as the nurse wheeled it into the room.

They both helped Sarah from the bed, steadying her as she turned to sit in the chair. Alex leaned down and kissed the top of her head before he left.

The nurse leaned over and whispered, "Is that Lord Rutherford, the actor?"

"Yes."

"You're a very lucky girl."

"Yes, I am."

CHAPTER 35

"Can I get you anything?" Alex asked as he plumped the pillows behind Sarah's back. They'd just returned from the hospital to the Knightsbridge apartment.

"Yes. You. You can please stay with me. I want to talk—"

"Sarah—"

"No. We've put this off long enough. Sit. Please."

He unwillingly sat on the bed next to her, his eyes wary, his lips drawn into a straight line.

"Alex, why didn't you tell me about the movie? When were you planning to tell me?"

"There were so many times I'd resolved to tell you, but circumstances would always interfere. I wanted to tell you, but I couldn't find the right time. It was wrong of me, and I'm so sorry if I hurt you. It was never my intention."

He looked deeply into her eyes, and she knew he was sincere.

Reaching up, he gingerly cupped her face in his hands, as tears filled his eyes. "Oh God, Sarah. If I had lost you . . ."

"Shhh. I'm here." She pulled his head down to kiss his mouth. He returned the kiss hesitantly, as if afraid she might break. Lowering his head to her chest, he pressed his ear to her heart, breathing deeply.

Sarah was so moved by his reaction that she felt tears welling in her own eyes. "I love you, Alex."

"I love you, Sarah." He raised his head, taking her hand in his. "Listen, I know you think I've undermined your success by producing the movie, that I'm biased and thus incapable of making an impartial decision." He turned her hand over, absently tracing the lifeline in her palm. "And to be completely honest, when an unpublished novel was presented to me, I wasn't terribly interested," he hesitated, wincing as he spoke, "until I found out you were the author."

He held up his hands before she could berate him. "Now don't get your knickers in a twist. I took a look at the manuscript because it was yours, but I optioned it because it was, well, marvelous. You know me. I wouldn't put my money or my reputation on the line if I thought it was rubbish."

She gave him a dubious look, but before she could speak, he continued, "I won't deny that an added benefit of optioning your work was seeing you again. I'm not finished," he said as he placed a finger over her open lips. "And I won't deny that that prospect didn't have anything to do with choosing to read your manuscript." He paused, waiting for her to speak, and when she didn't, he added, "Okay. I'm done."

"Alex, I am so sorry about our argument. After the train accident and having faced the possibility of never seeing you again . . . well, it has put a lot of things in perspective for me. Some things just aren't important in the grand scheme."

Thinking of her father's advice, she said as she picked at the blanket across her lap, "But on the train, before the accident, I'd been thinking about it, and I realized it was my stubborn streak that made me so angry. I have to let go of this need to do everything on my own. I have to allow people to help me, especially you. Isn't that what partners are for? And I'm going to start right now. I could use a little help to the bathroom." She smiled reassuringly into his bewildered face. He recovered, laughing at her inaugural request for help.

Shaking his head, he helped her out of bed and to the bathroom, before giving her some privacy. "Call me when you're ready to walk back to the bed."

Sarah held onto the wall, still a little unsteady on her feet. When she opened the door to ask for his help back to bed, he sat on the bed looking at his hands, a frown on his face.

"Alex, what's wrong?"

He rose, walking over to assist her back to the bed. After getting her settled, he sat on the bed again. "I have one more confession, and then I promise never to hide the truth from you again."

She stiffened, her first thought of Brooke. Telling herself to remain calm, she said, "Okay. I'm listening."

He heaved an enormous sigh. "This flat is mine."

"What? Yours? Why would you vacate your home for me? I'm sure there were hundreds of other places where I could have stayed." Yes, she reminded herself, too many coincidences.

"But I knew you would be comfortable here." The frown returned. "No. That's not the whole truth. The truth is that I relished the thought of you here . . . in my home . . . in my bed."

"Oh." Why did that jumpstart her heart? "That explains the food in the kitchen. I wondered how someone knew my favorite foods."

"Yes. I wanted everything perfect for you."

"Lord Rutherford, you are something else." She couldn't help laughing, but not too hard because it hurt her head.

"You're not upset?"

"Well, I guess under the circumstances you couldn't tell me until now, because your entire house of cards would have collapsed, though I'm glad you finally fessed-up. Come here."

As he leaned down, she took his face in her hands and kissed him tenderly at first, and then more insistently. She tried to ignore the throbbing in her head as her heart broke into a sprint.

He clung to her, remembering the pain, the uncertainty, but his brain overruled his heart . . . and his libido.

All too soon, he pulled away. "Sarah, remember what the doctor said: no rigorous activity—"

"Oh bollocks."

He raised an eyebrow at her use of British profanity.

"I'm fine." She reached for his face again, but he grabbed her wrists, stopping her.

"No. I promised Dr. Smithwick you would follow all his orders. I'm keeping that promise." He stood up, placing her hands primly in her lap. "You must be hungry. What can I get you to eat?"

"There's only one thing I'm hungry for."

He only shook his head, smiling at her corny cliché, but chose to ignore its meaning. "Sliced strawberries and mascarpone cheese on toast, with a side of extra-strength Panadol, it is."

She groaned in disgust as he left the room. She hated to admit it, but he was probably right. As her pulse slowed down to normal, the throbbing in her head eased. She smiled. She'd give it a couple of days and try again.

∾

"*U*gh."

"What's wrong?" Alex's concerned voice came from the kitchen.

"I'm so bored." Even reading no longer pacified her. She wanted to toss her book across the room, and she'd never felt that way about books. "I'm tired of being cooped up."

Alex walked into the living room, where she lay propped up on the sofa, wiping his hands on a dishtowel. "You mean you don't enjoy being cooped up with me?" His face wore a look of mock distress. "I'm hurt."

"I'd love being cooped up with you if our activities were a little more . . . rigorous." She hoped her seductive smile was enough to persuade him.

"You only want me for my body." Another mocking expression.

"Well, not *only* for your body, but yes, right now, I want your body."

"You're exasperating. It's only been a week since you got home from hospital."

His voice was placating, but it only served to aggravate her more. "But I'm going stir-crazy. Can't we at least go for a stroll, nice and easy, nothing hardcore?" Her voice became whiny.

He looked thoughtful for a moment. "If you're a very good girl and take it easy the rest of today, we'll go for a walk tomorrow, weather permitting." He sat next to her on the sofa, wrapping his arm around her. "How's that sound?"

Like you're talking to a child, she thought. But she was willing to take anything at this point. "Okay," her voice going from whiny to petulant. Hey, I've got an idea! I bet you have your movies lying around here somewhere. We could watch those." She was excited for the first time in a week, but from his expression, he wasn't too fond of the idea. "Why not?"

"You really are bored," he said, a little self-conscious.

"Oh come on. Do you think I haven't seen them?"

"You have?" He didn't know why that surprised him.

She could feel the heat in her face when she thought about the circumstances under which she'd watched the movies, over and over again, staying up all night and crying in self-pity. But he didn't need to know that. "Of course I did," she said, nonchalant in her response.

"Well . . . ?"

It dawned on her that he was waiting for her verdict. She snuggled up to his chest. He wrapped his arms around her hugging her tight.

"Oh Alex, I loved them." She could feel his body relax. "How could I not? You really are a very talented actor, and you make the most handsome, sexy Jude, Edmund, and Angel in history. Even though I haven't seen *Fitzwilliam Darcy*, I can say without reservation you made the most handsome Darcy ever." She sat back abruptly, startling him. "That's what I'd really love to see. Do you have that one?"

"I'm sure it's here somewhere . . . if that's what you really want . . ."

"Yes. Then I'll be a good girl, and we can take a walk tomorrow."

He kissed the top of her head. "Okay, but first I have to run out. Your concussion obviously hasn't impacted your appetite. We're out of everything in Sarah's basic food groups: Chocolate, berries, cheese, and oh yes, chocolate." He laughed as he walked back into the kitchen.

"What do expect?" she scoffed. "If you take away one pleasure, it must be replaced by another, even if the replacement pales in comparison."

"You're incorrigible," he muttered from the kitchen.

"I heard that."

He grabbed his keys. "I'll be back shortly. Try to rest a little while I'm gone."

She rolled her eyes. Like she could do anything else. "Get some popcorn for the movie."

He blew her a kiss before he closed the door.

She looked around the flat that had become her second home, more so now that she shared it with Alex. She could see herself living here, at least part of the year. Home would be wherever Alex was. They hadn't discussed anything more about their relationship since the day she left the hospital, and she didn't want to bring it up, sensing that he wanted to wait until she was recuperated.

But from her perspective, it was growing, deepening into a full-fledged significant-other kind of relationship. Would it progress to the next steps, whatever those were? She would bide her time, wait until he felt comfortable discussing it.

But she'd meant what she'd said to him about the accident putting things in perspective. She would no longer be afraid—of failure, of change, of love. She would put her heart out there for him, and the spotlight be damned. Furthermore, she would embrace her new career, and face the challenges it would undoubtedly bring.

Thankfully, aside from the day of the accident, the filming hadn't missed a beat. Other than the U.S. shoot, all of Alex's scenes were done. The first unit had wrapped up and was departing for the U.S., where they would begin shooting the final scenes. The second unit was currently in Oxfordshire filming the stunt work, inserts, scenery, and cutaways. The dailies were uploaded to a website each day so that Alex could watch them, keeping everything on schedule.

With clearance from the doctor, she and Alex would fly to Atlanta, the location for the U.S. shoot, at the end of next week. Her headaches were less frequent, and the dizziness was all but gone. Her memory of the events surrounding the accident was still spotty, but pieces were returning. Unfortunately, some of those pieces returned in the form of nightmares, something she hadn't had since she was a child.

She sometimes woke at night in a cold sweat, the smell of smoke sharp in her nose, the sound of the explosions ringing in her ears, and her heart racing in fright. Alex would instinctively roll over, wrapping his arm around her, comforting her even as he slept. She hoped the nightmares would recede soon. She was sure the concussion wasn't the only cause of the overwhelming fatigue she felt each day by late afternoon. She slid down on the sofa to a more comfortable position before drifting off to sleep.

The sound of Alex's keys in the door woke her.

"I'm sorry, did I wake you?" His arms were full of bags. He could have had his assistant take care of the shopping, or had the groceries delivered, but he insisted on doing it himself.

"Yes. But that's okay." She pushed herself up, a little groggy. "If I sleep too long, I won't sleep tonight, and since there's nothing more interesting to do at night, I might as well sleep." Even she winced at her tone of voice. She sounded like an irritable old crone. She probably looked like one too, dressed in an old T-shirt and workout pants, no makeup, her hair a mess. No wonder he wasn't interested.

"Again with the sex," he said from the kitchen where he was putting away the food.

"No, again with the lack thereof," she mumbled. What was wrong with her? You'd think she was a so-called sex addict.

"The only reason I'm showing this to you is because I promised I wouldn't keep anything from you again."

He walked toward her holding out what looked like a tabloid newspaper, the kind you see in the checkout line at the grocery store. "You read these?" she asked, surprised.

"No, but my mother does. Don't ask me why. She called while I was in the shop."

The paper was folded back, his finger pointing to a spot on the page. It looked like a gossip column, aptly named 'The Gossipmonger.' Glancing down the column, trying to figure out why he wanted her to read it, his name and then hers finally jumped out at her:

Romance on the Set?

Is Alex Fraser having an affair with American romance novelist Sarah Edwards? According to a reliable source, the two had what appeared to be a lover's spat on the set of the new movie The American and the Aristocrat *after Sarah caught the charming Fraser in a compromising position with sexy co-star Brooke Bellamy. Following the brief, but passionate, argument, Sarah stormed out of the house. Is the new romance already doomed?*

Sarah was so stunned she didn't notice that she'd dropped the paper to the floor until he bent over to pick it up. Don't panic, she told herself. Spotlight be damned, remember? This presented the first test of her new resolve.

Her eyes were wide as she looked into his angry face. He knelt on the floor beside the sofa. "I am so sorry. I can only guess who leaked this."

"Brooke." They both said it at the same time, his voice angry, hers flat.

He took her cold hands, chaffing them for warmth. "I'm sure there'll be more. Once these piranhas have their teeth in something, they don't let go." His voice was apologetic.

"At least it isn't a headline—"

"Yet. It'll make headlines if they get photos. I'm glad we're leaving for the states next week. I doubt the U.S. tabloids will pick it up since I'm a relative unknown over there."

He looked down at their entwined hands. "Sarah," he whispered her name. "I know how you feel about the spotlight, and I wouldn't blame you if you decided once and for all it's not for you," he finished, his voice gruff with anger and frustration.

"Alex, you remember the sonnet you recited to me in the hospital? 'Love . . . is an ever-fixed mark that looks on tempests and is never shaken.' I've given all of this a lot of thought, and I've decided I can handle it. As long as you're beside me." She continued with a determined smile, "An obnoxious tabloid journalist wannabe can't scare me off. If you can put up with my sometimes-irrational behavior, I can certainly deal with the minor annoyance of having my name in the papers." Before he could speak, she took his face in her hands. "I fell in love with a charming, handsome, sexy, warm, funny, kind man, who also just happens to be a wonderful actor, a very eligible bachelor, and, oh yeah, and according to Robert, reformed playboy. I guess it comes with the territory."

"I love you, Sarah Edwards." His face wore a suggestive grin. "I'd kiss you now, but I'm afraid where that might lead, so I'll settle for this." He kissed the back of her hand before replacing it against his cheek.

CHAPTER 36

"There, I think that's everything." Sarah sighed as she collapsed onto the bed in exhaustion. She'd just finished packing the clothing that would be shipped home. The remainder would go in her checked luggage for her stay in Atlanta.

Aside from short walks around Knightsbridge, it was the most physical activity she'd had in almost two weeks. If packing a couple of suitcases exhausted her, what would an international flight do? she wondered in frustration.

"Are you happy to be going home?" Alex turned from his own luggage to look at her.

"Well, it's not exactly home, but I am looking forward to finishing in Atlanta and getting home to see Becca and Ann. I've really missed them." She'd spoken to them both every day since the accident, texting or emails not enough for them, they had to hear her voice. Not that she minded.

He smiled indulgently. "It must have been very difficult to be away from them all this time. You three are extremely close." He sounded a little envious. He and Robert had had another heated exchange on the phone the day the tabloid article came out.

Sighing, she turned back to her luggage so he couldn't see the concern on her face. As long as Alex remained grist for the gossip rags, Alex's relationship with his brother would be a troubled one.

Attributing her sigh to cabin fever, Alex wrapped his arms around her waist, his lips nuzzled her neck as he whispered in her ear, "How would the invalid like to go on a real outing, not just a walk around the block?"

She spun quickly in his arms. "Really? Where? Oh, it doesn't matter. I think I'd be happy to go just about anywhere at this point." Her words poured out, thwarting any attempt on his part to answer her questions.

He laughed. "How would you like to meet my mother?" he asked a little hesitantly.

Her eyes widened. Meet his mother? Wow. That sounded like one of those next steps. An enormous one. She was torn between excitement and worry. *What if she doesn't like me?* she fretted. *What if they couldn't find anything to talk about?* Of course that was silly. They would have Alex as a popular topic of conversation. She needed to answer him before he recognized her apprehension. "That sounds great." Did that sound plausibly enthusiastic?

"We have a short window of time before she jets off on some other adventure. Besides, I haven't seen her since the spring, and knowing her, if I don't see her now, I might not see her again until next spring. We can drive up to Leeds tomorrow morning and return tomorrow evening."

"Great." She hoped she'd left something in the closet that was suitable for meeting the Countess.

~

*S*arah fidgeted in her seat, unable to get comfortable. If she didn't stop, her clothes were going to look like she'd slept in them by the time she got there. Having been involved in the running of her father's clothing store, Emma, or rather Lady Rutherford, would likely be attentive to clothing details.

Alex chuckled. "Will you please stop worrying? She's going to love you. Besides, we're almost there."

She pulled the visor down once more, anxiously checking her hair and makeup in the mirror for the umpteenth time. Going for a classic look that she thought matched Alex's taste level, she'd pulled her long hair back into a ponytail at the nape of her neck, tied with a paisley silk scarf that complimented the plum of her sleeveless mock turtleneck. She finished off the outfit with a pair of black trousers. Nothing too dull, but nothing too hip either.

"You look beautiful as always." He didn't even take his eyes off the road to look at her. It simply wasn't necessary to make this observation.

They turned onto a wide, tree-lined lane. It was the first time she'd noticed her surroundings, too focused on practicing what she would say when she met Alex's mother to even appreciate the scenery along the way.

"Emma moved from Rutherford to a one-bedroom flat after my brother and I were grown. With all her traveling, she's quite happy with a small home base."

They pulled up in front of an apartment building not unlike those in the States. "Are you ready?" He turned to look at her with an understanding smile. "You look more like you're going to a hanging. Smile."

Apparently her attempt at a smile failed.

"We've got to do something about your acting skills," he muttered as he got out of the car.

Ringing the door buzzer, Alex wrapped his hand around her waist and pulled her close. The door opened momentarily and the woman on the other side was nothing like Sarah had expected. She was about Sarah's height, so it was clear that Alex's height must have come from his father, but when she smiled, Sarah could see Alex's coffee-brown eyes crinkled at the corners and his dimples in her cheeks. She could even see his soft brown wavy hair in her short-cropped locks, now salted with gray, but she was dressed like she was going on an outdoor excursion, complete with hiking shorts, Teva sandals, and T-shirt. Not a stitch of makeup, not an ounce of hairspray. She was . . . earthy.

"You must be Sarah," she said in a softly clipped accent. "Please, come in."

Alex's hand was reassuring on Sarah's back, guiding her into the small entrance.

Emma stepped forward and gave Sarah a motherly hug. "I've heard so much about you from Alex." She stepped away, holding Sarah at arm's length. "You were right," she said, turning to Alex, "she's a stunner."

"Mum, you're embarrassing her," he chided as he kissed her cheek.

"What are mothers for if they can't embarrass their son's girl-friends? I looked like you once, playing the role of countess, but I found that weeks in the wilderness of New Zealand or the canyons of Utah were not conducive to make-up. I simplified my life." She shrugged, indicating her appearance.

Lady Rutherford may have come from the working-class, but her manners were polished and her accent cultured. Neither of which fit her appearance. It finally occurred to Sarah that so far all she'd done was stand there like a mute. Where were her manners?

"Lady Rutherford, it is such a pleasure to meet you. Alex speaks of you often and fondly."

"He's a good son," she said absently as she took Sarah's wrist, pulling her into the small living room. "You must call me Emma." She turned to Alex. "Now go find an occupation so Sarah and I can talk. Sit here." She indicated the sofa, sitting facing Sarah like they were best girlfriends.

Alex smirked at the look of alarm on Sarah's face, his expression apologetic.

"Your brother will be here in an hour—"

"What? Why?" His brows pulled down, and Sarah could see the storm clouds gathering.

She gulped. She wasn't sure if she was ready for another encounter with Alex's brother. Talk about trial by fire: meeting the mother with the disapproving brother looking on.

"There's a silly question. Does he have to have a reason? Are you two fighting again?" she asked, tilting her head to the side in a way that reminded Sarah of Alex. She waived him out of the room, and although he looked a little concerned with leaving Sarah alone with his mother, he did as he was asked.

"Those two . . . they're always fighting over something. As toddlers it was toys, as teenagers it was sports, and as men it's politics, and Alex's career. Opposite ends of the spectrum."

Alex had never been vocal about his politics, but her statement confirmed what she thought: Alex would not vote for his brother.

"My mother-in-law, Lady Clara, has been a very vocal supporter of yours," Emma was very direct in her address. Sarah had no doubt that she would know where she stood with her at the end of their visit. She was sure the same would be true of Robert, politician or not.

"Yes. Lady Clara and I had the opportunity to become well-acquainted last year when I attended classes with her at Christ Church."

"And that's where you and Alex met, at one of his favorite pubs," she said, her face intent. Sarah could see where Alex got his intuition. It felt as if she could read her face as well as he could.

So he'd told her about that. "Yes."

"Now then, Sarah, tell me about yourself."

❧

*A*lex sat in the kitchen then, paced a while, before making a pot of tea and settling at the kitchen table. He looked around the small, but cozy flat. Though she was Countess, his mother wouldn't turn her back on her humbler roots. He respected that. He often thought that's where he got his reticence to play the Earl.

Laughter erupted from the sitting room, relaxing the muscles in his neck that he hadn't realized were knotted. With all the reassurances he'd given Sarah, he'd been nervous as well. He didn't need his mother's approval, but he wanted it just the same.

He and Sarah had some thorny issues to resolve, but resolve them they would. He wanted Sarah in his life, and if that meant moving to the U.S., he would go. If it came to that, he would even consider relinquishing his title to his brother. Although possible, it would be diffi-

279

cult to run the estate from across the Atlantic, and it wouldn't be fair to dump the obligations on Robert without the benefit of the title. He and his brother had their differences, but he loved him, and he knew Robert would manage the affairs brilliantly.

More laughter from the sitting room. What he wouldn't give to know what was being said. He winced as he thought of all the stories Emma could tell of his childhood.

Like the time when he was fifteen, he'd gone skinny-dipping in the stream that ran through the estate, only to be caught by Fletcher's daughter. She'd taken advantage of the situation to seek retribution for putting a frog in her book bag. Confiscating his clothes, she'd stashed them in a known Adder hole nearby before going on her merry way.

Alex hadn't been too fond of snakes, still wasn't for that matter. He'd had to either overcome his fear, however momentarily, in order to regain possession of his clothes, or walk back to the house naked as the day he was born. Encountering the snake had seemed less terrifying than explaining to his grandmother the reason for his state of undress. He'd been forced to confess what had happened, when later that night he'd come down with a nasty case of dermatitis on his nether regions, likely from the euphorbia plant.

Alex looked up as Sarah and his mother joined him in the kitchen.

They'd talked for an hour or more, and Sarah could see the look of relief on Alex's face as they entered the room laughing.

"She's absolutely charming." Emma wrapped her arm around Sarah's waist. "Don't let her get away," she admonished, making Sarah blush.

"I don't plan to."

Sarah blushed even deeper, as he looked up at her from his seat at the table, his eyes fixed on hers, pride and love beaming from his face.

The front door slammed and footsteps thudded down the hall to the kitchen. "Mum?"

"In the kitchen."

Storm clouds gathered over Alex's brow, but he was determined to give his brother the benefit of the doubt. Although they'd argued over the recent article, he was grateful for his brother's help in finding Sarah in the chaos following the train accident.

Robert strode into the kitchen, stopping to buss his mother's cheek. "Hello, Mum. Sarah." He nodded briefly, then walked over to Alex and handed him a stack of newspapers. "Have you seen these?"

Alex tensed for a fight. "No. Remember, I don't read them."

"Well, you and Sarah are a hot item. I just thought you should know so you can take precautions for Sarah's sake."

Alex frowned. He had no idea what the articles said, but this was not the attitude he'd expected from his brother.

Sarah glanced at Alex, her face confused and wary. He opened his arm to her, and she joined him at the table.

"Sarah and I can handle it. But thank you for the warning."

Emma appeared just as confused by Robert's calm demeanor and apparent concern for Sarah, as Alex and Sarah were.

"How about a beer, Alex?" Robert walked over to the refrigerator, and without waiting for a reply, pulled out three beers, offering one to Sarah.

Sarah and Alex took what amounted to the proverbial olive branch from Robert.

Emma looked at her two sons, and then at Sarah. She didn't know if Sarah had precipitated this change, but she was pleased to see her boys getting along for a change.

⁓

*T*abloid newspapers, courtesy of Robert, were scattered around Sarah on the bed. She couldn't believe what they said. Privacy was a thing of the past, and anyone who thinks their private life is private needs to wake-up to reality. Alex was right. Once they got their teeth in a story, they didn't let go. Now she was shacking up with him.

Shacking up? Is American author Sarah Edwards living with Alex Fraser, Lord Rutherford? Edwards, who was one of those injured on the tube in last week's accident has reportedly been staying with Fraser in his London flat. I don't know about you, ladies, but I'd love to play doctor with the charming, sexy Fraser.

In another column, her time last year with Alex was revisited, as well as the fact that he was her inspiration for Christen:

The Gossipmonger has just learned that the Fraser/Edwards romance may have bloomed long before their meeting on the set. A source has come forward stating that she saw Fraser skulking out of a popular Oxford inn in the wee hours of the morning last August. We have it on good authority that Edwards was a guest at that very inn on the same date. Was she the mystery woman in the Port Meadow Picnic? I guess the cat's out of the bag now.

There is also some speculation that Fraser was the inspiration for the hottie Christen Hare in the upcoming movie The American and the Aristocrat, *based on Edwards' book. Anyone who's read the book can see that they're a dead ringer for one another? Hello? No wonder Fraser is perfect for the part! It was written for him. Sarah, you sly girl.*

She shuddered to think what else would be written about them. Aside from the exaggerated first story, the others were all true, so it wasn't like she or Alex could claim defamation. It was good that they were flying to Atlanta tomorrow. Maybe in their absence the papers would lose interest. Out of sight, out of mind.

"Why are you reading that rubbish?" Alex stood in the doorway wearing nothing but his shorts, leaning against the doorjamb with his arms folded across his bare chest, his hair damp from the shower.

Her righteous indignation over the gossip column fled, replaced by something infinitely more desirable. All she saw was him. He sauntered over to the bed. It had been too long. She wasn't taking no for an answer tonight.

She tossed the tabloids aside then, rose to her knees on the bed in front of him, wrapping her arms around his neck, her silky nightgown the only barrier between them. He smelled of cinnamon and citrus, and his own unique male scent.

He gave her a questioning look.

"Do you know what tonight is?" At his confused expression, she said, "It's been exactly two weeks since I came home from the hospital. Do you know what that means?"

"I'm sure you're going to enlighten me." He wore a provocative grin as he wrapped his arms around her waist drawing her closer.

She sighed with pleasure at the unyielding contact.

"I can return to . . . rigorous activity." She pulled his lips down to hers, taking his bottom lip between her teeth.

"And what type of rigorous activity did you have in mind?" he asked against her mouth.

"Hmm. I thought maybe a brisk run through the park . . ." Her fingers threaded in his hair, holding his mouth to hers.

"That's too bad. I was hoping you had something a little more . . . amorous in mind." The scent and taste of her assaulted his senses. Two weeks of restraint with her in close proximity had been sheer torture. Tasting her now was akin to a parched man getting his first sip of cool water. It only made him want more. Sliding the thin strap of her nightgown off her shoulder, he kissed his way down her neck to her collarbone.

Her breath shortened to shallow gasps, her pulse thickened, as the familiar warmth curled in her belly.

Lifting her off her knees, he gently pressed her back onto the bed, his free arm swiping the discarded newspapers from the bed, sending them fluttering to the floor.

"Well, I suppose this qualifies as an aerobic activity," she murmured.

"Very aerobic."

"Robert was very pleasant, even charming, this evening."

"Yes, maybe those anger management classes are paying off," Alex said, tongue firmly in cheek.

"Well, maybe he should focus more on anger management and less on your love life," she said with disapproval.

Alex chuckled. "Perhaps you're right. Maybe he should consider hiring you as his political advisor."

Lying in bed, luxuriating in the feel of their entangled bodies, they recounted the evening's odd turn of events.

Alex's fingers ran down her spine as if he were stroking a cat. It wouldn't have surprised her if she'd started purring.

By the end of the evening, he and Robert were sitting at the kitchen table laughing and joking over a beer, regaling Sarah with stories of their tumultuous childhood relationship. Emma looked on the whole scene with an affectionate smile. Robert was a gifted story-teller, a gift of gab being an important characteristic in a successful lawmaker. Sarah had finally learned the story behind the rugby grudge.

When Robert and Alex were teenagers, the two had been playing rugby on opposing teams, with Alex's team ahead. Alex was running with the ball when Robert hit him with an illegal elbow to the chin, busting open a gash. The wound required stitches. Robert had admitted to Sarah that he was a sore loser, especially when it came to losing to his big brother.

Sarah and Alex were content to lie in each other's arms for a time, each lost in their own thoughts.

Sarah's giggle broke the silence. "Been skinny-dipping lately?"

"She didn't!"

"Oh, yes she did!"

Alex groaned, as he put a hand up to cover his face. "Did she tell you . . . everything?"

"Poor Alex. What a terrible place to have a rash. Let me see," she said, as she lifted the sheet. "Did it leave any scars?"

"Come here, you saucy minx." He rolled over, pulling her underneath him, promptly ending any further conversation.

CHAPTER 37

As Sarah waited for Michael to instruct the actors and crew, she asked herself why she'd written such a romantic final scene. She couldn't have ended with a handshake? Thank God she hadn't written a sex scene! Note to self: Any future books where Alex may cast himself as the hero will have no sex scenes. Strictly PG.

The location manager had found a cozy little 1920s bungalow in Berkeley Park, a lovely neighborhood just west of mid-town Atlanta, to serve as Aunt Millie's house.

Christen comes to Atlanta in search of Amelia and finds her living in her aunt's modest house, despite having inherited over two million dollars. The exterior scene where Christen unexpectedly appears at Amelia's door had already been shot, and the crew had moved into the tiny living room.

Brooke, Alex, and Sarah had managed to reduce the tension to a low hum, but Sarah wasn't sure which of them, Alex or herself, had it worse: while he had to act like he loved her, Sarah had to watch while he kissed her.

"Okay, let's block the scene." Michael took his seat next to Sarah's. "Brooke, you walk into the room stopping in front of the sofa and turn to face Alex. Alex, you follow Brooke, hesitating in the doorway, then you make up your mind to tell her that you love her, and persuade her she loves you, whether she wants to admit it or not."

Brooke and Alex followed Michael's direction, but in place of their lines, Brooke asked, "Alex, do you think you can play this scene convincingly?"

"Brooke, I'll play my role with consummate professionalism, and everyone who watches will believe I'm totally captivated by you, but make no mistake, I'll detest every minute of it," he growled.

Their expressions and body language were at odds with their words. If this were a silent film, the audience would think they were confessing their undying love for one another.

"Okay. Let's roll," Michael instructed.

This was followed by the assistant director's instructions. "Quiet everyone. Roll sound. Roll camera."

Amelia, pain and confusion on her face: "Christen, I don't understand why you're here. We can't possibly have anything more to say to one another—"

Christen, approaching Amelia with determination: "I beg to differ. I think we have a great deal to say to one another—"

Amelia: "Did you fly all the way to Atlanta to berate me for my despicable behavior toward Lady Victoria? If so, save your breath. I know I was horribly rude and conveyed my apologies in a letter to be given to her by Margaret, although I'd understand if Lady Victoria refused it." Amelia turns her back on Christen.

Christen walks up behind her, placing his hands on her shoulders: "Amelia." He whispers her name. "I didn't come to berate you. Quite the contrary." He turns her to face him, placing his hands on either side of her face. "I came to make you believe that I'm in love with you, notwithstanding what Charles led you to believe. I've been in love with you from the moment you called me a pompous, condescending blue-blood and I pointed out that pompous and condescending were redundant." Christen smiles.

Amelia is speechless.

Christen, still smiling: "Apparently I've discovered how to leave you speechless. All I have to do is say 'I love you.' I'll have to remember that when we next argue."

Amelia recovers her capacity for speech: "You're taking a great deal for granted, aren't you? I haven't declared my feelings for you—"

Christen, complacently: "Oh, there's no need. You love me, too."

Amelia, shaking her head: "Arrogant to the last—"

Christen cuts off her words with a kiss. She puts her arms around his neck. He pulls back. "I love you, Amelia Hampton."

Amelia jumps up, wrapping her legs around his waist, exactly the type of behavior Christen would have abhorred before. Instead of chiding her, he places his hands under her bottom, laughing and spinning her around. She pulls his face to hers and they kiss.

"Cut. Print. Great job."

Breathe. At least that take was done. Knowing Michael, only twenty more to go. Sarah's relief was short-lived, however. As she looked on, Brooke's legs were still wrapped around Alex's waist, her lips still pressed to his. She knew Brooke was only doing it to aggravate her, but it rankled nonetheless.

"Brooke," Alex spoke against her mouth, "if I wasn't a gentleman, I'd drop you on your despicable little ass. Now let go before I forget my manners."

"Oh, did Michael say 'cut?' I guess I didn't hear him." She dropped her legs from his waist, and stepped back, wearing a smug expression on her pretty face.

Sarah groaned. This was going to be a long day.

~

"How do you do it?" At his confused expression, Sarah continued, "Make people believe you're madly in love with someone you actually despise?"

They were finishing a light dinner in their hotel suite. After the tabloid articles, there was no point in pretending their relationship was a secret, plus Sarah was sure Brooke had already enlightened everyone.

It was after midnight, late to be eating, but they didn't wrap up until after ten, the goal being to finish the principal photography today, four months to the day they started filming.

"It's what I do. How do you conjure beautiful, complex characters out of thin air, or create breathtaking settings with words? We have both found our calling, and when that happens, we often exceed our own expectations. You're willing to do the hard things in order to perfect your craft."

"But what I do seems easy by comparison. My work is solitary. I don't have to deal with troublesome people on a daily basis."

"Mind over matter I guess." He shrugged, taking a sip of his Southern iced tea, something he'd recently discovered in Atlanta. "You remember the actress who played Fanny Price? She reeked of garlic every day." He made a face wrinkling his nose.

"Ooh." Sarah made a similar face. "Yet you made me, and millions of others believe that you, or rather Edmund, were in love with her."

"Well, I'm not sure about millions, but there you have it, mind over matter, or in that case mind over odor."

They both chuckled.

"Should I be concerned that it's mind over matter with me?" Sarah said it teasingly, but a part of her was serious.

"Sarah, I could never be anything but myself around you." He reached across the table and took her hand, rubbing his thumb across her knuckles. "It's inescapable. When I tried to act angry around you, I failed. I couldn't sustain an emotion that was contrary to my actual feelings. After all day pretending emotions I don't really feel, being myself with you is . . . liberating." His eyes held hers. "No. I cannot act with you. It is always undeniably real."

CHAPTER 38

The movie, as they say, was 'in the can.' Of course, that phrase was no longer technically correct, since production companies no longer use celluloid, but Sarah thought it was fun to say, nonetheless. Post-production, including film and sound editing, sound and visual effects, and musical score, would begin next week.

Alex was flying out to California for a couple of weeks to work with Michael, the editors, and other members of the post-production team. Although she'd like to go as well, after four months away, she needed to go home and relieve Ann and Becca from their caretaker duties.

Alex would be back in time for Thanksgiving, his first taste of the American tradition, and Sarah wanted to make it extra special. With her family, as well as Ann's joining them for the celebration, she had her work cut out for her.

Sitting at the vanity, putting the finishing touches on her appearance, Alex walked up behind her and moving her hair aside, placed a kiss on her neck below her ear.

"I don't believe I tell you enough just how beautiful you are." His warm eyes met hers in the mirror. "I also believe I've been remiss in my gift-giving. The only gift you've ever received from me is that dodgy Jane Austen cross. It's time to rectify that."

From his fingers dropped a gorgeous dime-sized topaz pendant set in gold filigree. The exquisite gem swung from his hand, catching the light, flashing bronze, then gold, then amber. Sarah was dumbfounded as he unfastened the clasp and wrapped the delicate chain around her neck. It felt warm against her skin as it nestled in the hollow at her throat. She raised her fingers to touch the golden stone, tears welling in her eyes.

"Careful Sarah, you'll spoil your makeup." His face, which wore one of his brilliant smiles, was next to hers in the mirror. "Do you like it?" he whispered.

Sarah turned to kiss him, wrapping her hands around his neck, threading her fingers in his hair. He pulled her up from the chair, and turned her in his arms, kissing her so passionately that if it weren't for his arms around her, she thought she would lose her balance.

"I take it that's a yes," he murmured against her lips. He reluctantly withdrew. "You keep kissing me like that we'll miss the wrap up party." In keeping with tradition, Alex, as the producer, was holding a party for the cast and crew to celebrate the completion of the production phase.

"We can be a little late," she murmured as she pulled his lips back to hers. Much to her dismay, he retreated again, leaving his hands on either side of her neck.

"Sarah, it would be a shame to waste your *toilette*." He stepped back, dropping his hands from her neck, giving her an appreciative look. "You look stunning. I'll be the envy of everyone, but I have especially high hopes of galling Michael." He grinned mischievously. "At least allow me a few hours to flaunt it."

"If you insist we go," she said with a mock sigh. "I suppose as the host, you should make an appearance. After all, we wouldn't want to damage your reputation."

She checked her appearance in the mirror again. The topaz winked in the light. It was stunning in itself, but with her bronze chiffon dress, it was magnificent. That's when it dawned on her. "Is this why you insisted I buy this dress?" she asked as she turned from the mirror to face him, her eyebrow lifted.

"Guilty," he said, lifting his hands as if in surrender. "But, in my defense, that isn't the only reason." He took her hand and twirled her around so that the knee-length chiffon skirt floated out like a chocolate cloud. "It fits like it was made for you, and the color on you is dazzling."

"Alex, you really are too much. You keep offering such effusive praise I'll begin to believe it."

"I sincerely hope so, madam." He took her hand, and tucking it into the crook of his arm, escorted her out of the room.

～

The party, which was held in one of the hotel's smaller ballrooms, was in full swing, and true to form, the cast and crew were animated. The wine and champagne were flowing freely, with the volume of laughter rising in proportion to the amount of alcohol consumed.

As a waitress walked by with another tray of champagne, Alex took two glasses, handing one to Sarah. "Drink up, Sarah. This is a cause for celebration . . . your first book, your first movie." He raised his glass in a toast. "I'm so proud of you."

She raised the glass to her lips. She didn't need an excuse to drink champagne, this being her third glass. But who's counting. "Why Lord Rutherford, if I didn't know better, I'd say you were trying to get me drunk and take advantage of me," she said, mimicking the Southern accent of her ancestors and flirting in her best imitation of Scarlett O'Hara.

"On the contrary, Ms. Edwards, I prefer you in possession of all your senses when I take you to bed." He leveled a steamy gaze at her, reminiscent of Rhett Butler.

Oh. Her mouth formed the word, but nothing came out.

"The real celebration doesn't begin until we leave the party," he whispered seductively in her ear.

She shivered in response.

He flashed her his provocative smile. "Ponder that while I make a toast."

He stepped to the front of the room and clinking his glass with his Christ Church ring, miraculously gained the attention of the boisterous group. He was so handsome, so poised, commanding attention with little fanfare.

"Ladies and gentlemen . . . there are a few gentlemen here, I believe—"

"Very few," someone interjected to everyone's amusement, including Alex's.

"I want to take this opportunity to thank each and every one of you for your hard work and tireless dedication to this film. In my mind," he continued, "you are the best cast and crew with whom I've ever had the pleasure of working. This project was flawless, on schedule, and on budget. For that, I salute you." He raised his glass to the room and everyone drank.

"I would also like to thank Michael for his gifted directing. He captured the essence of the story in a way few could. Michael." Again, he raised his glass in toast, nodding his head in Michael's direction.

The room erupted in applause while Michael took a brief bow.

Alex turned to look at Brooke. "Brooke, what can I say, except that you're a brilliant actress?"

She preened at his words.

Sarah was hopeful that she was the only one who recognized the double entendre in Alex's words, having said them herself in her emails to Ann and Becca.

"I have no doubt you will go far in your career, and that we will see you on the silver screen for years to come."

Again, everyone drank a toast.

Yep, Sarah thought wickedly, especially if she sleeps with her directors.

"Finally, to the woman without whom this project would not have existed." He turned to Sarah, glass raised, eyes sparkling. "Thank you for writing this brilliant novel and for creating characters that will live on among those in other great works of literature. I love you, sweet Sarah." His eyes held hers as everyone sipped their drink, before draining his own glass.

Sarah was embarrassed over the attention, but she raised her glass to his generous praise, mouthing the words 'I love you' in response.

He set the glass down on a table as he made his way through the crowded room toward her, moving gracefully among the throng. When he reached her, he removed the glass from her hand placing it on the table behind her. "Come Sarah, it's time for our private cele-bration." Taking her wrist, he pulled her willingly from the room.

CHAPTER 39

After two weeks at home, Sarah's to-do list was still as long as the Florida Peninsula, and with Alex arriving tomorrow, she was running out of time. Car keys in hand, she was on her way out when the doorbell rang. Muttering something about timing, she yanked open the door, ready to give who she assumed was Ann a piece of her mind.

"Adrian!" She stepped back in surprise. She hadn't seen or heard from him since their divorce almost two years ago. He looked like hell.

"Hi, Sarah." He dragged his hand through his uncharacteristically unkempt hair. She'd never seen the polished Adrian Mills looking so . . . disheveled. "Can I come in?"

She hesitated. What on earth could he possibly want? But curiosity got the better of her. She held the door wider, indicating he could come in. "Sure."

He paced the foyer, unsure where to go. "You look like you could use a cup of coffee," she said, indicating the direction of the kitchen.

"So this is what the divorce settlement bought?" he said as he looked around. "Nice house."

"Thanks." She put the coffee on. "Adrian, you clearly didn't just drop by to see how I was living. So let's have it. Why are you here?"

He paced again. "Sarah . . . I did want to see you again . . . I've been thinking about you a great deal lately."

"What does your lovely wife think about your . . . preoccupation?" She raised a brow in disdain.

His face hardened. The beautiful surgeon's hand combed through his hair again. One corner of his mouth turned up into what could only be called an ironic smile. "My lovely wife is having an affair."

Sarah struggled not to crack the same ironic smile. "This is what some would call poetic justice." Did she say that out loud? "Hurts, doesn't it?"

"Yes . . . I guess I deserve that," he said, taking the proffered cup of coffee. Black and robust, the way he liked it.

"No wonder you look like hell."

"Well, that and a fourteen-hour surgery I just finished."

"Adrian. That still doesn't tell me why you're here. Did you come looking for a marriage counselor, a sympathetic ear, what?"

"I don't know." He turned his back to her, his voice barely audible. "I just knew I had to see you again. My car seemed to head in this direction of its own volition. I didn't even know which house was yours—I just guessed."

Sarah was tired of trying to pry his motivation out of him, so she just waited.

"I guess I came to apologize . . . for everything. The lies, the arrogance, the affairs, the way I treated you."

She couldn't help the cynicism that crept into her voice, "The good doctor got a taste of his own bitter medicine and had an epiphany."

He turned to look at her again, only there was pain in his pale blue eyes.

"Water under the bridge, Adrian." She shrugged.

He strode over to her. "Is it?"

She backed up against the counter and froze as he raised his hand to cup her face. She saw it coming but couldn't get out of the way. He pulled her roughly to him and kissed her, his lips hard and demanding, tasting of strong coffee.

She tried to push him away, but the harder she pushed, the tighter he held her. His lips crushed hers, as if he were taking out his anger and frustration with the two-timing Cheese on her. When his other hand slid up her ribcage to grope her, she bit him. Hard. And to her satisfaction, tasted blood.

"Ow!" His hand came up to his now-bleeding lower lip. "Goddammit!" He stepped back.

"How dare you!" Sarah moved around the other side of the island, putting it between them. "How dare you think you could assuage your bruised ego by attempting to seduce me!"

"Ow." He dampened a paper towel and held it to his lip, seemingly oblivious to her rant. "Damn, Sarah. Did you have to bite me so hard? I think I may need stitches."

"Then it's a good thing you're a surgeon. You can stitch it up yourself. Now get out!" she ground out, wielding a plastic spatula like it was Excalibur.

That's when he laughed. A deep-belly laugh that had him doubled over, and had her feeling ridiculous.

"Oh God, Sarah. I'm so sorry. Sorry for the kiss, sorry I made you feel you had to defend your honor with a . . . deadly spatula." He held up his hands as if in surrender then, turned, leaning against the counter with his head in his hands. "The trouble is, I love her, and I don't know what to do." His laughter was gone, and in its place was the voice of a man whose heart was breaking.

"Adrian . . . I'm confused as to why you came here, but if you came looking for advice . . . I don't have much to give, other than to say that if you truly love her, you'll find a way to work this out . . . confront her, forgive her, give her a second chance."

"You never gave me a second chance . . ."

"I don't think I ever really loved you."

"Ouch. Just kick a man when he's down."

"I didn't say that to hurt you. It's just the unvarnished truth. And I don't think you ever really loved me, either. It took me a long time to realize that, and even longer to accept it. Without that love, relationships can't overcome the inevitable bumps in the road."

"Sarah, you were always more than I deserved. I mean that. I hope you will forgive me."

"I'd forgiven you long before I knew it. Now, how about some ice for that lip?"

~

It felt good to clear the air. She could put the past behind her without any regrets, and that could only benefit her relationship with Alex. Adrian had stayed for a couple of hours, nursing his lip, catching up on news. He was proud of what she'd accomplished, and happy to hear about Alex. When they parted, it was as cautious friends, but friends nonetheless.

CHAPTER 40

"Welcome to my home," Sarah said as she opened the door. She was a little nervous, a ridiculous reaction.

Alex stepped through the front door, setting his luggage down and looking around. He first walked into her office and then crossed the foyer to enter the dining room. "It's so . . . you. Elegant, tasteful, and warm. I love it, and I love you, Sarah. Airport greetings leave something to be desired." He grabbed the front waistband of her jeans and drew her to him. "Come here and let me give you a proper improper greeting." He wrapped his hands around her neck and lowered his mouth to hers.

She hungrily returned the kiss, as he groaned and pulled her tighter against his body.

"Oh God, Sarah, how I've missed you. Let's not do that again."

Alex had been in California two and a half weeks, the longest they'd been apart since their reunion in July.

Before she could respond, he threw her over his shoulder like a conquering hero with his spoils and carried her up the stairs. "I assume your bedroom is up here?" He turned left at the top of the stairs as if he knew which room was hers.

Sarah giggled like a smitten teenager as he tossed her onto the big four-poster bed. "Why, Mr. Fraser, it's the middle of the afternoon," she teased.

"All the better to see you, my dear," he said, grinning wickedly. But as soon as he removed his T-shirt and crawled across the bed toward her, all playfulness fled. The desire in his eyes scorched her skin like flames licking her body. He lowered his body to hers, nuzzling her neck, unbuttoning her blouse, his warm hands on her skin inflaming the passion.

He grabbed her wrists, cuffing them above her head. "Let me." With each button he opened, he placed a kiss on the newly exposed skin. "I want to worship you."

Gasping, Sarah arched her back to his caresses, reveling in his desire.

When her blouse lay open, he grazed his lips back up her body to nuzzle her neck and nibble her ear. "Sweet, sweet, Sarah, how I want you. All of you, heart, mind, body and soul. I'll always want you," he murmured against her skin. He lifted his face to hers. The love she heard in his voice was reflected in his deep brown eyes.

"I'm yours. Take all of me," she whispered.

He lowered his lips to hers and the lonely weeks apart were all but forgotten in breathy sighs and throaty moans.

~

*S*tepping out of the shower, Sarah heard Alex answer her phone. She smiled to herself. There was something homey and comforting about it.

"This is Alex. Who the hell is this?" He paused for conversation on the other end of the line. She stepped out of the bathroom in time to see anger and surprise register on his face.

"Alex, who is it?"

"It's Adrian." He stalked over and thrust the phone at her as if he would have preferred to throw it.

"Oh." Taking the phone, she watched as he walked over to the window, turning his back to her. "Hi Adrian—"

"Yes. That's great news. I'm glad it was all just a misunderstanding—"

"Adrian, can I call you back later?"

"Yeah, that would be good. Thanks. Bye."

Alex still had his back to her. "Your ex-husband came by yesterday? When were you planning on telling me?"

"I didn't exactly get the chance. What was I supposed to do? Hi Alex, welcome to my home, and oh, by the way, my ex-husband dropped by yesterday?"

"Christ, Sarah." He turned to face her, his brows drawn down in anger. "It would have been better to have heard it from you than to have heard it from him. Do you mind telling me what his visit and that phone call were all about?"

"He came by because he was at the hospital and wanted to talk to me about . . . his wife."

"Bloody hell. He doesn't have any contact with you for almost two years, and he shows up on your doorstep to talk to you about his wife? I don't buy it."

"His wife is cheating on him, or at least he thought she was, and he came looking for advice—"

"From the ex-wife he cheated on? No. I'll tell you what he came looking for, what he came hoping to find, a warm and sympathetic woman willing to repair his wounded self-esteem."

She could feel the blood drain from her face. How did he do that? How did he cut through the noise to find the truth?

"I'm right, aren't I?" He strode over to her and put his hands on her shoulders. "Did he . . ."

The blood that had previously drained from her face flooded her cheeks. "He . . . he kissed me—"

He dropped his hands from her shoulders as if they'd been burned. He was having an out-of-body experience. He knew his reaction was completely ridiculous, but he couldn't get a grip on these alien emotions.

"But that's it. I, I bit him before he could—"

"I'll kill him." Alex didn't hear anything else she said. He paced and ranted.

She hadn't seen him this angry since his brother all but called her a tart. She remembered the result and swallowed hard. Alex darted out the bedroom door and down the stairs, grabbing her keys off the table, before stalking to the front door.

"Where are you going?" She could barely get the words out over the congealed lump in her throat.

"To find Adrian." He slammed the front door before she could stop him.

~

Sarah paced the floor, still wearing her robe, her wet hair dripping, wondering what she should do. Call the police? Call Adrian? Call Ann and Becca? Instead, she called Alex's cell, and heard it ringing in the bedroom upstairs. Great.

She paced down the floor following the same path. Okay. She didn't want to call the police. She didn't want to get Alex picked up. But thinking about his altercation with his brother, she wondered if that wasn't better than him getting arrested for assault and battery. Then she realized the police wouldn't pick him up for just making a threat.

She paced up the floor again. She'd call Adrian. No. Why get him riled? Odds are Alex will never find Adrian in the first place. Even if he knew the city, Adrian's address is unlisted. Adrian should be safe.

Shoving her hair out of her face, she paced the floor again. Maybe she should call Ann or Becca. She groaned. That wouldn't help. The only thing that would accomplish is having two more people pacing the floor.

Maybe she should try looking for him? Since he didn't know the city, how far could he get? Then she remembered he had her car. "Ugh," she huffed out in frustration.

She collapsed onto the bottom step. The best course of action was to wait, but for what? Alex's call from the police station? She had to hope that Alex would calm down, that the drive would clear his head, and that he would have the presence of mind to pull over and call her when that happened.

~

It took Alex about half an hour to work off the mad, and another fifteen minutes to realize he was lost. What the hell had he been thinking? He had no idea where Adrian lived, no clue how to get around the city, and now no idea how to get back to Sarah's. And, he just realized, no mobile. "Bloody hell."

He pulled into a parking lot and shut off the car. Okay, he thought, I can do this. I have Sarah's address, I can ask someone, or buy a map, or . . . something. But first, he needed to figure out what had triggered such a colossal meltdown. He'd always prided himself on his ability to control his temper, except, of course, where his brother was concerned. He'd become acquainted with the uncomfortable emotion of jealousy when he'd witnessed Michael's attentions to Sarah. But his reaction today was the equivalent of jealousy on steroids. What was it about this situation that so enraged him?

He knew Sarah loved him. And of course he trusted her. He didn't trust Adrian, especially given the underhanded purpose for his visit. The man cheats on Sarah. Then when his new wife cheats on him, or so he thinks, he decides to cheat on her with the woman he cheated on in the first place!

His head hurt just thinking about it.

If he was honest with himself, it annoyed him that Sarah would have anything to do with him after what he'd done to her. In the end, he supposed that was her decision. He'd respect it. But it didn't mean he had to like it.

~

*A*fter two long hours of pacing, crying, worrying, and caffeinating, Sarah heard a knock on the front door.

"Alex?" She ran to the foyer.

Wrenching the door open, she found a police officer, with a chagrinned Alex standing next to him, hair disheveled more than usual. "Ma'am, does he belong to you?"

"Yes," she said, confused, and not a little worried.

"If he has a tendency to get lost, you might want to consider micro-chipping him," Officer Friendly returned, tongue clearly in his cheek. "Had a yellow lab who wandered frequently. Worked like a charm for her."

"Thanks," Sarah said, taking Alex's arm and pulling him into the house. "I might just do that. Good night."

Head down, hands in his pockets, Alex said, "I'd have been back sooner, but I got a little lost. And I didn't have my mobile. Am I still welcome?"

"Oh Alex. Like you have to ask." She wrapped her arms around his waist and laid her head on his chest. "I've been so worried." Just as he wrapped his arms around her, she shoved him away from her. "Alex Fraser, Earl or not, don't you ever do that to me again. What the hell was that about?"

He ran his hands through his hair. "I don't know . . . other than Michael's fruitless advances to you, I've never been a jealous man, but then again, I never had reason to be." He pulled her close again. "No one has ever meant so much to me. The thought of another man, especially your ex-husband, putting his hands on you, kissing you . . . against your will, well I just . . . cracked. It was a powerful emotion for me. Clearly, I didn't have the intellectual or emotional tools to handle it."

Pulling away, she said, "I guess I should be a little flattered, but right now I'm just emotionally drained." She sat down on the bottom step, where she'd kept her vigil when she wasn't pacing.

He hesitated and then sat next to her, his elbows resting on his knees. He looked up at her. "Sarah, I am mortified by my conduct, and deeply sorry for causing you any pain or worry. Can you forgive me?"

She leaned over and kissed him, nibbling at the corner of his mouth. "Yes. I guess you're entitled to a meltdown every now and then, especially if you're going to keep up with me."

The corners of his mouth turned up. "Tell me, have you forgiven him?"

"Yes. I have. What's done is done. And if you think about it, if he'd never been such a louse, I'd never have met you." She considered it a moment, "So, in a way, maybe I should thank him." She tilted her head and shrugged.

He hadn't thought of it like that. Maybe he should find him and . . . no, he couldn't thank Adrian. That was asking too much.

"Now come," Sarah held out her hand, "let me show you just how much I forgive you."

They turned to climb the stairs. "So, you bit him . . ."

"Uh-huh. I made him bleed."

"Good." Then he winced. "Remind me never to piss you off while I'm kissing you."

CHAPTER 41

"Don't cry, Sarah. It'll be all right," Alex said with mock concern.

Sarah sniffed again, and he laughed. "Here, let me do that."

Tears ran down her face from cutting onions for the dressing for tomorrow's Thanksgiving dinner.

He took the knife from her hand and using his hip, bumped her aside.

The kitchen was fragrant with a combination of pungent chopped onions and the smell of nutmeg, cinnamon, and cloves from the pumpkin pies that were already baking in the oven.

The huge bird was thawing, the fresh cranberry chutney was chilling in the fridge, and the vegetable chopping was underway. Two pecan pies stood ready for the oven as soon as the pumpkin pies were done.

Tomorrow Sarah would prepare the turkey, of course, and home-made biscuits, dressing, giblet gravy, green beans, and sweet potato soufflé. A true Southern Thanksgiving, of which her mother would have been proud.

"How many people are you feeding tomorrow? It better be the

whole neighborhood, considering the amount of food here." He shook his head at her excesses.

It was true. She was making enough food to feed an army. "Overeating on Thanksgiving to the point that you can only lie on the couch and groan while you watch football is an American tradition dating back to the Pilgrims. Okay, well maybe not to the Pilgrims." She wiped her watery eyes with the back of her hand. "I want you to get the full effect," she said, then giggled at her pun.

Standing at the island, a dishtowel thrown over his shoulder, he chopped the onions and celery like an expert. Tilting her head, recalling his skills in the kitchen in his flat, she asked, "How is it the Earl of Rutherford knows his way around a kitchen so well?"

He chuckled, the knife slicing deftly through the celery. "You've seen the flat. Not exactly the kind of place for a bevy of servants. I needed to take care of my own nourishment. But it started when I was a little boy, visiting Rutherford's kitchen where Mrs. Watson would bake cookies."

He wiped his hands on the towel and braced his hands on the island. "Like Pavlov's dog and the bell, I learned quickly that if I helped her with the baking, I got to lick the bowl." He grinned. "Before I knew it, she was teaching me other skills. By the time I figured it out, I realized I was enjoying myself." Picking up the cutting board, he scraped the diced celery into a bowl. "It paid off."

"You're just full of surprises." She turned to check on the pies. "I think I'm beginning to like surprises."

She liked the feel of her home with him here. She'd always been content in her home, but with his presence, a different feeling settled over her, something more than contentment, something she hadn't felt in a very long time: bliss; pure, unadulterated bliss. It permeated everything she did. Even the most mundane tasks were pleasant.

His previous meltdown was history, especially after the best make-up sex she'd ever had. They'd also ironed out the Adrian issue, whose wife was not cheating on him after all. It had all been a terrible misunderstanding. The man he thought she was seeing was actually an exotic car dealer. Turns out she was buying him a lovely little Alfa

Romeo for his birthday—with his money of course, since she'd promptly quit her job after marrying him.

That morning, Alex had helped Sarah water the garden and cut camellias for tomorrow's table arrangements. Before they could complete the task, he'd pulled her beneath a secluded, vine-covered trellis, slipping his damp hands beneath her shirt at her waist, making her squeal when his cold hands brushed her warm skin. The squeal quickly turned into a sigh once he started kissing her. This encounter led to a detour to the living room floor, the closest thing to privacy they could find in their haste. After all, they wouldn't want to shock Mr. Waters, her elderly widower neighbor.

"Sarah. What are you thinking about?"

She could hear Alex scraping vegetables from the cutting board. She realized she had stopped scrubbing the pot she held over the sink. Glad her back was to him so he couldn't see her blush, she used the one niggling factor that invaded her bliss as an excuse for her distraction.

"Are you nervous about tomorrow . . . I mean, about meeting my family and friends?"

"Should I be?" he asked, as his eyebrows shot up. "After all, I've spoken to Ann and Becca on the phone, and you've told me so much about them, it's not like we're total strangers."

"But you haven't met Mark and Rob, and of course the Admiral. Since . . ." she turned back to the sink, "well, they can be pretty protective of me." They'd been spitting mad at Adrian when they'd found out about his affair.

Wiping his hands on the towel, he crossed the kitchen to stand behind her and wrapped his arms around her waist, placing his chin on her shoulder. "Sarah, of course I want them to like me, but there's not much I can do about it either way. It's you I love, and it's you I want to make happy." He kissed her shoulder.

"You seem nervous enough for both of us anyway," he chuckled, turning her around to face him. "What's next, chef?"

"Um, can you put the eggs on to boil?"

"Yes, ma'am." He managed to mimic a Southern accent quite well. He kissed her nose before going to do her bidding.

She turned back to the dishes in the sink. "Alex?"

"Yes."

She hesitated, biting her lower lip. "I've been wondering . . ."

"What have you been wondering, love?"

"Well, it takes a large sum of money to produce a film, right?

"Yes, but one can also find other backers, so that the entire financial burden doesn't fall on one person. Of course, the producer is responsible for making sure the production doesn't come in at a loss to the financial partners."

"Is that what you did, had financial partners I mean?"

"Sarah, what are you dancing around?"

With a little more dancing on her part, she said, "Well, acting pays well I suppose, and the estate . . ." She didn't know what else to say about that, since she had no idea how that worked. "But the movie, the apartment, the car . . . those things add up, and well, I don't want you spending extravagantly on me. Those things aren't important to me." She shrugged, thinking of the topaz and diamond necklace he'd recently given her, and Christmas only a month away.

He chuckled, making her turn around to look at him. "Sarah, you're asking about my finances?"

"Yes, I guess I am." She flushed in embarrassment.

"That's a fair question. I'm surprised you didn't ask sooner. Acting does pay well, even the small films that I've done. And although the portion I take from the estate is relatively modest, the apartment and the car are both paid for. I've lived a simple bachelor's lifestyle and haven't required a large income." Wiping off the counter, he continued, "But you're right, acting, or at least the acting I've done thus far, doesn't pay well enough to cover the costs of producing a film. Costs I choose not to take from the estate's coffers. But with hard work, and a little luck, preparation meets opportunity," he reminded her. "Those investments will pay off." He put his arms around her waist again, kissing her nose. "So, you see, Sarah, I am quite capable of maintaining you in the lifestyle to which you've been accustomed," he said, with a teasing smile.

"'Money can only give happiness where there is nothing else to give it.' I have you to give me happiness, and thus lack for nothing else."

CHAPTER 42

The kitchen was crowded with Ann, Becca, Sarah's nieces, Eliza and Kate, and Sarah putting together the final preparations for Thanksgiving Dinner. Ann's kids, Michael and Lily, were out in the garden competing to see who could name the most bird species that visited the feeders.

"If y'all don't pipe down, you won't be identifying any birds, because you'll scare 'em all off," Ann scolded from the open window.

The men lounged on the sofas, watching an NFL game, trying to explain the rules to Alex. "Aw, come on. What kind of call was that? He stepped out of bounds," Rob grumbled at the television.

"College football is much more exciting," Mark said. "Next year we'll take you to a Gator game. Now that's football."

Sarah caught 'next year' and looked up at Alex, a little worried about Mark's assumption. Alex looked up at the same time, with a mysterious smile.

"Sarah, where's the cranberry chutney?" Becca interrupted their interaction.

"It's in the blue bowl, top shelf."

Sarah frowned as she watched Alex and the Admiral walk in the direction of her office, but the task of preparing the meal soon distracted her.

❧

*A*lex and the Admiral sat in the relative quiet of Sarah's office, sounds from the kitchen and the football game, accompanied by the occasional *whoop* from the other men, providing the background noise.

"Sir, thank you for interrupting your game to speak with me," Alex said, licking his lips and wiping his palms against his slacks.

The Admiral stretched out his legs, crossing them at the ankles, arms behind his head, enjoying the Earl's obvious discomfiture. He supposed that when it comes to asking a father for his daughter's hand in marriage, every man puts his pants on the same way, titled gentleman or blue-collar worker. And there wasn't a doubt in his mind that was the purpose of this private meeting. A charming, outdated ritual he'd never expected to participate in.

"Tell me what's on your mind, son."

"I love your daughter, sir."

"Yes. I can see that."

"And, well, I would like your permission to ask for her hand in marriage."

The Admiral hesitated, letting Alex squirm. "I see. And do you have reason to believe that she'll accept you?" Why not make the man work for it? Didn't his daughter deserve a man who'd love her, fight for her, respect her?

"I believe so. I hope so, because I can't live without her." He gave the Admiral a hesitant smile.

"You know, son, home is important to Sarah."

"Yes, sir. I've seen her interaction with her family and her friends. They are all very dear to her."

"We moved so many times early in my career that I lost count. My girl craves roots, stability."

"I've given that a great deal of thought, and if she wants to stay here, I'll stay with her. Pass my title to my brother."

"What?" Sarah stood frozen in the doorway. She clutched her hands to her stomach.

Alex wasn't sure how much she'd heard, but it was clear from her face that she'd heard the last thing he'd said.

"No." She shook her head. "Absolutely not."

Was she saying no to his marriage proposal? His heart dropped to his feet as he stood up. "Sarah—"

"Look, I don't know the totality of your conversation, but I do know that I would never let you give up your title for me."

She closed the gap between them. "The day we rode the grounds of Rutherford I saw the love you have for the land, for the people who still make their livelihoods there. I also saw the pride. You may not flaunt your title, but you carry it, and the burdens it entails, with an honor and dignity that I know would make your father proud. Rutherford is part of you, and you it. I could never take that away from you. That's a deal-breaker."

The Admiral walked over and kissed his daughter on the forehead. "Well, son," he said with a smile at Alex, "There you have it."

~

"*D*inner is served," Sarah announced to the group.

"Oh boy." Rob stood up and rubbed his stomach. "I've been saving up all week for this. Alex," he put his arm on Alex's shoulder, "you're in for a treat. Sarah is the best cook I know. Er, sorry, honey, you're a good cook too." Rob stammered in the face of Ann's irritation.

"You better eat up. This may be the last meal you get for some time." Ann smacked him with the dishtowel she held.

Everyone chuckled as Rob released Alex to wrap his arm around Ann's waist and place a repentant kiss on her cheek.

The mild, sunny Florida fall day was picture perfect. Taking advantage of both the weather, and the needed space, they dined *al fresco* on the back patio, where there was room to line up two long tables and enough chairs to accommodate the large group, not to mention the abundant food.

Once they were seated at the table, and the food was being passed around among murmurs of appreciation, Sarah glanced at Alex in his seat at the head of the table. He was relaxed, appearing to enjoy himself surrounded by those dear to her. She heaved a sigh of relief, both because her family and friends welcomed him, and because he fit right in as if he'd always been part of her life.

The discussion in the library ended with his solemn promise that he would not step down as Earl unless and until he believed he no longer wished to retain the title.

The feeling of bliss that returned was complete, no more doubts. Everything was perfect. As she looked around the table at her dear friends, dearer family, and dearest Alex, she realized George Sand, and Lady Clara, had been right. 'There is only one happiness in this life, to love and be loved.'

The Admiral raised his glass for a toast. "To my circle of friends, which now boasts our newest member, Alex, and to my dear family, Happy Thanksgiving." The adults raised their wine glasses, while the kids raised their iced tea glasses.

The quiet that descended as everyone dug in was only interrupted by the occasional compliment on the fare. Sarah gave credit where credit was due, telling everyone that Alex had a hand in the meal's preparation. Ann and Becca were suitably impressed, while Rob and Mark appeared chagrined at the looks from their wives.

Everyone lingered over dessert, simply enjoying the food, the company, and the soft afternoon. The sun began to set, filtering through the trees and casting shadows across the garden.

As the sun dropped behind the trees, it grew chilly. Sarah shivered a little and rubbed her arms, not wanting to get up and break the spell of this most perfect Thanksgiving.

Alex excused himself and rose from the table, caressing Sarah's shoulder as he passed. As any good actor knew, timing was essential to any memorable scene, and he wanted this scene to be memorable. The timing couldn't get any more perfect.

He returned a few minutes later with one of Sarah's sweaters, wrapping it around her shoulders. Becca raised her eyebrow at Sarah, again impressed. Sarah smiled at her and shrugged her shoulder imperceptibly.

"Could I have everyone's attention?" Alex stood behind his chair. "First, I want to sincerely thank you for opening your hearts to me and for making me feel like a welcome addition to your group. It means more than you know. Second, I want to thank Sarah for this bountiful meal in this tranquil setting, and for giving me the happiest five months of my life." He came to stand next to her.

Sarah looked at him askance, expecting him to lean over for a kiss.

"Which brings me to what I hope will be the day's grand finale." Taking her left hand in his, he knelt to the ground.

While there was a collective gasp from those around the table, Sarah's breath halted in her throat as Alex reached into his shirt pocket, pulling out a ring. She vaguely heard Michael whisper, "Mom, what's Alex doing?" and Ann's "shhh" in response.

"Sweet, Sarah. 'When I saw you, I fell in love, and you smiled because you knew.' I didn't realize it, but I'd been waiting my whole life for you. And now that I've found you, I can't let you go. Marry me?"

Sarah felt a jumble of sensations at once—elation, fear, shock, even embarrassment—because everyone was looking at her, holding their breath, waiting for her answer, especially Alex. All of these emotions passed in a split second, but the one that passed the quickest was fear. She cut her eyes to her father. He beamed, tears sparkling in his eyes.

Sarah inhaled slowly. "Alex, I never thought it was possible to be this happy, but you've shown me so many astonishing possibilities that I don't know why I should be surprised by that one. Yes, I will marry you," she whispered. "Yes!"

An elated, and relieved, Alex slid the ring onto her finger, kissing it before releasing her hand and pulling her to her feet for a tender kiss.

Everyone erupted into applause, and promptly formed a group hug around the two of them.

"This calls for a toast," Rob said as he headed for the kitchen. "I thought I saw some champagne in the fridge . . ."

Michael came up and asked Alex if he had to call him Lord Rutherford. Lily exclaimed that she couldn't wait to tell her friends that she had not only a real-life earl but a movie star in her family now.

Kate and Eliza were very grown-up in their congratulations to Sarah, a little shy in their congratulations to Alex. Mark slapped Alex on the shoulder and shook his hand. The Admiral proudly stood back and watched the whole scene as if he had orchestrated it.

Ann and Becca cried when they hugged Sarah, before asking to see the ring, a gorgeous oval amethyst set in platinum, flanked by two diamond trillions.

"Get you! A countess!" Ann curtseyed, eyes sparkling.

A nervous flutter briefly unsettled her at that thought, but she extinguished it just as quickly as it came.

"That has to be the most romantic proposal I've ever seen," Ann exclaimed, dabbing at her eyes with a tissue, "not that I've seen that many . . ."

"Oh honey," Becca said, "I'm so happy for you both. I've never seen you look more contented. He's good for you, but I've no doubt that you've each found your soulmate in the other."

"Yes," Sarah whispered, looking at Alex's handsome face amid the rest of her family and friends. "I guess soulmates really do exist."

EPILOGUE

Ohile Ann put the finishing touches on her hair, Sarah took the opportunity to reflect on the past two years. Her life had changed immeasurably in that time. Those two years weren't without their wrong turns, potholes, and seemingly dead ends, but she'd gone from being an unhappy woman uncertain of her future, her career, and more importantly her love life, to a woman whose life was on a path she could only have dreamed of.

Not only was she happier than she'd ever been in her life, she was more certain than she'd ever been in her life that what she was doing was right.

The movie was scheduled for release next month, she was halfway through her second book, and Alex was already talking about the movie. They'd agreed they would divide their time among her house in Florida, his flat in London, and Rutherford.

"How's that look?" Ann asked, still fingering a curl into place. She'd pulled front sections of Sarah's hair up and piled it into a mass of curls at the crown of her head, letting the rest fall down her back in a cascade of gentle waves, leaving a few tendrils to frame her face.

Becca walked up handing Ann a treasured sterling silver hair comb that had been their mother's. Ann placed the rhinestone starburst in her hair to the right of her crown.

"The perfect final touch," Becca said, her eyes welling with tears as she caught Sarah's eye in the mirror.

"Don't . . . you'll make me cry." Sarah smiled, taking her hand.

"Not so fast." Ann held out a lovely white leather box. "This is from Alex . . . his wedding gift to you."

Sarah took the box, hands trembling, and opening the lid found a strand of pearls from which hung a large amethyst teardrop pendant accompanied by matching amethyst teardrop earrings. There was a collective gasp from the three of them.

"They're magnificent," Sarah breathed. "Becca, would you put these on for me?" she asked, handing the strand to her. Becca fastened the necklace around her neck while Sarah put on the earrings.

"The amethyst matches your engagement ring," Ann said.

"Yes. Alex likes me best in purple." She didn't elaborate on the reason he loved her in purple: it was the color of the dress she'd worn when they'd gone to Stratford-upon-Avon, the night he said he fell in love with her.

There was a polite knock on the door, and then Lady Clara popped her head in. "Sarah? Oh gracious. You aren't even dressed yet. You must move along my dear, the ceremony is about to start."

"Yes, m'lady," Sarah said, using the nickname she'd chosen for her whenever she scolded her. "I'll only be a moment, nothing left but the dress."

Lady Clara left the room with a promise to return if Sarah wasn't out in five minutes.

Ann had already gone to the closet to retrieve the dress, a simple unembellished silk chiffon in ivory cut in a Grecian style. Stepping into it, the whisper of the cool satin under-slip across Sarah's skin raised goose bumps.

Becca buttoned the long row of covered buttons down the back, while Ann picked up the bouquet of Clara Louise roses, a pale lilac-colored rose Lady Clara's husband had named in her honor.

Sarah turned once more to look at her reflection. The dress's lovely deep V-neck framed the pearls beautifully. The empire-waist gave way to a chiffon skirt that fell to the floor like a cloud, her ivory satin-encased toes peeping out from underneath.

"Oh, Sarah. You look breathtaking," Ann and Becca spoke at the same time. "Jinx!" they both cried. They all laughed.

"We'd better go before Lady Clara sends in a footman to carry me bodily down the stairs," Sarah said with a smile.

Rutherford provided a perfect location for the wedding and the reception. It was secluded enough to keep the tabloid magazines away, and it offered luxurious accommodations to the limited number of guests, all of whom were thrilled to stay in a seventeenth-century manor house.

They heard the soft strains of Gluck's *Dance of the Blessed Spirits* played by the string quartet floating through the doors from the terrace.

The Admiral waited at the foot of the stairs, a smile so wide he thought his face might crack under the pressure. "Baby, you leave me quite speechless."

"Thank you, Daddy," she replied, reverting to her childhood name for him.

"Nervous?" Ann whispered on the way to the open French doors.

"No," Sarah said, without hesitation. "I have never been more certain of anything in my life." Even the thought of being in the spotlight was not a concern today. She knew she would have Alex by her side.

"That's good, because this is it," Ann said as she stepped to the doorway for the opening notes of Bach's *Sinfonia in G*.

Safely tucked behind the door so no one could see her, Sarah looked out at the intimate gathering. The late May day couldn't be more spectacular. The English countryside was in full bloom, the air was soft and warm, perfumed with the scents of lilac, freesia, and hyacinth.

Ann stepped out, followed by Becca, each in knee-length lilac chiffon gowns, walking slowly down the aisle between the rows of white brocade-covered folding chairs.

Emma had returned from trekking in Bhutan in time for the ceremony. She looked very well. She'd told Sarah, Ann, and Becca last night that she would actually set aside her hiking clothes for more elegant attire, and wear make-up and style her hair for the wedding.

Emma and Sarah's father had hit it off very well. It seemed that every time Sarah saw one, she saw the other. Looking at her father now, she hoped he would find love again. It seemed such an incredible waste of a generous heart if he didn't.

Lady Clara, who sat in the seat that would have been reserved for Sarah's mother, her face glowing with the same pride Sarah's own mother would have shown, looked lovely in a light blue dress and hat suitable for Queen Elizabeth herself.

Sarah and her father stepped into the doorway just as Ann and Becca reached their places, and the quartet began Bach's *Suite No. 1 in G*, their cue. As she began her slow march down the aisle beside her father, she looked at Alex's tall frame standing beneath a flower-covered trellis, his face beaming as soon as he saw her.

She was sure hers beamed as well. He was beyond anything she could ever have imagined, dressed in a simple light gray suit, white shirt and lilac tie. Next to him stood Robert, as his best man, and Trevor, both looking dapper in dark gray suits.

After that, Sarah only had eyes for Alex, who looked at her in way that made her heart tremble with love for him.

Sure, he was dreaming, Alex gave himself a mental pinch. Sarah looked like a Greek goddess come to life, all diaphanous beauty, slender grace, and timeless elegance. She glowed from within.

Alex stepped forward to take Sarah's hand from her father—but not before she turned to give her father a kiss on his cheek—and escorted her to stand beneath the trellis in front of Mr. Stanforth, the superintendent registrar who would solemnize the marriage.

"Ladies and gentlemen," Mr. Stanforth began, "we are gathered here today in the presence of these persons to witness the marriage of Alexander Tristan Sutherland Fraser, Lord Rutherford, to Sarah Anne Edwards. Alex and Sarah have duly given notice of their intention to marry in accordance with the laws of Great Britain. Are you,

Alexander Tristan Sutherland Fraser, free lawfully to marry Sarah Anne Edwards?"

"I am." Alex's silken voice carried over the small assembly.

"Are you, Sarah Anne Edwards, free lawfully to marry Alexander Tristan Sutherland Fraser?"

"I am." Sarah's voice surprised her in its strength.

"Before reciting the words that will lawfully bind them, Lady Clara Fraser would like to read an excerpt from *Letters to a Young Poet #7* by Rainer Maria Rilke. Lady Clara."

Lady Clara joined the wedding party, kissing first Sarah then, Alex on the cheek, before turning to their friends, family, and loved ones, and clearing her throat. In her refined accent and measured pace, she read the words:

"'That something is difficult must be one reason for us to do it. It is good to love, because love is difficult. For one human being to love another human being: that is perhaps the most difficult task that has been entrusted to us, the ultimate task, the final test and proof, the work for which all other work is merely preparation.'

"'Loving does not at first mean merging, surrendering, and uniting with another person, but rather it is a high inducement for the individual to ripen, to become something in himself, to become world, to become world in himself for the sake of another person; it is a great, demanding claim on him, something that chooses him and calls him to vast distances.'

"I have seen Alex and Sarah ripen and become something in themselves. I have seen them overcome life's obstacles, which have served as mere preparation for the ultimate task of loving one another. I wish them always only the best life and love can offer."

"Thank you, Lady Clara."

Mr. Stanforth turned to Alex. "And now, Alex, you may speak your vows to Sarah."

Holding both her hands in his, Alex looked tenderly into her eyes. "I, Alexander Tristan Sutherland Fraser, take you Sarah Anne Edwards to be my wedded wife."

He finished with a quote from Shakespeare he'd selected for the ceremony. "'So long as I can breathe or I can see, so long lives your love which gives life to me.'"

Mr. Stanforth spoke softly. "Sarah."

Not taking her eyes off Alex's handsome face, she said clearly and confidently, "I, Sarah Anne Edwards, take you Alexander Tristan Sutherland Fraser to be my wedded husband." And, paraphrasing Shakespeare, she spoke her chosen sentiment. "So dear I love you that with you, all deaths I could endure. Without you, live no life."

"Alex and Sarah will now exchange rings as a symbol of their union."

Alex pulled the ring out of his pocket, and sliding it over her left ring finger, said, "Sarah, I give you this ring, as a token of my love, and a symbol of our marriage. I vow to be loving, faithful, and loyal to you, throughout our lives together." He gently kissed her hand before releasing it.

Becca handed Alex's ring to Sarah and as she slid it over his finger, she repeated those words to him. "Alex, I give you this ring, as a token of my love, and a symbol of our marriage. I vow to be loving, faithful, and loyal to you, throughout our lives together."

Mr. Stanforth then spoke the words heard by thousands of brides and grooms every year, but never sweeter than now. "By the authority vested in me by the District of Cherwell, Oxfordshire County, I now pronounce Alex and Sarah husband and wife. Alex, you may kiss your bride."

Alex cradled her face, tenderly kissing her lips, before whispering, "I love you, Lady Rutherford, Countess of Rutherford, my wife."

His simple words sent a thrill through her.

"Ladies and gentlemen, may I present to you for the first time, Lord and Lady Rutherford." They turned to face the gathering of well-wishers.

This time Sarah didn't just choose change. She embraced it. Now she would reap its promise.

AUTHOR'S NOTE

Author's sometimes take a little liberty with facts when writing their stories, especially if those facts don't fit the story. I confess, I took a factual liberty when it comes to the British peerage. One of the many arguments Alex and his brother, Robert, have is over Alex's title. Robert would prefer that Alex disclaim the title, so that Robert can become earl instead—in part to advance his political career.

However, under the Peerage Act of 1963, Robert would not assume the title of earl in Alex's stead. The peerage would remain without a holder until Alex's death, and then it would descend to his heir in the usual manner. The only way in which Robert could assume the title, would be if Alex died without an heir.

Alex and Robert may have their issues, but I doubt even Robert would wish such an outcome in furtherance of his political career.

ABOUT THE AUTHOR

Rebecca Heflin is a bestselling, award-winning author who has dreamed of writing romantic fiction since she was fifteen and her older sister sneaked a copy of Kathleen Woodiwiss' Shanna to her and told her to read it.

Never quite sure what she wanted to be when she grew up, Rebecca didn't attend college until age 30, and earned her bachelor's in literature, before going on to complete her law degree.

Ever the late bloomer, Rebecca finally turned her attention to fulfilling her dream of writing, and published her first novel at age 48. When not passionately pursuing her dream, Rebecca is busy with her day-job at a major state university.

She and her husband are also co-founders of a non-profit organization, which raises money to help cancer patients and their families.

Rebecca's pen name is an abbreviated version of her great-great grandmother's name: Sarah Anne Rebecca Heflin Apple Smith. Whew! And you wonder why she shortened it.

Rebecca writes women's fiction and contemporary romance, and she is a member of Romance Writers of America (RWA), Contemporary Romance Writers, and Florida Writers Association. Rebecca and her mountain-climbing husband live at sea level in sunny Florida.

Sign up for Rebecca's monthly newsletter, Rebecca's Readers, for all the latest news on upcoming releases, appearances, and contests.

- facebook.com/RebeccaHeflinBooks
- twitter.com/RebeccaHeflin
- bookbub.com/authors/rebecca-heflin

ALSO BY REBECCA HEFLIN

RESCUING LACEY

<u>DREAMS COME TRUE SERIES</u>

<u>DREAMS OF PERFECTION, BOOK 1</u>

<u>SHIP OF DREAMS, BOOK 2</u>

<u>DREAMS OF HER OWN, BOOK 3</u>

<u>STERLING UNIVERSITY SERIES</u>

<u>ROMANCING DR. LOVE, BOOK 1</u>

<u>WINNING DR. WENTWORTH, BOOK 2</u>

<u>EDUCATING DR. MAYFIELD, BOOK 3</u>

<u>SEASONS OF NORTHRIDGE SERIES</u>

<u>A SEASON TO DANCE, BOOK 1</u>

<u>A SEASON TO LOVE, BOOK 2</u>

<u>A SEASON TO REMEMBER, BOOK 3</u>

<u>A SEASON TO GIVE, CHRISTMAS NOVELLA</u>